JEAN SIBELIUS

JEAN SIBELIUS

LIFE, MUSIC, SILENCE

DANIEL M. GRIMLEY

REAKTION BOOKS

Published by
Reaktion Books Ltd
Unit 32, Waterside
44–48 Wharf Road
London N1 7UX, UK
www.reaktionbooks.co.uk

First published 2021
First published in paperback 2025

Printed and bound in Great Britain
by CPI Group (UK) Ltd, Croydon CR0 4YY

A catalogue record for this book is available from the British Library

ISBN 978 1 83639 038 1

CONTENTS

Preface

Few composers can claim such a prominent and esteemed place in the concert hall, recording catalogues and public imagination as Jean Sibelius, and studies of his work traverse much familiar and well-trodden territory. There are nevertheless compelling reasons why a further volume is worthwhile. First and foremost, Sibelius's music is continually being discovered by new audiences and generations of listeners, and wider interest in his work shows no sign of slackening. Second, the emergence of a range of fresh biographical data, not least under the auspices of the ongoing research of the critical edition *Jean Sibelius Works*, has prompted renewed focus on matters of chronology and musical interpretation. And third, the fascination with Sibelius's career remains strong, and closer consideration of work raises issues of longevity, agency and the creative process. Basic biographical questions repay continued interpretative scrutiny, including the cultural, geographical and political contexts of his early life, the reception of his music across the twentieth century, and his symbolic and material role in Finland's spectacular transformation from aspirant young republic into one of the world's most dynamic musical nations.

This book does not seek to offer a comprehensive account of Sibelius's work; nor is it primarily intended as a scholarly text (although it is hoped that it will serve to stimulate and support ongoing academic research). Rather, it offers a broad introduction to Sibelius's life and his cultural milieu, the remarkably rich and diverse environments in which he lived and worked and which shaped his musical output. In particular, it seeks to emphasize the breadth of Sibelius's output, extending well beyond his most well-known scores to encompass his theatre music, songs and chamber works. And it offers cautious reflections on some of the most difficult problems that arise in his biography, including his relationship with Finnish nationalism, the story of his final decades and his position during the Second World War. Above all, this book is designed as a critical introduction to Sibelius's music, shedding fresh light on some of his most popular works as well as illuminating the artistic networks and communities with which he was involved, both in Finland and beyond.

Introduction

In a diary entry dated 3 March 1910, Sibelius wrote: 'my soul hungers and thirsts for music.'[1] Hear barely a single note of Sibelius's music and his identity is immediately apparent. But identifying and locating Sibelius as a biographical subject proves a more elusive challenge. He was, at various points of his career, a national hero; a nature poet; a bardic seer; a caring father; an ardent lover; an errant husband; a symbolist visionary; a rugged modernist; a bilious *bon vivant*; and (for the final years of his life) a seemingly silent enigma. 'A green-eyed god upon the earth', as his friend, the Norwegian novelist Knut Hamsun, described him in a scurrilous lyric, jotted down in Constantinople, 'a devil in all the North'.[2] Sibelius simultaneously embodied all (and more) of these contradictory personae. Few composers have provoked such a wide and frequently polarized range of popular and critical responses, from adulation to contempt, yet a growing consensus has emerged which acknowledges that Sibelius was among the most important and influential composers of his time. A principal reason for the widely divergent trajectory of Sibelius's reception was his sheer longevity. Born in a small army town around 100 kilometres (60 mi.) north of Helsinki, in 1865, when Finland was still part of the Russian Empire, he lived to the age of 91 and died in 1957, two years after Finland had joined the United Nations. Even if at times he seemed unreachably isolated and remote, supposedly an 'apparition from the woods' ('eine Erscheinung aus den Wäldern') as he described himself sardonically in 1910, Sibelius's life spanned some of the most turbulent and tumultuous events of the last 150 years, and his work is central to the wider story of late nineteenth- and early twentieth-century music.

Ever since his emergence onto the international scene following the performance of his First Symphony and the inimitable *Finlandia* at the Paris Exposition Universelle in 1900, Sibelius's music has been inextricably associated with Finland's struggle for independence and its search for a national creative identity. For centuries Finland had been a Swedish province, governed and controlled from Stockholm, with the country's wealth and power concentrated in the hands of a relatively small number of aristocratic Swedish families. In 1809, in the wake of the Napoleonic wars, however, Finland passed into Russian possession. Though Russian rule was initially benevolent and even fostered the first stirrings of Finnish cultural nationalism, partly in order to dilute the legacy of the country's Swedish-dominated past, futile attempts to impose a more centrally dictated control as the Russian empire itself began to fall apart at the end of the century inexorably led to more urgent and direct calls for Finnish self-determination. Although he was born into a Swedish-speaking family, Sibelius's music would come to play a direct role in this campaign for national sovereignty. His early songs and choral works responded intensively to the rhythmic patterns and inflections of the Finnish language, and one of the primary sources for his work was the *Kalevala*, a collection of Finnish folk tales compiled by the multi-faceted doctor, linguist and botanist Elias Lönnrot and first published in 1835, at the start of the Finnish national awakening. Iconic figures and places from the *Kalevala* recur throughout much of Sibelius's music, from the tragic hero of his first breakthrough work, the brooding choral symphony *Kullervo* (1892), to the wind-swept domain of the forest god Tapiola, the subject of his final symphonic poem (1926).

Understanding Sibelius's music solely through a national lens, however, would be excessively short-sighted. 'Am I really nothing more than a national curiosity?' he asked, tongue only partly in his cheek, in November 1910.[3] He was, in fact, an elegant and highly cultured man-of-the-world, whose imagination ranged far beyond the wooded boundaries of his country villa at Järvenpää. After graduating from the Helsinki Music Institute as a young man, he studied in Berlin and Vienna, and regarded Germany as his spiritual home throughout much of the 1900s, just as continental European music moved from the richly evocative symbolist milieu of the 1890s towards the more aggressively modernist sound-worlds of Schoenberg, Bartók and Stravinsky. He was later lauded in Britain and North America, where his music was associated with ideologically problematic assumptions about Nordic character and landscape,[4] and almost completely ignored in France (until his 'discovery' by a wave of spectral composers in 1970s). Sibelius was, in this sense, a transitional figure. But his music had a remarkable capacity to harness the creative energy of the world whirling around him, and his symphonies are driven by an acutely attentive feeling for the human condition, whether in the surging passions of the First (1899), the sombre shades of the oblique Fourth (1911), or the elliptical grandeur of the single-movement Seventh (1924), which proved to be his last despite compelling evidence that he finished an Eighth. This vital current can be traced as much in his smaller compositions – incidental music, songs, virtuosic showpieces, chamber works and his innumerable waltzes – as in his symphonies and tone poems, and no overview of Sibelius's creative output can be complete without taking into account his many works in these other genres alongside his more celebrated orchestral achievements. It is a potent and irresistible legacy.

Sibelius was obsessed by questions of social distinction. As a Swedish-speaking Finn, he always felt as though he was in a minority, and his middle-class provincial background brought its own set of standards and obligations. 'You are too aristocratic for our socialist times,' he once remarked to himself, and for much of his life he believed that he was descended from an ancient Swedish family line.[5] At times, this brought him into conflict with his country's fledgling aims and aspirations. In a newspaper interview in 1910, the poet Eino Leino, for example, stated: 'we have two cultures and nations, one Finnish, the other Swedish, which are moving fast apart.'[6] As Sibelius acutely realized, music might deepen those divisions or it could bring the nation together. Music-making had always been an intrinsic part of his childhood domestic routine. After the early death of his father, who passed away when he was barely two years old, Sibelius's close correspondence, especially with his uncle Pehr, recorded his unusually sensitive responses to the sounds of the garrison town of his youth and the countryside beyond. Indeed, Sibelius's immersive imagination was swiftly attuned to the way in which aspects of the modern world – the railway, industry and commerce – were beginning to encroach upon life in the Finnish regions. He was initially sent to study law at the University of Helsinki, but dropped out of his course within a year and enrolled at the Helsinki Music Institute (later renamed the Sibelius Academy), founded by Martin Wegelius in 1882. Here, Sibelius's colleagues included the Italian pianist and composer Ferruccio Busoni, who became a close friend and who shared many of Sibelius's aesthetic concerns and preoccupations. Sibelius was also deeply inspired by Robert

Kajanus, a Wagnerian composer and conductor who was one of the most dynamic figures in late nineteenth-century Finnish life. It was nevertheless Sibelius's postgraduate study abroad – first with Albert Becker in Berlin and later with Karl Goldmark in Vienna – that really widened his artistic horizons, and which led to his first major musical success: the premiere of his *Kullervo* Symphony in 1892. From the very outset, then, Sibelius's career was marked by an irresolvable tension: the creative stimulus provided by his encounter with an international music scene versus the catalysing influence of material drawn from a more local source (whether the *Kalevala* or the Finnish landscape).

Sibelius's interest in the Finnish language and its vernacular cultures was stimulated partly by the increasingly desperate political situation in which Finland found itself in the 1890s: the final years of the century saw increasingly hardline crackdowns on separatist activity. But it was also circumstantial. His wife, Aino, was a member of one of Finland's elite nationalist families, the Järnefelts, and an ardent proponent of the Finnish cause. She was always, in that sense, more politically connected and engaged than her husband. Sibelius's letters in their early correspondence, recently published, slip continually between Finnish and Swedish (the language in which he still felt most comfortable). Association with the Järnefelt circle also brought him into close contact with a group of artists, writers and intellectuals that included the painter Akseli Gallen-Kallela, who turned to Finnish folk materials (mythology, landscape and design) as a rich and fertile creative resource. Sibelius found himself, whether by accident or not, to be a key player in demands for an independent Finnish voice. But he swiftly realized that the nationalist route was itself a creatively limiting one, and he increasingly sought to present himself as an artist working on the broader international stage: a strategic decision that brought its own defeats and rewards.

Although he was awarded a modest state pension in 1896, Sibelius never held a regular salaried position. For many years, until the 1920s, his royalty earnings were not governed by any globally recognized copyright legislation. Sibelius was hence beset by financial worries throughout his professional career, not least as he sought to provide for his growing family and maintain their middle-class lifestyle. Access to the international music market brought significant opportunities, but it also brought the risk of exposure. German critics never entirely embraced his work: he was inevitably seen as a 'Heimatskünstler' (provincial artist), a patronizing but essentially positive descriptor when employed by a writer such as

Walter Niemann, but a term of opprobrium for later authors such as Theodor Adorno. Seeking to compete in the most elevated and prestigious of German genres – the symphony – Sibelius's work was judged by an elite and exclusive set of aesthetic criteria that he could never hope to satisfy entirely. This feeling of marginalization from the most canonic of musical institutions was only exacerbated by Sibelius's own insecurities: he suffered both from stage fright as a performer and also from a crippling degree of compositional self-criticism. 'It seems to me as if all I have accomplished is of no significance,' he once wrote, 'as if my life is completely flawed.'[7] He withdrew *Kullervo* swiftly after its first performances, and almost every later orchestral work, from *En saga* onwards, was either withdrawn or went through a painful process of redrafting and revision before Sibelius was satisfied with the score. Although this ruthless process of review became an integral part of Sibelius's working method – a compensation, he believed, for what he felt were the inadequacies of his formal academic training – it could also become a more destructively compulsive urge. And ultimately it was this obsessive desire to go back over his materials and comprehensively rethink his compositional choices and decisions that became one of the primary factors that led to the probable destruction of the Eighth Symphony.

Sibelius's response to this compulsive self-criticism and sense of inferiority was to draw inwards. This was partly a defensive reaction, a strategic gesture in which the need for artistic isolation became a means of shielding himself from the rigours and strains of his professional performing commitments and the commercial imperatives involved. But it was also, far more importantly, a source of creative enrichment. His intensely felt response to nature and environment was not merely a well-worn trope in his critical reception: it was a more drastic way of rethinking human subjectivity and our relationship with the natural world. Sibelius's diary entries and correspondence make frequent reference to environmental sights and sounds: birds, meteorological conditions, effects of light and the changing seasons. 'The richest and strongest thoughts and moods are when I am alone,' he wrote in June 1910, adding a couple of months later: 'The evening atmosphere wonderful. As always when silence speaks: a secret pull of eternal silence and – life's song.'[8] This is not an anachronistically Romantic gesture, seeking nothing beyond solace or escape in idyllic fantasy, but rather a more radically immersive and destabilizing process, a commingling of self and environment that sought to permeate and break down the boundaries between human agency and the shifting moods of the weather and the night sky. In drawing upon such natural metaphors in his work, Sibelius attempted to capture a deeper acoustic attentiveness, a response to sound and mood that was central to his symbolist aesthetics: the intimate correspondence between the human imagination and the world beyond.

This interconnectivity is the key to understanding Sibelius's music and his environment – both natural and historic. Yet it is only one of the many narrative strands that run through his biography. The symphonies inevitably comprise a recurrent thread in this sequence, and they serve as landmarks for the stylistic shifts and turning points of Sibelius's career, but the discussion that follows will be more discursive and wide-ranging than a simple commentary alone. Rather, this book will seek to place Sibelius within a more complex, fluid and interdisciplinary artistic environment, drawing attention at relevant moments to his relationship with trends in architecture, literature and the visual arts. It cannot resolve all of the problems or enigmas that emerge from a critical overview of his career, but it seeks to capture the richness of Sibelius's creative life and his dynamic legacy, both within Finland and elsewhere. It is precisely in its feeling for the human condition that Sibelius's music gains its greatest strength. Sibelius's work sustains: both in its particular feeling for texture, space and sonority, and, more figuratively, as a source of vitality and renewal. It is to tracing the origins of this sounding source that the first chapter of this book is now directed.

Hjalmar Munsterhjelm, *Häme Castle*, 1872, oil on canvas.

1

Country and City

For present-day travellers in Finland, hurrying on the fast train between Helsinki on the southern coast and the commercial and industrial hub of Tampere and the lake region to the north, Hämeenlinna (in Swedish Tavastehus) may seem a pleasantly attractive but otherwise unremarkable stop.[1] The origins of the city date from the ninth or tenth century AD, a period of significant population expansion across the Scandinavian and Baltic region. Its strategic location, at the intersection of two ancient trade routes running east-to-west and north-to-south across the country, was marked by the construction of a defensive fortress by the Swedes in the thirteenth century and later by the opening of Finland's first railway, connecting Hämeenlinna with the capital in 1862. Even though the urban fabric of the city has changed considerably since Sibelius's day, the basic outline of the nineteenth-century town is still readily recognizable: the grid-plan arrangement of the streets in the centre recalls Hämeenlinna's historical importance and its later role as a Russian garrison town, and the city has maintained its familiar low-rise skyline. Hjalmar Munsterhjelm's illustration for Zacharias Topelius's pictorial topography of the country, *En resa i Finland* (1872–4), presents a panoramic view of the castle, lake shore, church, provincial governor's residence and a steamship on the waters of Vanajavesi, surrounded by forest on all sides.[2] These four elements – the institutions of state, religion, commerce and the encompassing natural environment – provided the basic reference points for Sibelius's childhood and would shape much of his later career.

Sibelius was born into what should have been a comfortable middle-class family. His paternal grandfather, Johan Mattsson (1785–1844), was an entrepreneurially minded countryman from Lapinjärvi (Lappträsk) who acquired a shipping business based at the Baltic seaport of Loviisa (Lovisa), just to the east of Helsinki, and who changed the family name from Sibbe to the Latinate Sibelius (a relatively common practice among Swedish-Finnish families in the nineteenth century). Of his four sons, the eldest, Johan Matias Frederik (1818–1864), pursued a maritime career – and adopted the dashingly Gallicized soubriquet 'Jean Sibelius', redolent of salty adventures and exotic foreign climes. The second son, Pehr Ferdinand (1819–1890), settled in Turku (Åbo), Finland's second city and former capital in the Swedish-speaking west of the country, and later became the composer's first musical mentor and confidant. The youngest brother, Karl Edvard (1823–1863), was a professional surveyor but died young, whereas the third, Christian Gustaf (1821–1868), trained as a doctor and was appointed physician at the battalion headquarters in Hämeenlinna in 1859. Here, three years later on 7 March, he married the daughter of a local priest (who had died in 1855), Maria Charlotta Borg (1841–1897). Christian and Maria had three children in turn: a daughter, Linda Maria (born 1863), and two sons, the youngest named after his father, Christian (born 1869), and the middle child, Johan Christian Julius (called Janne by his family), born on 8 December 1865.[3]

Christian Gustaf was evidently a live wire, a gregarious social figure and a vibrant member of the town's cultural and musical life. Erik Tawaststjerna writes that 'the composer's childhood home at

Hallituskatu, Hämeenlinna: Sibelius's birthplace (now a museum) is on the left side of the street, in front of the two-storey building.

Residensgatan [now Hallituskatu] in Hämeenlinna was marked by a bohemian atmosphere rather than solid middle-class values. His father had bought books and music instead of bothering about the home; he had hired a fortepiano since he couldn't afford to buy one of his own.'[4] Christian, in other words, lived extravagantly beyond his immediate means, and his lifestyle had serious repercussions for his young family. The winter and spring of 1868 were unusually harsh, even by Finnish standards, and a disastrous crop failure later that year led to extensive food shortages across the country, coupled with a serious outbreak of typhoid. As an army doctor, Sibelius's father was exposed to the full effects of the epidemic, and he swiftly contracted the fever and died, in his late forties, on 31 July. The implications for his widow, expecting their third child, were immediate and immense: the family were forced to sell their home and move in with Maria's mother in order to try and settle Christian's debts, and they relocated several times during Sibelius's childhood before they were finally able to establish a permanent home and regain a sense of social respectability.[5]

The long-term effects on Maria and her children were considerable: Sibelius's later anxieties about money, his seeming inability to manage his own finances efficiently and aspects of his compulsive behaviour (not least his need for alcohol and cigars, and his fastidious attention to fashion and his appearance) were surely shaped by the social stigma attached to the circumstances of his own early upbringing and the need to uphold a certain dignity and family pride. In the socially conservative, claustrophobic milieu of nineteenth-century provincial Finland, such pressures must have felt particularly burdensome and suffocating. And the strongly pietistic strand of Finnish Lutheran life, shared by his paternal aunt Evelina and his mother's family, may have been a further contributory factor in Sibelius's often punctilious sense of duty and convention. Glenda Dawn Goss notes that 'the copious moralizing expressions that permeate the Sibelius-Borg family correspondence hold the keys to understanding not only Sibelius, but also the Finns', and argues that, in the nineteenth century, 'to be Finnish meant to be inculcated with the sounds of Lutheranism.'[6] Indeed, the sounds of bells and hymn-like passages are among the most striking features of Sibelius's mature work, as is the reverential quality of passages such as the opening of the Sixth Symphony, his music for *Jokamies* (Everyman), the late song *Törnet* (The Thorn) and the stirring *Andante festivo* for strings. At the same time, it is possible to speculate what impact the premature loss of

Sibelius's mother, Maria, with Janne (on her knee) and his sister Linda (left).

a male father figure may have had on Sibelius's sense of confidence and his later struggles balancing the demands of parenthood with those of a freelance artistic career. Brought up in an environment dominated by strong and remarkably resilient women, Sibelius later became a devoted father, but his diaries and correspondence often reveal his uneasiness in family circles, and he frequently wrote of his uncertainty about his ability to fulfil his expected roles and responsibilities as head of the household.

The legacy of Sibelius's early years was important in other ways. Although the household had fallen on hard economic times following Christian's death, the Sibelius family nevertheless attempted to maintain aspects of their middle-class life. The young Sibelius enrolled at the local school in 1872, and later attended the Normaalilyseo, the first grammar school in the country to use Finnish as a language of instruction, from 1876. Here, the curriculum included texts in Latin, French, Greek, Russian and German, as well as literature in Swedish and in translation from English.[7] Sibelius's finely attuned feeling for language, rhythmic diction, metre and intonation, qualities especially evident in his songs, may well have been shaped by his early exposure to a range of writing in very different languages as a child. It also offered him his encounter with a sophisticated body of literary works that would provide one of his sources of cultural reference: Finland, like the other Nordic nations, has always placed particular emphasis on literacy and reading, and the importance of literature would remain a central theme in Sibelius's wider artistic outlook, not least his sustained interest in spoken drama and the theatre.

The presence of a Russian army corps was a largely low-key aspect of Hämeenlinna's daily life (at least until political tensions began to intensify in the 1890s), but the visit by a high-level imperial delegation in 1875 did provide Sibelius with an early instance of the power of public ceremony and ritualized performance: a childhood sketch reveals a keen sense of detail and a youthful curiosity in the uniforms and other paraphernalia associated with the event.[8] The military infrastructure also supported other less spectacular forms of cultural distraction, not least the town's musical life. In a letter dated 19 June 1881, Sibelius wrote to his uncle Pehr asking for his permission to take up the violin, and later that autumn he began lessons with the local bandmaster, the violinist Gustaf Levander. Chamber music was an integral part of middle-class life and the social routine in Hämeenlinna, and Sibelius's thorough immersion

Sibelius's father, Christian Sibelius.

in the classical repertoire – primarily Mozart, Haydn and Beethoven, and nineteenth-century works up to Mendelssohn and Schumann – provided the basic foundation for his musical development. The Sibelius children formed a piano trio: Sibelius's sister, Linda, was a competent pianist (like their aunt, Evelina), and his younger brother, Christian, was a fine amateur cellist, even though he later pursued a high-level medical career. Holidays by the coast at the family's old stomping grounds in Loviisa provided a favourite opportunity to explore new musical works, as did his growing contacts with the neighbours and other local amateur musicians in Hämeenlinna, and Sibelius later spoke particularly fondly of the domestic warmth and intimacy of such events. Writing to his uncle with a blushing sense of youthful pride on 12 October 1882, aged sixteen, Sibelius could report:

> the good news that here in Tavastehus a string quartet has been formed to which I too belong, playing the second violin. Anna Tigerstedt plays first violin, Music Director Levander plays viola, and the pharmacist Elfsberg plays violoncello. Last Sunday I was at the Tigerstedts and Levander taught both Anna and me our parts. The quartets we are playing are by Haydn.[9]

By the end of the year he boasted that 'Aunt and I have played compositions by Haydn, Schubert or Mendelssohn every day.' Such direct hands-on experience with canonic repertoire gave the young Sibelius his preliminary musical training.

Hämeenlinna's railway link with Helsinki also enabled the town to benefit from concerts by visiting professional musicians. Such events clearly served to widen Sibelius's musical horizons at a crucial formative stage. Writing to his uncle as a fifteen-year-old in September 1881, for example, he recorded: 'I have been at a concert by the violinist Brassin and the pianist Pfeiffer; I have never heard anything like it before.' He went on to describe a performance of Beethoven's Sonata in A major (presumably the 'Kreutzer', op. 47), as his favourite item from the programme. Later visitors to the town included some of the leading Finnish musicians of the day: singers Emmy Achté and Abraham Ojanperä, both of whom would become significant interpreters of the mature Sibelius's work. It is little surprise, then, that late eighteenth- and early nineteenth-century music provided the stimulus for Sibelius's very first attempts at composition. His earliest acknowledged piece, a miniature duet for violin and cello entitled *Vattendroppar* (Water Drops) is a little Mozartian study in pizzicato textures with a simple Alberti (broken-chord) accompaniment. Tawaststjerna dates the piece from around 1875, but it is unlikely that it pre-dated the start of Sibelius's lessons with Levander: a more plausible date would be some time during the early 1880s. This is certainly consistent with Sibelius's growing ambitions as a young musician. For instance on 17 March 1883, aged seventeen, he confided to his uncle that he had begun to study harmony, and later that summer he wrote, 'I have made a small attempt to compose. One trio for two violins and piano is already completely ready; it is in G major and eight pages long. I am busy writing out the instrumentation for another trio.' Sibelius was characteristically defensive about the quality of his output, even if his attempt to divert potential criticism does not ring entirely true: 'the compositions are, of course, very bad, but on rainy days it is fun to have something to work on.' Clues as to the mature composer's musical style are frustratingly absent from these early compositions: they are arguably more important for their fidelity to the classical models with which Sibelius was then most closely acquainted. But what is perhaps more significant, given the trajectory of his subsequent career, is the first indication of Sibelius's responsiveness to sound and his ability to immerse himself completely in his musical imagination. It is the obsessive intensity of his acoustic engagement with the world around him that was to become such a prevalent theme in later recollections of the composer, and such a strong thread in his critical reception.

There are several instances in Sibelius's early years of this formative combination of concentrated attentiveness and creative fantasy. The mature Sibelius still possessed 'a highly refined ability to note-name and could even ascribe pitch to birdsong and other natural sounds'.[10] Walter von Konow, one of Sibelius's childhood friends and a figure to whom he remained close as an adult, provided an even more vivid account of the young composer's creative impulse:

> In the dusk Janne would amuse himself by spying on all sorts of extraordinary beings in the gloomy forest depths and if the mood took him to be macabre it could be rather eerie to wander through the dark forests by his side peopled by trolls, witches, goblins and the like. At times our imaginations became so fired that when the night closed in all sorts of terrifying shapes loomed out of their dark hiding-places.[11]

Von Konow's description recalls the enchanted world of nineteenth-century fairy tales: Sibelius's school reading included the Brothers Grimm as well as the Norwegian folk stories of Asbjørnsen and Moe and other collections. The fantastical element of such material would be one of the recurrent tropes in much of Sibelius's music, and one of his earliest works was an 'opera' based on a libretto by von Konow called 'Ljunga Wirginia', scored for violin, cello and piano duet (the music for which, puzzlingly, contains no indication of any vocal parts). An alternative way of understanding von Konow's memoir might be more specifically tied to its location: the proximity of the countryside on all sides of Hämeenlinna and the opportunity to slip away from the predictable routines of urban life must have been no less compelling. Throughout his life, Sibelius maintained an awkward relationship with institutional power and authority, despite the nagging sense of duty and obligation that he inherited from his Lutheran childhood, and music offered the most powerful form of creative escape.

Sibelius evidently also responded to the physical qualities of sound in an especially intense way. Writing to his uncle Pehr on 1 August 1882, for example, he reported that

> I could never have imagined that my violin could achieve such a sound in its timbre, such an artistic quality that I have never before heard in a violin . . . it is as though the insides of the music opened up to me, and Haydn's sonatas with their deep, serious sounds almost make it holy.[12]

Several years later, while a student in Helsinki, he would write in even more vivid terms of a futurist music generated by the sympathetic vibrations of adjacent tones produced by industrial machinery:

> If, for example, one imagines a city with several factories, the cotton factories could, for instance, have low C; the sawmills, the [minor] second, E-F; the iron factories, G-A flat; and all the other factories, C-D flat. Then the following chord would result:

Sibelius described this sonority as a 'sexdecim chord', which, he claimed, was 'not found in any music other than my experimental music'. Although the actual theoretical basis (and nomenclature) for his claim is unclear, much of Sibelius's mature work is indeed distinguished by its powerful feeling for the resonant frequencies of particular sounds and harmonies: it forms the basis for his characteristic approach to orchestration, the idiosyncratic arrangement of low sonorities and tones so that the higher instruments can pick up a range of upper partials and brighter sounds from the bass. Here, in 1888, he already seems to have developed an innate sense of the way in which different kinds of musical timbre can induce both a physical response and a change of atmosphere or mood. 'This chord has a highly peculiar effect upon people and animals,' Sibelius went on to explain, adding: 'I think that the many seconds vibrating in the air cause electricity, and this in turn is transformed into animal magnetism in people and animals which again remoulds the activity of the entire animal kingdom.'[13] Such patterns of thought, indebted to earlier nineteenth-century theories of acoustic perception and electromagnetism, never formed the foundation for a more rigorously scientific approach to composition in Sibelius's case. But music's affective power would remain one of his recurrent preoccupations, especially following his immersion in the symbolist world of the 1890s. And it is no less remarkable to think about the specific sources identified in Sibelius's letter: not the haunting silence of the Finnish forest, as later biographers would insist, but the clangorous din of modern industrial development, from the incessant hum of the automated cotton looms (Tampere, just north of Hämeenlinna, became the centre for the Finnish textile industry, the so-called 'Finnish Manchester') to the whining sound of the sawmills and the metallic clang of the iron foundry (which would in turn provide the inspiration for a younger generation of futurist composers such as Alexander Mosolov).

At the same time as he was immersing himself, physically and creatively, in aspects of his ambient environmental sounds, Sibelius also began to recognize the need for some kind of formal musical training. Whether prompted by his local teacher, Levander, or his uncle Pehr, in February 1884, aged eighteen, he obtained a copy of Johann Christian Lobe's *Compositionslehre* (1844), an extended theoretical primer that laid particular emphasis on thematic working, sentence structure and musical form. Lobe's treatise worked in exhaustive detail through the different kinds of formal structures associated with nineteenth-century instrumental music, from basic binary and ternary forms through to theme-and-variation, rondo and sonata forms. A particular feature of the first chapter was a forensic dissection of the opening theme from the finale of Haydn's Symphony no. 104 in D, the last of his so-called 'London' Symphonies, showing how the passage was strictly assembled from the smallest musical motif through a hierarchical ordering of musical units: 2-bar segment (in German: 'Abschnitt'); 4-bar phrase ('Satz') and 8-bar period. But the most enduring legacy of Lobe's textbook for Sibelius was not so much the rigid emphasis on periodic structure as the fundamental importance of motivic working as the basis for elaborating a full musical texture. The voluminous pages of sketches for much of his later music are concerned precisely with exploring the thematic possibilities of specific motifs or musical ideas. Sibelius evidently internalized the lesson from Lobe's insistence on the melodic integrity and logic of the classical musical form from the earliest stage.

This tight feeling for musical symmetry and balance is evident throughout Sibelius's youthful musical composition. Works such as the Piano Trio in G, JS 205 (from summer 1883, when he was seventeen), the Menuetto in F, JS 126, and the Piano Trio in A minor, JS 206 (from 1884), have a striking classical elegance and gracefulness: the principal theme of the opening Allegro of the G major trio, for instance, sounds especially Haydnesque, whereas the corresponding movement of the A minor trio suggests Mozart or Schubert. As Sibelius reached his final years at the Normaalilyseo, however, his artistic horizons inevitably began to expand. The school curriculum now included nineteenth-century Finnish writers such as Topelius and Johan Ludvig Runeberg, as well as other Nordic authors including Bjørnstjerne Bjørnsen, Henrik Ibsen and August Strindberg's bitingly satirical 1879 novel *Röda rummet* (The Red Room), based on a lightly fictionalized account of the writer's early career. Sibelius would remain a devoted admirer of Strindberg's work for the rest of his life, and Runeberg was his favourite poet, to whose verse he would continually return. The trajectory of Sibelius's early years hence becomes clearer: a childhood overshadowed by the tragedy of his father's early death and the family's straitened financial circumstances was followed by an upbringing in the socially restrictive but educationally ambitious and culturally outward-looking milieu of a small late nineteenth-century Finnish town. Sibelius did not in any sense come from the backwoods, as some of his later Anglo-American biographers sought to suggest. On the contrary, for all its provincialism and limited opportunity, Hämeenlinna effectively fostered Sibelius's intellectual curiosity and creative spirit, and his school years offered him a vital literary and philosophical grounding upon which he would continue to draw as a mature artist. Family trips to Loviisa in the summer fed in him the desire to explore beyond his immediate musical environment and strengthened his appetite for new repertoire and compositional models. It was in this spirit, then, that he left his home town and travelled to the Finnish capital, which would have a far deeper and more transformative effect upon his creative development.

When Sibelius arrived in Helsinki at the start of June 1885, on the cusp of his twenties, the city was in a remarkable state of transformation. Although the town had first gained its market charter in the mid-sixteenth-century, it had remained a small settlement of relatively little economic importance until 1819, when the new Russian authorities, who gained control of Finland in 1809, moved the Finnish senate from the former capital, Turku (Åbo) in the west, to a site closer to St Petersburg at the heart of Imperial Russian government. Helsinki was thus one of the youngest capital cities in Europe. The sudden shift of political authority brought with it a wave of development, as the new city was laid out on an ambitious scale with designs by the German architect Carl Ludwig Engel. The centrepiece of Engel's scheme was the senate square (Senaatintori), surrounded by the government palace (Valtioneuvoston linna, completed in 1822), the main building of the newly created University of Helsinki (originally founded as the Royal Academy of Åbo under Swedish rule in

Central Helsinki: the old market hall, harbour and Tuomiokirkko (Lutheran cathedral), *c.* 1890, photograph by Karl Emil Ståhlberg.

1640) and the Lutheran cathedral (Tuomiokirkko), which still dominates the Helsinki skyline from the southern harbour. A series of other institutions followed, including the city's first theatre, which opened in 1827, the inauguration of the Finnish Art Society (Suomen Taideyhdistys) in 1846, succeeded by the opening of the Drawing School in 1848, the publication of the Finnish newspaper *Suometar* in 1847, the construction of the Swedish Theatre in 1860 (replaced by a new building – Nya Teatern – following a fire in 1863), and the consecration of the Russian Orthodox cathedral (Uspenskin katedraali) in 1868. The arrival of the railway line from Hämeenlinna in 1862 was swiftly followed by a connection with St Petersburg in 1870 as the political and economic ties with Russia tightened ever more strongly.

During the course of the nineteenth century Helsinki's population grew steadily, although by the standards of other European capitals such as London, Paris or Vienna, it remained a relatively small city. Home to just over 22,000 residents in 1860, it had more than doubled in size by the mid-1880s, and the population exceeded 100,000 by the turn of the century. This expansion significantly changed the urban appearance of the town, a process that Sibelius would have witnessed at first hand and which was captured in photographs by his friend and contemporary Into Konrad Inha, among others. The austere monumental neo-classicism of Engel's original plans began to be augmented and transformed by other architectural styles and tastes. The Esplanadi park, first laid out by Engel in 1818, for instance, now became lined with elegant high-end apartment buildings and fashionable shops, modelled on the great boulevards of Baron Haussmann's Paris. A new green space, Kaivopuisto (Brunnsparken), was laid out at the end of the villa quarter at the end of Unioninkatu (Union Street), running directly north–south across the city centre: this was, in fact, where Sibelius and his family first resided when they moved to Helsinki, crammed into an apartment that must have always been too small for their needs. Two years after their arrival saw the opening of the Ateneum, the art museum located opposite the central railway station on Rautatientori (Railway Square) and designed by Theodor Höijer, which would later house significant works of art by many of Sibelius's friends and contemporaries. It also saw the construction of the Hotel Kämp at the western end of Esplanadi, in a luxurious building also designed by Höijer, which would become one of Sibelius's most regular (and notorious) haunts. The 1890s brought an even more striking shift of style, with the construction of four- and five-storey

Elegant café on the esplanade, Helsinki, 1893, photograph by Henry Pauw van Wieldrecht.

residential blocks with characteristic grotesque architectural features: carved stone mullions, architraves and porticos, often featuring details inspired by scenes from Finnish nature or the *Kalevala*. Helsinki was to become a major international centre for art nouveau design, on a comparable level with Vienna or Brussels, and its young architects such as Lars Sonck, Armas Lindgren, Herman Gesellius and Eliel Saarinen would have a lasting influence on Finnish design. Such was the impact of these new idioms upon the urban fabric that an early twentieth-century British visitor, writing barely two decades after Sibelius first arrived in the city, described Helsinki as having 'a strange, freakish personality that is alien to the rest of Europe, something that suggests the Japanese, or the Oriental, or the Egyptian', and added that 'with its fantastic skyline of domes, cupolas, and spires, its quaint balconies and perilously overhanging windows, its enormous granite portals and pillars, and its extraordinary decorations[, one] seems to have passed from the stern North into the land of the Arabian Nights'.[14]

Helsinki was also indelibly shaped by its role as a port city. Its cultural and economic life was underpinned by a dynamic mix of Russian, German,

Swedish and Baltic influences, alongside its growing sense of Finnish identity and its increasing importance as the nation's principal point of international arrival and departure. It was this rich cultural and economic through-flow, enhanced by its strategic position on the gulf between Stockholm and St Petersburg, which supported Finland's musical development during the nineteenth century. In particular, it was the German-speaking community who took a leading role in Helsinki's musical life. The Hamburg-born composer, violinist and conductor Friedrich (Fredrik) Pacius (1809–1891), for instance, who had studied with Louis Spohr and Moritz Hauptmann in Kassel, was appointed music teacher at the University of Helsinki in 1834, shortly after the institution moved from Turku in 1828, and the following year gave a large-scale performance of Spohr's oratorio *Die letzten Dinge* (1825–6). In the relatively tolerant climate of the 1850s, he was able to complete a series of large-scale popular works, including a violin concerto, a single-movement symphony (which was presumably left incomplete) and the first Finnish opera, *Kung Karls jakt* (King Charles's Hunt), with a libretto by Topelius, as well as a setting of Runeberg's poem *Vårt Land* (in Finnish, *Maamme*), which would later become the Finnish national anthem. Pacius also founded the Akademiska Sångförening (the Swedish-language Academic Male Voice Choir), based at the University of Helsinki, in 1838, and directed the first Finnish performances of Handel's *Messiah* and Haydn's *The Creation*.[15] The city's first Finnish-language male choir, Ylioppilaskunnan Laulajat (the Helsinki University Male Voice Choir), usually abbreviated to 'YL', was founded by Pekka Juhani Hannikainen in 1883: a further indication of the growing national pride in Finnish language and culture that was to become an increasing feature of the decade.

Helsinki's impact upon the young Sibelius was immediate. Writing to Uncle Pehr and Aunt Evelina on 2 June 1885, virtually as soon as he arrived, he declared, 'I am completely delighted with Helsingfors', and compared it favourably with his home town: 'once one gets a taste for it, Tavastehus [Hämeenlinna] is no longer good enough.' As the eldest son of a bourgeois middle-class family that had fallen on difficult financial times in his childhood, Sibelius was intended to pursue a respectable professional career rather than follow his artistic interests, and so in September he enrolled at the University of Helsinki to study law. It was nevertheless the city's range of musical distractions that most strongly attracted his attention. In his letter to Pehr and Evelina, for example, he wrote, 'I have been to four concerts and I particularly liked one of them,'[16] and he was keen to find a new violin teacher who would be able to support his desire to explore a wider and more demanding repertoire. Though he attended to his law studies dutifully for some months, his energies were always already divided: on 15 September, alongside his university entrance, he had enrolled at the Helsinki Music Institute (Helsingin musiikkiopisto), and it was soon apparent that music would become his full-time occupation.

Now known as the Sibelius Academy and widely recognized as one of the world's leading conservatoires, the Helsinki Music Institute had been founded in 1882 by Martin Wegelius. Born in western Finland in 1846, the son of an academic and administrator who would later become university bursar in Helsinki, Wegelius himself read literature and philosophy in Helsinki before pursuing musical studies in Vienna, Leipzig (where he studied at the conservatoire with Carl Reinecke) and Munich in the 1870s. He became an enthusiastic admirer of Wagner's work and drafted a three-hundred-page biography of the composer (which remained unfinished), as well as publishing a series of textbooks including a history

Sibelius's teacher, Martin Wegelius, 1890s, photograph by Daniel Nyblin.

of Western music (1893) and a primer in harmony and figured bass (1897).[17] Widely active as a teacher, accompanist, critic, conductor and choral director (he briefly led Pacius's Akademiska Sångförening), Wegelius's compositions included a cantata, *Den 6 Mai*, to a text by Runeberg, a violin sonata, an orchestral overture to the historical drama *Daniel Hjort* by Josef Julius Wecksell, the rondo 'quasi una fantasia' for piano and orchestra, and a large number of solo songs, choral works and folk-song arrangements. It is nevertheless as founder of the Institute that he arguably made his greatest contribution to the development of Finnish music. Wegelius's aims were twofold: to elevate musical training in Finland to a professional level comparable with that available elsewhere in Europe (inspired by his study trips in Germany and Austria), and to internationalize Finnish musical life by bringing teachers and performers from overseas to support the Institute's curriculum. Foremost among the staff he recruited, and arguably the most significant influence on Sibelius's career, was the remarkably gifted Italian pianist and composer Ferruccio Busoni (1866–1924), a fellow former student of Reinecke who was recommended by the German musicologist Hugo Riemann. Though Sibelius himself never held Busoni's compositions in high regard, there is no question that his ability as a pianist made a powerful impression, and Busoni's subsequent writings on musical aesthetics in many ways paralleled the direction that Sibelius's own work would pursue. Busoni in his turn would play an important part in introducing some of Sibelius's most significant works to audiences in Germany and beyond.

Wegelius's curriculum at the Institute combined formal instruction in harmony, counterpoint and music theory with practical instrumental performance. Sibelius's principal study was the violin, and he must at this point have been considering a professional career as a soloist or chamber musician. In mid-October, after his enrolment, he wrote to his uncle Pehr with a vivid account of his first violin teacher, Mitrofan Vasiliev, whom he described as 'delicate in appearance, rather tall, thin with black hair, a moustache and whiskers and two black eyes in his head'. According to Sibelius, Vasiliev 'plays with fire and life, and possesses a colossal technique'; though he spoke Russian, French and a little Swedish, their lessons took place in German.[18] Sibelius was hence trained in a tradition that combined elements of both the German and Russian violin schools, with an emphasis on depth and range of tone production, purity of intonation and a virtuosic dexterity of articulation. Sibelius's repertoire included concertos by Rode, Viotti and Mendelssohn, as well as the Beethoven

Romances, alongside études by Mazas and Kayser, and much of his later music for the violin points to his immersion in the technique and sound world of such earlier nineteenth-century violin writing: a significant but critically neglected part of his legacy. Even though he later progressed to study with the Institute's principal violin professor, Hermann Csillag (1852–1922), Sibelius evidently never gained sufficient confidence and security of execution to maintain a top high-level performing career. The gulf between his own ability and that of Busoni, who was a year younger than Sibelius, must have been especially apparent, although his uncle Pehr also noted that Sibelius was reluctant to invest sufficient time and effort in the sheer amount of sustained practice that a virtuoso career would demand. More important perhaps was the experience he continued to gain playing chamber music: as a member of the Institute's string quartet, he later took part in performances of works by Schumann and Anton Rubinstein, and in 1889, towards the end of his time at the Institute, he appeared alongside Busoni and Csillag in a performance of Schumann's Piano Quintet.

Though he therefore thought of himself primarily as a violinist during his early years at the Music Institute, Sibelius also continued to compose, and he studied counterpoint and later composition with Wegelius. His summer holidays provided further opportunities to write chamber music for domestic use, and the works he composed during his student years provide evidence of his growing creative ambitions. The so-called 'Hafträsk Trio', JS 207, written during the summer of 1886 while staying on Norrskata island at Korpo in the far western Finnish archipelago beyond Turku, for instance, presents a much more expansive musical frame than his earlier works. The opening Allegro Maestoso suggests Schumann or Brahms rather than the eighteenth-century composers who had been the primary point of reference for Sibelius's earlier music. The Andantino that follows is a lilting barcarolle, one of Sibelius's favourite idioms: the delicately rescored return of the opening theme evokes an elegant Biedermeier drawing room, whereas the Scherzo is a brilliant tour de force. The concluding rondo suggests a *danse macabre*, and seemingly comes to a complete stop after a series of hushed hymn-like chords, before a rapid return of the opening theme unexpectedly recalls the Mephistophelian flavour of the start. A work for the same forces written on holiday the following year (1887), known as the 'Korpo Trio', JS 209, is on an even grander scale: the exposition of the opening movement alone takes almost four minutes to perform, and the second movement

Jean, Linda and Christian Sibelius playing as a trio at the spa casino of Loviisa, late 1880s.

is an intense Beethovenian Fantasia that is broken down into several constituent parts, suggesting a hidden narrative or programme. The work's most striking gesture is the use of string harmonics and the piano's extreme upper register to create a chilling atmosphere, an effect unlike anything else in Sibelius's work to date. The guileless finale comes as an emotional release after the intensity of the Fantasia, and its nagging opening theme proves deceptively memorable.

Given the intensity and imagination of the 'Hafträsk' and 'Korpo' trios, and that of a third work, the 'Lovisa Trio', JS 208, written in 1888, it is curious that Sibelius never returned to the piano trio format later in his career: perhaps the forces were too closely bound up with his childhood and student years, and with precious memories of evenings spent playing chamber music with family members. Alternatively, perhaps he simply felt that he had already exhaustively explored the genre. He nonetheless continued to write music for piano and single strings – violin or cello – extensively. Sibelius's other student works included an austerely beautiful String Quartet in A minor, JS 183, his 'graduation piece' performed by an ensemble led by Csillag at the Institute on 29 May 1889, when Sibelius was 23, and which marks a considerable advance on his three piano trios, as well as a remarkable Violin Sonata in F major, JS 178, which he completed later that summer. Writing to his uncle Pehr, he described the opening movement of the sonata as 'fresh and daring as well as gloomy with some brilliant episodes', whereas the second movement was 'Finnish and melancholy; it is an authentic Finnish girl who sings on the A string; then some peasant lads perform a Finnish dance and try to entice her to smile, but it doesn't work; she only sings with greater sadness and melancholy than before.'[19] The Griegian finale was inspired by an altogether more cosmic phenomenon: the passage of a comet witnessed by Pehr himself and later recounted to the captivated young composer. Though the image of a meteor streaming across the Finnish midsummer night sky might seem an appealing metaphor for Sibelius's own early career following the completion of his studies at the Music Institute, that potential remained as yet unfulfilled despite the immense promise suggested by works such as the A minor String Quartet and the F major Violin Sonata. The outlook was inescapable: it was only by physically leaving Finland and pursuing his studies overseas, in the context of a much wider artistic and cultural environment, that Sibelius could begin to shape his own individual musical character in a manner that would sustain his mature composition.

2

Young Romantics

Sibelius's student years in Helsinki not only provided his first professional-level musical training, but introduced him to a circle of young artists, writers and musicians that brought significant social and cultural prestige. Foremost among this group were the three Järnefelt brothers: writer Arvid (1861–1932), painter Eero (1863–1932), and composer Armas (1869–1958), who studied like Sibelius at Martin Wegelius's Music Institute before spending much of his career in Sweden. Sons of a high-ranking former general in the Russian army and later governor of Vaasa Province, Alexander Järnefelt (1833–1896), the brothers had been brought up in a strongly patriarchal household that stressed loyalty to the Russian tsar, on the one hand, while insisting on equal rights for Finnish citizens and the Finnish language, on the other: a paradox that had seemed sustainable during the relatively tolerant years of Alexander II's rule, but which was to come under increasing strain during that of his more reactionary successor, Alexander III. The general's estranged wife, Elisabeth Clodt von Jürgensburg (1839–1929), was an important patron of the arts (and sister of the artist Michael Clodt von Jürgensburg, a founding member of the Peredvizhniki movement in Russian art and tutor at the Imperial academy in St Petersburg), who for several years hosted a literary salon, similar to those in other continental European cities, where the latest developments in Finnish, Russian and Scandinavian arts, politics, music and literature were intensively analysed and discussed. Brought up in St Petersburg, she was heavily influenced by Tolstoy's ideas, and after her husband's death purchased a farm at Vieremä in central Finland, modelled on Tolstoy's estate at Yasnaya Polyana south of Moscow. Though her Russian associations led to straitened circumstances after Finnish independence in 1917, the family was for a time at the forefront of the campaign for Finnish cultural and political self-determination. It was likely that Sibelius was first exposed to serious political debate, especially over the pre-eminence of the Finnish language, during his early years in the orbit of the Järnefelts. And it must also have introduced him to many of the most controversial topics in contemporary European thought and literature, not least the question of gender and sexual equality explored in Ibsen's dramas and the work of French realists such as Zola and Flaubert.

It was through the three Järnefelt brothers that Sibelius became acquainted with their younger sister, Aino (1871–1969), whom he first met in autumn 1888. Although Aino was at that time the focus of another young artist's attention – the author Juhani Aho (Johannes Brofeldt), who later wrote heartbreakingly about his sense of betrayal in his lightly autobiographical novel *Yksin* (Alone) – she became engaged to Sibelius, and they eventually married on 10 June 1892. Aino was a remarkable locus of domestic stability: their marriage was able to endure despite Sibelius's frequent shifts of mood and fragile confidence. She also gave the young composer access to an elite world that was among the best connected in Finnish society. Sibelius's association with the family not only channelled and supported his artistic interests and activities, but provided a degree of social and cultural privilege that would in turn feed into his growing anxieties about class, duty and public obligation.

Järnefelt family portrait, 1896: brothers Arvid, Armas and Eero (at rear); Aino and Elisabeth (front, left) and Sibelius.

As Sibelius approached the end of his formal studies at the Music Institute in Helsinki, it was clear that he would need to look further afield if he wished to pursue his education at a higher level. There was at that time no provision for postgraduate musical instruction in Finland. Furthermore, trips south across the Baltic to continental Europe had long been routine for aspiring young artists and musicians from across the Nordic-Scandinavian region. The painter Albert Edelfelt (1854–1905), for example, had studied in Antwerp and at the École Nationale des Beaux-Arts in Paris before returning to Finland (where his pupils included Léon Bakst), and Wegelius himself had spent time in Germany and later undertook study visits to France and Italy. When Sibelius applied for a stipend to travel abroad in early 1889, therefore, it was a perfectly normative expectation for an ambitious young Finnish musician, and on 7 September he departed Helsinki onboard the steamship *Storfursten*, bound for Berlin, in the company of a group of young colleagues, including Eero Järnefelt, Juhani Aho (his rival for Aino's affections), the literary scholar Werner Söderhjelm and a fellow musician, Ilmari Krohn, who would later become a distinguished ethnomusicologist and pedagogue, but without his future wife, Aino.[1] Writing to his uncle Pehr back in Finland, Sibelius reported on the boat's progress down through the Baltic – the furthest he had travelled away from home thus far – past the islands of Gotland and Bornholm, and recorded his hopes for his time in Berlin: 'I am going to study composition with Becker; he is a very capable composer and teacher. We'll see with whom I'll study violin. I am burning with desire to hear the most splendid orchestras one can imagine.'[2] It would prove to be the first of many occasions on which he would journey south in search of musical and aesthetic inspiration, a regular pattern of cultural exchange that would be disrupted only by the outbreak of the First World War.

The choice of Berlin as a destination was dictated partly by the city's strategic accessibility and active musical life (Sibelius and his friends attended a performance of *Don Giovanni* at the Kroll Opera on their first evening – the first time he had seen a live performance of Mozart's work), and also by the fact that it was already a centre of activity for young Scandinavian artists and musicians: among Sibelius's colleagues were the Danish musicians Fini Henriques and Frederik Schnedler-Petersen, the Norwegian composer Christian Sinding – then seen as potentially Edvard Grieg's most significant successor, but better known now as the composer of the Wagner-inspired piano miniature *Frühlingsrauschen* (The Rustle of Spring), op. 32/3 – and Finnish compatriots Alf Klingenberg and Adolf

Edvard Munch, *Artists Around a Table* (August Strindberg, Holger Drachmann, Gunnar Heiberg, Edvard Munch), *Zum Schwartzen Ferkel*, 1893, blue crayon on paper.

Paul. The Scandinavian Berliner circle gathered at a tavern at the western end of Unter den Linden and its corner with Neue Wilhelmstrasse in central Berlin known as 'Zum Schwarzen Ferkel' (The Black Piglet), close by the Brandenburg Gate. Its more notorious customers later included August Strindberg, the young Edvard Munch and the Danish poet Holger Drachmann, as well as the striking Norwegian author Dagny Juel, with whom both Munch and Strindberg became romantically entangled and who would later die in mysterious circumstances in the Georgian capital Tbilisi, aged only 34. Conversation revolved around issues of symbolism, human psychology and artistic inspiration, gender politics, eroticism and subjectivity, themes that would recur with particular frequency in much of Sibelius's work throughout the 1890s and the following decade. It was a vastly different cultural and aesthetic milieu from the pietistic Lutheranism of his childhood home in Hämeenlinna.

Among this remarkable group of artistic visionaries and practitioners, Adolf Paul (1863–1943) was almost certainly the least talented, and never succeeded in establishing a professional musical career either at home or abroad. But his breezy and thinly camouflaged autobiography, *En bok om en människa* (A Book About a Person), published in 1891, scandalized polite Helsinki society with its vivid descriptions of decadent life in a continental European metropolis, and provided a valuable insight into the group's artistic debates and preoccupations. Paul's book also offered an early glimpse of the hero worship that Sibelius's talent inspired in some of his contemporaries. Paul referred to Sibelius, lightly disguised in the novella as the composer 'Sillén', as 'Genibarnet' (or 'Wunderkind'), 'a truly natural genius, utterly individual, without the slightest relationship to anyone else', and presented a remarkable account of his musical method in dialogue with the book's principal protagonist (modestly modelled on Paul himself), a character called Hans:

> Once he told Hans how he composed. The moods that struck him with an impression were identified in his brain with a certain shade or colour, and only then, when mood and shade were clear to him, did the actual composition start. Then and only then did the motives, appropriate rhythms, and correct harmonies report for duty.
>
> ... For him there was a wonderfully mysterious connection between tone and colour, between the most secret perceptions of the eye and the ear. Everything he saw brought on a corresponding impression in the auditory organs – every tone impression was transferred and fixed as colour on the retina, and from this into memory.[3]

Paul's description was, of course, merely a second-hand and distanced attempt to capture in words what was inevitably a more complex and opaque (and at times prosaic) pattern of work and association in the young composer's mind. But for all the fantastical and over-exaggerated qualities of Paul's prose, it is curiously consistent with aspects of Sibelius's own elliptical commentary on his creative process, whether recorded in his diaries and correspondence or as reported by other writers. If Sibelius was never properly a synaesthete, as Paul's description attempted to suggest, he certainly maintained an extraordinarily acute associative capacity to link music, sound and other media with colour, mood and atmosphere ('Stimmung', or, in Sibelius's preferred Swedish coinage, 'stämning') – an ability to perceive the intimate correspondence between things and objects that was avidly discussed by the circle at Zum Schwarzen Ferkel and that provided the basis for Sibelius's symbolist worldview. At the same time, Paul also caught something of Sibelius's addictive personality. Writing of 'a refined egoist', Paul described Sillén as 'a great gourmet', who 'loved cigars more than he loved himself – which is to say, a considerable extent', and for whom 'pleasure was to be found not in possession but only in the satisfaction of such craving'. For Sibelius's patient and long-suffering fiancée Aino, reading such racy descriptions of her future husband must have been especially painful. For Sibelius, the city's diversions were a formative rite of passage.

Berlin thus provided the young composer with an intensely immersive creative environment and an opportunity for experimentation, both personal and artistic, that was beyond anything that Helsinki could then offer. In terms of formal musical tuition, however, Sibelius was evidently disappointed. Albert Becker was a pillar of the Prussian musical establishment: a stylistically conservative figure, born in Quedlinburg in 1834, who became professor of composition at the Scharwenka Conservatory and was best known for his liturgical music and songs, including the *Reformation* Cantata (1878), as well as a handful of chamber and orchestral works. He was later appointed director of the Königliche Domchor and dedicated his oratorio *Selig aus Gnade* to Kaiser Wilhelm II. The course of instruction through which he led Sibelius was based on strict counterpoint – effectively an extension of

Adolf Paul, 1886.

the curriculum that he had already followed under Wegelius in Helsinki – rather than free composition. For a young composer striving to identify his own individual artistic voice, such tightly circumscribed technical assignments must have felt especially frustrating. But for all his resistance to such musical routine, a note that Sibelius scrawled on the back of a receipt from Becker dated 14 October 1890 suggests that at the least he respected his teacher's commitment to artistic self-discipline and humility: 'Don't give in to passion but develop what gifts you have harmoniously. Don't imagine you are anything other than you are. Don't think of becoming a great man. Work intelligently. *Si male nunc et olim sic erit*.'[4] The injunction to work harder would remain one of the leitmotifs throughout Sibelius's career.

The musical results of Sibelius's Berlin year would nevertheless bear witness to a striking advance in terms of scope and ambition. Foremost among these works is the Piano Quintet in G minor, JS 159. It may have been Sibelius's friend and former colleague in Helsinki, Ferruccio Busoni, who provided the stimulus for the composition, Sibelius's largest and most complex to date.[5] Busoni encouraged the Finn to attend a performance of Sinding's Piano Quintet, op. 5, with the Brodsky Quartet in Leipzig on 19 January 1890, and this experience may directly have inspired Sibelius to start his own work. The step-change in mood and idiom is apparent from the quintet's opening bars: the tremolando effect of the piano writing has an entirely different quality from any of Sibelius's previous works, as does the strongly profiled contour of the first movement's thematic material and its spacious presentation. The central Andante revolves around two contrasting themes, a sombre opening melody, which returns with an imaginatively varied accompaniment, and a more cheerful, march-like idea that looks back to the idealized Biedermeier world of some of Sibelius's earlier chamber works. The two themes are combined in the final section of the movement: an imaginative and unexpected compositional conceit that leads to the most emotionally stirring music of the whole work. The slow movement is framed by a gentle intermezzo and a brief, dashing scherzo with brilliant *moto perpetuo* figuration. The finale provides a counterweight to the opening movement – an extended torrent of melodic ideas and figuration that incessantly drives the music forward towards a seemingly obsessive close. Despite the impressive quality and conception of the music, the quintet's early performance history was far from straightforward: Busoni took part in the official premiere at the Helsinki Music Institute on 5 May 1890, but only the first and third

Ferruccio Busoni, 1889.

movements were played on that occasion, and at a second performance in Turku (with Adolf Paul at the piano), the first four movements were given without the finale. The quintet was not performed in its entirety until 1965, the centenary of Sibelius's birth and 75 years after its first appearance: one of Sibelius's most important but neglected early scores.

Among the other major musical events of Sibelius's time in Berlin was, ironically, the performance of a work by one of his elder Finnish contemporaries: the symphonic poem *Aino* by Robert Kajanus (1856–1933). Almost a decade older than Sibelius, Kajanus had studied music theory and composition privately in Helsinki with Richard Faltin before enrolling, like Wegelius, at the Leipzig Conservatoire, where his teachers included Reinecke. After graduation he worked briefly in Paris (with the great Norwegian conductor and composer Johan Svendsen) and in Dresden, but on his return to Finland in July 1882 (in the same year as the inauguration of Wegelius's Institute) he founded the Helsinki Orchestral Society, later renamed the Helsinki Philharmonic Orchestra (Helsingin Kaupunginorkesteri or, in Swedish, Helsingfors stadsorkester), the country's first permanent orchestra and later one of the major ensembles in the Nordic countries. In the tight-knit and claustrophobic world of Helsinki's musical community in the 1880s, it was easy for strong personalities to fall out, and Kajanus and Wegelius quickly became rivals, especially when Wegelius failed to offer Kajanus a salaried position at the Institute. Sibelius's interactions with Kajanus before his arrival in Berlin would therefore have been limited, although he would certainly have been aware of Kajanus's efforts to create a professional orchestral standard of performance in the Finnish capital at a time when such opportunities were otherwise extremely limited. Kajanus, for his part, would become a stalwart interpreter and supporter of Sibelius's music, although rivalry would again figure prominently in their relationship, especially towards the end of the 1890s.

Kajanus's historical standing as a composer has certainly not equalled his reputation as a conductor, but his symphonic poem *Aino* is easily one of the most important Finnish works before Sibelius's *Kullervo* Symphony. Modelled on Liszt's famous series of symphonic poems, which often borrowed mythic or legendary themes as topics, Kajanus's

Robert Kajanus, 1906.

Aino was based on an eponymous female character from the Finnish epic the *Kalevala*, and first performed in Helsinki at a gala event organized to celebrate the epic's fiftieth anniversary in 1885. Musically, *Aino* is remarkable not only for its richly Wagnerian harmonic idiom, apparent especially in the winding chromaticism of its opening bars, but for its command of instrumental colour and texture. After the statement and elaboration of a broadly heroic theme, invoking pride in the image of a shared cultural-historical legacy, the full orchestra is joined in the closing passage by a male voice chorus, whose words act as a form of collective declamation: 'Soi, soi, nyt kannel, mun murhe jo murtanee. / Soi, soi, se mun sydäntäni virvoittaa' (Resound, resound, kantele, my sorrow breaks me / Resound, resound, it revives my heart).[6] For the young Sibelius, the scale and ambition of Kajanus's work – and the spectacle of a large-scale choral piece written and performed by one of his Finnish contemporaries in a major continental European city – must have been overwhelming, and it may have been one of the primary reasons why he began to think about his own first orchestral scores the following year.

Stimulated by the musical and artistic opportunities that Berlin had already offered, Sibelius may originally have intended to spend a second year in the city. But he was already tempted to spread his wings even further afield, and so, after returning to Finland over the summer, he travelled south again in autumn 1890, this time with the intention of studying in Vienna. As before, his plan was to undertake a course of academic study, although his hopes of working with Anton Bruckner were swiftly dispelled by the older composer's ill health. Instead, Sibelius took lessons with Robert Fuchs (1847–1927), professor of music theory at the Vienna Conservatoire, whose other pupils comprised a roll call of musicians who would go on to achieve significant careers, including Mahler, Wolf, Alexander Zemlinsky, Erich Korngold and the Anglo-French composer Maude Valerie White. Nicknamed 'Serenaden-Fuchs', after the popular success of his five orchestral serenades, Fuchs also wrote symphonies and operas. But, as with his experience with Becker in Berlin, Sibelius found Fuchs's teaching painfully dry and limiting. More liberating perhaps were his occasional consultations with a second Viennese figure, Karl Goldmark (1830–1915), a Jewish composer born in Keszthely at the western end of Lake Balaton, who achieved notable success with his four-act opera *Die Königin von Saba* (The Queen of Sheba), first performed at the Hofoper in Vienna in 1875. Goldmark was a very different character from either Fuchs or Becker. He was more open-minded and less didactic in approach, and interested in a wider range of musical idioms and repertoires. His track record as an opera composer was matched also by his orchestral music, including the splendid 'Ländliche Hochzeit' (Rustic Wedding) Symphony of 1876, a work that certainly influenced the young Mahler. Sibelius's meetings with Goldmark, which did not take place on a regular or frequent basis, do not ever appear to have followed a formal plan or systematic programme of work, but he may have been an important sounding board for the Finnish composer, and he was able to provide introductions into the otherwise impenetrable Viennese musical network, a seemingly intractable challenge for a young musician in a foreign city at the start of his career.

Sibelius's letters home nevertheless focus on performances of music by other composers who were to have a more obviously direct influence on his development. Writing to Wegelius on 21 November 1890, shortly after his arrival, for instance, he recorded: '*Tristan and Isolde* was mounted at the opera in so brilliant a fashion that I would not have conceived it possible.' The following month he wrote to Aino about a concert at which Bruckner was booed by partisan members of the audience caught up in the polemical debates between supporters of Wagner versus Brahms, and confided:

> to my mind he is the greatest of all living composers . . . It was his D minor symphony (no. 3) that was played and you cannot imagine the enormous impression it has made on me. It has its shortcomings like anything else but above all it has a youthful quality even though its composer is an old man. From the point of view of form it is ridiculous.[7]

Such formal reservations aside, it was evidently Bruckner's handling of orchestral colour and texture that made the most vivid impression, particularly the hymn-like writing for brass choirs and the variety of tremolo and ostinato figuration for strings, both of which feature prominently in passages from *Kullervo*. At the same time, as with the performance of Kajanus's symphonic poem *Aino* in Berlin, Sibelius's thoughts during his time in Vienna appear to have been drawn back to Finland. In a letter to Aino from the end of the year, dated 26 December 1890, he reported: 'I am reading the *Kalevala* a lot and am already beginning to understand much more Finnish. The *Kalevala* strikes me as entirely modern and to my ears is pure music, themes and variations.' Sibelius's letter has frequently been read as indicating that he was still insecure about his proficiency in Finnish. Swedish was his mother tongue, and his correspondence frequently switched between the two languages. Given the strongly pro-Finnish sympathies of his future family-in-law, gaining greater confidence and fluency in Finnish would certainly have been a priority. But there is another way of reading Sibelius's note, which suggests that he was concerned not so much with matters of vocabulary and grammar, but rather with what he identified as a distinctively Finnish idiom and mindset, a way of thinking about the world. In that sense, his new-found concern with the *Kalevala* aligned with his existing symbolist sympathies: 'its story is far less important than the moods and atmosphere conveyed,' he continued in his letter to Aino. Drawing perhaps also on his recent immersion in Wagner's work, he explained 'the gods are human beings: Väinämöinen is a musician and so on.'[8] As Glenda Dawn Goss has argued, the heady, intoxicating world of *fin-de-siècle* Vienna, the city that gave birth to Gustav Klimt's shimmering paintings and Sigmund Freud's theories of the unconscious and the return of the repressed, surely only intensified Sibelius's interest in the *Kalevala* as a form of mythic discourse that offered privileged access to the inner workings of human psychology and behaviour.[9] Hence the apparent paradox between his time in the Habsburg metropolis, far south of Helsinki, and his sudden preoccupation with such archetypal Finnish literary and artistic materials need not seem so contradictory after all: on the contrary, it was a fortunate and opportune commingling of otherwise independent creative preoccupations that was to bear almost immediate fruit.

That does not imply that Sibelius's year in Vienna was an unequivocal professional success. Precisely the contrary, in fact. Early in the new year, on 9 January 1891, Sibelius auditioned unsuccessfully for a rank-and-file position in the Vienna Philharmonic, and the rejection came as a crushing blow that was one of the hardest disappointments of his musical life. Always a nervous performer in public, Sibelius was ill-equipped to perform optimally in the high-pressure environment of an audition. And, as his uncle Pehr had noted just a few years earlier, Sibelius had never properly invested in the intensive and all-consuming instrumental drills that a career as a professional performer would demand. In another sense, however, the audition was a timely reminder that Sibelius's creative energies were better channelled in another direction. Had he been hired as a violinist in Vienna, he may never have pursued composition as a full-time occupation. The musical results of this renewed set of priorities are startling: the premiere of a new string quartet, in B flat, op. 4, at the Helsinki

Music Institute on 13 October 1890, led by Johan Svendsen, had been further evidence of Sibelius's growing confidence with large-scale form and instrumental texture. Arguably more significant, however, were his two first orchestral compositions, an Overture in E major, JS 145, and a symphonic poem entitled *Balettscen*, JS 163, which both date from early 1891. Whether or not the two pieces were seriously intended as parts of a multi-movement work such as a symphony,[10] they present a strongly contrasting pair. The overture opens with a similar sense of breadth to that which characterizes the first movement of the piano quintet, and has many passages, especially in the development, that anticipate later works such as the *Karelia* music. The sudden broadening of the tempo at the reprise is an early instance of Sibelius's interest in manipulating the feeling of musical time and space at a crucial moment of structural articulation. The *Balettscen* is a very different conception, a brilliant orchestral waltz with exotic writing for percussion (including castanets) and a sweeping melodic momentum. It is in one sense a genre picture, a symbolic representation of the swinging rhythms and pulses of modern life, and a vital soundtrack for the modern city with its escapist dreams and fantasies. Sibelius had long been fascinated by the waltz: many of his early chamber works include waltz-like sequences, or comprise miniature dance-sets, and he continued to compose in the idiom until his very final published work. Few composers since Chopin have been as obsessed with the dance and its expressive world. For symbolists in the 1890s, the waltz was also freighted with an alluring sense of erotic danger. The protagonists in Edvard Munch's famous 1899 painting *The Dance of Life*, for instance, present a characteristically bleak and emotionally fraught allegory of human relationship and sexual encounter. The apex of Sibelius's *Scène* likewise suggests an abrupt moment of crisis, a paralysing spasm of pain or self-realization that threatens to derail the music. And written almost three decades later, the whirling figures in Maurice Ravel's wistfully nostalgic *poème chorégraphique*, *La valse* (1919–20), eventually spiral out of control towards self-destruction and collapse. The music at the end of Sibelius's dance, in contrast, simply evaporates enigmatically into thin air, suggesting not so much a dramatic decline and fall but that the dance merely continues elsewhere in an unceasing dynamic motion.

Sibelius's freshly awakened interest in Finnish cultural materials during his year in Vienna took a number of forms. First and foremost was his ongoing work on a grand choral symphony based on the tragic legend of Kullervo, an ill-fated orphan, from Runos 31–6 of the *Kalevala*.

Edvard Munch, *The Dance of Life*, 1899–1900, oil on canvas.

Second was his continuing enthusiasm for the poetry of Johan Ludvig Runeberg, his favourite writer from his school days in Hämeenlinna. Just as the *Kalevala* had gained a new, deeper significance for Sibelius in the context of the symbolist circles in which he moved in Berlin and Vienna, so too must Runeberg's luminous poetry have taken on a new psychological intensity. That is certainly the case in the settings of three Runeberg poems that Sibelius completed during spring 1891. The first, 'Drömmen' (The Dream), is an abruptly concise narrative poem that recounts how a young lover seeks refuge from their sorrow in sleep, only for their beloved to appear to them in a dream: as they rise to meet her lips in a kiss, the dream evaporates, the beloved long departed 'bort om land och sjöar' (across the land and lakes), and the protagonist is left alone in abandonment and guilt. What might possibly have seemed a mawkish story of infatuation in Sibelius's hands becomes a writhing turmoil of frustrated passion and barely suppressed erotic longing: the unsettled arpeggio accompaniment of the opening gives way to an icy stillness as the dream descends, only for the return to be savagely abbreviated as the protagonist is brought back down to earth. Musically, the song is interesting not only for the way that Sibelius pivots on the enharmonic equivalence of D flat and C sharp to effect the modulation that initiates the dream sequence, but for the strong rhythmic profile of the opening phrase. The asymmetrical stress pattern of the initial phrase suggests the influence of sung Finnish on the articulation of Runeberg's Swedish text: early evidence of Sibelius's attempt to create a hybrid musical language combining both sides of his national poetic heritage and his interest in folk song.

Three settings of Runeberg – 'Drömmen', plus two further songs, 'Hjärtats morgon' (The Heart's Morning) and 'Våren flyktar hastigt' (Spring Is Flying) – were performed by the esteemed baritone Abraham Ojanperä, whom Sibelius had heard singing as a child in Hämeenlinna, at the Helsinki Music Institute on 19 October 1891.[11] Sibelius had spent the summer with his family in Loviisa on his return from Vienna, and then returned to the Finnish capital to try and earn a living from teaching, composition and performance. His first major appearance on the podium, to direct a performance of his Overture in E major and *Balettscen* at one of Kajanus's concerts, was well received, not least as evidence of the results of his study trips abroad. But later in November he travelled to Porvoo (Borgå), an ancient medieval city on the coast 50 kilometres (30 mi.) east of Helsinki, in the company of the sociologist and literary scholar Yrjö Hirn (1870–1952), who from 1910 was Professor of Aesthetics and Contemporary Literature at the University of Helsinki. The primary objective of the visit was to meet a well-known Finnish folk singer, Larin Paraske, and record some of the melodies that she performed. Paraske had been born in Ingria in 1833, an area close to St Petersburg at the far eastern end of the Gulf of Finland between Lake Ladoga and Estonia. Her

Albert Edelfelt, *Larin Paraske*, 1893, oil on canvas.

extensive knowledge of indigenous Finnish folk stories, performed through a form of highly repetitive unaccompanied recitation known as runic singing, attracted the attention of a cleric, Adolf Neovius, who began to transcribe her melodies in 1887. When Neovius moved to Porvoo in 1891, Paraske followed him, and she became acclaimed for the range of her repertoire and the power of her performance. She was the subject of portraits by both Edelfelt and Eero Järnefelt, and was belatedly granted a pension by the Finnish Literature Society (Suomalaisen Kirjallisuuden Seura) in 1901, but died in poverty in Sakkola (now Russian Gromovo) in 1904. Paraske had first appeared at the Literature Society in March 1891, where her singing had aroused considerable interest, and Sibelius may have heard her later that summer before travelling to Porvoo in the autumn. Although her appearances by this time were to a greater or lesser extent carefully choreographed, wearing specially purchased folk costumes, for example, Sibelius was evidently moved and impressed by her performance, and it fed into his continuing work on *Kullervo* as well as his growing awareness of the latent potential of Finnish vernacular musical traditions.

The depressing trajectory of Paraske's career – born into a hard-working lower-class agrarian family, marrying young, being 'discovered' by middle-class ethnographers and performing for an elite group of artists and scholars, but ultimately unable to escape economic hardship and destitution – points to the tensions and ambiguities that characterized many nineteenth-century European folk revival movements. Regarded as possessing privileged native knowledge, an increasingly valuable form of cultural capital at a time of rising politically engaged nationalist activism, artists such as Paraske occupied a liminal position at the sharp edge of different class and social boundaries. In the complex historical political context of nineteenth-century Finland (supposedly autonomous but in reality a distantly administered region located at the extreme western edge of a sprawling empire), the systematic collection and curation of Paraske's music and its adoption in high-art idioms was a form of inward colonial appropriation, bound up with assumptions about ethnic character and identity. It was never simply a neutral transaction or reciprocal process of exchange.

Sibelius himself never aspired to a professional ethnographic career, and in later years sought to distance himself from the idea that he had ever used actual Finnish folk melodies in his work.[12] There is no evidence that he was ever interested in runic singing or other forms of Finnish folk music as a child. His sympathies were rather with the late eighteenth- and early nineteenth-century art music repertoire. But for a short while during the 1890s he certainly undertook ethnographic excursions with more serious collectors such as Hirn and the distinguished folklorist Kaarle Krohn, and he played an active role in the fashion for folk-inspired creative work as part of the attempt to shape and define a distinctively Finnish aesthetic idiom. At the time of his marriage to Aino in 1892, for example, he combined plans for their honeymoon in the east of the country with further opportunities to hear runic melodies, writing on 2 June: 'in the morning I got a "catalogue" from Krohn of all the runic singers he knows. I went to him and asked about it. After then we selected an itinerary.'[13] Later the following month, however, he could write with only partially successful news about his trip: 'So far I've heard no more than two singers and nothing at all from *Kalevala*. Half of them are dead and the other half have moved away. I've only just returned from walking (1 mile) to one who was gone. I hope for better luck tomorrow at Tjokki.'[14] As Glenda Dawn Goss has shown, Sibelius consulted two existing collections of Finnish folk song as he was working on the score of the *Kullervo* Symphony in 1891: the first was Emil Sivori's *Folk Songs of Mäntyharju* (*Mäntyharjun kansanlauluja*), and the second is likely to have been a Russian anthology (possibly the famous 1806 collection edited by Nikolai Lvov and Ivan Prach, if not a more recent source).[15] Given the permeability of the Russian-Finnish border at the time, the irony of using a Russian publication to access Finnish folk materials may not have been as awkward as it now seems. In other ways, however, Sibelius struggled to clarify the shape and form of the composition as it developed. In a letter to Aino dated 17 December 1891, for instance, he confided: 'there is much in my Kullervo introduction which has taken all of my soul, but other things which still aren't so good.' At the same time, he already had a clear vision for the emotional crux of the symphony at the centre of the third movement: 'the culmination is when Kullervo sets forth in his sledge and seduces his sister. I have imagined this as a broad melody (a hundred bars) for violins, violas, and cellos in unison with some low rhythmic accompaniments (in the trombones and so on).' Three days later he wrote again about the same passage: 'I am still unclear whether to have a narrator or not and turn it into a melodrame (in which case the wonderful duet between Kullervo and his sister would lose its impact) or to have two singers (Ojanperä and Ms. Achté) to portray the characters and describe everything else purely in musical terms.'[16] Sibelius eventually abandoned the idea of narrator, placing the burden of the musical narrative exclusively on the orchestra in movements 1, 2 and 4; but the passage at the heart of the third movement would prove to be the most powerful he had yet conceived.

It is difficult to overstate the impact that the premiere of the symphony had upon both the reputation and career of its 26-year-old composer and the idea of a national music in Finland. As early as April 1891, when he was first working on the score, Sibelius described the symphony to Aino as 'completely in the Finnish spirit', and wrote, 'this UrFinnishness has gotten into my flesh and blood. I succeed best in this manner. Besides, Finnish for me has become sacred.'[17] The performance took place on 28 April 1892 in the ceremonial great hall of the University of Helsinki, located at the heart of the Finnish capital on Senate Square, and was conducted by Sibelius himself with two of the country's leading soloists, baritone Ojanperä and soprano Emmy Achté (mother of the great Wagnerian diva Aino Ackté, for whom Sibelius later wrote his great tone poem *Luonnotar* in 1913). The significance of the event was marked by its illustrious audience, including a pantheon of Finnish dignitaries, and by its critical reception, which was unreservedly enthusiastic. Oskar Merikanto, for example, proclaimed that 'we recognize these tones as

University of Helsinki's Great Hall, 1907, photograph by Signe Brander.

ours, even if we have never heard them as such' in an article published on the day of the premiere.[18] Another influential writer, Karl Flodin, wrote after the performance that, in *Kullervo*, 'Sibelius has established his own voice . . . and with it creates his *own* music in our *own* music'.[19] Yet after the initial run of performances, Sibelius withdrew the score and it was never heard in its entirety again for the rest of his life: he only permitted selected extracts to be revived for celebrations to mark the centenary of the *Kalevala* in 1935. If *Kullervo* was a breakthrough, at least on a national platform, it was simultaneously also the first in the series of artistic crises of confidence or abrupt changes of stylistic direction that would characterize much of the remainder of Sibelius's career.

What was perhaps most striking for its contemporary audience in 1892 was the prominence of the symphony's Finnish-language text. Although Kajanus had already used a male chorus in the closing sequence of his symphonic poem *Aino*, the use of the chorus in *Kullervo* is far more prominent and integral to the work's impact. Although the chorus effectively serves the distanced role of narrator, as in Greek tragedy, the spectacle of the sung choir must have fostered an intense sense of involvement with the work's trajectory. *Kullervo* is a shockingly raw drama of lust and male sexual violence. Its title character appears only briefly in the first version of the *Kalevala*, published in 1835, but his darkly tragic tale is narrated at greater length in the revised 1849 edition, from which Sibelius took his libretto. Abandoned by his parents and brought up in an abusive foster home, Kullervo travels across the northland's desolate wastes in search of female company. Rejected by the first two women he encounters, Kullervo enjoys more success with the third, who, in Sibelius's version of the story, is lured fatefully into his sledge not because of the promise of money ('raha', as in the original version) but because of longing and desire ('halu', Sibelius's sole emendation to the text).[20] Only after Kullervo and his conquest have spent the night together does he realize the awful truth – that he has unwittingly seduced his sister. She casts herself into the foaming rapids out of shame, and Kullervo swears terrifying vengeance on his foster family, who he discovers have betrayed him. After cutting them down ruthlessly, Kullervo throws himself upon his own sword in a bloody act of contrition.

Whether Sibelius somehow associated himself with Kullervo's story – an orphaned boy who tragically gives way to illicit physical desire and then faces the world's bitter slings and arrows with a stoic determination – is unclear, although it would explain the work's searing impact and brutalizing intensity. Sibelius covers the key elements of Kullervo's story in five movements, the third and fifth of which are choral. The opening movement is a brooding character portrait that opens with a sombre motto-like theme in E minor. In his letter to Aino on 17 December 1891, Sibelius described the movement as being in a 'strict sonata form', and a meditative second subject group leads to a harmonically adventurous development before the opening motto returns. The movement closes with a sense of oppressive defeat, foreshadowing the outcome of the entire work. In contrast, the second movement, entitled 'Kullervo's youth', is a lullaby in a softly radiant B major, with two contrasting pastoral episodes dominated by stylized nature sounds in the woodwind. Adapting the same strophic model as the one he had already developed in the central Andante of the G minor Piano Quintet, in which two themes are repeated with a variety of rhythmic and textural variations (culminating here in a stormy passage of surging strings and craggy brass interjections), 'Kullervo's Youth' is the most distinctive and innovative movement in the whole work.

The third movement is the longest and most complex in the symphony. A scurrying orchestral introduction in F major depicts Kullervo's wild ride across the desolate northern heath. The male choir's unforgettable first entry (in a modally inflected D minor) introduces the work's eponymous hero figuratively for the first time: 'Kullervo, Kalervo's son / the old man's child' (Kullervo Kalervon poika / Sinisukka äijon lapsi). The rhythmic and harmonic tension rises as his initial attempts at seduction are unsuccessful. The love scene with the third young woman whom he does not yet recognize is an ardent passage in C sharp major, with a soaring melody in the upper strings and pulsating brass accompaniment, some of the most explicitly erotic music that Sibelius ever wrote. The sister's anguished lament after her fall from grace is achingly captured in an extended monologue, a showstopping set piece for the soprano soloist, after which Kullervo angrily curses his fate in a blunt F minor.

Following the emotional apex of the middle movement, the fourth is a glitteringly macabre scherzo in C major as Kullervo prepares for war and glorifies in its bloodshed, a brilliant percussive clash of iron and steel. The finale deals hauntingly with the massacre's consequences; after Kullervo returns to the site of his original crime, the chorus seemingly urge him on towards his grisly end. In the final bars Sibelius calls back the opening motto from the first movement, leading the work in cyclic fashion to its seemingly inevitable conclusion. For Sibelius's audience, the remorseless oppressiveness of the symphony's dramatic unfolding inevitably called to mind Finland's own political status, increasingly burdened under the yoke of Russian imperial rule. But the composer's own equivocal attitude to the work indicates a more characteristically ambivalent response. Now that *Kullervo* enjoys a much more prominent place in the repertory – indeed, it is currently played more often than at any point during its history – the symphony can perhaps be best understood as offering a salutary glimpse of the originality and brilliance of the young composer's compositional imagination. But *Kullervo* also points to the creative life experience of Sibelius's formative years in Berlin and Vienna, and his immersion in the symbolist world of erotic anxiety, sexual desire, psychological angst and myth that he encountered in his conversations and dialogues with contemporary Nordic artists and writers on the continent. It is a moving tribute to Sibelius's remarkable ability to gather up such seemingly disparate materials and impulses – from Bruckner's solemn symphonic textures to Larin Paraske's runic singing – and synthesize them in such a way that a wholly characteristic and compelling musical vision emerges as the result. And it also points to Sibelius's feeling for how to shape a musical narrative and drama over an extended span that would never find its outlet in full-length operatic form but would nevertheless support his sustained interest in writing for the theatre. Finally, the symphony's premiere established Sibelius's profile as one of the nation's leading artistic heroes at a crucial moment of cultural and political struggle and resistance. It was a legacy that would both serve to advance and promote Sibelius's reputation as a young musician seeking to establish his professional career, and become an increasing burden in its own right. In its grand mythic sweep, *Kullervo* captured Sibelius's creative opportunity and his artistic fate in a single devastating instant.

3

Sagas, Swans and Symphonic Dreams

One of the most well-known, indeed notorious, works in late nineteenth-century Finnish art is Akseli Gallen-Kallela's 1894 painting *Symposium*. Alternatively titled 'The Problem', Gallen-Kallela's tableau depicts three figures who are clearly the worse for wear, seated at the end of a dinner table surrounded by half-filled glasses and empty bottles and overseen by a self-portrait of the artist behind the table towards the left. Gallen-Kallela and two of the figures on the right – Sibelius, and his friend, colleague and rival Robert Kajanus – avoid the viewer's glance but instead stare implacably into the open wings of an unseen creature at the left edge of the picture: a harpy, sphinx, angel or other mythical being. In the background, the moon rises above a star-filled lake, as a rolling red mist drifts slowly across the waters, and in the far top right-hand corner, the lake reflects a shadowy forested shore. Gallen-Kallela's gilded frame encloses the whole scene with a stylized Egyptian relief that might either echo the fan-like wings of the mythical beast who haunts the left edge of the image or could suggest the stylized rays of a rising sun. In an alternative version of the picture, which Gallen-Kallela painted the same year and titled *Kajus Tableau* ('Kajus' was Kajanus's nickname), the third seated figure is recognizable as the composer and critic Oskar Merikanto: although the winged beast to the left is absent, a ghostly human form rises across the face of the moon, arms outstretched and raised towards the heavens.

The precise meaning of Gallen-Kallela's picture remains elusive: the disconcerting contrast between the strong realism of the individual portraits and the surreal symbolist imagery within which they sit is indicative of the artist's remarkable technical proficiency as well as the

Akseli Gallen-Kallela, *Symposium*, 1894, oil on canvas.

diverse range of influences and artistic traditions upon which he drew: Assyrian mythology, Platonic idealism, the paintings of Arnold Böcklin and the spirit of Friedrich Nietzsche's aristocratic radicalism.[1] At the same time, the painting captures a number of themes that were recurrent throughout much of Gallen-Kallela's work and that of his contemporaries, including the astonishingly talented Helene Schjerfbeck, during the 1890s. Those themes include a preoccupation with art as a form of revelation or mystical communion with an unseen spirit, alongside a fascination with human mortality, a penchant for dark, intense colours and a relentless sense of self-scrutiny. Equally striking is the aloof bearing of the group, dressed in formal evening wear at the end of some exclusive (and exclusively male) occasion and seemingly disdainful of the everyday world and its mundane routines. For Sibelius's family, as he struggled to earn a viable living from bits of teaching and performance on his return from Europe that could support their middle-class lifestyle, the bohemian character of the group and the all-too-obvious state of intoxication indicated by the dishevelled appearance of its participants must have been a cause for concern, not least following the birth of the composer's first daughter, Eva, on 19 March 1893. Yet the image also gives a good indication of the social and artistic circles in which Sibelius moved in the years following the premiere of *Kullervo*, and of the shared aesthetic preoccupations that were to feed into his music and ideas at the time. In the first instance, it is not nationalism or Finnish folklore that emerges as the single predominant concern from Gallen-Kallela's painting, much as they were to figure prominently in his other work from the decade, but rather the idea of the artist as a symbolist visionary, a medium for a fantasy world of ghostly shades and moonlit landscapes, an esoteric philosopher hovering on the boundary between life, death and the world beyond.

Sibelius's immersion in this symbolist fantasy world, with its alluring darkness and obscurity, is vividly manifest in the series of works that he completed in the wake of *Kullervo*, written partly while on a belated honeymoon with Aino in eastern Finland in the summer of 1892, aged 26. In the first of his Runeberg Songs op. 13, 'Under strandens granar' (Beneath the Pine Trees at the Shore), for example, the muse takes the form of the malevolent shape-shifting water spirit or 'Näcken', a common figure in Nordic mythology (and in European traditions elsewhere), who lures unwary passers-by to their death in the waters of the fabled Saimaa, Finland's largest lake in the far east of the country. The rippling piano *tremolando* of the opening bars suggests the brimming waters and a heightened state of expectancy. The Näck appears first to entice a young boy playing by the shoreline, disguising himself as a white pony in order to draw the child into the waves. When the boy's mother appears, the Näck transforms himself into an image of her child: as she rushes forward to embrace him, the Näck drags her down into the depths, the stridently brilliant chords of the coda celebrating the Näck's grisly triumph. In a later song, 'Till Frigga' (To Frigga), the muse is an idealized image of feminine beauty, for whose affection the poet would gladly forsake all the treasures of Africa and the ocean's pearls. Sibelius responds to Runeberg's erotically charged verse with a dazzling waltz, like an intensified version of his earlier *Balettscen*, which whirls towards its ecstatic high point as the narrator imagines himself falling into his beloved's arms. In both songs, then, the muse's siren call is fraught with danger, a sobering but simultaneously thrilling reminder of the perils of sinking too far into that escapist realm of longing and desire from which there can be no return.

'Under strandens granar' was not the first time, in fact, that Sibelius had been drawn to the mythical image of the water sprite hidden within the depths. Five years previously, while a student at the Music Institute in

1888, he had set an extract from a longer setting of Gunnar Wennerberg's poem *Näcken* (The Water Sprite), for which his teacher Wegelius had written most of the music. Sibelius's setting of the Näck's song had again invoked the waltz. The piano figuration has characteristic charm and the violin and cello suggest the Näck's resonant 'strängespel' (sounding strings): Scandinavian mythology often associated the Näck with waterfalls, and with the spellbinding strains of a fairy harp or fiddle that it was believed could be heard within the sound of the cascade (Stephen Sinding's well-known 1901 statue of Norwegian violin virtuoso Ole Bull in Bergen invokes precisely the same mythic imagery). But it was to Runeberg that Sibelius turned in 1893 for his melodrama *Svartsjukans nätter* (Nights of Jealousy). Conceived on a more ambitious scale than either *Näcken* or the individual Runeberg Songs from the op. 13 collection, *Svartsjukans nätter* is in effect a tone poem for chamber ensemble: a sustained study in nature sounds, woodland murmurs and frustrated love, which anticipates the trajectory of many of Sibelius's later orchestral works, notably the *Lemminkäinen Legends* and *Pohjola's Daughter*. The melodrama was written for a festival to celebrate Runeberg's birthday held at the Helsinki Music Institute on 5 February 1893, and Sibelius was so taken with the music that he re-used some of the material in his *Impromptus* for solo piano, op. 5, nos 5 and 6, works he later rescored for string orchestra. The piano arrangements capture different aspects of the melodrama, especially its enchanted invocation and wistful repose, and also point to Sibelius's growing confidence in writing for the instrument, inspired perhaps by his friendship with Busoni. The melodrama begins with a sustained introduction in E major, suggesting a blissful immersion in nature. The text specifies 'en nordisk sommarqväll' (a Nordic summer evening), a time of seemingly endless light and amplified sensory awareness. A rustling tremolo, like the start of 'Under strandens granar', suggests a sense of anticipation, prompted by the evening glow, which gives way to a sudden melancholy, 'ett stilla qval' (a silent pain). Out of this meditative state emerges a distant sound, heard from afar: at first the stylized sound of lute strings, later joined by a female voice (the wordless solo soprano). This triggers an involuntary memory in the narrator, the voice and image of his beloved. As his memory becomes stronger, he recalls her name, 'det var Minnas röst' (it was Minna's voice). In his imagination, they are united once again, and the melodrama drifts into a state of ecstasy. It is only the very last clause that shatters the illusion, the return to cold reality brusquely realized by Sibelius's abrupt final cadence.

Sibelius's attraction to melodrama was a prominent part of his early career and an interest he maintained throughout his active compositional life, and might be explained partly by the intimacy and intensity of the genre. Invariably smaller and more self-contained as a form than opera, melodrama was particularly well suited to the brevity and concision of Sibelius's musical style, and also to his preoccupation with evoking a particular mood or atmosphere ('stämning'), which was one of the founding principles of his work. But he was also compelled by the act of storytelling or narration, often from the distanced perspective of a poet or narrator, with which melodrama was often concerned. This combination of *stämning* and storytelling had been the basis for his first substantial engagement with the *Kalevala*, in *Kullervo*, and it would also become the platform for his next major orchestral work, the tone poem *En saga*, premiered on 16 February 1893, whose title (A Saga) simply refers blankly to the narrative genre itself without any further reference to the precise details of the story it purports to unfold. As would become a pattern in later life, Sibelius was deliberately cagey about the origins of the work and its possible sources of inspiration. According to his secretary Santeri Levas, many years after the work's composition Sibelius suggested that

> *En saga* is psychologically speaking one of my most profound works. I could almost say it encompasses my entire youth. It is the expression of a certain state of mind. When I composed it, I had undergone many shattering experiences. In no other work have I revealed myself so completely. Therefore I find all interpretations of *En saga* totally alien.[2]

Sibelius's German biographer Walter Niemann employed almost exactly the same turn of phrase in his description of the work: 'It is rather a question of a state of mind, the musical atmosphere a saga engenders in the listener, irrespective of whether it is Icelandic, Swedish or Finnish.'[3]

Levas's testimony needs to be handled cautiously, given the historical distance between the date of composition and that of his reported conversation with Sibelius. But the possibility that *En saga* might be at least partly autobiographical offers a potentially irresistible insight into Sibelius's personal and creative struggles and disappointments – as well as his subsequent reluctance to say too much about the work's meaning and significance. As Gallen-Kallela's *Symposium* painting had suggested, the boundaries between life and art could become fatally blurred. But, as Glenda Dawn Goss has argued, a closer contemporary source might present an alternative reading of the tone poem's subject-matter. A short story entitled 'Aleksis Kiven satu' (Aleksis Kivi's Tale) by the novelist Samuli Suomalainen (1850–1907) includes a passage in which a young composer called Johannes Seppälä (or 'Janne' for short, Sibelius's own Christian name) discusses the revision of a large-scale composition with the conductor Robert Kajava (the thinly disguised Kajanus), and reveals that the work's plot was based on the lynx hunt sequence from Chapter IX of Kivi's satirical folk tale 'Seitsemän veljestä' (Seven Brothers, 1870).[4] Kivi's novel is one of the most influential works in Finnish literature after the *Kalevala*, even though its portrayal of Finnish rural culture was far from flattering or idealized, so the idea that it may in fact have formed the basis for Sibelius's orchestral composition is not completely implausible. And Sibelius did indeed revise *En saga* extensively after its first performance, so Suomalainen's story has at least some historical credence. But more important than trying to pin parts of the music down to specific elements in Kivi's plot is emphasizing the work's concern with atmosphere and with the act of storytelling as a particular rhetorical device or mode of performance. Indeed, the work's ambiguity – its feeling of allusiveness without ever clarifying exactly what or who is being portrayed – is precisely what makes it such a powerful and effective piece in the concert hall, the quality that aligns it most closely with Sibelius's other works from the decade.

Like much of the orchestral writing in *Kullervo*, *En saga* is characterized by the widespread use of rhythmic ostinatos and circular, insistently repetitive motivic ideas, usually of a severely restricted melodic range, whose purpose is to generate precisely that incantatory mood or atmosphere which Sibelius conceived as the basis of his symbolist aesthetics. Although its revision excised some of Sibelius's more imaginative and experimental instrumental textures,[5] the later, more streamlined version of the score foregrounds the symbolism of the work's underlying tonal structure: the 'tragic' pairing of C minor and E flat major, two keys associated with musical representations of the Romantic hero ever since Beethoven's *Eroica* Symphony (where the super-confident E flat major music of the opening movement is followed by a sombre C minor funeral march). The tone poem's introduction begins remotely in A minor with a shimmering string accompaniment: the impression is of different narrative strands or storylines gradually being woven together, like the three Norns at the opening of Wagner's *Götterdämmerung*. The music's first significant chromatic alteration is D sharp, the enharmonic equivalent of E flat, the pitch that later plays a central role in the work's basic tonal argument (the constant modal drift from C *major* to C *minor*) and which becomes its eventual harmonic goal. Out of this sombre invocatory music a broad spacious theme emerges, which, gradually gaining greater confidence and assurance, serves as the tone poem's first principal melodic group. The main body of the work is subsequently divided into two broad phases: an extended exposition and counter-exposition or development, followed by a third strophe (a dark brooding passage in C minor) that combines elements of development and reprise. Despite its dynamic sense of purpose and forward motion, suggesting an eagerness to join a quest or some heroic pursuit, the introduction's epic theme does not return in its entirety until the end of the reprise, a thrilling ride that ultimately leads to a dramatic climax on an anguished *Tristan* chord. Following this catastrophic collapse, the tone poem closes with an extended epilogue, in which the clarinet soliloquy intones a chilly version of the original epic theme from the introduction in a dark-hued E flat minor.

Even without a detailed programme, it is possible to hear *En saga* plausibly as the vivid portrayal of heroic struggle and defeat against a

Akseli Gallen-Kallela, *En saga (Satu)*, 1894, gouache and watercolour on paper.

wild, storm-tossed landscape: a reading that aligns Sibelius's tone poem with other closely contemporary works such as the opening movement of Gustav Mahler's Second Symphony (1888–94, which Mahler originally entitled 'Totenfeier', or 'Funeral Rites', referring to the protagonist of his First Symphony), or the first part of Richard Strauss's *Tod und Verklärung* (1889). Unlike Mahler and Strauss, Sibelius permits no hint of salvation or redemption, and his hero remains crushed by his tragic fate. For Gallen-Kallela, however, the music inspired a different kind of fantasy: a painting entitled *En saga*, completed in 1894, depicts a half-length portrait of the composer alongside a stylized, enchanted winter landscape, whose exotic details suggest an imaginary hybrid Finnish–oriental scene. A third panel, intended to contain a musical quotation from the tone poem, remains blank – Sibelius evidently did not wish to subscribe quite so firmly to Gallen-Kallela's correspondence between music, mood and visual imagery – but the painting nonetheless hung on the walls of the composer's villa for many years, and it remains one of the most striking artistic responses to any of Sibelius's compositions.[6] The picture is less an attempt to depict what *En saga* might be about, and rather an allegorical representation of its symbolic affect. In other words, it shifts focus away from narrative or storytelling per se towards a more ecological conception of what Gallen-Kallela saw as the vibrant hidden connections between music, art, myth and the natural world.

Gallen-Kallela's work points to Sibelius's fascination with fantasy, theatricality and historical spectacle (whether real or imagined). The composer's strongly visual imagination, and his intensive feeling for the relationship between sound, mood (*stämning*) and symbolic form, had already underpinned much of his earlier work, not least *Kullervo*, and it found a very different outlet in the music that he composed for an evening entertainment arranged by the Viipuri Student Association on 13 November 1893, the month before Sibelius's 28th birthday. Held at the Seurahuone (Society House), the elegant building designed by Engel on the harbour front in central Helsinki that is now the City Hall, the evening comprised a grand lottery accompanied by a series of *tableaux vivants*, directed by Kaarlo Bergbom (the founder of the Finnish National Theatre) with set designs by Gallen-Kallela, Emil Wikström and Eliel Saarinen. The performers included a star turn from Larin Paraske, whose presence gave the evening's representation of Finnish folk traditions a suitable aura of authenticity (despite the highly contrived nature of the event). Modelled on the format of a previous set of entertainments from March 1891 (when Sibelius was abroad in Vienna), and arranged ostensibly as a fundraising initiative in support of public education, in reality the evening was a focal point for pro-nationalist Finnish sentiment and a thinly coded call for self-determination at a time when Russian government oppression had become increasingly heavy-handed and intolerant. As originally conceived, the 1893 event consisted of eight linked tableaux, recounting the story of Finland's historic past from its mythic origins in the age of runic song to the siege of Viipuri in 1710 and the union of Karelia with the rest of Finland in 1811 (after the country had been ceded from Sweden to Russia), and closing with a rousing rendition of Pacius's national anthem, 'Maamme/Vårt land' (Our Land).[7]

Sibelius's score readily reveals his skill in writing vivid and evocative music for theatrical performance. The original overture that opened the evening is a suitably mouth-watering potpourri, like a cinematic trailer that musically foreshadows the scenes that are to follow. The initial bars set out with an irresistible sense of momentum, before the mood momentarily darkens and time seems to pull back into an earlier age of ritual and mystic incantation. On the manuscript, Sibelius wrote symbolically of 'a soul who seeks happiness', crossing out the name 'Karelia' and adding: 'Seeks but does not find. He gets anxious. He goes away and tries to destroy happiness. Bacchanal. He goes in search of solitude by the side of a distant forest lake. It is evening. A lonely water bird sings its sad song.'[8] The first tableau stages an 'authentic' act of runic singing, possibly inspired by accounts of Karelian runic singers holding hands dating back to Henrik Gabriel Porthan's 1778 account as much as by more recent ethnographic reports of vernacular performance,[9] suddenly interrupted by the sounds of encroaching warfare, a visceral reminder of Finland's violent and contested political past. The second tableau focuses on the founding of Viipuri castle in 1293. Barely 130 kilometres (80 mi.) northwest of St Petersburg, Viipuri (in Swedish Vyborg) occupied a crucial strategic location and was an early centre for the spread of Christianity across the Karelia region. The powerfully built medieval fortress still stands on a rocky island next to the old town. Sibelius's use of fugato textures at the start of the tableau suggests an appropriate sense of antique ceremony, whereas his music for the following scene, improbably depicting the taxation of the Käkisalmi District in the fourteenth century, borrows from the music of the overture to create a bustling activity. The intermezzo that follows is familiar as the opening movement of the so-called *Karelia Suite* that Sibelius later extracted from the complete incidental music and published as an independent piece: here, in its original setting, its distant echoing horn calls serve a more obviously theatrical purpose, evoking a feeling of medieval pageantry and festive pomp. The 'Ballade' that follows, accompanying the fourth tableau (a portrait of the defeated Swedish king Karl Knutsson at Viipuri castle, soothed by the song of a court troubadour), is likewise familiar as the second movement of the *Karelia Suite*. Both the fifth and sixth tableaux, separated by the famous 'Alla marcia' with which the *Karelia Suite* concludes, are characterized by an intense foreground figuration, Finland's historical status once again in turmoil and upheaval. The final tableaux bring a greater sense of poise and stability, the entry of the national anthem in the closing sequence carefully calibrated so as to achieve maximum dramatic effect. The soaring bars that conclude the Second Symphony may well owe their origin to this earlier apotheosis, a gesture whose political allegory is so transparent that it is hard to understand how the score ever escaped the attention of the tsarist authorities.[10]

There is no question, of course, that Sibelius was animated and excited by the general enthusiasm that motivated the campaign for Finnish independence in the closing decade of the nineteenth century. His immediate circle, including Gallen-Kallela and the Järnefelt family, were ardently pro-Finnish, and he socialized also with the group of writers and activists known as the 'Young Finns' (*Nuori Suomi*), associated with the first daily Finnish-language newspaper, *Päivälehti*, published from 1889 until it was closed by the Russian authorities in 1904. But nationalism was not the only factor that captured his interest in the Viipuri Lottery project. No less attractive, artistically speaking, was the potential it offered for depicting historical scenes and events, and their associated moods and atmosphere. The colour and spectacle of the *Karelia* music hence poses the question why Sibelius did not compose a full-length opera: the one-act operetta *Jungfrun i tornet* (The Maiden in the Tower), which he completed in 1896 to a mock-medieval libretto by the Swedish-Finnish author Rafael Hertzberg, was his only completed operatic score, but hardly suggests any sustained commitment to the genre. The likely answer is complex. Despite the emergence of a number of high-quality operatic singers in Finland, and the efforts of earlier musicians such as Frederick Pacius, there was still no professional opera company in the country. Kaarlo Bergbom's initiative at the National Theatre in the 1870s had been short lived, and a more permanent repertoire company was not established until 1911, so the genre offered limited domestic opportunities for a young composer barely thirty years of age and at the start of his career. More significant in the long term was the difficulty of breaking into the international opera market, centred in Paris, Italy and, more locally, St Petersburg. Sibelius's later decision to focus much of his most important work in symphonic composition brought significant challenges given the weight of tradition attached to this most prestigious of instrumental forms, especially in Germany, and so competing in a second major genre must have seemed a forbidding proposition. But Sibelius may also have been swayed by his long-standing interest in the theatre and spoken word as a more malleable and effective means of exploring musical action and stage drama. Theatre in Scandinavia and the Nordic countries, after all, had already established a reputation as a progressive and innovative medium, not least in the wake of Ibsen and Strindberg's work, and it readily appealed to Sibelius's underlying concern with the fleeting shifts of human mood and character that was closely attuned to his symbolist sympathies.

A further factor in his conflicted relationship with opera may well have been the overwhelming burden of the Wagnerian legacy that appears to have affected almost every member of the compositional generation born in the 1860s, who grew up precisely in the years when the reception of Wagner's works was at its height. In a letter to Aino dated 9 July 1894, shortly before his trip to Bayreuth, for example, Sibelius wrote: 'I have bought piano scores, *Tannhäuser* and *Lohengrin*. I am studying *Lohengrin* closely. Luckily Achté [Aino Ackté] has the score of *Walküre*; I will borrow it when I am abroad. That is very fortunate! It would have cost 200 mk ... I shall copy some of it at least.'[11] Later, in a famous letter to his wife from Bayreuth dated 19 July, in which he copied out the opening bars of Wagner's vocal score, he wrote: 'I have just heard *Parsifal*. Nothing in the world has ever had such an impact upon me. It just speaks to my innermost heart.'[12] Profoundly moved as he was by the sight and sound of Wagner's work, however, Sibelius evidently already harboured doubts. The outline for the plot of a verismo opera that he sketched out later that month, telling the story of a young student's betrayal of a country girl to whom he was betrothed, after a liaison with a dancer during his study year abroad, for instance, feels remarkably remote from any Wagnerian drama (and also feels uncomfortably autobiographical).[13] Sketches for his own mythic opera based on an episode in the *Kalevala*, entitled *Veneen luominen* (The Building of the Boat), begun in connection with a competition run by the Finnish Literature Society (Suomalaisen Kirjallisuuden Seura, or SKS), never came to fruition. Hence, by 19 August 1894, aged 28, he could write to Aino from Munich:

> I think I have found my own self in music again. Now I have faced the facts. I really am a musical painter and poet. I mean that Liszt's musical stance is closest to me. Hence the symphonic poem (that is what I meant by poet) is particularly dear to me right now.[14]

Sibelius's ambivalent feelings about Wagnerian music drama did not lead to an immediate outright rejection of Wagner's influence. Rather, he appears to have channelled his Bayreuth experience synthetically into his next major compositional projects (to which he alluded in his letter to Aino quoted above). Those projects comprised three related works based on the poem *Skogsrået* (The Wood Nymph) by the Swedish author Viktor Rydberg (1828–1895), which he wrote in 1894–5, and the four mighty *Lemminkäinen Legends*, op. 22, a cycle of tone poems that constituted his most extended symphonic work since *Kullervo*. *Skogsrået* draws on familiar territory to that which Sibelius had already explored in 'Under strandens granar' and *Svartsjukans nätter*: a young hero named Björn is enticed into the sighing woods by a sense of restlessness and adventure, only to be waylaid by a hauntingly beautiful supernatural creature who beckons alluringly out of a forest pool. His heart is stolen and he returns to the real world a broken man, his spirit wrecked by an inconsolable grief ('oläkeligt ve'). Sibelius had used the poem first as the basis for a full-length orchestral tone poem and solo piano work, before turning the work into a melodrama, first performed at an evening event hosted by the Finnish National Theatre in March 1895. All three versions share the same narrative outline. Björn sets forth with a swaggering confidence, and delves recklessly into the rustling sounds of the twilit forest. His fatal encounter with the nymph is depicted with a sudden change of texture and dynamic level, and a seductive feeling of complete immersion, a passage that contains some of Sibelius's most radiant and erotically charged music. But the illusion gives way to a tragic funeral march as Björn returns home broken and bereft. As in *En saga*, in spite of his rugged endeavours, the hero's quest ends only in heartbreak and defeat.

A very different fate would await the hero of Sibelius's next major orchestral work, the dashing Lemminkäinen of his *Four Legends*, op. 22. Conceived on a much broader and more ambitious scale than either *En saga* or *Skogsrået*, the *Legends* recount the adventures of one of the *Kalevala*'s more irrepressible characters, based on Runos 14, 15 and 29 of the epic. In the opening number, *Lemminkäinen and the Maidens of the Island*, the young Don Juan-like Lemminkäinen finds himself in an enchanted nature idyll, a land of 'leafy groves for frolicking, level meadows for dancing', where he performs his magical songs, conjuring the 'sands to pearly beads, pebbles into shining jewels, all the trees to golden red, all the flowers to lovely blooms'.[15] Suitably impressed, the local female inhabitants invite him to join them for a feast, where he is pampered and indulged until the island's menfolk return, at which point Lemminkäinen beats a hasty retreat. Sibelius's tone poem does not follow the *Kalevala* story slavishly, although the relevant lines from the epic were published alongside the programme note at the work's premiere.[16] Rather, it is concerned with evoking the underlying atmosphere and mood of the events: the tone poem's introduction, for example, is wistfully evocative *stämnings-musik* that conjures up the alluringly exotic natural surroundings of the island where Lemminkäinen lands. The work's initial horn call, which strikingly anticipates the opening of the Fifth Symphony, composed two decades later, is followed by a series of echoes and distant nature sounds, out of which emerges a gentle dance-like rhythm that foreshadows the festivities to come. This increasingly lively dance music gives way to a more turbulent, romantically charged passage, whose twisting chromatic lines once again signal the simultaneous threat and allure of erotic entanglement. The second half of the tone poem simply restates and amplifies this basic pairing: the earlier dance music now has a feverish energy, and the romantic melody that follows becomes an extended rising sequence that slowly accumulates textural and harmonic pressure, an ecstatic 'Liebestod'. Just as this sequence reaches its surging climax, the horn call from the opening returns and the tone poem achieves its long-awaited cadential closure, after which Lemminkäinen can sail narratively away into a glowing sunset. Though this outline plan offers merely a reductive account of a more complex process of motivic variation and development, Sibelius's music is equally remarkable for its rich and finely graduated orchestration, a notable advance on anything in his preceding works (even allowing for the score's revision in the 1930s), and also for its formal clarity and relative concision: the tight relationship between the tone poem's introduction and its softly nostalgic postlude is especially satisfying and effective.

The ordering of the two inner movements gave Sibelius some cause for confusion. At the premiere of the *Legends* on 13 April 1896, Lemminkäinen's erotic adventures on the island were followed immediately by his descent into Tuonela, the Finnish Hades. Goaded by Louhi, the old woman of the north, into attempting to shoot the sacred swan that swims upon the murky waters of the dark river that flows turbulently around Tuonela, Lemminkäinen is ambushed by the blind cattle-herder Märkähattu ('Wet-hat') and his body dismembered and cast into the stream, 'spinning in the downward spiral, to the dwellings of the dead'.[17] The coursing string tremolos and craggy brass entries that summon the whirlpools and rapids of Tuonela's river are among the most striking textural effects in Sibelius's music, and an early instance of the representation of the power of natural forces beyond human capacity or control. It is an image that would recur not only in his following work, an orchestral setting of A. Oksanen's poem *Koskenlaskijan morsiamet* (The Rapid-shooter's Brides), but in later tone poems such as *The Oceanides* and *Tapiola*, as well as his music for Shakespeare's *The Tempest*. The heart of *Lemminkäinen in Tuonela* is a startling contrast. A sudden shift in register and dynamic evokes the chillingly enigmatic image of the icy daughter of Tuonela whom Lemminkäinen encounters during his passage through the underworld, music of a strangely remote and austere beauty. The turbulent ostinato figuration of the outer sections of *Lemminkäinen in Tuonela* is in similarly stark contrast to the mirror-like stillness with which the famous *Swan of Tuonela* opens. So familiar and well known has this tone poem subsequently become, not least on account of its famous cor anglais solo, that it is hard to understand why Sibelius may have harboured doubts about its placement in the four-movement scheme of the *Legends* after early performances. Initially third in the sequence, he later reversed the order of the inner movements so that the swan appeared before Lemminkäinen's descent. The magical scoring of *The Swan*'s opening bars, with its multiply divided voicing for strings, points to the influence of the Act 1 Prelude from Wagner's *Lohengrin* – a story likewise concerned with mythic heroes and the appearance of a magical swan – and the doleful procession that follows in the final section of the tone poem might suggest Siegfried's Funeral March from *Götterdämmerung*. But Wagner is not the only significant (or even the primary) musical source in the *Lemminkäinen Legends*. Sibelius's newly acute feeling for orchestral and harmonic colour might equally well have reflected his growing exposure to recent Russian music across the gulf in St Petersburg, especially Rimsky-Korsakov, Liadov and Tchaikovsky, as well of course as his fascination with the symbolist imagery of painters such as Böcklin (whose 1880 painting *The Isle of the Dead* – another version of Tuonela – would later inspire Rachmaninov in 1908).

The shadows that enshroud both *The Swan* and Lemminkäinen's orphic passage through the underworld are decisively banished by the final number in the sequence, *Lemminkäinen's Homeward Journey*. Brought magically back to life by his mother, who rakes the waters of Tuonela's dark river for the pieces of her son's body and then sews them back together, Lemminkäinen is resuscitated by a drop of honey from a passing bee and then recounts his adventures in the realm of the dead. Although in the original text his return is described with a characteristically laconic sense of equivocation, in Sibelius's rendering it becomes a furiously galvanized homecoming, a wild orchestral ride that never slackens or loses pace even as it enters the familiar sunlit realm of E flat major, the heroic key in which the first of the *Legends* began. The *Lemminkäinen Legends* hence represent both a narrative and an artistic triumph, even if their success was hindered by the rather mixed reception that the work received after its initial performances, which led Sibelius to withdraw and revise two of the movements. In terms of imaginativeness of design and textural refinement, as well as motivic rigour, the *Legends* are a significant step forward, and arguably Sibelius's most important score before the First Symphony, a work that is likewise concerned (though in a less explicitly programmatic way) with heroic struggle and endeavour.

It is tempting to speculate how far Sibelius mapped different aspects of his own personality onto some of the *Kalevala* characters that formed the basis for his early works, whether the wanton Lemminkäinen or the wise old seer (and musician) Väinamöinen, or the psychologically damaged and orphaned Kullervo. Aspiring to the status of such fictional literary figures may have offered some sense of legitimation, elevating his choice of vocation to the level of a mythic quest, or it may simply have been an escapist fantasy, a role-playing performance that drew attention away from the more quotidian demands of sustaining a freelance professional career alongside a young family. This tension becomes sharper in light of his references to other literature. A diary entry dated 22 August 1896, for example, records that he had been reading the work of the pioneering Swedish female novelist and gender equality campaigner Fredrika Bremer (1801–1865), and then notes guiltily: 'tried to compose but it was without *Schwung* [verve or momentum]. I wonder whether this *Schwung* comes so seldom nowadays because the *excess in venere* has caused paralysis in my soul (or *in baccho*).'[18] Sibelius was evidently torn between his desire to work productively, the fleeting and contingent nature of artistic inspiration, and the bilious lure of the *Symposium* circle who had gathered in Gallen-Kallela's painting.

The need to ensure some form of stable economic income now that he had entered his thirties could also have been a reason why Sibelius chose to apply for an academic position – the first full-time professorial chair in music at the University of Helsinki – later that autumn. Sibelius was interviewed alongside Kajanus and another friend and contemporary, the ethnomusicologist Ilmari Krohn, and as part of the appointment process was invited to give a trial lecture. The title of this talk, which he read on 25 November, 'Some Viewpoints Concerning Folk Music and Its Influence on the Musical Arts', highlights the slightly speculative nature of Sibelius's subject and his relative lack of professional expertise: although he had gained some experience working with vernacular singers, as the history of the compositional genesis of *Kullervo* had shown, he never sought to maintain an intensive and sustained level of scholarly ethnographic interest in the field. Sibelius's application was nonetheless successful, not least because of his rapidly rising prominence as a composer, and he was offered the position before the end of the year. Kajanus, evidently offended by the decision to award the post to a younger man, appealed against the decision and took his complaint directly to the government's highest authorities – then located, of course, in St Petersburg. Although recourse to the Russian establishment was a risky strategy at a time of growing political unrest and disquiet, Kajanus's appeal was eventually successful, and he was finally awarded the chair later the following year (1897).[19] In recompense, Sibelius was awarded a government pension for life in order to support his compositional work. Though the pension provided a regular income of sorts, it was insufficient by itself to support Sibelius's lifestyle, including his desire for regular foreign travel to the continent, and it scarcely sustained his middle-class tastes.[20] Its effect, in other words, was to increase Sibelius's sense of obligation and dependency, and it may even, at worst, have increased his already sharp self-criticism and lack of confidence.

The creative results of Sibelius's newly awarded pension were not immediately forthcoming, though it may have helped him begin to play a slightly longer compositional game. During 1897 he had been working on an orchestral work tentatively entitled *The Tree of the North*, possibly inspired by Heine's famous two-stanza poem 'Ein Fichtenbaum steht einsam' (A Fir Tree Stands Alone), and on 25 August he mentioned a 'Forest Song' in a letter to Aino, which presumably refers to the same piece.[21] Meanwhile he completed a set of arrangements for A. A. Borenius-Lähteenkorvas's collection of runic melodies, issued by the Finnish Literature Society, and signed his first contract with an overseas publisher, the prestigious German firm Breitkopf & Härtel, based in Leipzig. This association with the continent's oldest music publishing house was a material sign of Sibelius's growing international reputation, but it also brought its own pressures and expectations, in terms of both quality and genre. Chief among these was the absence, hitherto, of a symphony, the category of instrumental work that occupied the most hallowed and esteemed position in the German musical hierarchy. Sibelius had of course completed works on a symphonic scale, including both *Kullervo* and the *Lemminkäinen Legends*, so size alone was not the issue. Rather, Sibelius had not yet written a work that explicitly addressed itself to the German canon. Part of the issue was perhaps the slightly fluid contemporary status of the genre itself: though Sibelius had been moved by the spectacle of Bruckner's symphonies in Vienna and had attended performances of Brahms's music, his aesthetic sympathies at that moment lay more with Liszt and the New German School, who were broadly antithetical to the idea of the symphony as an 'absolute' musical work, and arguably also with the theatre. Among the works he finished in early 1898 was the incidental score for a play by his friend and former colleague at the Helsinki Music Institute, Adolf Paul, based on the story of the Danish king Christian II, who ruled briefly over the whole of Scandinavia under the Union of Kalmar in 1520–21 and was responsible for the Stockholm massacre, before being deposed and sent into exile by Gustav Vasa (the future Gustav I of Sweden). Despite the slightly indifferent quality of Paul's text, the production was a considerable success, not least on account of Sibelius's music. Four numbers in particular have since entered the repertoire: the eloquent and beautifully scored 'Elegy' for strings, which acted as an overture to Act I; the 'Musette', with its imaginatively 'historic' scoring for clarinets and double reeds; the radiant 'Nocturne', performed after the end of Act I; and the brutal 'Ballade', which brought Act IV to an urgently compelling close. It was Breitkopf's decision to purchase the score of the *King Christian* music that initiated Sibelius's relationship with the German publisher, and it afterwards became one of the most important works in his early international reception.

Sibelius's thoughts were nonetheless preoccupied with large-scale symphonic designs. At the beginning of April 1898, for example, he noted down the scheme for a 'Musikalisk Dialog' (musical dialogue), comprising four movements or episodes with brief programmatic titles or subheadings. Fabian Dahlström has traced the first, 'Det blåser kalt, kalt väder från sjön' (The Wind Blows Cold, Cold Weather from the Lake) to a medieval Swedish ballad entitled 'Havsfrun' (The Mermaid), reprinted in a collection published in Helsinki in 1887, and a further possibility may have been a second ballad entitled 'De två systrarna' (The Two Sisters), in which the same refrain recurs alongside the image of a magical harp;[22] the second movement looked back to Heine's 'Ein Fichtenbaum steht einsam', 'Nordens fura drömmer om söderns palm' (The North's Fir Dreams of the South's Palm); the third was titled simply 'Vintersaga' (Winter's Tale), alluding possibly to Shakespeare; and the fourth, 'Jormas Himmel' (Jorma's Heaven) referred to a sequence from Juhani Aho's 1897 novel *Panu*, in which the runic singer Jorma describes heaven as a forest domain populated by characters from the *Kalevala*. Although Sibelius even jotted down a plan of keys for each of the movements (starting and finishing in F major), the planned work never materialized, and its fate remains unclear, although materials from the project probably ended up in the First Symphony.[23] He had evidently drawn inspiration for his symphony from a number of sources: a performance of Berlioz's *Symphonie fantastique* in Berlin earlier in February 1898, for instance, had prompted excited ideas about a work based on 'En drömmares lif' (A Dreamer's Life), and Tchaikovsky's 'Pathétique' Symphony was performed in Helsinki in 1894 and 1897, representing the most up-to-date and advanced model of symphonic design and a trenchant vote of confidence in the status of the genre as a progressive and cutting-edge musical form.

Composers' first symphonies often mark an auspicious threshold: the combination of expectation, innovation and respect for received tradition can make for an especially compelling creative mix. But it can also represent a considerable burden, as the case of Brahms most famously shows. Sibelius's caution about engaging with such an elite and high-pressure genre is therefore understandable, not least given the uncompromising standards inculcated by his teachers such as Wegelius. The First Symphony is nevertheless a remarkable entry into the symphonic canon, and one that reveals a characteristically dazzling synthesis of different stylistic ideas and impulses. At the time of the work's premiere, conducted by Sibelius on 26 April 1899, attempts to consolidate and extend Russian authority by the hardline governer-general Nikolai Bobrikov had intensified political tensions across the country, especially following the declaration of the so-called 'February Manifesto', which sought, among other things, to conscript Finnish soldiers into the Russian army, and writers immediately associated the symphony with contemporary debates about Finnish self-determination and the demand for greater autonomy. In this context, the symphony was readily heard as an allegory of Finnish oppression and heroic resistance. But many commentators have since drawn attention to its obvious debt to Russian musical models: Sibelius borrowed Tchaikovsky's preference for cyclic structures and use of motto figures, and the work's tragic narrative trajectory points especially strongly to the 'Pathétique'. Like much of Tchaikovsky's music, however, the underlying stylistic argument in Sibelius's symphony can be more clearly understood as a dialogue between different modes of musical behaviour: a feeling of linear goal-direction or forward motion characteristic of the post-Beethovenian symphony following the first movement of the *Eroica*, and the iterative circularity of much contemporary French and Russian music. The First Symphony is therefore a hybrid work, one wedded closely to its particular historical context, but readily revealing a more complex (and at times almost contradictory) interplay of voices and musical identities.

Underlying tensions between circular and linear musical trajectories are apparent from the symphony's opening bars. The long desolate clarinet solo with which the work starts creates a sense of structural and expressive ambiguity, hardly the manner in which one might expect a symphony to begin. Though this gesture returns, transformed, at the start of the finale, binding the work together at the most basic thematic level, sketches show that it was in fact a late addition to the score – a compositional afterthought rather than the catalyst from which the whole work emerged.[24] Tonally, the solo starts in mid-air, hovering uneasily around the symphony's dominant (B natural), before tending chromatically towards B *flat*, suggesting G minor. The opening of the Allegro suggests a modal brightening (to G major), and scarcely touches the work's 'true' tonic, E minor, which is only reached fatefully in the movement's closing bars. Stephen Downes has described the opening movement as 'the opening act in an erotic symphonic drama', whose 'sensuous moments and narratives of seduction leading to possession or destruction interact with and "deform" the symphonic paradigms of development, synthesis and resolution'.[25] Aspects of this binary model of seduction and collapse can be mapped onto the tonal dualism (G versus E) that underpins the whole work, as well as its prevailing chromatic instability. The second subject group with its pastoral woodwind thirds, for example, pivots on the enharmonic transformation of the opening solo's B flat (that is, A sharp), casting the music momentarily into an enchanted nature realm. The development attempts to address the music's chromatic problems from a different perspective, out of which the recapitulation emerges almost imperceptibly: an early instance of Sibelius's skill at assembling carefully graduated transition sequences in which the musical ground moves almost imperceptibly yet still leads towards a distinctive tonal or thematic goal. The coda, in contrast, takes the form of a sudden fading away, the return of the second subject's folk-like circularity followed by the brutal imposition of tonic closure. The brusque pizzicato chord with which the movement ends resounds like a giant harp or *kantele* (a Finnish zither), rhetorically closing the book on a bardic narrative or saga tale.

The key and atmosphere of the second movement (E flat) suggest a sudden shift of environment and mood, 'a transference or sinking into the timelessness of the mythic world'.[26] Like the corresponding movement in Gustav Mahler's Sixth Symphony, which shares the same key, the Andante is a dream-like fantasy, an escape from the battle-weary drama of the first movement. It begins with a soft lullaby, like the movement entitled 'Kullervo's Youth' from the *Kullervo* Symphony, and, as in the earlier work, the remainder of the movement consists of a series of strophic repetitions and intensifications of this opening material. The cumulative effect of these cycles generates a considerable volume of chromatic energy that spills over into the reprise, initially oriented towards C minor. The return of the opening is consequently abbreviated, the sense of calm disturbed by shadows of earlier chromatic instability, which here gain a powerfully nostalgic glow. The Scherzo is a genre piece, the stylized invocation of a folk idiom or country dance familiar from earlier symphonic models. But the music simultaneously reinforces the symphony's basic underlying chromatic problems, in particular the chromatic instability of B natural/B flat and the work's prevailing minor/major modal ambivalence. The outer sections of the movement are an energetic round dance, marked by the timpani's incisive rhythmic interventions and fugato writing for strings and woodwind. The trio, however, again suggests withdrawal into another time and space, like the preceding Andante, a luminous collage of rustling woodwind calls and nature sounds that evokes the familiar Nordic topos of the midsummer night.

The finale brings a further change of colour and temperament. Elements of the first movement's opening are brought back and recontextualized from a more impassioned and seemingly war-torn perspective.

The rest of the movement, 'quasi fantasia', seeks to reduce the symphony's underlying tensions to polarized opposition: a bustling mass of chromatic figuration and pithy motivic work, similar to the 'Ballade' that brings the *King Christian* music to its brutal conclusion, but which fails to generate any sustained textural stability. The contrasting episodes are dominated by an extended cantilena for strings that drives optimistically forwards. The second occurrence of this passage anchors itself on the dominant, suggesting the long-delayed arrival of a definitive statement of the home key with hopeful brass fanfares and expectant string accompaniment, as though the symphony's troubled state can finally achieve some sense of attainment and release. Yet, just as victory appears to be within grasp, decisive structural resolution is once again evaded, the music instead fleeing from the scene with parting glimpses of previous moments of chromatic unrest. The tragic hero of Sibelius's symphony, his energy ultimately spent, sinks to the ground in defeat.

Allegorical readings of the symphony are hard to resist, despite the score's intricate motivic and harmonic detail. Such readings are given even greater credence by Sibelius's other significant creative project in the closing months of 1899: music for a series of historical *tableaux vivants* staged as part of a lottery in aid of press journalism at the Swedish Theatre on 4 November with texts by the poet Eino Leino and theatre supervisor Jalmari Finne and stage design by Kaarlo Bergbom, founding director of

Swedish Theatre, Helsinki, 1906, photograph by Karl Emil Ståhlberg.

the Finnish National Theatre. As with the Karelia celebrations from six years previously, the scenes for which Sibelius was asked to provide music were strategically drawn moments from the history of the Finnish nation.[27] After a solemn prelude in the form of a ceremonial procession, the opening scene, for example, depicted the ancient *Kalevala* hero Väinämöinen with his *kantele*, playing for a group of nature spirits and semi-divine characters from the epic including Tapio (the Finnish god of the forests), Ahti (the god of the ocean), Ilmarinen the smith and Lemminkäinen's long-suffering mother. Sibelius's music, which he later reused as the opening number of his *Scènes historiques*, op. 25, evokes the summoning of the group with a mounting sense of excitement and expectation. The second tableau illustrated Finland's conversion to Christianity through ritual baptism, and Sibelius's score combines a recurrent striking bell with rich, chorale-like writing and a stylized archaic counterpoint. The third scene was set in the sixteenth-century court of Duke John, the son of Gustav Vasa, at his castle in Turku (Åbo): the otherwise incongruously Iberian quality of Sibelius's score was explained by John's fascination with Spain and Spanish culture. The fourth tableau shifted focus to a more turbulent episode in Finnish history: the start of the Thirty Years War. The quiet domestic mood of the opening is soon ruptured by more energized military signals. If the emphasis in the fourth tableau was on Finnish stoicism in the face of political upheaval, the sombre and grief-stricken tones of the fifth illustrated the nation's suffering during the period of conflict between its larger neighbours, Sweden and Russia, known as the 'Great Hostility' (Isoviha), a thinly veiled reference to the nation's current parlous state.

The culmination of this carefully staggered narrative of nation building was the sixth and final tableau, 'Suomi herää' (Finland Awakens), which depicted Finland's emergence in the nineteenth century as a modern state capable of surviving on its own resources. Starting with Tsar Alexander II's benevolent support for the first generation of Finnish Romantic writers and philosophers, including Lönnrot and Runeberg, it celebrated the community-forming power of education and industrial development. The most elaborate and fully scored movement of the set, Sibelius later extracted the music and performed it as a free-standing piece, under various titles such as *Finaali* and *Suomen herääminen/ Finlands uppvaknelse* (Finland's Awakening) and even (outside Finland only) 'Impromptu', before it began to appear in its more famous guise as *Finlandia*. The emotive opening strains of the 'Finlandia hymn' that forms the ostensible second subject theme of 'Suomi herää' were most likely modelled on a patriotic choral work by the Finnish composer Emil Genetz (1852–1930), with the title 'Herää, Suomi!' (Awaken, Finland!). Even without such a musical paratext, Sibelius's treatment of the tune, first played reverentially by the strings and then taken up with swelling ardour by the wind and later the full orchestra, may already have filled its contemporary listeners with a growing sense of confidence and pride. During the final section of the work, the stage was dominated by the entry of a papier-mâché railway engine, epitomizing Finland's new-found economic power. For Sibelius, who had grown up in a small town connected to the capital by the country's first railway link, the image must have been especially stirring. The surging and affirmative force of the work's final bars could then be heard, as James Hepokoski suggests, 'as a declaration of the identity of tonal and national attainment, and as a launch into the new century of the now-realised spirit of a fully "awakened" Finland – a Finland coursing locomotive-like, into what was hoped to be a promising liberated future'.[28] There were probably few in the audience, Sibelius included, who could foresee just how difficult that journey towards liberation would prove to be, or how costly and traumatic negotiating the challenges and obstacles en route would become. But, for a brief moment at the very end of the century, Sibelius's music enabled his listeners to share in that vision with an optimism that would ultimately prevail.

Finnish Pavilion, Exposition Universelle, Paris, 1900.

4

New Dawns

Although the closing months of 1899 had resounded with the uplifting strains of the *Finlandia* coda, a signal of defiance amid the growing political tension between Finland and Russia, the new century began on a far bleaker personal note for Sibelius and his family. On 13 February, their third daughter, Kirsti, died during a typhoid epidemic, a victim of the same disease that had killed Sibelius's father in 1868, and a sobering reminder of the historical rates of infant mortality across the Russian empire and the dangers of infectious disease in the days before widespread quarantine and vaccination protocols were in operation. Music may have offered some sort of emotional release, and in the following month Sibelius wrote his sombre duet *Malinconia* (Melancholy) for cello and piano, op. 20, dedicated to his colleague the cellist and conductor Georg Schnéevoigt (1872–1947). Though Schnéevoigt gave the work's premiere and would later become an important interpreter of Sibelius's orchestral works, Sibelius must surely have composed the cello part with his brother Christian's playing in mind, his memory drifting back to their childhood summers playing piano trios in Loviisa. The work's elegiac opening swiftly gives way to more virtuoso passagework, as though attempting to dispel its underlying grief through sheer force of musical will. Despite such energetic activity, however, the chromatic shadows are never entirely dispelled, even in the cello's final radiant cantilena, and the mood ultimately remains introspective and withdrawn. *Malinconia* is among Sibelius's rawest and most powerfully direct scores, and a further indication of his ability to bury the experience of death and personal loss within a musical text.[1] The opportunity to spend sustained compassionate time with his family was limited, however, and Sibelius was swiftly required to devote his musical and emotional energies elsewhere. A National Song Festival, held in Helsinki on 18–20 June, provided a grandly public platform for new work, and Sibelius performed a series of occasional pieces including the brass septet *Tiera*, and an arrangement for mixed chorus of his rousing patriotic choral song 'Isänmaalle' (To the Fatherland).

At a time of such personal domestic tragedy, the prospect of a change of scene must have seemed especially attractive, and the chance to join the Finnish cultural delegation to the Exposition Universelle in Paris later that summer was one that Sibelius eagerly grasped. For cosmopolitans, commentators and trendsetters at the turn of the century, whether artists, artisans, politicians, scientists or industrialists, all eyes and minds were figuratively turned towards the French capital. The Exposition Universelle was laid out across a grand 112-hectare (277 ac) site on either bank of the Seine, connected by a new bridge dedicated to Tsar Alexander III in honour of the recent Franco-Russian alliance. The Exposition featured grand halls dedicated to the latest developments in engineering and industrial manufacturing, a giant telescope, a cinéorama projecting the illusion of a hot-air balloon ride over the city, and a Phono-Ciné theatre, devised by Henri Lioret de France and Clément-Maurice Gratioulet in competition with the pioneering work of the Lumière brothers, where film images were shown synchronized with phonograph recordings. It offered the almost 50 million visitors who entered through its grand *porte monumentale* a dazzling array of fashion, innovation and enchantment that would prove irresistibly alluring.

The Exposition Universelle was not simply about promoting the idea of Paris as the centre of the modern world, however. On the contrary, it was also an opportunity for other countries to demonstrate their cultural and economic prowess. Among the show's attractions, accessible via a mechanical moving walkway, were forty pavilions arranged along a 'rue des nations' bordering the river. Each pavilion sought to reflect the character and history of its particular nation. The Russian building, for example, was modelled on the Kremlin, whereas the British pavilion was designed by the distinguished English architect Edwin Lutyens and took the form of a mock-Jacobean mansion. The fact that Finland was able to host a pavilion of its own was a remarkable diplomatic coup, given that the country was officially still a sovereign part of the Russian empire. The building had been planned by the ambitious young architect Eliel Saarinen, who was awarded the commission despite only being in his late twenties. Saarinen had already begun to create a name for himself with his striking art nouveau designs, and his scheme for the pavilion envisioned a hall with a steeply pitched roof, arranged around a central atrium crowned by a lantern tower with a distinctive stylized conical cap. Inside, the walls were ornamented with decorative murals painted by Gallen-Kallela, depicting scenes from the *Kalevala*. Erected as a proud statement of Finnish ingenuity and endeavour, it was also a bold assertion of the nascent country's independence, and was accompanied by a programme of exhibitions, displays and artistic events. Among the visitors to support the Finnish delegation was the Helsinki Orchestral Society, who performed in the grand surroundings of the Palais du Trocadéro under the baton of their founding conductor, Robert Kajanus. Accompanying the orchestra were the celebrated diva Aino Ackté, who scored the greatest success with French critics, and the 34-year-old Sibelius.[2]

Kajanus, Sibelius and the orchestra had arrived at the Exposition on the back of a lengthy tour of northern Europe, playing to largely positive critical notices in Stockholm, Kristiania (now Oslo), Copenhagen, Lübeck, Hamburg, Berlin, the Netherlands and Belgium. Although Kajanus exclusively occupied the podium and Ackté received most of the plaudits in Paris, Sibelius was well represented on the programmes, with movements from his *King Christian Suite*, *The Swan of Tuonela*, *Lemminkäinen's Return* and *Finlandia* (billed as 'Vaterland' or 'La patrie') performed alongside the First Symphony. This sustained international exposure of this music was to have a transformative effect: though French critics described him condescendingly as a 'Finnish Grieg', his music was well received, and his time in the French capital opened his eyes (and ears) to a completely new set of social and artistic conventions.[3] Equally important was the German response to his symphony in Hamburg and Berlin: writers were cautious and conservative, as one would expect from such an inward-looking market, but Sibelius's treatment from the critics was not as wholly negative as many figures from outside the German sphere might normally endure.[4] Significantly, as a result, Sibelius's ambitions could shift from being solely a leading national figure to a musician capable of competing on a genuinely international stage.

On his arrival to home soil, however, Sibelius swiftly returned to his by now familiar patriotic vein in a rugged setting of Viktor Rydberg's ballad *Snöfrid*, the stormy tale of a proud hero who seeks the 'noble poverty of battle' ('kämpens ädla armod') rather than the false comfort of 'renown won from selfish deeds' ('namnfrejd, vunnen i självisk ävlan').

The contemporary allegory of the work would have been immediately apparent to Sibelius's audience at its premiere, conducted by the composer on 20 October, though the score has not since maintained a permanent place in the repertoire. A more lasting contribution was the series of songs that Sibelius composed in late summer and early autumn, including his brooding response to Runeberg's 'Den första kyssen' (The First Kiss), with its desolate sense of the loss of innocence and naivety in the aftermath of young love: the song's pivotal moment of self-realization is captured by an angular *Tristan* chord that radically destabilizes the narrator's sense of poise. In contrast, there is a feeling of containment at the opening of his setting of Josef Julius Wecksell's 'Marssnön' (March Snow), which gathers greater strength and gravity as the song proceeds, forecasting the fate of the spring season: 'the stronger you shall blossom / the richer you shall die' ('dess mäktigare skall du blomma, / dess rikare skall sen du dö'). Another Wecksell setting, 'Demanten på Marssnön' (The Diamond upon the March Snow), has since become one of Sibelius's most popular songs. The alluringly delicate figuration of the piano's opening filigree gives way to the swaying rhythm of the vocal line and a gentle ecstasy: 'O, fairest fate to love / The highest that life brings, / to glisten in its radiance, / and die, amid its smile' ('O, sköna lott att älska / Det högsta livet ter, / att stråla i dess solblick / och dö, när skönst den ler!'). A fourth song, 'Säv, säv susa' (Reeds, Reeds, Sigh), to a text by Gustaf Fröding, asks the rustling sedge by the lake shore to recount the tragic story of a young girl deliberately drowned for her beauty. Sibelius's music recalls the opening of his Runeberg setting 'Under strandens granar' from the op. 13 collection, a song similarly concerned with fateful immersion, but it is hard to escape a much heavier sense of poignancy with the recent death of his daughter Kirsti so close at hand.

It was perhaps for this reason, and eager to build upon the success of his Paris trip, that Sibelius was keen to take his family away from Finland again in the latter half of the year. The choice of Italy as destination had been suggested by a new supporter, Axel Carpelan (1858–1919), a minor Swedish-Finnish aristocrat and amateur musician who became one of Sibelius's most valued correspondents and, despite Sibelius's often insensitive and self-possessed behaviour towards him in person, one of his closest friends. In his relationship with Carpelan, Sibelius found a sounding board, confidant and cheerleader, and, above all, 'a mirror that reflected his soul's tiniest vibrations'.[5] Carpelan would propose ideas for future projects to the composer, advising him in a letter dated 28 February 1901, for instance, that Shakespeare's plays might make a suitable subject for musical treatment (anticipating Sibelius's score for *The Tempest* by over two decades). And on 13 March 1900 he had written anonymously to suggest that Sibelius spend late autumn and winter in Italy: 'that land where one can learn cantabile, moderation and harmony, plasticity and symmetry, where everything is beautiful – even the ugly. Remember what significance Italy had for Tchaikovsky's development, and for Richard Strauss.'[6] Sibelius was evidently strongly taken by Carpelan's idea, not least because his friend began to fundraise for the trip. Accordingly, Sibelius left Finland with his family barely a week after the premiere of *Snöfrid*, heading south on 27 October. Their first stop was Berlin, where Sibelius was keen to try and cement his relationship with German publishers and critics following the performance of his symphony in the summer. At that time Richard Strauss was musical director at the Staatsoper, and his friend and former colleague from the Helsinki Music Institute, Ferruccio Busoni, was also in the city and energetically promoting new music. He also took the opportunity to visit the conductor Arthur Nikisch (1855–1922) in Leipzig, musical director of both the Gewandhaus and the Berlin Philharmonic, who would later come to conduct many of Sibelius's most important works. And at a musical soirée organized by Otto Lessmann, chief editor of the *Allgemeine Musikalische Zeitung*, one of Germany's most important music periodicals,

Axel Carpelan, *c.* 1900.

the Finnish soprano Ida Ekman performed the premiere of a new song: another Runeberg setting, 'Flickan kom ifrån sin älsklings möte' (The Girl Came from Meeting Her Beloved), which once again recounts the perils and heartbreak of young love.

Sibelius's stay in Germany was so prolonged, in spite of the fact that he was burning through the money Carpelan had raised at an alarming rate, that it was not until February 1901 that he and his family finally crossed the Alps and arrived in Italy. Their destination was the Villa Molfino, a fine old house in Rapallo on the Ligurian coast, halfway between Bogliasco and Chiavari and less than 32 kilometres (20 mi.) east of Genoa. Here, surrounded by citrus trees and herb-scented hillsides and with the distant sound of the Mediterranean crashing against the cliffs, he was able to begin work on his next large-scale project. As was so often the case, however, his first thoughts about the composition appear to have shifted several times. Sketches exist for a series of four tone poems ('fyra tondigter'), along the lines of the *Lemminkäinen Legends*, entitled *En fest* (A Festival or Celebration). Among Sibelius's sources of inspiration, partly inspired by his Italian sojourn, were the legend of Don Juan (the basis for Richard Strauss's famous 1888 tone poem and also for Mozart's opera), Dante's *Divine Comedy* and Liszt's oratorio *Christus* (1866), which Sibelius and Aino had heard in Berlin.[7] As his thoughts developed, Sibelius sketched a more elaborate scenario for the Don Juan work, drawing on the image of the stone guest who calls to summon Don Juan to his fate: 'Sit

Ernest C. Peixotto, *View of the Rapallo Harbour and Castle*, 1902, engraving.

in the twilight in my castle, a guest enters. I ask who he is – no answer. I make an effort to entertain him. Still no answer. Eventually he breaks into song and then Don Juan notices who he is – Death.'

The symbolist preoccupation with human mortality and the esoteric was once again prominent in Sibelius's plans, alongside the idea of a reckoning or being called to account – an image that would recur more prominently later in his career. But work on the tone poem proved difficult, and Sibelius was increasingly distracted by the presence of his young family. Eventually in late March he abandoned Rapallo, leaving Aino and their daughters behind, and fled to a hotel in Rome, where he found he was able to work more freely. From a historical distance, it is difficult to empathize with Sibelius's decision, and far harder to understand how Aino could have sustained the family under such conditions. Sibelius once again appears to have been crushed by the burden of creative expectation and his domestic responsibilities. But he and the family returned to Finland together in May, and he was able to report positive progress on the new work to Carpelan in August, when they were staying with Sibelius's mother-in-law in the Finnish countryside. It was only in November, however, that he began to refer to the composition as a symphony, and he heavily revised the score at the end of the year before the music finally received its premiere under Sibelius's direction on 8 March 1902 in the Great Hall of the University of Helsinki, where the first performance of *Kullervo* had taken place a decade earlier.

The Second Symphony would always remain in many senses Sibelius's 'Italian' Symphony. The journey across the Alps had figuratively triggered a significant shift of stylistic orientation and perspective in his music. In Rome, Tawaststjerna suggests, Sibelius 'finally freed himself from his Wagner crisis, while Tchaikovsky's pathos began to seem more and more remote'.[8] Elements of the ideas that had first formed the basis for Sibelius's thoughts – the legend of Don Juan and Dante's *Divine Comedy* – can still be traced in the finished work. The opening movement, for example, might figuratively be heard as a spring hymn sung on arrival in the south from the cold gloom of a northern winter. The rhythmic impetus of its opening bars generates a series of cumulative melodic paragraphs which open and unfold like a gradual sunrise, gaining depth, colour and intensity as they progress. Sibelius's sketches show that this opening gesture originally started precisely on the downbeat of the first bar, but his subsequent decision to syncopate the idea against the music's underlying metre by delaying its start just for a single crotchet helps to generate the movement's characteristic forward momentum. Sibelius had perhaps modelled this opening gambit on the start of other recent D major symphonies with which he would certainly have been familiar, not least from his time in Vienna: both Brahms's Second Symphony (1877) and Dvořák's Sixth (1880) commence in a similar vein, and are likewise radiantly pastoral scores. Similarly, the extended introductory passage of the second movement, with its pizzicato walking bass and chant-like melodic lines, could depict a solemn pilgrim's procession, much like the corresponding movements in Mendelssohn's 'Italian' Symphony (similarly in D minor) or Berlioz's *Harold in Italy*. Sibelius pencilled the word 'Christus' on one page of sketches for the movement, possibly referring to an ascending motif that resembles the 'crux fidelis' figure employed by earlier composers from Mozart and Mendelssohn to Liszt. The movement's violent contrasting material might represent the conflict and struggles of a Straussian adventurer, a character whose amorous encounters are consummated with cinematic candour in the languorous trio of the Scherzo (where the principal theme cleverly anticipates the finale's sweeping summative theme which lies ahead). The outer sections of the third movement, meanwhile, unleash a whirling saltarello, scored with characteristically carnivalesque virtuosity, whereas the finale represents the hero's ultimate march to victory and breathtaking apotheosis in the brilliant light of a southern sun.

Other programmatic accounts of the work need not rely solely on its Italian associations. For many writers, from Sibelius's early Finnish champion Robert Kajanus onwards, the dark mood of the Andante and the spirit of redemption and release through adversity of the symphony's finale suggested an obvious contemporary political metaphor, a fervent call for Finnish independence from the tyranny of Russian rule and occupation. For another contemporary Finnish critic, Evert Katila, the symphony charted a Nietzschean journey, similar to that charted in the philosopher's *Also sprach Zarathustra*, 'a portrait of a great hero, of a real Overman who reveals therein the various richness of his spirit in all its human sublimity'.[9] Such conflict-liberation trajectories have suggested darker political ideologies to many later writers, notably Theodor Adorno, who witnessed how narratives of heroic endeavour and liberation were swiftly co-opted by the far-right forces of fascism. Yet it is equally possible, as Tawaststjerna implies, to understand the work as an abstract essay on the nature of the symphonic project, particularly the elaboration of the process of 'crystallisation of thought from chaos',[10] which Sibelius would explore increasingly closely in later works, from the Third Symphony (1907) onwards. Heard from this perspective, the Second Symphony is concerned, above and beyond its various programmative associations, with a process of musical goal direction, the articulation of a definitive structural cadence in the tonic major attained only in the work's very final bars. The soaring statement of the D major hymn with which the symphony concludes is a dramatic resolution of the music's underlying tonal opposition (D major/minor versus its two related mediant key centres: B flat and F sharp or G flat). In this sense, the finale serves both as a powerfully predetermined destination and simultaneously as an open gateway or threshold. In this musical double-vision, looking both forwards and backwards, or north and south, lies the symphony's compelling feeling of equilibrium regained, its searingly affirmative spirit. In that way, the symphony's greatest achievement is to resurrect the hallowed Beethovenian symphonic model of *ardua per astra* (or struggle-to-victory), elevated for the modern age.

The premiere of the symphony in Helsinki was followed by four sell-out repeat performances later that month. Its first performance overseas was in Stockholm in November 1903, when critical reviews were once again glowing, and the work received its American premiere in Chicago in January 1904, alongside performances in Hamburg and St Petersburg. Sibelius's friend Busoni invited him to conduct it at one of his new music concerts in Berlin in 1905, and the symphony received its first British outing at a Hallé concert in Manchester directed by the distinguished Wagnerian conductor Hans Richter. In other words, riding on the back of his appearance at the Exposition Universelle, the Second Symphony became one of Sibelius's first major works to achieve a significant international breakthrough, and it was the score that definitively established his reputation abroad as the pre-eminent Finnish composer of his generation. It was also a substantial technical advance on his earlier orchestral music, both in terms of the formal precision of the first movement with its remarkably abbreviated reprise and also the carefully graduated transition that seamlessly links the end of the Scherzo and the beginning of the finale. The two-phase plan of the fourth movement, with a preliminary play-over of the principal theme and then its glowing return at the close after a turbulent period of cyclic accumulation, would become an important structural pattern for later works, not least the Fifth Symphony written over a decade later.

From this point on, Sibelius's career faced a double challenge: maintaining his domestic reputation at home in Finland, where his audience already strongly associated his music with the patriotic cause, and simultaneously striving to retain his profile overseas as a significant new voice in a highly crowded and competitive international market. Meeting these two objectives would become an increasingly demanding emotional and logistical task for a creative artist who was, despite his regular government stipend, still essentially a freelance musician. It was with these opportunities in mind, for example, that Sibelius returned to Berlin in June 1902 to meet Nikisch and a leading Austrian conductor, Felix Weingartner, whom he hoped to interest in his new symphony. He was back again in November later that year, to conduct the revised score of *En saga* at one of Busoni's concerts (in a programme that also included the original version of the tone poem *Paris: Song of a Great City* by Frederick Delius), after which he wrote excitedly to Aino: 'the main thing is that I *can conduct* a world-class orchestra. And do it well! That's what they all said!'[11] At such moments, even after what was otherwise a significant musical success, Sibelius's fragile self-confidence and anxiety became all too readily apparent, and his use of addictive substances (principally alcohol and tobacco) to manage his stress became ever deeper. It was a tension that would become an increasing source of friction both in his relationship with Aino and in terms of his musical output.

The start of 1903 was nonetheless a far more positive event, marked by the birth of Sibelius's fourth daughter, Katarina, on 12 January. Sibelius was now 37, rapidly approaching his forties. With a growing family, and with the international prospects for his music seemingly brightening, Sibelius had already begun to think about moving out of his cramped rented accommodation in Helsinki, and Aino hoped that geographical distance from the cafés and bars of the capital might also lead to a more settled domestic routine. The death of his maternal uncle, Axel Borg, meant that Sibelius had sufficient funds to put down a deposit on a substantial loan to support the purchase. Sibelius's brother-in-law, the painter Eero Järnefelt, had already built a villa named 'Suviranta' on a plot of land next to Lake Tuusula (Tuusulanjärvi), a small stretch of water next to the town of Järvenpää (whose name in Finnish simply means 'Lake End'), about 40 kilometres (25 mi.) north of Helsinki on the main railway line, joining Juhani Aho and his wife Venny Soldan-Brofeldt, another painter, who had moved there in 1897. A further artistic friend of the family, Pekka Halonen (1865–1933), designed and built his own residence, 'Halosenniemi', at Järvenpää in 1901–2, incorporating an elegant ground-floor studio with living quarters above. After scouting for a suitable site, the Sibeliuses bought their own plot of land in the same neighbourhood on 18 November 1903, and soon became part of a growing artists' colony benefiting from semi-rural seclusion, yet still within touching distance of the amenities and cultural resources of the city.

Sibelius remained musically active during the summer, completing a series of shorter works including the six little Finnish folk song arrangements for piano that he subsequently published without an opus number. These tiny improvisatory sketches may have been modelled on the pattern of many of Grieg's *Lyric Pieces* – easy works for amateur pianists based on familiar national materials – but their tone and intensity belies their diminutive size. The opening number, 'Minun kultani' (My Darling), for example, has a heavy sense of melancholy, and a similar mood prevails in the second, 'Sydämestäni rakastan' (The Heart's Beloved). The rippling ostinato accompaniment in the fourth number, 'Tuopa tyttö' (That Girl) is inspired by the transparent sound of the *kantele*, the Finnish zither, but the churning left-hand figuration in the fifth, the ominous 'Velisurmaaja' (Fratricide), suggests a much darker and more obsessive compulsion. The spirit is only partially lifted in the final number, 'Häämuistelma' (Wedding Memory), which suggests a wistful nostalgia. Taken as a whole, the set comprises a miniature tone poem that reflects on the common themes of love, desire, jealousy, attraction and death, topics similar to those that motivated the Don Juan-esque drama of the Second Symphony but explored here on a far more intimate and no less compelling scale.

The remainder of the summer was taken up by two more settings of poems by Viktor Rydberg, both of which evoke an intense nature mysticism. The first, 'Höstkväll' (Autumn Evening), is a drama of strange weather, fading light and changing seasonal cycles. It is also an intensive study in acoustic ecology. The poem's desolate landscape is animated by sound: sighing forests, screaming gulls, the day's whispering farewell tones ('Dagens viskande avsked tonar'), voices called forth by the storm from the woodland's depths. And yet, despite this windswept arena, the narrator listens with pleasure as they seek solace in the wilderness: 'Does his soul feel in harmony / with the song that raised by the starless night? / Does his sorrow die like a gentle note / in the autumn's mighty lament?' ('Känner hans själ en samklang / med sången, som höjes av stjärnlös natt? / Dör hans ve som en skata ton / i höstens väldiga sorgedikt?'). Sibelius's response is on an expansive, almost orchestral scale. Indeed, he later arranged the song for voice and orchestra, so that its striking similarity with his later tone poem *Luonnotar*, likewise an evocation of a bleak, storm-wrecked world, becomes all the more apparent. The first two verses are dominated by the descending contour of the opening line, 'The sun goes down' ('Solen går ned'), followed by the vocalist's soaring re-ascent, suggesting the bird's distant view of the ground below. The start of the third verse has a tremulous excitement, evoking rainfall or the rippling waters of the lake below, culminating in a piercing cry of pain, while the fourth stanza brings an overwhelming climax at the soul's moment of communion with the surrounding landscape, followed by a feeling of resignation and acceptance if not relief. 'På veranden vid havet' (On a Balcony by the Sea) is likewise an outburst of existential angst, the poet casting their glance despairingly upwards in search of divine grace, but only silence answers: 'shore and sky and sea, all as though sensing God' ('stränder och himmel och hav, allt som i aning om Gud'). Sibelius's setting broods upon its opening chords, the chromaticism reminiscent of the bleak coast at the opening of the third act of Wagner's *Tristan und Isolde*, one of the works that had been such a formative influence on the young composer searching for his true creative voice.

The symbolist preoccupation with nature, love and human mortality in Rydberg's poetry runs like a thread throughout much of Sibelius's work in the wake of the First and Second Symphonies, and it was shared by many of his contemporaries, including his brother-in-law, the writer Arvid Järnefelt (1861–1932). When Sibelius agreed to write incidental music for a production of Järnefelt's play *Kuolema* (Death) in late 1902, he completed six short movements for the premiere at the Finnish National Theatre on 2 December. Järnefelt's play is a form of dramatic *Bildungsroman* that tells the story of its male protagonist, Paavali, from the death of his mother, through his marriage and middle age, up to his own death. After its premiere, the initial production ran for only six nights. Though the participation of celebrity singer Abraham Ojanperä, and of Sibelius himself, guaranteed a certain degree of critical interest, there was little indication that the play's opening musical number, 'Tempo di valse lente', later evocatively retitled 'Valse triste', would soon become Sibelius's calling card. It is a cruel irony that a composer's most popular work can often be among their least commercially rewarding outputs. Edward Elgar suffered particularly harshly when he naively sold his early salon piece *Salut d'amour* to his publisher, Schott, for a knock-down fee, and waived his rights to the royalties in perpetuity. He was haunted by the experience for the remainder of his professional life.[12] Sibelius experienced a similar fate with 'Valse triste', after he agreed the customary modest terms with his Finnish publisher, Helsingfors Nya Musikhandel,

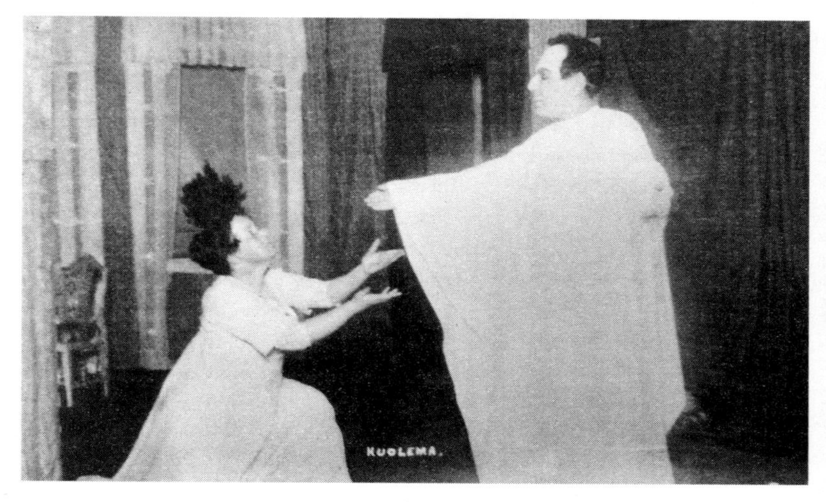

Scene from Arvid Järnefelt's *Kuolema* (Death), undated photograph.

who later sold the work as part of a package to the German firm Breitkopf & Härtel.[13] Had he instead retained his commercial interests in the piece, he would have been able to retire comfortably on the income.

In retrospect, it is perhaps easy to understand why 'Valse triste' became such a well-loved work. Sibelius had already explored his fondness for the waltz in earlier scores such as the *Balettscen*. Both works share a spirit of nostalgia mixed with nihilism: their circularity swiftly becomes destructive, so that the waltz effectively becomes a dance of death. This is explicitly evoked in Järnefelt's play: Paavali's mother lies delirious on her deathbed, watched over by her son, who has momentarily fallen asleep. In her dreams the woman imagines herself at a formal ball, dancing a final waltz with friends from her youth. As the dance gathers pace, a mysterious figure enters the room, and suddenly brings the waltz to a halt: the shadowed figure is Death. As Paavali awakes, he realizes that his mother is now dead. Sibelius's music traces the action in Järnefelt's play closely. The wistful opening gives way to a mood of chivalrous elegance as the waltz begins, only for the dance to become increasingly strained and frenetic as it reaches its dramatic denouement. A fragment of the opening is recalled at the very end to bring the dance to a close, but its return sounds merely empty and prosaic, a bleak summing-up of life's trials and tribulations. Sibelius's other numbers for *Kuolema* never attained anything like the popularity of 'Valse triste', although one particular sequence, the 'Scene with Cranes', has been programmed as an independent concert piece: the characteristic polyphonic writing for upper strings at the start of the score creates a feeling of immense luminosity, while the birds' trumpeting call is evoked by a pair of clarinets. Sibelius's compositional imagination had once again been stimulated by the fragility of the human condition and his immersion in the natural world.

The shadowy figures of life, death and desire that move through the pages of *Kuolema*, the Rydberg songs and the Second Symphony also animate Sibelius's next large-scale work: the Violin Concerto. It is surprising given his close personal relationship with the instrument that Sibelius waited so long before writing a concerto, and that despite later attempts to revisit the form he ultimately completed only a single work in the genre. From his earliest musical experiences shared with his uncle Pehr, through his studies at the Helsinki Music Institute with Mitrofan Vasiliev and Hermann Csillag, to his unsuccessful audition for a place in the Vienna Philharmonic Orchestra, the violin had been central to the way in which Sibelius thought about aspects of colour, rhythmic articulation and melodic line, and he had been for many years a proficient (if not virtuosic) performer. And although his chronic anxiety and stage nerves eventually took their toll on his performing career, which Sibelius instead deflected into conducting his own works, the violin evidently remained an intrinsic part of his musical imagination, as well as part of his own sense of self-being. As late as 1915, as he was working on his sparkling Sonatina in E, op. 80, for example, he noted wistfully in his diary: 'dreamt I was twelve years old and a violin virtuoso'.[14] The genesis and early reception of the Violin Concerto, however, were to prove especially difficult, partly because of the inherent compositional challenges in achieving an optimal balance between the genre's expectations of bravura solo display and Sibelius's increasing preoccupation with tightness of structural design and formal innovation, and also because of his bungled attempts to secure the work's premiere. Though Sibelius was perhaps burnt by the experience, the Violin Concerto would always remain an exceptional work in his catalogue.

Initial thoughts about the concerto appear to have emerged in 1902 during one of Sibelius's regular trips to Berlin, when he was in close contact with the violinist Willy Burmester, former concertmaster of the Helsinki Orchestra. Sustained work began while Sibelius was on holiday in the Baltic resort of Tvärminne on the Gulf of Finland. In a letter to Aino dated 10 September, for example, he wrote urging himself to compose more at the writing desk and less at the piano; 'yet there is this in me that wants to be a violin virtuoso and this "impulse" [utöfvanda] always takes such a strange form within me. Piano tinkering and doodles etc. It all has the same root. That is completely clear to me now.' Such self-chastisement seemed to work, because barely a week later, on 18 September, he revealed, 'I've got some marvellous themes for a violin concerto.'[15]

The first two movements of the concerto were ready in short score by early 1903, with the finale drafted in the summer; the full orchestral score was complete by the end of the year. Sibelius had initially promised the work's premiere to Burmester, but for reasons that remain unclear he changed his mind at the last minute, and the first performance instead took place in Helsinki on 8 February 1904, with Viktor Nováček, a teacher at the Helsinki Music Institute but an inferior player, as soloist. Burmester generously offered to perform the piece for the second time in Helsinki later that year, but Sibelius withdrew the manuscript, dissatisfied with the work's shape and stung by some of the negative press the concerto had initially received. Burmester was eventually passed over on a third occasion, when the revised version of the concerto was finally unveiled in Berlin on 19 October 1905, conducted by Richard Strauss with the Czech violinist Karl Halíř. Though German critics were largely positive (thanks perhaps to Strauss's advocacy), the concerto initially struggled to gain ground, and it was not until Jascha Heifetz took up the score in the 1930s that it finally gained a permanent place in the repertoire. It is now one of Sibelius's most popular and frequently recorded works.

The concertos of Mendelssohn and Bruch were important models for Sibelius's approach to the genre: Sibelius had learned both works as a student, and the significance of Mendelssohn's celebrated E minor concerto, for example, is particularly evident in the hazy, impressionistic opening of Sibelius's score. Sibelius may equally well have had Tchaikovsky's concerto in mind, which he got to know in Helsinki in 1893, although he does not appear to have heard the Brahms concerto until after drafting his own. Questions of influence nevertheless detract from the more innovative aspects of Sibelius's score. The first movement, in its revised form, is a remarkably compressed sonata design. The violin's atmospheric principal theme is not immediately taken up by the orchestra, as might normally be expected, but leads instead into an improvisatory cadenza, an early instance of the importance of Bach's unaccompanied violin works with which Sibelius was also familiar. The first tutti entry leads into the second subject group, marked *Largamente*, with the soloist's affective parallel sixths suggesting a more languorous exoticism. The orchestra's response is a furious *Allegro molto*, with sharp brass fanfares and bustling string ostinato figuration. The development section that follows is essentially a self-contained cadenza for the soloist, exploiting more of the neo-Baroque polyphonic writing from the exposition alongside wistful reminiscences of the opening theme. The reprise is texturally rescored and begins on the subdominant – the opening theme is initially given to the bassoons before being picked up once by the soloist, on the instrument's lowest string. The second subject returns, briefly landing on the tonic major, but the orchestra's rhythmically motoric music from the close of the exposition leads into a tempestuous coda and a dashing final glimpse of the soloist's first entry, seemingly cast into the roaring winds of an orchestral gale.

The second movement brings an immediate change of mode and musical terrain. The tonally unstable writing for the woodwind with which the movement begins swiftly settles in B flat major, and the soloist's warmly expansive first entry, marked *sonoro ed espressivo*, suggests a restrained and dignified idyll after the turbulence of the preceding movement. The end of this first melodic phrase is marked by a darkening shift of tone, and the orchestra's increasingly restless chromaticism. The demanding two-part writing for the soloist, with triplets syncopated against an elaboration of the opening melodic idea, leads into an ecstatic return of the primary subject, played fleetingly by the whole ensemble, and a hushed, nostalgic coda.

The brilliant figuration and technical wizardry of the final movement swiftly blows away any lingering shadows from the preceding Adagio. Donald Francis Tovey's affectionate description of a 'polonaise for polar bears' is hard to resist, although the music is characterized more by a *Zigeuner*-like spirit of playfulness and invention than by fantastical zoological images of the far north well beyond Finland's physical borders. The mood is closest, in fact, to that of Sibelius's later *Humoresques* for violin and orchestra, miniature gems that readily reveal his debt to the Mephistophelian showpieces of Paganini and Wieniawski. As the soloist's increasingly spectacular runs in the final bars drive the concerto towards its characteristically brusque conclusion, it is poignant to trace the distance the work has travelled: from the young provincial fiddler dreaming of a glamorous international performing career, to the mature composer who would eventually grasp the musical world in the palm of his hand.

In a letter to Axel Carpelan dated 8 March 1904, a month after the concerto's unsuccessful premiere, Sibelius wrote: 'life is splendid enough although we are set to suffer. In my opinion, he who can suffer the most is richest. My *allein Gefühl* has been stronger than ever. Death approaches ... I have many new ideas!'[16] While Sibelius's thoughts were preoccupied once again by intimations of mortality alongside the waxing and waning of his creative spirit, work was proceeding on his new property at Järvenpää. The plans for the house, which Sibelius named 'Ainola' in honour of his wife, were drawn up by the young architect Lars Sonck (1870–1956), whose later projects would include the Helsinki Stock Exchange and the Kallio church, which remains an imposing landmark on the city's skyline. Sonck's design is characterized by its distinctive steeply pitched roof and heavy wooden window frames, referring to traditional elements of vernacular Finnish architecture. On 24 September Sibelius and his family finally moved into the villa, which was surrounded by a sensitively landscaped garden stocked with fruit trees and bushes that would be carefully maintained by Aino for many years. Living accommodation was originally limited to the ground floor only (which is the space accessible to visitors today). Sonck later converted the attic into additional space and remodelled the outside of the building with the distinctive white timber cladding in which it now appears. The purchase and construction of 'Ainola' was a significant financial burden on Sibelius, and he would not repay the mortgage loan fully until he was in his sixties. But it would remain the family home for the rest of his life, and was only sold to the state in 1972 (fifteen years after his death), opening as a museum two years later.[17]

A violent reminder of the fragile state of events in the world outside the domestic sphere flared up briefly in the summer. On 16 June an ardent young Finnish nationalist, Eugen Schauman, assassinated the Russian Governor-General in Helsinki, Nikolai Bobrikov, before turning the gun on himself. Widely despised in Finland for his imposition of censorship and suppression following the February Manifesto in 1899, Bobrikov's death was celebrated by the nationalist side and Schauman was regarded as a hero. The Russian response, distracted by its war with Japan on the other side of the empire, was unexpectedly muted, and the feared reprisals and crackdown after Bobrikov's death never materialized. But the event foreshadowed the more widespread violence that was to occur across Russia in the wake of the general strike the following year. Sibelius was sympathetic to Schauman's cause, and briefly considered writing a requiem in his memory, although he quickly abandoned the project.[18] His compositions of the year otherwise strike a strangely escapist note. On 5 March, for example, he conducted a short piece to accompany a *tableau vivant*

Jean and Aino Sibelius with daughters Margareta, Katarina and Heidi in front of Ainola, 1915, photograph by Eric Sundström.

based on Heinrich Heine's famous poem 'Ein Fichtenbaum steht einsam', in which a lone northern pine chillingly draped in ice and snow dreams longingly of a southern palm, far away in the eastern desert sands. Heine's poem had inspired many musical responses, including two songs by Franz Liszt as well as settings by Rimsky-Korsakov, Agathe Backer-Grøndahl, Delius and Grieg. Sibelius's score plays on the geographical polarization implied in Heine's poem by juxtaposing a mysteriously atmospheric slow introduction with a curiously light-hearted waltz. Though the dance's contrasting central section recalls the unsettled mood of the introduction, the waltz's reprise promises a return to more sunlit lands, but the minor turn in the very final bars brings the work to an abruptly ambivalent close. Sibelius swiftly edited and arranged the piece for piano, and later published a revised version of the orchestral original, now entitled *Dance intermezzo*, in 1907. The other work to emerge during the summer was also something of an anomaly. *Kyllikki* is a three-movement suite for solo piano, based on a female character from the *Kalevala*, although Sibelius later claimed that the work had no specific programmatic associations. It is among Sibelius's most ambitious works for the instrument, inspired perhaps by his friendship with Busoni, and the blustery first movement in particular is indicative of his expansive approach to register, texture and broad melodic sweep. Among Sibelius's youthful enthusiasms was Schumann's *Kreisleriana*, and elements of Schumann's imaginary musical characters – Florestan and Eusebius – might be heard transfigured in the shifting personalities of much of Sibelius's piano work. The hymnic chords at the start of the second movement suggest a dignified calm that gives way to more trembling figuration as the movement progresses, like shuddering ghostly echoes from a Schubertian song. The finale is essentially a playful polonaise, though darker and more malignant shadows never remain too far from the music's elegantly skittish surface.

It was just as Sibelius was moving at last into Ainola in autumn 1904 that he accepted a commission from the Swedish Theatre in Helsinki to write incidental music for a production of Maurice Maeterlinck's 1893 symbolist play *Pelléas et Mélisande*. First performed at Offenbach's Théâtre des Bouffes-Parisiens on the rue Monsigny in Paris, directed by the acclaimed actor and stage designer Aurélien Lugné-Poe (who had been the leading advocate of Ibsen and Strindberg's work in France), Maeterlinck's play had received a scathing review from the critical press but soon proved to be a remarkable success, not least because of its innovative staging and scenography. The play quickly attracted musical responses: most famously Claude Debussy's opera (1901–2), but also Gabriel Fauré's elegantly stylized incidental score (written for a production in London in 1898 and orchestrated by Charles Koechlin) and Arnold Schoenberg's sweeping tone poem of 1903. The attraction of Maeterlinck's drama lay not so much in its narrative or plot, which must have always seemed rather thin, but rather in its preoccupation with what would become recurrent *fin-de-siècle* themes of adolescent love, sexual violence, jealousy and existential despair, as well as in its alluring, atmospheric setting of gloomy forests and dolorous old castle walls. It was a striking antidote to the naturalism that had dominated much French literature in the 1880s.

Pelléas et Mélisande was Sibelius's most ambitious theatre project since the *King Christian* music of 1899, and further evidence of his keen concern with the creative potential of music, stage drama and the spoken word. The overture, which Sibelius later titled 'At the Castle Gate' when he prepared his concert suite from the score the following year, provides a suitably stirring opening number with its strong chorale-like writing for strings and bold festive cadences, gestures that echo the music he had provided for many of the Helsinki historical *tableaux vivants* in the 1890s. The Prelude to Act I, Scene 2, which follows Golaud out into the forest where he discovers Mélisande sitting weeping beside a spring, is another melancholic *valse triste*: the soft swaying motion of the dance captures the young girl's fragility and introversion. The melodrama 'At the Sea Shore' from Act I, Scene 4 is a brilliantly evocative tone picture, anticipating Sibelius's music for *The Tempest*, which suggests the insistent rocking swell of the water that carried the ship on which Pelléas fatefully arrives, and the deep echo of the waves within the sea caverns to which he and Mélisande descend. The Prelude to Act II, Scene 3, is a more cheerful, light-filled interlude, though Sibelius's characteristic double-bass writing suggests that danger is lurking and ever-present: this threat is amplified by the Prelude to Act III, where the music's obsessive repetitiveness is driven figuratively by the rotary mechanism of Mélisande's spinning wheel. The increasingly taut thread replicates the drama's rising tension, which almost reaches breaking point before gradually losing momentum and winding down once more. The song in Act III, Scene 2, 'The Three Blind Sisters', is the sole vocal number in the score: Sibelius's accompaniment has a particularly restrained quality, softly written for strings and lower winds so as not to overload Mélisande's voice on stage. Meanwhile, the melodrama in Act III, Scene 4, is a glowing pastoral, and one of Sibelius's most beautifully judged miniatures, a heart-breaking portrait of youthful innocence and vulnerability. The Prelude that opens Act IV is a busy entr'acte, suggesting childhood games and fairy-tale adventure, the world of the young boy Yniold; only towards the end of the central section do shadows briefly threaten once more. The final bars recapture the end of the 'Castle Gate' overture – a fleeting reference to the location where the play's fateful denouement, Golaud's bloody revenge for what he perceives as Pélleas's betrayal, will shortly take place. The Prelude to Act V, Scene 2, which gives onto Mélisande's deathbed scene, has a suitably otherworldly quality. Here, and elsewhere, Sibelius may have been influenced by Grieg's music for Ibsen's *Peer Gynt*, which Lugné-Poe had produced at the avant-garde Théâtre de l'Oeuvre in Paris in 1896. Grieg's music for Åse's death, for example, has a similar elegiac quality to that of Sibelius's score, and Sibelius had always been deeply influenced by Grieg's approach to writing for massed strings. The second half of the number, however, has a barely sustainable feeling of grief and loss, the very briefest glimpse of an emotional release before the castle twilight descends once more and gloom envelops the stage.

It is remarkable and instructive to compare the distance between the shimmering delicacy of Sibelius's score for Maeterlinck's drama with his bold, raw-edged representation of violence, obsession and sexual desire in earlier works such as *Kullervo*, *Skogsrået* and even the *Lemminkäinen Legends*, written barely a decade earlier. Now, perhaps writing as a father and thinking of his own daughters, his attitude had changed. In his music for *Pelléas et Mélisande* the emphasis is never on an overt expression of passion or physical longing, but rather on the shifting moods and elusive atmosphere of Maeterlinck's text. The remoteness of the play's historical location becomes a cipher for the obscurity of its protagonists' emotions, and ultimately for the inscrutability of the human soul. It was precisely this impenetrability that the symbolists paradoxically embraced, and which proved so alluring for Sibelius's musical imagination. Yet for all its fleeting moments of radiance and insight, and its captivating immersion in the forest shadows of Maeterlinck's mythic Allemonde, there is something wistfully retrospective about the tone and quality of Sibelius's music that belongs more properly to the 1890s than to the new century. The following years would bring a significant change of direction in his work and, for a brief time, a brighter light, even as the clouds of political conflict, turmoil and upheaval would begin to gather on the horizon once more.

5

Along Modern Lines

If Aino had hoped that relocating to their new villa at Järvenpää in September 1904 would lead to a quieter and less disrupted daily routine, she was mistaken: with his restless nature, Sibelius swiftly began planning his next visit overseas, even while they were still unpacking the moving crates. His first destination was Berlin, the city where he had studied and made his initial contacts with German publishers and which, for the time being, was the primary focus of his international musical attention. Is was also one of his key cultural reference points: memories of alcohol-fuelled symposium evenings at Zum Schwarzen Ferkel with Adolf Paul, Munch, Gallen-Kallela, Sinding and others would always remain a strong draw. He had been invited by Busoni to conduct a performance of his Second Symphony with the Philharmonic on 12 January 1905, and arrived at the start of the month in order to begin rehearsals. The concert was very warmly received: Sibelius was often acclaimed for directing performances of his own work, even if he showed little interest in conducting other music. Though he found the Berlin schedule exhausting, he also gained a great deal professionally from working closely with the orchestra. Either side of the concert, the visit provided an opportunity to catch up with old friends as well as to make new acquaintances (such as the American dancer Isadora Duncan). It also gave him the chance to hear a range of music, including some new works – significantly, Richard Strauss's *Ein Heldenleben* (1898) and the *Symphonia Domestica* (1902–3) – as well as more familiar repertoire such as Tchaikovsky's Fifth Symphony and the amiable *Ländliche Hochzeit* (Rustic Wedding) symphony by his former Viennese teacher Karl Goldmark, which now struck Sibelius as particularly quaint and old-fashioned.

Mindful of the pressures of their shared domestic commitments in Finland, Aino must have been dismayed to read Sibelius's proposal, in a letter sent on 16 January, that he should in future spend two or three months at the height of the winter season every year in Berlin in order to hear new music, 'otherwise', he suggested, 'I shall get out of touch':[1] at crucial moments, music, for Sibelius, evidently came before family, as his sudden flight from Rapallo while working on the Second Symphony in Italy had already indicated. Alongside Strauss's new compositions, he noted that he was studying Mahler's work (the Fifth Symphony, which had received its first performance only the previous October in Cologne), as well as Sinding's String Quartet in A minor, published in Leipzig the previous year. Tawaststjerna has suggested that it may have been the mighty funeral march ('Wie ein Kondukt') at the head of Mahler's symphony that later inspired Sibelius's tone poem *In memoriam* (1909).[2] In addition, Sibelius heard Brahms's Violin Concerto ('too symphonic'),[3] just as he was finishing the revisions to his own following its unsuccessful premiere in Helsinki the previous year. And he particularly admired a performance conducted by Arthur Nikisch of Schubert's 'Great' Symphony in C major, a piece that he would play at home with Aino in its four-hand piano arrangement, and which 'always sounds new'.[4] Perhaps it was this nostalgic thought of his own private music-making at home in Ainola that first suggested the idea of a C major symphony in Sibelius's mind, a concept that would soon bear more significant fruit in the coming years.

As well as his concert engagement, Sibelius was keen to explore other professional opportunities during his stay in Berlin, one result of which was a contract with the publisher Robert Lienau that required him to produce four new works each year. Although this commercial endorsement by one of the leading German publishing firms (and Breitkopf & Härtel's rival) was a significant expression of confidence in the international market for Sibelius's music, he swiftly found the terms of the contract unsustainable, and it became an additional burden on his already fragile self-belief. At the same time, Sibelius was scoping other potential audiences for his works: the English conductor and composer Granville Bantock (1868–1946), for example, attempted to persuade him to travel to England in March to conduct a concert with the Liverpool Orchestral Society, although in the event Sibelius instead returned to Finland and directed the premiere of his music for *Pelléas et Mélisande* at the Swedish Theatre in Helsinki, where it proved the biggest success of the season.

The Queen's Hall, London, on a postcard, *c.* 1912.

Although he had declined Bantock's initial approach, Sibelius's first visit to England did not have to wait too long. Travelling down through the continent via Berlin and following an aborted concert in Heidelberg later in the autumn, he crossed the English Channel on 29 November and was fined '2 pund 6 schilling' for illegally bringing undeclared cigars across the border at Dover. Despite this initial glitch, England immediately made a 'pleasant and aristocratic impression' upon Sibelius, not least because Bantock had generously arranged accommodation at the elegant Langham Hotel on Regent Street in central London, adjacent to the Queen's Hall, which was then the city's leading concert venue. While in the capital Sibelius was introduced to Henry Wood (1869–1944), co-founder with Robert Newman of the Promenade Concerts (later the BBC Proms), who had conducted his First Symphony in 1903, as well as Hans Richter (1843–1916), principal conductor of the Birmingham Festival and director of the Hallé Orchestra in Manchester. Journeying north via the School of Music at the Birmingham and Midland Institute (now the Royal Birmingham Conservatoire), where his visit coincided with that of Busoni who was over from Berlin, Sibelius conducted his First Symphony and *Finlandia* in Liverpool and was very favourably impressed by the orchestra ('10 double basses'), before returning to London where he met the music critic Ernest Newman (1868–1959), who would later become an important commentator on his work. Sibelius returned to Finland via Paris in December, struck again by England's cultural history and aristocratic hierarchies and traditions, and with the promise of many further performances already secured.[5] And thanks to the advocacy of Bantock, Wood, Newman and others – especially the remarkable writer and critic Rosa Newmarch (1857–1940), who already had extensive interest and expertise in Russian music – England would swiftly prove to be a far more congenial and receptive environment for Sibelius's work than either Germany or France.

Energized by his trips abroad, and already under pressure from his new contract with Lienau, Sibelius had been preoccupied for much of 1905 with a major new large-scale work: an oratorio entitled *Marjatta* (Mary), based on the final section of the *Kalevala* that recounts the arrival of Christianity in Finland. The writer and theatre director Jalmari Finne, who had supplied much of the text for the 1899 Press Lottery Celebrations for which Sibelius wrote *Finlandia*, had drawn up a lengthy scenario and drafted an extended libretto, and it is fascinating to speculate what form the final work might have taken had Sibelius followed his plans through to completion.[6] He had, of course, been greatly taken by a performance of Liszt's oratorio *Christus* in Berlin, and Edward Elgar had recently discovered new creative potential in the genre in his setting of Cardinal Newman's revelatory poem *The Dream of Gerontius* (1899), so Sibelius's interest in the form is not implausible. By mid-December, however, he had abandoned the oratorio, and instead focused energies on a work entitled *Luonnotar*, based on the creation myth that appears at the very start of the Finnish epic. Sibelius had first mentioned the idea of *Luonnotar* in a letter to Aino as early as 28 July 1894, when he was grappling with the challenge of how to respond to Wagner's music dramas, and he had already returned to the theme at the time of his work on the Second Symphony in 1901. Ultimately, a finished score carrying the title 'Luonnotar' would not appear until 1913, when he composed his tone poem for Aino Ackté and the Three Choirs Festival in Gloucester. The immediate fate of *Marjatta* and *Luonnotar*, however, is illustrative of Sibelius's complex and often convoluted working method: themes, motifs and ideas would evolve over a number of years, often in conjunction with very different and contrasting compositional schemes and ideas, before they eventually reached their final and definitive form. Sibelius's sketchbooks are evidence both of the fluency and flexibility of his creative imagination, and also of the persistence of certain basic characters and figures, musical and symbolic: a quality that gives his work a strongly intertextual dimension and means that the boundaries between individual pieces are often more permeable than they first appear.

The threads that had become entangled in *Marjatta* and his preliminary sketches for *Luonnotar* were eventually tied together in a third project: the tone poem *Pohjola's Daughter*. As Timo Virtanen has shown, the genesis of *Pohjola's Daughter* was among the most protracted of any of Sibelius's compositions, and material for the piece was drawn not only from the abortive work on *Marjatta* and *Luonnotar* but from sketches for what would later become the Third Symphony. Based on Canto 8 of the *Kalevala*, the tone poem tells the story of an encounter between the epic's primary creative figure, the ancient seer Väinamöinen, and the beautiful daughter of the Northland, who resists his amorous advances and sets him a series of impossible tasks, including tying an egg in invisible knots and assembling a boat from a splinter of her spindle. Sibelius had initially proposed 'Väinamöinen' as a possible title, but it was Lienau who eventually preferred 'Pohjola's Daughter', and who insisted on printing explanatory verses from the *Kalevala* at the head of the score.

The tone poem is among the most detailed and intricately conceived of Sibelius's orchestral works. The G minor introduction, with its gloomy scoring and sombre cello solo, evokes a darkly incantatory state, a feeling of mythic time and primeval forces underpinning the earth. Out of this murky beginning emerges a growing sense of anticipation, led first by soft woodwind dialogues and then picked up by the strings. As the music gains life and momentum, it initiates the first climactic statement of a craggy brass-heavy cadence, perhaps a representation of the dignified Väinamöinen, that attempts to assert B flat as a bold new tonic key, but which is harmonically deflected at the very last moment, leading into a more reflective, pastoral episode in F sharp minor. The heart of the tone poem depicts Väinamöinen's increasingly stormy and frustrated struggles with the tasks that the Northland's daughter has challenged him to accomplish. Eventually, after intensive motivic development and a drastically compressed reprise, the texture accumulates once more and Väinamöinen's proud fanfare returns with a renewed hope and expectation, only to be thwarted for a final time as the hero's ambitions evaporate into the Northland's mists just as his prize appears to be within his grasp. The desolate coda is a series of slowly ascending string lines, haunted by the enharmonic shadow of F sharp (G flat), as Väinamöinen returns to his lonely fate. Like his earlier tone poems, *En saga* and *Skogsrået*, as well as the First Symphony, the heroic quest in *Pohjola's Daughter* thus ends in exile and defeat, which can be heard at least in part as a further brooding reflection on Sibelius's own struggles with his creativity (and a very different vision of artistic conquest from that in Strauss's *Ein Heldenleben*). But at the same time, the tonal structure and motivic sophistication of the score was a significant accomplishment, one that has since drawn many admirers (notably Arnold Bax), and *Pohjola's Daughter* has proven to be one of Sibelius's most popular works in the concert hall. Väinamöinen himself would surely have acclaimed such ingenuity.

The composition of *Pohjola's Daughter* had proven so demanding, both in terms of time and creative energy, that it must have come as a shock when Sibelius realized that this was only one of the four pieces that he was contractually obliged to deliver to his new publisher, Lienau, on an annual basis. He had been working on other less significant projects in the meantime. The vividly scored miniature *Pan and Echo*, for example, was a character piece written for another fundraising *tableau vivant* held at the Seurahuone in Helsinki on 24 March, which provided ample opportunity for splashes of instrumental colour and escapist fantasy. The patriotic cantata *Vapautettu kuningatar* (The Captive Queen), based on Paavo Cajander's thinly veiled historical ballad, meanwhile, was a more obviously politicized piece, opening with a drumming, military beat like a call to arms and concluding with the long-awaited sounds of liberation and release, a trajectory calibrated to the hopes and aspirations of its local audience. At the same time, Sibelius was aware of the need to sustain wider international interest in his work. The set of six German songs that he published with Lienau as his op. 50, for example, was clearly intended for export to the continent. The two opening numbers, 'Lenzgesang' ('Spring Song', to a text by Alfred Fitger) and 'Sehnsucht' ('Longing', by Emil Rudolf Weiss) form an extended upbeat to the three strongly Schubertian songs that lie at the centre of the collection, which comprise a miniature cycle or Liederkreis. These songs are linked thematically, tonally and symbolically: 'Im Feld ein Mädchen singt' (A Young Girl Sings in the Field) is a soft, pulsating lament in B flat minor as a woman mourns her recently deceased lover. Twice, at the end of each stanza, the texture unfolds as the twilight glows and the meadows stand still and empty, Sibelius's setting dwelling on the insistent false relation A natural/A flat like an unresolved dart of pain and loss. Those same pitches form the centre of the tonal argument in the following number, 'Aus banger Brust' ('From a Troubled Heart', by Richard Dehmel). A restless account of frustrated longing and erotic desire, the song's schizophrenic tonal structure revolves around the tonic, D minor and the enharmonic equivalence of its tritone pole, A flat/G sharp (the pitch on which the vocal line ambiguously ends). A second Dehmel setting, 'Die stille Stadt' (The Silent Town), textually riffs on one of Heine's poems set by Schubert and published posthumously as part of his *Schwanengesang*, the image of a bleak, silent and seemingly deserted town that forms the backdrop for the narrator's existential angst. Sibelius's setting returns to B flat, the key of 'Im Feld ein Mädchen singt', creating a strong correspondence between the two songs. The piano's soft, insistent ostinato gives way only at the very end, the acoustic image of a child's prayer offering just a glimmer of hope amid the desolation. The final number, 'Rosenlied' ('Song of the Rose', to a text by Anna Ritter) is a curiously blithe scherzo in E major that suggests one of Mahler's *Wunderhorn* lieder. After the sorrow and introspection of the central songs, it is an equivocal reminder of the essentially fleeting and transient nature of life and beauty, and of the fickleness of love. Embrace the warm night: the only certainty, the final line concludes, is that all shall ultimately pass into the grave.

The ambivalent character of the op. 50 songs, with their frequent intimations of human mortality amid more seemingly innocent and naive gestures, in some senses reflects the wider political mood in Finland at their time of composition with its strange feeling of the calm before the storm – precisely the phrase, in fact, that Sibelius used in a letter to Aino dated 9 August.[7] Bobrikov's murder had heightened tensions, but Russian attention had been almost entirely preoccupied by its war with Japan over imperial control in Manchuria and the Korean peninsula, and subsequently by the fallout from the general strike and revolution in December 1905, which resulted in the creation of the Duma (the Russian parliament) and the declaration of the 1906 constitution. For a brief moment, life in Finland seemed quieter and less antagonistic than in previous years, although Sibelius took the opportunity to meet the dissident socialist author Maxim Gorky, who was in exile from St Petersburg and who briefly stayed with the Järnefelts in Järvenpää.[8] It was at this moment that he received a second commission from the Swedish Theatre in Helsinki, following the success of his music for *Pelléas et Mélisande* the previous season. The topic on this occasion was *Belsazars gästabud* (Belshazzar's Feast) by the Swedish-Finnish journalist, poet and bon viveur Hjalmar Procopé (1868–1927). Procopé's play, based on the well-known biblical story (Daniel 5:1–30) but owing much, in fact, to Oscar Wilde's *Salomé* (1891), had been published in 1905 and dedicated to the leading Finnish actress and impressaria Ida Aalberg (1857–1915), who would for a time be one of the leading figures at the Finnish National Theatre.

The timing of *Belsazar*'s premiere, on 7 November 1906, was propitious: the first staging in Finland of Wilde's play had been given at the National Theatre in 1905,[9] the same year that Richard Strauss's opera *Salome* was premiered in Dresden. Procopé's work thus capitalized on the vogue for Wildean fantasy in alluringly Eastern settings. But the greater significance of the work was located both in its choice of performance venue and in its place within the delicate language politics that were unfolding in early twentieth-century Finland, in particular the tense relationship between Swedish-speaking and Finnish-speaking communities in the context of Russian colonial rule. Procopé was a member of an artistic circle based around the Finnish music journal *Euterpe*, founded in 1902 by critic Karl Flodin, whose fellow members, including the writers Bertel Gripenberg, Oscar Levertin and Gunnar Castrén, were committed to a positively international perspective (directed especially towards Paris).[10] With their aristocratic sense of detachment from the everyday world and their decadent outlook (marked equally by aesthetic refinement and self-indulgence), it was a group to which Sibelius was inevitably drawn and felt sympathetic, not least as he began to distance himself from the blunter, more overtly Fennomane nationalism of Gallen-Kallela and Juhani Aho.

In total, Sibelius composed eleven short numbers for the play, none of which last longer than three minutes in performance. Conditions for performing music in the Swedish Theatre were far from ideal. Sibelius conducted the ensemble behind the wings, and the work was scored for a group of barely twenty players – light woodwind, two percussion players and strings. Alongside Strauss's glitteringly opulent *Salome*, Sibelius's evocation of Babylonian excess was on an altogether more modest scale. He nevertheless cared sufficiently about the music to extract a suite of four movements with a lightly expanded orchestration from the complete score that he then offered to Lienau and performed relatively frequently abroad. As one might expect, the setting and themes of Procopé's text, with its crude and racially deterministic representations of the Middle East, offered Sibelius ample opportunity to explore conventional musical orientalist gestures of the kind familiar from nineteenth-century opera and ballet. The opening march, for example, has a swirling sense of the exotic, with its janissary percussion and ostinato rhythms, as does the bustling prelude to Act III, depicting the festive preparations at Belshazzar's court. Elsewhere, however, the score has a more affective sense of mood and atmosphere: the delicate nocturne that depicts the hanging gardens of Babylon at the start of Act II, for instance, has a radiant beauty, and the 'Judiska flickans sång' (Jewish Girl's Song) at the end of the act, performed by an offstage singer rather than by the character of Leschanah herself onstage, has a particularly moving wistfulness, supported by a gossamer-thin inverted pedal in the upper strings and sparing use of the bass. Sibelius's score ends not with a bang, comparable to the death of Salomé's in Strauss's opera after she has bewitched Herod with her 'Dance of the Seven Veils', but rather with Khadra's wry and whimsical dance of life and death: another of his seemingly effortless and beguiling waltzes. Although the staged regicide with which Procopé's play concludes might have been a dangerously provocative gesture in the context of a Russian empire that was seemingly inevitably tumbling towards its own bloody end (not least given the obviously allegorical subtext of Sibelius's earlier score for Paul's *King Christian II*), the well-heeled audience of the Swedish Theatre in 1906 appears to have been more-or-less oblivious of any wider political ramifications. For a brief moment, as they strolled down the elegant pavements of Esplanadi after the performance, such worldly and material concerns seemed little more than an ominous shadow on the distant horizon.

Scene from Hjalmar Procopé's *Belsazars gästabud* (Belshazzar's Feast), 7 November 1906.

Sibelius's work on his score for *Belsazars gästabud* was further evidence of his continuing interest in music and the theatre. But it was ultimately a distraction from progress on his next major large-scale project, the Third Symphony. Expectations of the new work at home in Finland were running particularly high given the success of the First and Second Symphonies, with their sweeping narratives of struggle and (in the latter work) triumph over apparent adversity. The crisp, streamlined contours of the Third hence came almost as a shock to Sibelius's audience. The symphony is in many ways among his most radical conceptions. One of the central stylistic points of reference for the work had been his conversations with Busoni. In 1907, the same year that Sibelius finished the score, Busoni published the first edition of his polemical *Entwurf einer neuen Ästhetik der Tonkunst* (Sketch for a New Aesthetics of Music), in which, among other things, he called for a fresh approach to musical form that was no longer reliant on outdated tonal procedures or structures, and for a freer approach to musical fantasy informed by a more refined tonal and harmonic system (advocating the use of both older modes and quarter-tones and micro-tuning). The spirit of the *Junge Klassizität* (young classicism) that Busoni would later formulate in the 1920s, in parallel with similar movements in architecture and the visual arts, was already anticipated by the strongly linear, more strictly contrapuntal layout of Sibelius's new symphony, although Sibelius later wrote disparagingly about his impressions of Busoni's *Fantasia Contrappuntistica*, lamenting: 'why does this great piano artist compose?'[11] Even the simple idea of writing a symphony in C major was in itself a radical decision for a symphonic composer in the first decade of the twentieth century. An almost overwhelming historical weight rested on the key's symbolism (from Mozart's final symphony, the 'Jupiter', K 551, through Beethoven's First, Schubert's 'Great', which Sibelius had recalled playing fondly with Aino, and Schumann's Second), so that there can scarcely have seemed any creative space for a new work, especially in such an elevated and hallowed genre. But this is precisely where Sibelius's opportunity for innovation could be found, in reconceiving the idea of a C major symphony in a fresh and progressive fashion (much as Stravinsky would do more than thirty years later when he came to write his own Symphony in C in 1938–40). By paring back the forces required for the performance, recalibrating the music's form and tonal structure, and creating a strong sense of goal direction or teleology across the first and third movements, Sibelius succeeded in remodelling the symphony compellingly along modern lines: it is a dazzlingly original achievement.

Elements of the *Marjatta* oratorio project can still be heard distantly within the work's trajectory. The frequent recourse to hymn-like writing, the gentle lullaby motion of the second movement, and the sense of excitement and spiritual elevation in the finale are all consistent with the narrative arc of the proposed choral work, even if no firm evidence survives to support any direct thematic link between the works.[12] At another level, however, the symphony feels entirely *sui generis*: an exemplar of the creative fantasy for which Busoni had called so energetically in his *Entwurf*. The first movement begins distinctively with a rhythmically alert figure, immediately suggesting forward propulsion (Sibelius might have had the opening of Beethoven's 'Waldstein' Sonata in his mind as he sketched this initial gesture). A prominent feature of the opening bars is the strong emphasis on F sharp, a note that lies outside the diatonic C major scale but which plays an increasingly important role as the work progresses. The initial effect of this dissonant intrusion is to pivot the music into a modally inflected B minor. The circular cello theme that dominates the second subject is the first glimpse of a melodic idea (a minor third) that will eventually generate the hymn-like apotheosis in the finale. The central development section is concerned almost exclusively with musical motion – the impression is of travelling through a hazy landscape at speed, in search of familiar landmarks or signposts. The recapitulation brings a sense of territory regained, and the movement closes with a feeling of arrival and pealing bell sounds in the horns and woodwind.

After the breezy, sunlit diatonicism of the opening Allegro, the second movement plunges into G sharp minor, icily remote from the symphony's home key. The Andantino is a lullaby, oscillating gently between triple and duple metres. The brooding repetitiveness that had characterized the Allegro's second subject is here applied as a formal principle, so that the whole movement can be heard as a series of strophic transformations of its opening material. There are two contrasting interludes, the second of which evokes the luminous light of the Nordic midsummer night, but the initial passage returns to suggest that the gently rocking cradle-song of the opening bars has become a cortège, and the music finishes tersely, in a mood of emotional restraint and withdrawal.

The finale begins with a fairy-tale Scherzo, whose teasing playfulness banishes the shadows of the previous movement. Echoes of the Andantino are briefly heard in the opening paragraph, alongside enharmonic transformations of its dark tonal centre (G sharp/A flat). As the music attempts to gather together its various melodic and textural strands, however, it becomes marooned in a mysterious half-lit realm, dominated by woodwind calls and dusky woodland sounds, underpinned by an uneasy rocking string ostinato. A second play-through of the exposition brings a sense of lighter terrain, and a stronger feeling of structural direction. The passage that follows is a dense and highly chromaticized development, with seemingly no fixed point of tonal reference: it is the most difficult music in the whole work. As this central section dissipates, a seemingly new melodic idea emerges magically in the lower strings. This stirringly diatonic hymn provides the basis for the remainder of the movement, as Sibelius literally drums out the symphony's remaining problematic pitch element, the dissonant F sharp from the opening bars. Subsequent play-overs of the hymn tune generate a thrilling momentum, alongside greater textual weight, with horn trills and pulsing string accompaniment. It is hard to resist the image, first evoked in the closing section of *Finlandia*, of a railway locomotive at full steam, driving the symphony irresistibly forward across a wide landscape towards the C major destination of the closing bars.

Although the new symphony was politely rather than enthusiastically received by Sibelius's domestic audience in Helsinki following its premiere on 25 September 1907, at least one critic recognized the importance and significance of the score. Karl Flodin pointedly described Sibelius as 'a classical master', and noted that 'the new work meets all the requirements of a modern symphony, but at the same time it is, at a deeper level, revolutionary, new and truly Sibelian'.[13] The radical nature of the work came into even greater relief in the wake of the most prominent musical visitor to Helsinki later that autumn, Gustav Mahler, who had been invited to conduct the Orchestral Society by Kajanus. Sibelius met Mahler on a number of occasions during his stay, although his memories of the event are only recorded apocryphally. But the two composers could scarcely have been further apart, in terms of both personality and world view.[14] Their professional careers had taken very different pathways: Mahler had succeeded in establishing himself as one of the leading international conductors of his generation, although his compositional work remained controversial and was at that time less widely acclaimed (not least because of the nagging antisemitism that remained a persistent thread in German music criticism), whereas Sibelius's compositional reputation was rapidly rising while his conducting was essentially a means to an end – he very rarely directed repertoire other than his work. Moreover, it is illuminating to reflect on what the idea of a symphony in C would have meant for Mahler, who had only recently completed his colossal Seventh Symphony (which ends with an extended C major rondo), alongside the taut design and concision of Sibelius's Third.[15] As a genre, the symphony had reached a significant crossroads, at a point of departure between the post-Romantic demand for a universalizing sense of scale and scope (exemplified by Mahler's work) and a more modern desire for balance, rigour and formal clarity (the approach increasingly favoured by Sibelius). Although it would be a mistake to conceive of this tension as a simple binary or opposition, since the future of the symphony lay in synthesizing elements of both tendencies, the cutting-edge quality of Sibelius's Third Symphony becomes much sharper in this context, and it perhaps explains why the two men did not forge a closer personal connection.

Sibelius travelled twice to Russia in short succession at the end of 1907 in order to showcase his new symphony, first to St Petersburg at the invitation of the pianist and conductor Alexander Siloti (1863–1945), who had studied with Liszt in Weimar and later worked closely with Tchaikovsky, and later to Moscow, which Sibelius found 'enormously interesting'.[16] Critical reception, as in Germany, was rather guarded and reserved. Sibelius's anxieties were exacerbated by his growing concerns about his health. His heavy alcohol and tobacco consumption had begun to take its toll, and he was increasingly bothered by problems with his throat that would soon require surgical intervention. He was nevertheless able to make a second trip to London in late February the following year, where he stayed again at the Langham Hotel, to conduct the Third Symphony at the Philharmonic Society. Unlike their colleagues in Russia, English critics were very positive, and Sibelius dedicated the score to Bantock in recognition of the role he had played in promoting his work. A postcard of Westminster Bridge and the Houses of Parliament that Sibelius sent to Aino on 27 February was signed by Rosa Newmarch, Breitkopf & Härtel's agent in London, Otto Kling and Bantock, and annotated with a short musical extract from the finale of the symphony and a cartoon sketch of an empty wine bottle floating in the Thames: perhaps a semi-conscious reference to Gallen-Kallela's *Symposium* portrait in which Sibelius had appeared sixteen years earlier. In fact, he was to give up smoking and alcohol for nearly the next eight years, a period that would correspond with the most creatively productive phase of his life. His old habits, he might have reassured Aino, were now water under the bridge.

Gustav Mahler, 1907, photograph by Moritz Nähr.

Sibelius's compositional thoughts had been stimulated instead by the prospect of working with one of his literary heroes, August Strindberg. The idea of the collaboration had come via Harriet Bosse (1878–1961), the gifted Norwegian-Swedish actress who was for a short time Strindberg's third wife and muse. Bosse had played the role of Mélisande in the 1906 Helsinki production for which Sibelius had provided music, and so it was she who may have first suggested his name when Strindberg was planning a performance of his fairy-tale drama *Svanehvit* (Swanwhite) in Stockholm. *Swanwhite* might at first glance seem a curious choice of text, given Strindberg's more obviously innovative work in plays such as *Fröken Julie* (Miss Julie), *Ett drömspel* (A Dream-play) and the *Till Damascus*

(To Damascus) trilogy. But *Swanwhite*'s similarity to Maeterlinck's play was surely one factor in the decision, and the text's imaginary medieval setting spoke to precisely the aspect of Sibelius's creative imagination that was powerfully attracted to historical fantasy. It was also a play that offered particularly rich opportunities for musical symbolism and nature mysticism.[17] The plot revolves around the fate of a young princess, the eponymous Swanwhite, who lives with her wicked stepmother and father (the duke), and who falls in love with a young prince, the messenger of the king to whom she is formally betrothed. At the start of the second act, Swanwhite's deceased mother appears in the magical guise of a white swan in order to comfort her daughter, who has been imprisoned in the blue tower. Her beloved prince is banished and drowns when his ship is wrecked on the return voyage, but the evil spell that has cursed the stepmother is lifted, her crimes forgiven, and Swanwhite's kiss brings the dead prince's body miraculously back to life.

The premiere performance of *Swanwhite*, conducted by Sibelius, took place at the Swedish Theatre in Helsinki on 8 April 1908, and comparisons

Harriet Bosse as Indra's daughter in Strindberg's *Ett drömspel* (A Dream-play), 1907.

were inevitably drawn with his music for *Pelléas* and *Belsazars gästabud*. Much of the score consists of short numbers, sometimes little more than a single chord or musical gesture designed to evoke a particular atmosphere or state of mind (for instance, the sound that twice marks the passing flight of a white swan), but a handful of movements are more extended, such as the Comodo, which evokes the sound of the peacock that wanders the castle grounds and whose tail forms one of the play's recurrent symbols. Another is the sound of the harp that magically begins to play in the princess's chamber in Act II, whereas the mother's wistful memory of her youth is a gentle pastoral scherzo preceded by a lingering slow introduction. The portrait of the prince alone has a brooding obsessive quality, and the stepmother's attempts to lure him into a false marriage are accompanied by a slow, dark waltz. As Tawaststjerna observed, there are some details of the score that anticipate figures in the Fifth Symphony: the horn call at the end of Act II that symbolizes the prince's chivalry as he lies down in bed with Swanwhite, separated by his sword, echoes the rising motto with which the symphony famously begins, and the music to accompany the king's departure at the start of Act III bears a striking resemblance to a key phrase in the symphony's second movement.[18] A more direct one-to-one correspondence between the symphony and the incidental score in the form of a hidden programme is unlikely. However, the feeling of enchantment and fantasy that underpins both, and the symbolism of the natural world that pervades Strindberg's text, is evidence that Sibelius was sufficiently moved by his engagement with the drama that its sound world lingered in his mind long after its first appearance.

Swanwhite's magical story of young love and rebirth may have appealed especially strongly to Sibelius at a moment when his own health had seemingly reached a crisis point. An operation to remove a throat tumour, which took place partly in Helsinki and was then followed up by a visit to a specialist in Berlin, only heightened awareness of his own mortality as well as adding considerably to his financial pressures. *Swanwhite*'s bird symbolism may also have been an influence on one of his following vocal works: *Jubal* is a setting of a poem by the visionary Swedish poet and artist Ernst Josephson, born in 1851, who had died less than two years previously, on 22 November 1906. The song recounts the eponymous story of a naive Parsifalian youth who (like Lemminkäinen) recklessly shoots down a swan and then sings of its death, paraphrasing the bird's own dying swansong. Sibelius's response opens with a spectacular vocal cadenza, tracing the soaring arc of the swan's flight. The gentle arpeggios of the piano accompaniment in the central section suggest the ringing strings of Jubal's bow, and the opening cadenza returns at the song's climax as Jubal promises to return each evening to the place where the bird fell. Distant horn calls resound in the piano's left hand as Jubal seeks comfort in the 'string music's sweet consolation' ('strängaspelets ljuva tröst'), and the twilight descends. Life, death and creativity, as so often in Josephson's work, seem inextricably intertwined. A setting of an unpleasantly misogynistic poem by the Euterpist author Bertel Gripenberg, 'Teodora', could not be more different. If Sibelius had avoided the grislier sides of Babylonian decadence in his music for *Belsazars gästabud*, his interpretation of 'Teodora' more than compensates with its grinding, furtive piano accompaniment and almost feverish vocal line. The obvious comparison with Strauss's *Salome* is well made: Sibelius's evocation of the degenerate world of Gripenberg's lurid text makes the flesh creep. Despite their incongruity, Sibelius published both 'Jubal' and 'Teodora' together under the same strangely out-of-sequence opus number (35): a salutary indication that Sibelius's own work lists were rarely a reliable guide to his music's actual chronology.

The figures of life, death, and physical and creative rejuvenation that were foregrounded by *Swanwhite*, and which had been recurrent threads in Sibelius's work ever since the 1890s, also found their way into his next major composition, the tone poem *Nightride and Sunrise*, sketched in autumn 1908 for performance the following year in St Petersburg. The piece has remained one of Sibelius's most enigmatic works, despite its seemingly obvious pictorialism. Sibelius's explanation to Rosa Newmarch, for example, offers little in the way of a substantial or specific account:

> The music is concerned . . . with the inner experiences of an average man riding solitary through the forest gloom; sometimes glad to be alone with Nature; occasionally awestricken by the stillness or the strange sounds which break it; not filled with undue foreboding, but thankful and rejoicing in the daybreak.[19]

To his secretary Santeri Levas, however, he reportedly proposed an alternative reading, claiming that the music was inspired by a nocturnal sledge journey from Helsinki to Kerava (Kervo), just outside Järvenpää, around the turn of the century, during which the dawn created 'a sea of colours that shifted and flowed producing the most inspiring sight until it all ended in a growing light'. To Karl Ekman, meanwhile, he claimed it had been inspired by his first sight of the Colosseum in Rome in 1901 after he had abandoned his family in Rapallo, and this was how he referred to a motif from the work in a thematic table that he later compiled in 1915.[20] There may also be other compelling biographical explanations for the music's shape and design. Sibelius's recovery from his successful throat operations, for example, could have felt symbolically akin to a prolonged night-time journey followed by a re-emergence into the light. And no less significant may have been the birth of his fifth daughter, Margareta, on 10 September; having already lost one daughter in early childhood, the birth of another would inevitably have felt particularly fraught and anxious. The hymn-like final section of the tone poem could then be heard figuratively as a thanksgiving for safe deliverance, and a blessing to welcome a new arrival into the world. These accounts need not necessarily be mutually exclusive, of course, since Sibelius was always eager to disclaim any single deterministic reading of his work, but they serve to illustrate the potential extramusical richness of the tone poem's basic binary design, over and above issues of programmaticism alone.

The conductor at the first performance on 23 January 1909, Alexander Siloti, evidently struggled to gain a strong grasp of the score, and he made a number of unauthorized cuts in the work for the concert. Siloti's confusion is hard to understand, since the tone poem's formal structure is remarkably straightforward. The piece is divided into two halves, corresponding to the night-time journey and dawn awakening of the title, each half of which is then subdivided into two large-scale phrases or cycles. Tonally, the music traces a familiar darkness-to-light trajectory, from C minor to E flat major (the same progression as *Lemminkäinen's Homeward Journey* from the *Legends*, op. 22, in fact, and a common Romantic pairing of keys). One of the tone poem's most remarkable features is the very opening gesture, a thrilling brass cadence in E flat that is swiftly deflected downwards, initiating the extended ride sequence that follows. Sibelius's sketches show that he recast this opening several times, sharpening the cadence's harmonic edge and clearing out the scoring so that it has maximum impact. The motivic fragments left behind after this explosive start gradually coalesce to form a more stable texture, at which point Sibelius begins to modulate the music's underlying phrase rhythm from an unstable two-bar pattern to a more regular four-bar scheme. This subtle shift of musical gear (known as phasing) begins to expand the listener's feeling of passing time, as though moving through a landscape at greater speed (or remaining stationary as objects or events fly past more swiftly). The process is repeated by the second phrase of the ride, reaching a stormy climax as the multiple ostinato layers begin to pile up on top of each other, before the music comes to a halt with a momentary pause for breath and reflection. The sunrise that follows is announced, in the first instance, by a soft, glowing horn chorale, featuring the 'crux fidelis' figure that Sibelius had pondered using elsewhere in the Andante of the Second Symphony: a representation of the dawn in its 'purest' timbral state. In the climactic second statement, the chorale is first divided between the trumpets and trombones, and then restated by the trumpets in unison, so that the melody becomes stronger and brighter as the sunrise proceeds. A brief clarinet flourish brings forth a burst of light in the strings and a moment of silence, perhaps a sudden intimation of the divine, after which the brass section returns to resolve the ride's opening cadence and bring the work to a radiant conclusion.

With its firm but gentle sense of affirmation and deliverance after a prolonged period of artistic struggle and inward self-reflection, *Nightride and Sunrise* moves within the same symbolic and musical world as the Third Symphony, one that marks a distinct break from Sibelius's works of the preceding decade. And in its sophisticated attention to musical time and timbral transformation, it also anticipates many of the most innovative features of his later compositions. The final bars of the tone poem seem to face the future with a remarkable poise and openness: for almost the last time, Sibelius could look out upon a musical environment that held seemingly limitless potential and opportunity, even as world events around him were sliding inexorably into greater turmoil and confusion. It was a creative challenge that, for a short while yet, he would confront directly.

6

At the Summit

The start of 1909 saw Sibelius on the move once more. Although he did not travel to St Petersburg for the premiere of *Nightride and Sunrise* in January, the following month he journeyed south and made his third visit to England, where he conducted performances of *En saga* and *Finlandia* at the Queen's Hall on 13 February. Sibelius's admiration for the capital had only increased since his second visit, the previous year. He spent time sightseeing, including a tour of the British Museum, which made a powerful impression. And he was increasingly moving within some of the country's elite social and artistic circles, a glamorous, well-heeled (and at times tedious) world of aristocratic patrons, wealthy music-lovers and professional agents. Sibelius stayed initially at the Langham Hotel, before travelling across the country to conduct *Finlandia* and *Valse triste* with the Cheltenham Philharmonic Society on 17 February, admiring the scenery and spring flowers en route.[1] Returning to London, he lodged at a private house on Gloucester Walk in South Kensington, and was invited by Alfred Kalisch to an evening reception of his music at the Royal Academy of Music in Hanover Square under the auspices of the Concert-goers' Club, where the performers included Myra Hess, Lionel Tertis, York Bowen and the young Arnold Bax.[2] These musical contacts appear to have been the most important element of Sibelius's visit. In a letter to Axel Carpelan, he wrote:

> I have seen and heard much. It has even done me some good – many things that were previously obscure are now clear. The personal meetings with Debussy and d'Indy, Bantock, Barth and Dale and other composers, together with many new works,

> including Elgar's new symphony which I shall tell you about when we meet – also Bantock's *Omar Khayyám*, Debussy's new songs and the orchestral suite *Nocturnes*, etc., have all reinforced my thoughts about the path I have chosen to follow, and have to take.[3]

Just as Sibelius's meeting with Mahler in Helsinki prompts reflection about the state of the symphony in the early years of the twentieth century, so the fact that he had the opportunity to listen to an early performance of Elgar's First, which had only recently been premiered by Hans Richter in Manchester on 8 December 1908, reinforces an awareness of both the commonality and distance between the two composers. Elgar's creative approach to the genre had arguably taken a more complex and protracted path than that of Sibelius, and, as with Mahler's Seventh, his First Symphony offers a very different vision of the form's shape and trajectory from that of Sibelius's Third. Sadly, Sibelius's thoughts about Elgar's work do not survive in written form: he would surely have recognized and admired Elgar's adaptation of a Tchaikovskian cyclic model (similar to his own First), even if the sheer textual density and depth of Elgar's orchestration would have felt far removed from the direction of his recent work. And the mood of wistful nostalgia that movingly permeates Elgar's score, especially at the end of the third movement, must also have felt simultaneously familiar and foreign to Sibelius's ears. For both men, the idea of the symphony as the most elevated and prestigious of musical institutions was weighted with an exceptional burden of historical and aesthetic expectation.

More significant even than his encounter with Elgar's music was Sibelius's meeting with Debussy, which took place after a performance of the *Prélude à l'après-midi d'un faune* and the *Nocturnes* at the Queen's Hall on 27 February. The identity of the 'new songs' that Sibelius mentioned in his letter to Carpelan is not entirely clear: presumably the *3 Chansons de France*, settings of texts by Charles duc d'Orléans and François l'Hermite that Debussy had completed in 1904, which could have been performed as part of an evening reception jointly hosted by the Concert-goers' Club at the Aeolian Hall. Debussy was already suffering from symptoms of the cancer that would kill him nine years later, and he had been forced to cancel concerts in Edinburgh and the north of England, but Sibelius found him 'interesting' and appreciated the compliments that the French composer paid him when they met. Sibelius's opinion of Debussy's music was at times equivocal. In a diary entry dated 21 October

1910 that referred to Debussy's G minor String Quartet, for example, Sibelius described him as 'a "minor" composer! Refined but, I believe, small.'[4] But he must have been struck by the sophisticated approach to texture and harmonic colour in works such as 'Nuages'. Sibelius's own orchestral music began to gain much greater transparency and lightness in the following years, and passages in both *The Oceanides* and *Tapiola* suggest that he had been deeply moved by the sonic allure of Debussy's work.

Despite the lavish care and hospitality with which he was received, Sibelius was beset by insecurity and anxiety throughout his trip, writing at the end of March of 'Delius the serpent', and lamenting what he felt had been Bantock's betrayal: 'I never thought that I should lose him'. Slowly but surely Sibelius sensed he was sliding towards his inimitable fate: 'alone, ruined, in shame and sorrow!'[5] It is hard to credit any basis for Sibelius's fears, especially given Bantock's continued generosity and enthusiastic advocacy for his work. Rather, such outbursts may have been caused by displaced stress from his creative compositional work, as well as the pressures of maintaining a high-profile and exposed professional career. During his time in England he had been working on a string quartet, and he continued to wrestle with the score after he had left London for Paris and Berlin, finally writing melodramatically in his diary on 15 April: 'Quartet finished. I – my heart bleeds! – why this tragedy in life. Oh! Oh! Oh! That I exist! My God! People with the eyes of children and a wife's [two deleted words] look upon me, ruined man! What have I now done?'[6] As was so often the case with Sibelius's large-scale works, reaching the finishing line of a major project proved to be an almost unbearable task, the satisfaction of completion already inescapably bound up with feelings of inadequacy and failure.

The Quartet is in many ways a singular work, not unlike the Violin Concerto. It was Sibelius's only mature essay after his youthful interest in the genre, despite his extensive experience as a chamber music player, and he never produced a canon of quartets comparable with that of his Scandinavian contemporaries Nielsen and Stenhammar to stand alongside his symphonies, songs and theatre scores. The work's poetic subtitle, *Voces Intimae* (Intimate Voices), refers specifically in Sibelius's autograph manuscript to the series of strange, otherworldly *pianississimo* E minor chords that punctuate the texture of the quartet near the start of the central slow movement, a gesture that feels as though it comes from a completely different time and place, like the sound of an antique viol consort. But the subtitle also points in other symbolic directions: to the inward, conversational discourse of the ensemble itself; to the music's seemingly remote, abstract non-linguistic character – its ability to move listeners and provoke an emotional response, despite resisting any fixed programme or form of representation; to the mysteriously opaque and often elusive processes of artistic inspiration with which Sibelius perpetually struggled and whose insight he continually sought but feared losing; and perhaps also to the idea of music as historical memory, both biographical and imaginary. The quartet was inevitably accompanied by a weight of generic expectation no less demanding than that for symphonies and opera, and its pages were marked by the presence of weighty canonic precursors and musical forebears. It was perhaps for this reason, and for the challenge that the medium posed to composers working in the unstable and rapidly shifting musical environment of the late nineteenth and early twentieth centuries, that many of Sibelius's colleagues, such as Grieg, Delius, Elgar, Fauré, Debussy and Ravel, likewise only completed a single mature quartet. For this group of musicians, with their prescient sense of an imminent change of stylistic orientation and aesthetic direction, the concentration and intensity of the genre were both an irresistible opportunity and a stifling prospect.

The most formidable historical ancestor lurking behind Sibelius's engagement with the quartet tradition was the figure of Beethoven, and the score of *Voces Intimae* has an obviously Beethovenian seriousness and density of argument. Beethoven may also have been the inspiration for the quartet's five-movement layout: three of Beethoven's late quartets, notably opp. 130, 131 and 132, expand the basic four-movement classical scheme in formally innovative ways, and Sibelius's decision to append a curious fairy-like scherzo to the end of the first movement, which he referred to as movement '1½', may have taken its point of departure from Beethoven's practice.[7] In other ways, the quartet's consciously classicizing tone is consistent with the stylistic direction that Sibelius had been pursuing in his Third Symphony, especially in the formal clarity and concision of the individual movements. The quartet opens with a lonely question-and-answer exchange between the first violin and cello, a gesture that simultaneously suggests periodic classical syntax as well as the antiphonal pattern of runic singing. The Allegro molto moderato that follows begins expansively with a series of rising melodic waves in contrary motion, one of the movement's basic motivic shapes or patterns. The second subject shifts immediately to the dominant major, another consciously classicizing strategy, but is elided with the development. The return of the opening antiphonal gesture likewise runs on at the start of the reprise (one of Schumann's favourite devices), so as to create the impression of a single, sustained line of thought. It is only at the coda, in fact, that the movement pauses for breath: a sudden broadening, like that at the end of the first movement of the Third Symphony, which lends the coda a feeling of solemn formality.

The second movement playfully riffs on themes and ideas from the preceding Allegro, extending the idea of elision across individual movement boundaries in a way that Sibelius had explored elsewhere in a finale context. Its sudden stops and starts can seem skittish or quixotic in equal measure. At the same time, the Scherzo serves as a formal and affective buffer between the opening movement and the emotional heart of the work, the central Adagio di molto. The aspirant, ascending contour of the Adagio's opening theme contrasts sharply with the repetitive, circular design of its second subject, first heard in the tonic minor, which initially seems little more than an accompaniment but swiftly becomes an intensifier, driving the music continually forward. The movement as a whole consists of three broad phrases, each initiated by the opening melody, which grow in range and expressive depth as they proceed. As the third phrase reaches its climax, the music becomes increasingly focused around a single motivic pitch, D flat, and its enharmonic equivalent (C sharp), a dissonant note in the tonic major but part of the minor mode (and the leading note of the outer movement's home key, D minor). When the intimate E minor chords return, for example, they are transposed to C sharp minor, and this is one of the last dissonant pitches to be resolved before the movement's idyllic close. In retrospect, it is possible to realize that the same pitch (C sharp) is also one of the movement's first chromatic interventions, in the opening melody's very first ascent. Sibelius thus brings the centre of the quartet full circle. Perhaps it is this insistent, heart-tugging dissonance that is the true origin of the quartet's 'intimate voice'?

The Adagio is in many ways the quartet's most radical innovation. It is a single sustained slow movement of a kind that Sibelius had not written before, clearly modelled on a Beethovenian prototype but more modern-looking in its distinctive and idiosyncratic design. Its closest counterpart might in fact be the corresponding movement of Elgar's First Symphony, which Sibelius had only just heard in London, likewise an Adagio, and a movement that had its origins (unbeknown of course to Sibelius) in sketches for a string quartet.[8] Over his Adagio's coda, Elgar had written 'the rest is silence', referring to Hamlet's dying words in Shakespeare's play (v.2, line 301). A similar motto might well have been applied to the closing bars of the slow movement in Sibelius's quartet. The Allegretto that follows hence has the quality of a stern fortitude regained, the determination to face the world and suffer fortune's slings and arrows once more. The austere rhythmic tread of its opening bars becomes a flying waltz as the movement develops. Any lingering doubts are then swept away by the finale, which pursues a similarly energized course to that of *Lemminkäinen's Homeward Journey*, an increasingly hectic pursuit that demands virtuosic playing from the ensemble and which somehow ends in forceful defiance amid the storm. At the same time there is a devilish glee in the movement's furious activity, a dark brilliance that burns within the final bars and becomes a wild, untrammelled dance. Closure is seized at the very last minute just as the world appears thrillingly to be in free fall.

Even if Sibelius's time in London, Paris and Berlin had been overshadowed by anxieties concerning the composition of *Voces Intimae*, and by lingering health worries following his throat operation, his mood was evidently not exclusively negative. A letter from Germany to Aino dated 9 April 1909, for example, noted with delight that he had recently met the Canadian pianist and dancer Maud Allan (1878–1956), 'the Englishman's goddess', who had gained notoriety in London for her erotically charged performances as Salome in a skit based on the 'Dance of the Seven Veils' from Wilde's play and who later became the victim of a pernicious homophobic libel attack by the British politician Noel Pemberton Billing. Sibelius was initially strongly attracted by the idea of working with Allan, a former pupil of Busoni, writing revealingly in his correspondence with Aino that 'the scenario is very attractive for me because it is just pantomime with music, my genre (not opera!)'.[9] He went on to admire Allan's commercial success in the box-office: 'last year she danced 345 performances to a full house', but, as so often when Sibelius was approached by strong creative personalities, the project somehow never materialized, although the idea of a ballet-pantomime was one that he would pick up a few years later in his remarkable music for *Scaramouche*.

Momentarily distracted by the abortive collaboration with Allan, Sibelius in the meantime directed his attention to a further work for Lienau: the *Eight Songs with Texts by Ernst Josephson*, op. 57. Returning to Josephson's work, a year after the composition of his soaring setting of *Jubal*, must have been a welcome stimulus after his struggles with *Voces Intimae*. The songs offer a characteristically fantastical mixture of nature imagery, fairy-tale escapism, and pointed irony and loss. The surging waters of the forest stream batter the poor snail that clings to a moss-laden rock in the first number: when a young boy comes to harvest mussels along the shore, he cracks open the snail's home and finds a glittering pearl within that adorns the breast of a fair queen. The second song has a folk-like innocence: a flower picked by the wayside is abandoned and withers in its vase, forgotten by its friends. The outer sections of 'Kvarnhjulet' (The Mill Wheel) are driven by the rotary action of the old wheel's mechanism, but the ancient gears and worn drive shaft no longer turn as regularly as they did once, and the wheel stops to rest: 'Nu är jag trött; / gladde edra fäder' ('Now I am tired; / I once gladdened your fathers'). 'Maj' (May) is a gentle pastoral, a simple expression of joy in the return of spring. A very different seasonal wind blows through the boughs of 'Jag är ett träd' (I Am a Tree). Josephson's poem is a paraphrase of Heine's 'Ein Fichtenbaum steht einsam', which Sibelius had first considered setting as early as 1897, and which later became the basis for his curious *Dance Intermezzo* (1904). 'Jag är ett träd', by contrast, is a storm-lashed study in existential angst and inner resolve, one of Sibelius's finest songs. The three verses capture the inner mind of an ancient tree, stripped bare by the winter gales, who longs for death's cold snowy embrace rather than standing alone surrounded by the foliage of summer. Sibelius's setting has a persistent, obsessive triplet rhythm, like a beating pulse, that becomes increasingly weighty and persistent as the song proceeds. The final cadence has a feeling of desolation comparable to the conclusion of 'Höstkväll': the tree's death-drive is simultaneously a creative release. 'Hertig Magnus' (Duke Magnus) is in the same key (D minor), but assumes the manner of a medieval ballad: the nobleman looks out over the waters of Lake Vättern in southern Sweden, and is entranced by a young nymph. He is later found slumbering in the reed beds by the lake shore. A more dangerous threat lingers in the final song, 'Näcken' (The Water Sprite), the same familiar mythic figure from Runeberg's 'Under strandens granar' who lures the unwary into a watery grave. Sibelius's setting of Josephson's poem is a study in musical insanity: the frequent shifts of key and rapidly changing textures create an impression of irrationality, a chain of musical non sequiturs despite the strict strophic design of the song. The only firm point of reference is the final stanza, as the narrator dismisses the image of the water sprite as nothing more than a figment of his imagination, but it is hard to forget the song's underlying restlessness, a nagging nervousness that something remains out of balance and unresolved.

With the completion of his Josephson songs on 18 May 1909, Sibelius had fulfilled the terms of his contract with Lienau. But the burden of producing four substantial new compositions a year had proved unsustainable, and after a meeting with the publisher three days later, the contract was not renewed by mutual consent. Separation was amicable and Lienau commissioned a set of small piano works along the model of Grieg's best-selling *Lyric Pieces* as a sign of continued confidence in his music, although Sibelius soon began to resent the task, commenting that 'piano technique always seems rather foreign to me.'[10] Sibelius's mood on his departure from Berlin was therefore equivocal, noting in his diary on 21 May: 'must return home. It is no longer possible to work here. A change of style?!'[11] Although freed from his obligations to Lienau, he had nevertheless lost his single most sustainable source of income, and his arrival back in Järvenpää was accompanied by the usual flurry of bills and demands for payment. The light evenings of a precious summer were spent with his family and working on the Lienau piano pieces, which he finished on 28 August and felt were, technically at least, an improvement on his earlier works for the instrument (and an indication also of the sheer diversity and range of the numbers within the collection). Other projects included revisions to the score of his sweeping *Romance in C* for strings, originally composed, as Sibelius noted wistfully, in happier times alongside the first version of his Violin Concerto, as well as the first draft of his large-scale funeral march, *In memoriam*. With his characteristically macabre sense of humour, Sibelius noted in his diary, 'strange to think that it will probably be played when I am dead'.[12] The music was indeed played at his funeral (in its later revised form), though Sibelius could scarcely have imagined in 1909 that it would be almost half a century before that event would take place.

A further commitment over the summer months was to provide incidental music for the production of Mikael Lybeck's play *Ödlan* (The Lizard), the story of an ill-fated love triangle between the heir of a venerable old estate, Alban, the evil temptress Adla and the pure-souled Elisiv. Lybeck (1864–1925) was one of Sibelius's friends from the *Euterpe* circle, and the commission came from the Swedish Theatre, where the production premiered on 6 April 1910. Sibelius's score responds especially intensively to what Jeffrey Kallberg calls 'the threshold states between life/death, waking/sleep, consciousness/unconsciousness that the drama repeatedly asks us to contemplate'.[13] In that way, it has much in common with his music for Maeterlinck's *Pelléas et Mélisande* and Strindberg's

Svanehvit, likewise written for productions at the Swedish Theatre. But the forces used for *Ödlan* were greatly reduced – essentially a small string chamber orchestra – and the music is drastically pared back and austere. Though much of the work is underscore, it has a strange, uneasily shifting quality that both captures the elusive mood of Lybeck's drama and also anticipates his later theatre scores, most notably *Jokamies* (Everyman), as well as the Fourth Symphony.

The change of style to which Sibelius referred in his diary entry of 21 May might have reflected the strongly classicizing path that he had chosen to pursue in *Voces Intimae*: a very different field of stylistic reference from his earlier symbolist works. Or it could more likely have referred to his next large-scale project: the work that would eventually become the Fourth Symphony. As with its predecessor, the new symphony had a complex gestation bound up with plans for other works before it emerged in its final definitive form. In this instance, Sibelius's thoughts had been preoccupied for some time with Edgar Allan Poe's darkly gothic poem 'The Raven'. Whether he had first encountered the poem in German during his time in Berlin or in Viktor Rydberg's Swedish translation is unclear (he later claimed that Rydberg's version 'reads rather better than the original'),[14] but Poe's evocation of the bird's mythic status as a trickster and the harbinger of fate strongly appealed to Sibelius's melancholic frame of mind. In a diary entry dated 28 August, as he noted the completion of his piano pieces for Lienau, he added (in Swedish) the poem's famous tagline: 'Quoth the raven: "nevermore"', casting an ironic glance in his own direction and forecasting what would become one of the closing gestures of the symphony.

Sketches exist both for a setting of Poe's text and also for a further string quartet which may have been connected with the 'Raven' project,[15] but Sibelius's inspiration was pulled in a completely different direction by a trip that he took with his brother-in-law, the painter Eero Järnefelt, to far-east Finland in October. Here, as autumn began to change the colour of the birch and larch trees, they stayed at a well-known beauty spot in northern Karelia, close to a long, isolated ridge known as Koli that rises above the shores of Lake Pielinen. Given Finland's generally low-lying topography, scoured by the glacial action of retreating ice sheets at the end of the Pleistocene era less than 12,000 years ago, any significant difference in elevation is rare, and the Koli ridge afforded exceptional panoramic views of the surrounding countryside. Now a protected park managed by Metsähallitus, the Finnish forestry corporation, Koli had

Eero Järnefelt, *Landscape from Koli*, 1930, oil on canvas.

already gained the status of a 'national landscape' at the time of Sibelius's visit, as much for its cultural heritage value as its natural beauty: at the time of writing this present study, it forms the basis for an immersive environmental installation inside the international terminal at Helsinki's Vantaa airport, offering visitors and residents alike a technologically enhanced experience of 'Finnish nature' on arrival and departure from the country. In that sense, then, Koli was already a symbolically laden location, and a heavily artistically mediated site, rather than a pristine wilderness untouched by any human presence. It is precisely this concentration of artistic energy, as well as the opportunity to immerse himself in the elements – wind, sun and autumn rain – that is likely to have attracted Sibelius's attention as he accompanied Järnefelt.

Work on the symphony nevertheless proceeded far from smoothly. On 3 October 1909, for example, Sibelius had noted: 'At Koli! One of the greatest impressions in my life. Planning "La montagne"!', but then immediately he began to complain, 'sick. Affairs.'[16] The precise identity of the work called 'La montagne' is not clear, whether intended for a symphony or a tone poem or another project altogether. Sibelius may well have had Liszt's symphonic poem *Ce qu'on entend sur la montagne* (1848/9, revised 1854), based on Victor Hugo's text of the same title, at the back of his mind as he first contemplated the composition, in which case it was a long way from his recent preoccupation with Poe. The return to his daily routine at Järvenpää was inevitably accompanied by another shift of mood. 'How infinitely remote I am from that rational work that fills life and satisfies the practitioner and those around him,' Sibelius wrote on 23 October, but on 3 November he returned to the mountain metaphor with his spirits seemingly rejuvenated ('Mood lifted – a Himalaya again!'), only to fall back into a deep decline just five days later ('Have been in Hades. A depression like never before.')[17] Tawaststjerna suggests that it may have been the experience of his recent health scare, and his decision to give up alcohol and tobacco, that had prompted Sibelius's frequent references to his own mortality:

> both *Voces Intimae* and the Fourth Symphony reflect his inner life during the years immediately after the operation when he had passed through the shadows of the valley of death. There are inevitably problems when stepping back, as it were, from the edge of the abyss and returning to the rhythm of everyday life.[18]

But seeking a direct one-to-one correspondence between life and work is never straightforward in Sibelius's case; nor is it consistent with his essentially symbolist outlook, in which such connections always remained necessarily tangled or occluded. Sibelius in fact revealed more in his correspondence with Axel Carpelan, writing dismissively of 'those Kapellmeisters with their circus pretensions' when comparing himself with some of the contemporary musicians he had met on the continent (although their identity remains unclear), and praising instead what he called 'that wonderful logic (let us call it God) which governs a work of art.'[19] What is important here is not so much that supposed force of logic, which for many years dominated attempts to develop an analytical theory of Sibelius's work, but rather the seemingly arbitrary, divine nature of such inspiration, and the very day-to-day struggles with his compositional routine that Sibelius evidently endured throughout much of his career. Carpelan in turn served as a source of confidence, advice and support, writing in return to Sibelius: 'Yes, I have thought a great deal about the symphony – what you played me from "The Mountain" and "Thoughts of a Wayfarer" were the most impressive things I have heard from your pen.'[20] Carpelan's faith in Sibelius, and in the Fourth Symphony, would be well repaid.

This complex mixture of emotions, part blackly humorous and ironic, part nihilistic and part gentle self-parody – succinctly captured in Sibelius's own diary entries (and in his particularly characteristic use of Swedish) – runs throughout the music that he composed alongside work on the Fourth Symphony. The two little settings for voice and guitar of Feste's songs from *Twelfth Night*, his first attempt to set Shakespeare, for example, point readily to his waxing and waning moods. The first number, 'Kom nu hit, död!' ('Come away, come away Death'; II.4, lines 50–65), revels in Shakespeare's luxuriant melancholy with its images of cypress trees, white drapes and black coffins, whereas the second, 'Hållilå, uti storm och i regn' ('Hey ho the wind and the rain'; V.1, lines 383–402) has a blustery good cheer. The songs that make up his op. 61 collection, all written during the late spring and summer of 1910, are similarly varied, although often dark-hued. The modal mixture of the opening number, a setting of Karl August Tavaststjerna's 'Långsamt som kvällskyn' (Slowly as the Evening Sky), suggests an autumnal melancholy, the only brightening prompted by the memory of the girl's song from across the skerries ('tonen af skärflickans sång'), which once gave life its colour, whereas the flickering exotic figuration of the striking 'Vattenplask' (Lapping Water) evokes the play of light upon the waves of a Venetian canal. 'När jag drömmer' (When I Dream), to another Tavaststjerna text, is a nocturnal fantasy of poplars and willow trees swaying in the cool summer night's breeze. Sibelius was moved to write of the poem's curiously alluring ambiguity in a diary entry on 17 May as he was working on the song, referring to its key and final line: 'In a strong mood. "E minor and the nightingale".'[21] The three central songs are also settings of Tavaststjerna: 'Romeo' is a mischevious serenade, which constantly lands on the wrong tonal foot, whereas 'Romans' (Romance) has a declamatory expansiveness as a captive prince appeals to his distant beloved. 'Dolce far niente' is a sunlit pastoral in praise of new love, but the song's contentment and well-being are swept away by the dramatic storm-tossed waves of 'Fåfäng önskan' (Vain Wishes), a setting of a poem by Runeberg, as the narrator imagines themselves cast adrift and battered amid the surging billows of a raging sea. The collection's feeling of ambivalence is sustained even in the final number, 'Vårtagen' (Spring Thrall) by another Euterpist poet, Bertel Gripenberg, the author of *Teodora*. As the nights brighten and the scent of pinewoods fills the air, the narrator feels energized once more, but spring brings its own equivocation: 'my soul gathers sorrow, my soul gathers joy / in the languishing evening's light' ('Min själ blir sorgsen, min själ blir glad / i trånande kvällar ljusa').

In an oft-quoted diary entry from 13 May 1910, Sibelius wrote anxiously: 'Do not let all these "novelties", triads without thirds, etc. lead you from work. Anyone can be a "pioneering genius".'[22] Sibelius's hesitation about indulging such musical novelties is rather belied by the op. 61 collection, which is among his most adventurous and innovative, not least in terms of the virtuosic demands of the piano accompaniment and the poise it requires of its performers. But Sibelius's intense self-criticism remained unrelenting: he described the premiere of *In memoriam* as 'a great defeat', and its orchestration as 'hellish', withdrawing the score immediately for revision. He had similar comments after attending a rehearsal of *Voces Intimae*: 'the melodic elements are splendid but the sound could have been more transparent and, surely, more "quartet"-like', adding that his criticism might be taken '*cum grano salis*' (with a grain of salt).[23] A more exceptional insight is provided by a further diary entry, from 9 June, as he was working simultaneously on the op. 61 songs and the new symphony. Praising the first volume of Fritz Volbach's treatise *Das moderne Orchester in seiner Entwicklung* (The Modern Orchestra and Its Development), which had just been published in Leipzig earlier that year, Sibelius outlined his own approach to orchestration, drawing on his empirical experience working with various ensembles across the continent:

> The 'epic' in instrumentation. The 'narrative'. Do not interrupt the colour earlier than necessary.
>
> With instrumentation, one must be careful as a principle to avoid passages [*satsen*] without string instruments. A 'ragged' sound. Wind instruments have different qualities in different countries and different cities, different string configurations etc. make the relationship between the wind and string sections uncertain, variable, and circumstantial. The sound to a large extent depends upon the purely musical passages; its polyphony, etc. Separate what the dynamics indicate.
>
> In smaller orchestras, for example, the oboe, which usually sounds poor, should be handled with equal caution as the trumpet.
>
> In various orchestras the bassoon is not a quiet instrument in its middle or upper register. The very deepest notes can be used quietly.
>
> In these orchestras the low flutes are almost exclusively loud. The woodwind and brass are usually equally unreliable at the

> beginning of a note in terms of purity and precision. The entry should accordingly be emphasized. Take care when the melody passes from one wind instrument to another.[24]

Sibelius rarely, if ever, sought to codify or theorize his compositional practice, and so the diary entry is revealing, both for what it says about his approach to instrumentation and because of the very direct relationship between composition and the pragmatics of early twentieth-century performance. In some ways it is also a surprisingly conservative document, especially given his recent encounter with Debussy's work in London in which instrumental colouring (especially the woodwind) was much more variegated. It is unclear whether Sibelius was seeking to capture some aspect of his working method for future reference, or preparing notes for private pupils: since his early days at the Helsinki Music Institute he had not held a full-time teaching position, but he offered a more consultancy-like provision to a few select musicians such as Erkki Melartin, Toivo Kuula and Leevi Madetoja. But his repeated injunctions to himself in his diary as he was working on the symphony and the op. 61 songs and going over the score of *In memoriam* bear witness to his continual restlessness and dissatisfaction with his own music, and to his fears about what he perceived as his lack of technique and methodological grounding. 'The most beautiful moment', he wrote on 25 July, 'is when I finally have a particular composition planned and I have it in my heart. Work is a battle between "life and death". And this is because of self-criticism or deficient talent.'[25]

As the summer of 1910 progressed, Sibelius's thoughts about the symphony began to take an increasingly defined and focused shape. But the actual business of composition remained burdensome. Writing on 12 August, for example, he noted in his diary, 'worked splendidly – on the development in the first movement of the symphony. "Do not let go of life's pathos".' But just five days later he recorded: 'Crossed out the whole of the development. It needs more beauty and genuine music! Not sequences [*combinationer*] and dynamic crescendos, with stereotyped figures – "Full speed ahead"! "Now or never!"'[26] The first movement was finished on 30 August, and he began work immediately on the second, interrupting progress in early September to travel into Helsinki for business: as always after such visits, Sibelius returned to Järvenpää exhausted and depressed, feeling patronized and publicly shamed. He had noted his dire financial situation in his diary in June: his annual expenditure amounted to about 22,000 Finnish marks, of which 12,000 were living expenses, 4,000 were mortgage payments and 6,000 were interest payments on his debt; yet having given up his contract with Lienau, he had no regular replacement income beyond some royalties and his freelance work, leaving a significant shortfall of over 10,000 marks per annum. It was only thanks to Axel Carpelan's discreet fundraising efforts behind the scenes on his behalf that he was able to regain any kind of financial stability.[27] Composition gradually picked up again towards the end of the month. On 15 September, in one of his characteristic mood upswings, he noted, 'have the feeling of being a genius. Hammered away at III [the third movement]', and three days later: 'forged the theme in IV. Splendid day: in dreams and fine moods,' but then added the following day, 'think the theme in IV is not good. It needs more idealism.'[28] An autumn trip to the Norwegian capital Kristiania (now Oslo) to conduct a performance of the revised version of his cantata *Tulen synty* (The Origin of Fire) and the Second Symphony allowed him to visit an exhibition of contemporary French painting at the National Gallery: he was especially impressed by Matisse, and noted, 'what power this French art has upon the senses. In music, Debussy!'[29] The following day he spent the evening with the Norwegian painter Gerhard Munthe and the Arctic explorer and politician Fridtjof Nansen, though he described the occasion as 'empty and elegant'. In place of alcohol, he took a small dose of a bromine-based sedative to try and steady his nerves before the concert's first general rehearsal, though feared that he had taken 'too little' for it to be effective. By the end of the month he was in Berlin, still working, as he reassured Aino, on the symphony despite the many social diversions the city provided (not least in company with Busoni). Here he heard music by Rachmaninov, which he found 'sonorous, cultured, but tame', Arensky ('splendid, naive') and Reger ('national, German, too ornate and long-winded, but purely on the basis of its Germanness, good'). Sibelius returned to a wintry, snow-covered Finland in November and felt re-energized by the silence of his surroundings, writing in his diary just over a month before his 45th birthday: 'a symphony is not a "composition" in the ordinary sense. It is really a confession of the different stages of one's life.'[30]

Just as Sibelius was reaching the final phase of work on the symphony, a new opportunity unexpectedly emerged that became a further source of distraction. A meeting with the opera star Aino Ackté in Helsinki on 8 November resulted in his promise to supply a new composition for her to perform at concerts in Munich and Prague the following spring. Against his better judgement, knowing that his energies were already stretched with the symphony, Sibelius agreed to resume his setting of Poe's 'The Raven', and for just over a month Sibelius attempted to work on the two scores simultaneously. The pressure swiftly proved unsustainable: Aino became ill, and as early as 12 November, just a couple of days after his meeting with Ackté, Sibelius noted 'doubts about *The Raven*'.[31] At the end of the month he found himself 'Wrestling with God! The Raven!', and by 4 December he had reached verse 9 of the text. But a week later the pressure had finally broken, and he abandoned work definitively on the Poe project, leaving Ackté in the lurch but allowing himself proper time to focus on the symphony: 'have cast away a month', he noted bitterly in his diary, 'my heart weeps.'[32] By the end of the year he was making strong progress on the symphony once more: 'a Himalaya again', and on Christmas Eve he noted excitedly: 'an elk crossed our grounds three times!' It was, he felt, an auspicious sign.

The start of the new year brought two further sets of concert engagements, first in Gothenburg, where he was a guest of Wilhelm Stenhammar (whose Fourth Quartet he admired), and then in Riga across the Baltic. But on 28 March he recorded, 'battling for my life with the symphony. Carry your "compositional cross" with virility!', and on 2 April, the day before its premiere, he was finally able to note 'the symphony "ready"'. Sibelius was exceptionally nervous about the new work's reception. The day after the first performance he noted, 'performed well, everything in confusion . . . Aino steady! I am expectant and restless! B[reitkopf] & H[ärtel]? Axel C[arpelan] here and full of understanding.'[33] The critical reception was indeed mixed – Karl Wasenius, writing under the pen name 'Bis' in the Swedish-language newspaper *Hufvudstadsbladet*, for example, published an extended description of the symphony as an account of an imaginary journey to Lake Pielinen and the Koli ridge, in which the first movement 'depicts Koli and the impression it makes', and the third a panorama of the hillside 'bathed in moonlight', while the finale was a homeward journey through the 'darkening shadows of an approaching snowstorm'.[34] Other critics were more cautious. Heikki Klemetti, for example, wrote, 'everything seems so strange. Curious transparent figures float here and there, speaking to us in a language whose meaning we cannot grasp.'[35] Evert Katila, meanwhile, described the symphony as 'a sharp protest against the general trend in modern music', and yet hailed the work as 'the modern of the modern, and in terms of both counterpoint and harmony, the boldest that has yet been written'.[36]

Robert Thegerström, *Wilhelm Stenhammar*, 1900, oil on canvas.

The context for Sibelius's violent rejection of Klemetti's explicitly programmatic account of the work can be discerned in his diaries and correspondence. On 14 March, three weeks before the premiere, for example, he had noted: 'have my doubts about the "descriptive" [*skildrande*] in the music of our time',[37] and elsewhere he always retreated from attempts to apply an overly deterministic narrative to any of his supposedly abstract instrumental works. His resistance might have been prompted especially by Richard Strauss's tone poems, or, as Tomi Mäkelä suggests, the work of lesser luminaries such as Siegmund von Hausegger, whose Lisztian *Natursymphonie* (with its choral finale setting Goethe's *Proömion*) dates from precisely the same year as Sibelius's Fourth.[38] Sibelius was prompted to write a formal letter of complaint to *Hufvudstadsbladet* on 8 April, the day after the premiere, objecting to the particularity of Klemetti's account and claiming that its topographical details came from a private communication he had shared only with close friends.[39] Yet aspects of Sibelius's musical landscape thinking can nevertheless be discerned throughout the work, most notably in its exploitation of rich, dark instrumental colours, and the music's overwhelming sense of space and its subtle manipulation of passing time. The symphony opens with a groaning motto in the lower strings, outlining the interval of a tritone, a figure that several writers have identified with Sibelius's musings on his own mortality. Out of this seemingly primordial sound world emerges an incantatory figure on the solo cello, which is gradually enfolded within an austere, slowly oscillating texture that evades any fixed harmonic reference point. Initial attempts by the horns to achieve stability (in C major!) are undermined by dissonant elements from this opening passage (especially C sharp/D flat and F sharp), leading to a series of craggy chordal blocks in the heavy brass that eventually die away in faint echoes. The wispy writing for strings in the development recalls the wandering, existentially vagrant music from *Ödlan* and belies the symphony's origins as a string quartet. The movement gradually regains its opening territory and offers a brief telescoped reprise with the return of the chordal brass blocks, but the final bars are inconclusive, and the music drifts away into nothingness.

The Scherzo (placed second) brings an immediate change of musical mood and colour, even though motivically it is closely derived from the concluding pages of the preceding movement: the final note of the Moderato becomes the long-held oboe pitch with which the Scherzo begins, harmonically recontextualizing the enigmatic conclusion of the preceding movement's coda. The Allegro's character is initially pastoral, with prominent writing for strings and solo woodwind (notably the first oboe). The atmosphere darkens, however, as the trio develops, the distinctive tritone figure becoming prominent once more, and the expected return of the Scherzo is reduced to a fleeting glimpse of the opening phrase, caught almost incidentally in the first violins as the movement draws to a sudden, disconcerting close.

The third movement, marked *il tempo largo*, is the emotional heart of the entire work: an intense, sustained processional whose slow, C sharp minor tread recalls that of *In memoriam*, composed just a year or two earlier. It begins with a series of lonely isolated fragments in the solo woodwind, interspersed by a pair of solemn chorale-like passages for the horns and strings, often charting obscure modal territory that feels remote from any fixed tonal centre. The movement is divided into three broad arcs or large-scale phrases. As these develop, the alternating woodwind cadenzas and chorale sequences become increasingly integrated and gain a feeling of forward momentum, ultimately resulting in a passionate rising theme in the strings. The crushing climax of the movement is the return of the tritone motif from the very beginning of the symphony, played *fortissimo* by the trombones, after which the music dies away in a bleak coda, with brief fragments of its opening material. Along with *In memoriam*, the Largo was among the pieces played at Sibelius's funeral.

If the third movement offers a compelling portrait of heroic struggle and tragic defeat, the finale briefly promises salvation, only to end in an austere, resolute acceptance. The opening pages are initially playful – the symphony's tritone motto reduced almost to an ornamental decoration – and the strings swiftly generate a characteristic excitement and expectation. But the writing gradually becomes mired in harmonic ambiguity, as though lost in a vaporous tonal mist without any obvious structural landmarks. Attempts to regain a sense of direction are momentarily successful with a return to the opening material in transfigured form (briefly in C major, but then more properly in A), but as the music's sense of energy grows, so the level of dissonance increases, and the movement again becomes disorientated and fragmented. Like the repeated mocking cry of the raven, 'nevermore!' (or, in German, 'Nie du Tor!'), in Poe's poem, the closing pages are dominated by a chain of harsh birdcalls in the woodwind and anguished string passages. Somehow the strings manage to regroup and draw a seemingly prosaic veil over proceedings. The final bars are marked *mezzo forte dolce*, one of Sibelius's most ambivalent and puzzling but ultimately courageous musical gestures.

The confusion and bewilderment of Sibelius's contemporary Finnish audience is easy to understand. For listeners who were still enamoured by the (one-sided) image of Sibelius as national hero and musical patriot, the composer of *Finlandia* and the Second Symphony, the challenging formal and tonal elusiveness of much of the new symphony, and the uncompromisingly equivocal quality of its closing bars, must have felt strangely unfamiliar and threatening. For Sibelius, who had struggled with the shape and design of the work throughout and immediately withdrew the score for revision and review before sending it to Breitkopf & Härtel for publication, trying to mediate the lukewarm public reaction with his own faith in the score proved a struggle. Part of the difficulty lay in the question of how the symphony – and the rest of his production – related to wider musical trends on the continent. On 16 August, for example, as he was looking over a theme by his pupil Erkki Melartin, he noted: 'If one distances oneself from this "modernity" [*detta moderna*], it is certain that many beautiful things will be gained. It is possible that at present I am too narrowly committed to the "simple".

And yet – I can take an even greater step forwards.' And the following month, on 23 September, he wrote, 'Find myself to be un-modern, ignored.'[40] His perceived isolation, largely more apparent than real, was both a strength and a weakness, and could serve as a source of inspiration as much as intensifying his feelings of marginalization and neglect. And, as had so often been the case, immersion in the natural world served as a form of consolation and symbolic escape. On 8 October, he noted, 'walked and enjoyed the cry of the flying cranes – that sound, whose glory most closely resembles the sound of my own soul.'[41]

Sibelius was always powerfully attracted to the sight and sound of migratory birds, partly because he associated them with the poignancy of arrival and departure and partly because he envied their apparent sense of freedom and ability to move at will. Restless as ever, he left Finland for the continent again in late October, travelling first to Berlin, where he narrowly missed hearing Enrico Caruso in concert, and then to Paris, where he stayed at the Grande Hôtel de Malte on the rue Richelieu.[42] Back in the French capital, where he had so recently struggled with the composition of *Voces Intimae*, he worked on an arrangement and revision for string orchestra of his early choral piece *Rakastava* (The Lover), a set of three short movements that originally set texts from the *Kanteletar*: Sibelius had composed the initial version in 1894 for a competition hosted by the YL male voice choir at the University of Helsinki, for which it won second prize. The first movement begins with an evocation, as the narrator summons his beloved; the second captures the idyllic memory of their meeting; and the third is a radiant, softly lyrical farewell. In the string orchestra arrangement, the music's elusive tonal-modal ambiguity and subtle polyphony are intensified, so that the work's mood and atmosphere become even more alluring. 'There is something of the black soil in this work,' Sibelius wrote in early December, referring to its low register and quiet understatement: 'Earth and Finland.'[43] Meanwhile, he again took the opportunity to hear a range of both new and less contemporary music, including Stravinsky's *Scherzo fantastique*, Paul Dukas' Symphony in C (which he described as 'a brilliant work'), and Boieldieu's opera *La dame blanche*. Of Boieldieu's work, he wrote: 'of its kind, it is a masterpiece. But the opera form has always been and remains conventional. I believe the subjective does not have its place there.'[44] Dukas' work was much more obviously consistent with his own musical sympathies. He was nevertheless impressed – and simultaneously horrified – by a performance of Richard Strauss's *Salome* starring Gemma

Bellincioni, the Italian soprano who had taken the lead role of Santuzza at the premiere of Mascagni's *Cavalleria rusticana* and was one of the most celebrated singers of her day. 'Don't think of me as old fashioned,' Sibelius wrote to Aino, 'but I cannot get excited or feel engaged by a Salome who kisses, fondles and hugs the head [of John the Baptist]. Yet it is brilliantly done. That much is certain. In particular, the 120-player orchestra is excellently handled.'[45] By the side of Strauss's work, Delibes' ballet *Coppélia* seemed ponderous and naive, but Sibelius enjoyed meeting the American opera singer Minnie Tracey, whom he admired more as a person than as an interpreter of his songs, and the musicologist and critic Michel Calvocoressi, who would become best known as an expert on Russian music and a member of *Les Apaches*, the avant-garde circle that also included Debussy, Ravel, Florent Schmitt and Stravinsky.[46] Sibelius was in the meantime busy correcting proofs of the Fourth Symphony, a process that for once appeared to reinforce his faith and confidence in the score: 'I love that work,' he wrote to Aino on 16 November, 'it is perfect'.[47]

After his return to Finland at the end of the year, Sibelius received an unexpected offer, a post as Head of Composition at the prestigious Akademie für Musik und darstellende Kunst in Vienna. Sibelius's memories of his ultimately unsuccessful application for the professorship in Helsinki in 1896 (and his failed audition for the Vienna Philharmonic in 1891) may still have lingered darkly in the mind, but he could not fail to have been flattered by the invitation from one of the continent's leading music conservatories. He was also tempted by the thought of leaving behind what he regarded as the provincial bourgeois mindset of his compatriots in Finland, burnt perhaps by the reception of the Fourth Symphony and tired of having to trawl round banks and wealthy patrons to ask for loans.[48] The prospect of a permanent institutional position would never have appealed, however, especially given Sibelius's highly informal approach to teaching and his insecurities about what he perceived as his own pedagogical shortcomings (surely more imaginary than real). In the end, he turned down the position at the beginning of March. His thoughts instead turned to more domestic concerns at the start of the year: an old photograph unearthed by his brother Christian reawakened Sibelius's interest in genealogy and family history, including the supposed venerability of his surname, which he believed to be 'at least 1,500 years old!' And in conversation with his brother-in-law and neighbour Eero Järnefelt, his companion on his trip to Koli and Lake Pielinen, he reflected on his recent music and recorded: 'I have thought too much about the inherited forms and their demands. They sound decent – and, why not – brilliant, and yet – it isn't – a cheerful art. An art that, however it is produced – has a profound effect. A middle way between inspiration and artistic work is necessary.'[49]

Sibelius's thoughts were partly a reflection of his own working methods and his painful awareness of the apparent fragility of his musical imagination. But they also corresponded with his growing struggle to locate himself, stylistically speaking, within a rapidly changing artistic environment beyond the Finnish borders, one which, he sensed keenly, was already on the brink of a significant aesthetic shift. His hopes of being able to steer a stable course between artistic extremes, however, would come under increasing strain, not least from the tightening political tensions at home in Finland. In February, for example, the composer, music critic and founder of the Finnish-language student choir Suomen Laulu, Heikki Klemetti, who had been so puzzled by the 'curious transparent figures' in the Fourth Symphony, wrote to Sibelius to protest against the continued promotion of Runeberg as Finland's national poet, 'when he is worshipped above all by those elements who have turned their backs on national unity with us. It is at [Alexis] Kivi's grave and [Elias] Lönnrot's statue that Finnish students should assemble, undisturbed by Swedish nationalists.'[50] Klemetti's letter sought to justify his decision to refuse to permit Suomen Laulu to perform at the country's annual Runeberg festivities, but opening up Finland's bitter language and class divisions at a time of growing political unrest was a provocative gesture, and one that Sibelius, for whom Runeberg had always been a treasured point of cultural reference, was keen to avoid. Instead, he sought solace in his creative work. 'A new symphonic mission plays in my thoughts,' he noted on 19 April, before turning criticism inward upon himself once more: 'how little, infinitely little understanding and encouragement have my symphonies gained out in the wider world! It often strikes me now as if the whole of my symphonic endeavour has been in vain. But this work and this task has had the greatest educational importance for me.' Here lies music's double-bind for Sibelius: in the feeling of compulsion or obligation that it engendered, an irresistible calling or vocation to which he felt beholden, versus the day-to-day struggle to maintain his artistic and commercial profile both at home and overseas. In the face of such a steep challenge, Sibelius found himself 'small and unimportant. A small, unimportant talent.' But the world stage would not share his sense of diminishment, even as events beyond Ainola slid seemingly inexorably towards conflict, revolution, war and unimaginable human loss. For now, at least, Sibelius could wander through his garden and take comfort in the weather, 'a splendid day, like summer!', casting his eyes upwards once more: 'in the evening, stars! Stars!'[51]

7

Summoning and Reckoning

As Sibelius gazed up at the stars in the spring night sky from his garden at Ainola, various fresh compositional thoughts were already beginning to circulate in his imagination. On 2 March 1912, with the nights brightening but still a very cold month in Finland, he noted: 'forged new ideas. A symphony V. A symphony VI: Luonnotar! Remains to be seen whether these projects take hold. Orchestral troubles worse than ever.'[1] The troubles to which he referred were caused by the Russian authorities' attempts to implement severe budget cuts on Finnish cultural institutions following a dispute about the country's annual contribution to the Imperial army in lieu of general conscription. Robert Kajanus, by now in his mid-fifties, travelled to St Petersburg to intercede on behalf of the Helsinki orchestra, but the punitive effects of the cuts proved severe: a sign of darker times ahead.[2] Sibelius's list of prospective compositions gives some indication of his ambitions following the Fourth Symphony, and also of his tendency to conceive of several works simultaneously. At the same time, the issue of genre and the burden of historical expectation continued to weigh heavily upon his mind, especially as he considered the next stages in his symphonic canon. On 23 April, for example, he wrote: 'the symphonic fantasy [that is, not the symphony] is my domain!! With or preferably without programme. But – the musical thoughts, which is to say the motives, should shape the form and determine my path.'[3] Sibelius's diary note reflects a long-standing pedagogical and aesthetic tradition, reaching back to Johann Christian Lobe's emphasis on the motif as music's basic structural unit or building block – a lesson he had learnt as a teenager seeking to teach himself the rudiments of composition – and Adolf Bernhard

Marx's elevation of the fantasy as the highest form of musical art. At the same time it also reflects a more contemporary, modernist position: the search for new forms of expression and the avoidance of predetermined structures or formulae.

This fundamental tension – between the need to respect certain seemingly immutable musical laws while at the same time appearing innovative and progressive – is one of the determining characteristics of Sibelius's work and that of many of his contemporaries throughout the decade.[4] Writing on 8 May 1912, for instance, Sibelius noted: 'I imagine allowing the musical thoughts and their development in my mood determining the form. No other solution to this problem can be found. Arnold Schönberg's theories interest me. But I find him one-sided! Perhaps I won't when I get to know him!'[5] Sibelius's comments significantly predate Schoenberg's rationalization of the twelve-tone method and hence refer to his early theoretical writings, such as the *Harmonielehre* (dedicated to the memory of Gustav Mahler), which had only been published the previous year. Unlike Schoenberg, Sibelius was never interested in assembling a formal theory or system of composition, nor did he share Schoenberg's didactic interest in music as a pedagogical discipline. But Sibelius had begun to encounter Schoenberg's music during his earlier visits to Berlin, where he had presumably also discussed his ideas with Busoni, and he evidently sensed that they shared some kinship or common outlook. A later visit to Berlin, at the start of 1914, gave him an even greater opportunity to immerse himself in Schoenberg's work, with not entirely positive results. On 28 January, for example, one of Schoenberg's songs made a 'deep impression', but after a concert on 4 February he wrote at greater length:

> Mahler v [Fifth Symphony] and Schönberg: *Chamber Symphony*. I suppose one can see things that way. But it is painful for the ears. A result achieved through intellectual over-exertion. It whistles and shrieks. Not for the weak-minded, such talents. They certainly put their stamp down. Something great lies in the background. But Schönberg has not yet accomplished it.[6]

In a letter to Aino, Sibelius referred to the Chamber Symphony as 'interesting cubism in music'.[7] But despite such equivocation, he continued to admire aspects of Schoenberg's work. A performance of Schoenberg's genuinely path-breaking Second Quartet, op. 10, on 9 February, alongside songs by Henri Duparc and Korngold's Piano Trio, gave Sibelius 'much to think about . . . He interests me enormously.'[8]

For all that he remained curious and intrigued by works such as the Second Quartet, Sibelius himself did not feel able or inclined to pursue the kind of wholesale stylistic and syntactical revolution that he perceived in Schoenberg's music. His reluctance was partly generational – he was almost a decade older than Schoenberg, at a moment when musical fashions were changing extremely rapidly. But it may also have been a reflection of their respective geographical contexts. The career trajectory and experience of a musician based in part of the European continent that was usually regarded (fairly or not) as peripheral to mainstream sites of artistic activity and aesthetic debate presented very different challenges and opportunities from someone at the very centre of modernism's two great metropolises (Vienna and Berlin). For Sibelius, this sense of working on the margin was always both an obstacle and, in some ways, an advantage. Though it inevitably created the impression of a higher threshold, it also gave him a different route of access to the most canonic and esteemed musical genres. This explains his continued interest in the symphony, beyond the point at which the conjunction of Mahler's Fifth and Schoenberg's Chamber Symphony might seemingly have rendered it redundant.

As he was contemplating the early stages of his next major symphonic works, however, Sibelius's attentions were characteristically distracted by smaller projects. An orchestral concert in Helsinki at the end of March featuring a further performance of his Fourth Symphony, for instance, was accompanied by the premiere of the revised string orchestra version of *Rakastava* and a new set of *Scènes historiques*: a vivid little triptych of tone poems whose pictorialism looked nostalgically back to his *tableaux vivants* music of the 1890s.[9] Later that summer he completed the three elegant Sonatinas for piano, op. 67, which are among his most inviting works for the instrument but very different in range and scope from the virtuosic accompaniments of some of his op. 61 songs such as 'Vattenplask' or 'Fåfäng önskan'. The opening of the first Sonatina in F sharp minor in particular has a delicate modal ambiguity, hovering between D major and the tonic minor, and a sensitive use of register and spacing. Busoni had just finished his own first Sonatina for piano in 1910, although his work makes far greater demands upon its performer than Sibelius, so it is possible that the two men exchanged ideas about small-scale piano works when they met in Berlin that spring, even as they discussed Schoenberg's latest theories.

Sibelius's mood was as ever subject to seasonal cycles and shifts of weather, as well as perceived changes in his musical fortunes. On 14 September, as the summer drew to a close and autumn approached once more, he noted in his diary, 'the day rainy and sad – how overcast I am as an artist. Utterly forgotten. And now this with my IVth Symphony. It is too subtle and tragic for our sordid world. My own production – is it merely a drop in the ocean or does it have any significance?'[10] His fourth visit to England later that month must surely have allayed some of those fears. The Langham Hotel, his usual haunt in London, was fully booked, so he stayed instead at the Hotel Richelieu on Oxford Street, before travelling up to the Midlands to conduct the Fourth Symphony as part of the Birmingham Festival. Rosa Newmarch gave him a tour of historic sites in Stratford-upon-Avon: he spent a night at the half-timbered Shakespeare Hotel on Chapel Street, next to the plot once occupied by the playwright's house, New Place, and visited the bard's grave in Holy Trinity Church, retaining the entry ticket as a souvenir.[11] The concert itself was part of an ambitious programme of contemporary music that included the premiere of Elgar's *The Music Makers*, a desolate self-referential setting of Arthur O'Shaughnessy's 'Ode', lamenting the transient ebb and flow of the creative spirit and the essentially solitary vocation of the artist, alongside Delius's *Sea Drift*, which had only recently received its first performance in 1906 at the Essen festival in Germany. A planned performance of Scriabin's *Prometheus* that was to have completed the programme was cancelled, unsurprisingly, because of the lack of sufficient rehearsal time. All three composers were present for the occasion and heard each other's work. Delius, who remained a firm admirer of Sibelius's music throughout his career, wrote to his wife, Jelka, the day after the concert:

> Elgar's work is not very interesting – & very noisy – The chorus treated in the old way & very heavily orchestrated – it did not interest me – Sibelius interested me much more – He is trying to do something new & has a fine feeling for nature & he is also unconventional – Sometimes a bit sketchy & ragged[.] But I should like to hear the work again – He is a nice fellow & we were together with Bantock before & after the Concert.[12]

Delius's letter suggests that whatever tension may have flared up between the two men during Sibelius's last visit to England in 1909 had long since burned itself out. More interesting are the parallels and divergences in their respective responses to landscape and nature: Delius was just drafting his tone poem *The Song of the High Hills*, inspired at least in part by his experience of hiking in the Norwegian mountains, much as Sibelius's Fourth had drawn on his trip to the Koli ridge at Lake Pielinen.[13] For both composers, the evocation of a particular nature space was associated with an existential state of being, a feeling of instantiation that was marked also by an acute awareness of the fragility of the human condition. Such environmental immersion could be liberating and ecstatic, a privileged site of sensory awareness and revelation, or, in equal measure, an experience of desolation, abandonment and loss. What they shared was an acknowledgement of nature's fundamental indifference, the seeming immutability of the elemental forces that shaped and animated the natural world and the contingency of human presence. Whereas Delius drew his inspiration from Whitman and Nietzsche, Sibelius could point to Runeberg, Rydberg and Josephson. Yet for both musicians music operated over and above any literary form of representation. Contemplating landscape became a form of close listening or attunement, a merging of the musical self with the idea of being-in-place. For his part, Sibelius described the Birmingham concert as a success. Critics were largely negative and confused, but he noted some exceptions, including Ernest Newman's extraordinary review in the *Birmingham Daily Post* and the unsigned note in *The Times*, which described how the music 'seems to dream of old half-forgotten memories and new unrealized visions of the future. Its harmony and its orchestral colour alike strange, yet really so simple that time must make their beauty clearer.'[14] Newman in particular would become a staunch advocate for Sibelius's music, founding the Sibelius Society in 1932. Sibelius meanwhile prosaically rated his visit as a break-even trip at best, or 'possibly a couple of hundred marks in deficit',[15] further indication of the tight financial pressures he faced as a composer.

Sibelius returned to Finland excited by the prospects for his work in England, but coolly realistic about the commercial returns it might offer. English audiences in turn would have to wait less than a year before another major Sibelius performance – and this time a world premiere. In the meantime, however, Sibelius's energies were distracted by another orchestral project. The compact and understated tone poem *Barden* (The Bard) had its origins in a work provisionally entitled *The Knight and the Naiads*, based on the story in Ernst Josephson's poem 'Duke Magnus', which Sibelius had set as one of his op. 57 songs. At some point during the early stages of the composition, however, the topic shifted from Josephson to Runeberg: an easy modulation for Sibelius, since both writers were especially close to his heart. Runeberg's lyric poem 'The Bard' is a portrait of an orphic hero from an imaginary feudal past, whose singing enchants the world and its inhabitants and yet whose life seems untouched by everyday worries and concerns until winter greys his hair and he gives up his soul to his ancestors. The poem's mood, characteristically for Runeberg, is one of nature mysticism and gentle resignation, precisely the qualities that attracted Sibelius. He completed the first version of the work in the spring, and it was premiered in Helsinki on 27 March.[16] But by the end of the following month he had already begun to have second thoughts about the piece, reconceiving the work not as a single uninterrupted movement but rather as a two-part scheme or 'intrada and allegro'.[17] Precisely what motivated the change of mind is unclear: whether, as Tawaststjerna suggests, it was because Breitkopf & Härtel were unwilling to publish the work in its shorter form because they believed it was commercially unviable, or because Sibelius briefly saw further potential in an expanded version of the story. By early June he was now thinking of a triptych for orchestra, and even noted that the score was 'complete'.[18] But no trace survives of this larger multi-movement work, and Sibelius's attentions were suddenly directed more urgently towards his next tone poem, *Luonnotar*, which he had promised for Aino Ackté later that autumn. He only returned to *The Bard* the following year, and it received its premiere in this revised and definitive form on 9 January 1916.

Despite its brevity, *The Bard* is one of Sibelius's most beautifully scored and alluring works. The revised version bears no direct relationship with Runeberg's text, beyond the orphic presence of the harp that plays a seemingly obbligato role throughout and the mood of quiet thoughtfulness and contemplation that it engenders. Although no remnant of the multi-movement scheme remains, the work revolves around two subtly differentiated ideas. The opening *Lento assai*, with its distinctive semiquaver commentary in the strings (in fact a sped-up version of the rising third with which the tone poem opens), is followed by a rising sequential idea, first played as a soft, flickering string tremolo at the *Poco stretto*, a barely noticeable shift of emphasis. This dual pattern is expanded and repeated, the rising sequential idea now gaining greater force and momentum until it generates a new idea: a dramatic sunrise motto in the trumpets and trombones, which ascends radiantly out of the orchestral texture. With this brief moment of revelation achieved, the heavy brass withdraw and the strings bring the tone poem swiftly to a close with a series of hymn-like cadences and a brief snatch of the opening prelude.

Sibelius could well have imagined himself as the bardic poet at the work's centre: he had the opportunity, after all, to portray himself in various guises throughout earlier tone poems, whether the dashing Lemminkäinen of the *Legends*, the ancient seer Väinämöinen in *Pohjola's Daughter*, or the anonymous traveller in *Night Ride and Sunrise*, without ever committing himself to a musical autobiography of the Straussian kind. But more significant is the way *The Bard* crystallizes a structural and expressive paradigm incipient in his earlier music that was to become increasingly central to much of his later work: that is, an iterative process starting with an introductory prelude, an intensified repeat (or set of strophic variations on this initial material), leading to either a revelatory moment of return or some other elementalized gesture of resolution or arrival, and a brief retrospective close. James Hepokoski has codified this pattern as 'rotational form', allied to a goal-directed process of 'teleological generation', and presents it as one of Sibelius's hard-won solutions to the problem of how to achieve a structurally innovative musical design while respecting certain basic formal-syntactical principles.[19] In the context of *The Bard*, this idea of a varied 'strophic form' feels especially appropriate given the symbolic weight associated with the imaginary character of the eponymous hero in Runeberg's text. In that way, *The Bard* was no less than Elgar's *The Music Makers* a sustained meditation on the allegorical figure of the creative artist, its quietude and inwardness a commentary on the inescapable isolation that, for Sibelius, seemingly accompanied (and was indeed necessary for) the intense concentration that such visionary work required.

The idea of creation as an essentially bleak, lonely pursuit was one that Sibelius would take up again immediately. He had contemplated a work based on the figure of Luonnotar, the nature spirit who appears in the opening chapter of the *Kalevala*, ever since the early 1890s, and the image had occurred repeatedly in his mind at various stages of his career. The request to provide a new piece for Aino Ackté, whom he had treated so badly when he abandoned work on his setting of Poe's 'The Raven', to perform at the prestigious Three Choirs Festival in Gloucester, offered the perfect opportunity finally to fulfil his plans. The *Kalevala*'s account of the creation of the world is characteristically wild and fantastical: Luonnotar has floated in the void for centuries, but

Aino Ackté as Salome, 1910.

finally descends to the world ocean, whose waters are whipped into a fury by the east wind. Calling out to the sky-god, Ukko, for assistance, she raises her knee out of the water, upon which a passing bird (a golden-eye, *Bucephala clangula*, in Finnish 'sotka') makes its nest. As the nest becomes warm, Luonnotar flexes her leg and the bird's eggs fall into the depths and shatter: the lower half becomes the earth and the upper half the sky, the white becomes the moonlight and the yolk forms the sun, whose pale glow illuminates the cold ground below. Sibelius's setting captures the pain and suffering of birth vividly. The string's opening ostinato figuration suggests a gathering storm, and in fact contains the intervallic components of the work's climax. The soloist's first entry arcs upward from this initial idea, climbing as far away from the tonic (F sharp minor) as it is possible to reach (C major) before falling back to earth. This pattern of statement, recitative and exchange is repeated before the tone poem's first contrasting episode, a dark *tranquillo assai* in B flat minor that suggests an uneasy calm. The duck's wild cries as it rides the wind, desperately seeking a place to land, form the animating idea in the second strophe. The third strophe then raises the orchestral storm to full strength, the singer momentarily inundated by giant waves of sound that swiftly crest and break. As the storm's energy subsides, the new world emerges during an extended closing recitative, based on the contrasting episode from the first strophe. Marked *visionarico*, it is a strange, rocking lullaby that comes to rest uneasily on the work's tonic without resolving any of its underlying dissonances. The violin's gleaming final sonority, which transforms B flat into the raised third of the tonic chord (A sharp), depicts the icy gleam of the stars in the vaulting heavens above.

Among the musicians most affected by Sibelius's startling image of a brave but chilly dawn was Vaughan Williams, whose Sixth Symphony closes with a similarly bleak and post-apocalyptic epilogue. Vaughan Williams later sent Sibelius a copy of the score, who replied gratefully and described the work as 'a masterpiece'.[20] *Luonnotar*'s premiere took place on Wednesday 10 September, not in Gloucester Cathedral, where it would surely have made an overwhelming impact, but at the Shire Hall: an elegant early nineteenth-century building constructed in a dignified Greek revival style, and the regular venue for the festival's non-sacred orchestral concerts. With the tone poem's premiere, and the remarkably early performance of the Fourth Symphony in Birmingham the previous year, England had now heard two of Sibelius's most advanced and original scores in relatively quick succession. For audiences that had enthusiastically embraced his earlier works such as *En saga*, the *Lemminkäinen Legends*, the *King Christian* music, *Finlandia* and the first two symphonies, the austere and apparently remote style of Sibelius's later music must have seemed a hard sell. But for a younger generation of British composers, not only Vaughan Williams but Gustav Holst and Arnold Bax, it was to become a central point of reference and a sustained source of inspiration. *The Times* described it as 'the musical conception of an intensely imaginative mind working on purely independent lines', and noted that 'those who have admired the delicate orchestral suggestions of his Symphony in A minor will delight in the atmosphere with which the orchestra surrounds the voice in this poem. But it is a work to hear often before one dare attempt to describe, much less criticise it.'[21]

Sibelius awaited news from *Luonnotar*'s Gloucester premiere anxiously, but was delighted with the reports when they arrived, noting with satisfaction that Ackté took six curtain calls after the performance. Back at home, the Helsinki concert season brought the opportunity to hear some interesting new works: he was especially impressed by the Finnish premiere of Carl Nielsen's Third Symphony, the radiantly vital *Sinfonia Espansiva*, which he described as a 'splendid work', although he felt that it somehow lacked 'compelling themes': an odd comment given the broad, striding melody that frames the finale and forms its apex. Sibelius's admiration for Nielsen was nonetheless sincere: 'he is a complete artist, that man'. The following month he heard Erkki Melartin's elegant Violin Concerto, op. 60 – so very different from his own – as well as Elgar's new 'symphonic study' *Falstaff*, op. 68, which he found 'rather confused'.[22] Then, on 17 December, Dan Godfrey, chief conductor of the Bournemouth Municipal Orchestra (later to become the Bournemouth Symphony Orchestra), whom Sibelius referred to as 'that courageous man', gave the second English performance of the Fourth Symphony at the Winter Gardens, where it received a generally more sympathetic reception than its outing in Birmingham the previous year. Bournemouth's association with Sibelius's work proved to be warm and long-standing: among the orchestra's later directors was the distinguished Finnish conductor Paavo Berglund, who was especially admired for his interpretations of his countryman's music.

Sibelius's energies had been taken up for much of the autumn with a major new theatre score: his music for the ballet-pantomime *Scaramouche*, which had been commissioned by Poul Knudsen for the Royal Theatre in Copenhagen, and for which rights had already been agreed with the Danish publisher Wilhelm Hansen. When he first accepted the commission, Sibelius had casually assumed he would need to provide no more than a couple of short dance numbers: in reality, the project demanded a complete score lasting over an hour.[23] Difficulties had further increased when it emerged that Knudsen's scenario was modelled more or less directly on Arthur Schnitzler's *Der Schleier der Pierrette* (Pierrette's Veil), which had only recently opened at the Königliches Hoftheater in Dresden, directed by Max Reinhardt and with music by

Ernst von Dohnányi.[24] Sibelius's attempts to extricate himself from his contractual obligations proved unsuccessful, and he eventually delivered the complete manuscript to Hansen on 19 December. To rub salt into his wounds, the premiere was delayed and did not take place until 1922. *Scaramouche* is nevertheless a remarkable and striking score, and offers further evidence of Sibelius's skill in writing for the theatre. Knudsen's storyline reflects the immense early twentieth-century interest in puppets, clowns and the *commedia dell'arte*, the same phenomenon that produced Stravinsky's *Petrushka* and Schoenberg's *Pierrot Lunaire* at almost exactly the same moment. Knudsen's plot revolves around a tragic love triangle. Leilon and his wife Blondelaine are hosting an elegant ball. An unexpected guest arrives: the hunchbacked dwarf Scaramouche, who tunes up his viola and begins to play. Blondelaine is bewitched by his performance and beings to dance wildly. After Scaramouche's departure, the ball guests proceed to dinner, but Blondelaine suddenly hears Scaramouche's viola in the distance and is irresistibly pulled away: the guests search for her in vain. In Act II Leilon laments his loss. Blondelaine reappears, unable to explain her absence. Scaramouche is revealed hiding behind the door, and Blondelaine seizes Leilon's dagger and stabs him; Leilon and his wife can now be happily reunited, but just as their love seems complete, Blondelaine hears Scaramouche's viola once again, calling from beyond the grave. Seized with horror, she begins to dance once more, becoming increasingly frenetic until she collapses dead on stage.

Although the composition of *Scaramouche* gave Sibelius significant cause for worry, it is nonetheless one of his most fascinating and neglected scores.[25] The delicate minuet with which the work opens gives way to a more rhythmically charged bolero, with its threateningly erotic overtones: Sibelius had been very moved, like so many composers of his generation, by the drama and intensity of Bizet's *Carmen* and by its exotic Spanish setting. Scaramouche's entry is cleverly dovetailed with further rounds of the bolero, so that he slips into the orchestral texture almost unnoticed. The dramatic and highly articulated instrumental dialogue as he seeks to entrap Blondelaine is especially powerful, followed by the physical abandonment of her wild dance: the strangely dissonant horn writing gives a sense of the violence to follow. Blondelaine's reappearence in Act II is accompanied by a beautifully shaped solo flute melody, but ominous chromatic shadows appear once more in the bass as Leilon's interrogation gains urgency and the texture becomes gradually ever more fragmentary. Sibelius's writing for the strings, in particular the double bass, as Scaramouche's hiding place is discovered, is remarkable for its detailed texture and affect. Leilon and Blondelaine's love music after Scaramouche's death has a surging passion, but the elegance of their final waltz soon grows dark once more as Blondelaine is haunted by the sound of Scaramouche's viola. Her fatal dance reaches a swift and brutally abrupt close, her death marked by three solemn woodwind chords and the dull sounds of the string pizzicato.

Sibelius's approach to the scoring of *Scaramouche* owes much to his early experience with melodrama – the ability of a single strongly characterized musical gesture to evoke a distinctive atmosphere, mood or state of mind. But his ballet music also responds to characteristic early twentieth-century concerns about gender, erotic desire, degeneration and the body: topics that had haunted his work ever since *Kullervo* and which were seemingly a perennial subject for debate within modernist circles in Berlin. When he returned to the city in early 1914 for the second half of the winter season, he could immerse himself in the current trends in contemporary music once more. On 24 January, for instance, he noted: 'Delius is a poet, but rather a stranger to the orchestra in the highest sense'. Precisely which piece he was referring to is unclear, although Theodore Spiering had conducted the Berlin premiere of *In a Summer Garden* at the start of November, and Sibelius was keen to try and interest Spiering in his Fourth Symphony. The following week, on 1 February, he was especially struck by a performance of Mahler's early cantata *Das klagende Lied*, a work that may have appealed to his own interest in medieval ballads, alongside some of Brahms's vocal quartets. Yet again, however, he felt himself to be increasingly out of step with the times. 'Regarding novelties', he mused on 26 January, 'it is remarkable how few contemporary composers can create anything vital based upon the church modes. Since I am closer "by virtue of my birth" I am made for them.'[26] It was further evidence of the divergent path leading away from Schoenbergian modernism he believed he should now pursue, and of the artistic implications of his Finnish background: the legacy of his maternal family's pious Lutheranism perhaps still lingered in his mind, as did perceived notions of centre and periphery.

Sibelius had been disappointed when Breitkopf & Härtel paid barely half (1,000 marks) of what he had originally hoped for *The Bard*.[27] In the interim he offered them a little set of piano pieces, of which the first, a gentle *Eclogue*, was finished on 9 February, alongside a new collection of songs. Tragically, the autograph manuscripts of the first two of the op. 72 songs were lost during the First World War, but fortunately the remaining four survived, including a radiant setting of Larin Kyösti's *Kaiutar*, another Finnish nature spirit who wanders the moors lamenting her deserting lover. Breitkopf paid over twice as much for the piano pieces and songs as for the orchestral work, a commercial decision based purely on their sales potential alone. At the end of the previous summer, on 27 August 1913, however, Sibelius had received a lucrative commission from the United States: $1,000 (equivalent to over 5,000 marks) to write a new symphonic poem for the summer music festival in Norfolk, Connecticut. The following April, the prospect of the visit was enhanced even further by the offer of an honorary doctorate at Yale University. Sibelius celebrated in his diary by showing off his best school Latin: 'Facultas filosofiæ vult me doctorem nominare. Honoris causa! Evoe! Evoe! Venus Baccusque omnesque Dei. Ars mea!' ('The Faculty of Philosophy have elected me to an honorary doctorate! Hurrah, hurrah! Venus, Bacchus, and all the gods. My art!') In light of Sibelius's perpetual middle-class insecurity about his own slightly sketchy academic history, the distinction was one he particularly treasured. He left for the United States on 19 May on board the SS *Kaiser Wilhelm II* of the Norddeutscher Lloyd line from Bremerhaven, travelling via Southampton, and noted excitedly in his diary as he was about to embark: 'America, the land of the future. – I have scored a great victory for the Finns!'[28]

Music Shed, Norfolk, Connecticut, *c.* 1906.

In New York Sibelius stayed at the Hotel Essex on Madison Avenue and East 56th Street, before rehearsing *Pohjola's Daughter* and his new tone poem with a specially chosen group of orchestral players at Carnegie Hall. He travelled up to Connecticut on 29 May, and the concert in Norfolk took place on 4 June. His hosts were significant patrons of music and the arts in New England: Carl Stoeckel was the son of Gustave Jacob Stoeckel, the first professor of music at Yale University, and his wife Ellen (née Battel) was the daughter of a musical philanthropist and sponsor of the professorial chair at Yale held by Horatio Parker. The Stoeckels had founded the Litchfield County Choral Union in 1899 to promote music in Norfolk, shortly after which the festival became a regular annual event. Sibelius was thrilled by the performance, writing to Aino after his New York rehearsals: 'my new composition is splendid. I live in it. You know, dearest, it is as though I find myself more and more. The Fourth Symphony was just a beginning. But in this piece everything is enhanced. There are places in the score that drive me crazy. Such poetry!!!'[29] *The Oceanides* had a particularly complex compositional gestation. Sibelius had begun work on a piece entitled *Rondo der Wellen* almost as soon as he received the commission. Manuscript sources for two movements from a three-movement suite survive, the third of which contains material that would eventually find its way into the final score. As Andrew Barnett suggests, it is possible that these two early movements were the missing parts of the mysterious triptych that Sibelius mentioned in connection with *The Bard* in June 1913: that could explain the speed with which he was able to work on both *Luonnotar* and the American commission simultaneously as the year progressed. In the event, Sibelius worked up an independent draft of the *Rondo*, now entitled *Aallottaret* (The Oceanides), and sent the score ahead of his voyage by prior agreement on 3 April 1914. With time rapidly running out before his departure, he decided to revise the work, completing it at the very last minute so that he spent part of his trip across the Atlantic checking the copyist's instrumental parts. After his visit, Stoeckel deposited the original single-movement version of *The Oceanides* in the university library at Yale and it has since been recorded, facilitating detailed comparison of the two scores.

Sibelius's frequent revisions normally took place after a work's first performance, and most commonly involved compression, both of scoring and of formal layout. His default editing procedure, from the revised version of *En saga* onwards, was always to seek greater clarity and concision of expression, and to achieve significantly deeper impact out of fewer resources. Exceptionally, that rule does not hold in the case of *The Oceanides*, where the revision pre-dated the premiere, and involved a significant expansion and broadening of the material, as though seeking to capture a wider oceanic horizon in sound. The other significant change was one of tonality, transposing the music from a dark, rich D flat major up a semitone to D major – a much easier key for the string players, and resulting in a brighter, more translucent sound. Formally speaking, *The Oceanides* is assembled from a series of musical waves, building from the small, oscillating ripples with which the work opens and climbing through three grand accumulating cycles until breaking with tremendous energy and force just before the final bars. The melodic current pulls in two directions: the first is the opening woodwind figuration, which essentially remains playful and benign throughout, and the second is a rising sequential idea that has a much greater affective undertow. As with *The Bard* and *Luonnotar*, *The Oceanides* is concerned with the gathering of elemental forces and the idea of nature not merely as a representational device but as a fully immersive state of being. Human presence is once again figured not as a controlling agent. Rather, the impression is of a more contingent state of flux, subject to the ebb and flow of a deeper, more powerful tidal motion.

Less than two years earlier, on 1 August 1912, Sibelius had compared the symphony to a river:

> It emerges through an infinite number of small streams, from which it proceeds. The river discharges broadly and powerfully into the sea. But these days the channel is dug broadly and powerfully – one can easily make a river. Yet where does the water come from? In other words, one does not allow the motives, the musical impulse, to determine the form. It is all very well making the form strong and powerful and then trying to 'fill' it. But from where does one get the water – the music? You, splendid ego, have already realized this.[30]

Sibelius left only very brief records of his impressions of Niagara and the Atlantic crossing: both, he wrote, were 'unforgettable', as were the Norfolk performance of *The Oceanides* and the Stoeckels' generous hospitality. But the metaphor of the symphonic watercourse must have particularly appealed in the wake of *The Oceanides*, not least because it corresponded with Sibelius's frequent reliance on nature imagery to try and explain his working processes: composition was always more than simply a form of hydrological engineering, seeking to channel the surging flood of ideas that could appear almost arbitrarily from an unseen source and directing them towards their final, oceanic destination. And being swept creatively away by the flood's waves revealed a further danger, namely the risk of over-inundation or of becoming wrecked on unseen obstacles in the watercourse. Composition, as Sibelius vividly recognized, always remained an inherently hazardous enterprise. When asked by Stoeckel whether he had considered using Niagara as the basis for a musical work, he is reported simply to have replied: 'I have given up the idea. It is too solemn and too vast to be represented by any human individual.'[31]

Sibelius returned from the United States with wind in his sails, excited by the prospects for his music in North America, and determined to return the following season to renew his acquaintances and make the most of the opportunities it appeared to present. Breitkopf offered him 3,000 marks for *The Oceanides* – three times what they had paid for *The Bard* – as well as congratulating him on his honorary doctorate. A visit by the choreographer Maggie Gripenberg at the end of July led to discussions about a possible ballet-pantomime, *Karhun tappajaiset* (The Bear Hunters), based on a story from the *Kalevala*. The summer weather warmed up and the wind turned to the east, bringing hot air from across the Russian border with heat and smoke from forest bush fires. Then, in his diary on 29 July 1914, Sibelius noted: 'War declared. Austria-Serbia.' The consequences would prove immense. The following day he recorded: 'The war has begun. – What will it mean for me? My family needs money; including my children. My German publishers cannot send anything because of the war situations. How to cope?' And on the final day of the month he wrote: 'In Helsinki in expectation. War hangs in the air. Impossible for me to negotiate money. Retreat in every direction. Strange! It is as though I was completely out of the game.'[32] Without any warning at all, Sibelius had seemingly lost his most valuable sources of income, the cultural networks he had spent decades assembling, and access to the overseas musical communities (performers, critics and audiences) on whom his whole livelihood relied.

Somehow, amid the political chaos, he found time and space to compose. Towards the end of June, while still in the United States, he wrote, 'a wonderful theme captured!', and again on 25 July, barely four days before the outbreak of war on the continent, he noted that he had got 'a splendid theme!' Although it is not certain which theme these comments referred to, or which work, on 1 August he observed, 'the new symphony begins to stir itself,' before adding with his customary sense of self-pity, 'why will I *always* be disturbed, *never* achieve what my spirit seeks to create?' and lamenting his outstanding financial debts (still in the region of 90,000 marks).[33] The Fifth Symphony, in other words, already owed its origins to a moment of crisis and panic so soon after his American triumph.

Desperate for money, having lost touch with his German publishers, Sibelius was forced to divert time during the autumn from working on the symphony to completing sets of smaller piano works that he could more easily sell to local Finnish music firms, Westerlund and Lindgren. The op. 75 'tree' pieces might easily be dismissed as little more than a financial expediency, occasional works written at short notice for purely pecuniary gain. But that would be to undervalue their particular beauty and attractiveness. One of the number, 'Den ensamne furan' (The Lonely Fir), might refer to Heine's famous poem 'Ein Fichtenbaum steht einsam': a text that had already inspired Sibelius on a number of occasions, and which must have assumed an even greater poignancy as he reflected on his wartime position in Finland, suddenly isolated from friends and colleagues further south. The fourth number, 'Björken' (The Birch), which was in fact the last to be completed, is a gentle *perpetuum mobile* that suggest the swaying branches of the trees scattered across the northern forests: the second half is a wistful *misterioso*, as though listening ever deeper to the quiet sounds of the woods within. The final piece, 'Granen' (The Spruce), is one of Sibelius's most beguilingly nostalgic farewells, a slow, heartfelt and dignified waltz that closes sombrely in the tonic minor. A sixth number, *Syringa* (The Lilac), was withdrawn and reworked later as the popular *Valse lyrique* for orchestra, op. 96a: Sibelius perhaps sensed that 'Granen' offered a more moving point of departure.[34] The individual pieces in the diverse op. 76 collection of thirteen little movements, in contrast, were written over several years rather than conceived together as a single set: 'Carillon' has a delicate control of register and texture, and the *Affetuoso* is one of Sibelius's most beguiling songs without words.

Even as Sibelius was writing these smaller pieces, his thoughts were continually turning back to the new symphony. As was so often the case, his initial ideas underwent several transformations. Writing in his diary in October, for example, he noted 'Planning an orchestral suite for Hansen', referring to a loose collection of movements rather than a symphony as such. He added bleakly that 'it appears as though my mission here at home is finished. But – I think it as though the real "Jean Sibelius" begins now. Wonder whether that name "symphony" damages rather than benefits my symphonies. Ponder intensely how to allow my inner self – my fantasy – to speak.'[35] By the following month he was writing again of 'a splendid theme. The adagio of the symphony – earth, masks, and misery, fortissimo and mutes, many mutes! And the divine sounds! Jubilation and freezing shivers when the soul sings.'[36] The 'splendid theme' to which Sibelius referred on several occasions in his 1914 diary presumably corresponds to the swinging horn melody that was to become the principal idea in the finale and which was to be the symphony's primary motivic point of reference. Sibelius's musical sketchbooks of 1914–15 contain extensive drafts for the melody alongside ideas and materials that would later find their way into the Sixth and Seventh Symphonies and *Tapiola*.[37] From the outset, however, the symphony appears to have been associated with a feeling of ambivalence. The muted quality of the music is a constant refrain in Sibelius's references to the score, and a quality that always undercuts the outwardly sunny, optimistic tone of the much of the work's surface.

The other prominent and recurrent theme in Sibelius's references to the symphony, and one of the work's distinguishing qualities, is its concern with landscape and environment. Sibelius had of course been moved by the sight and sound of birds in several earlier works, notably *The Swan of Tuonela* from the *Lemminkäinen Legends*, the cranes in his score for *Kuolema*, Svanehvit's mother in his music for Strindberg's play, and Jubal's swan. But his notes on the Fifth Symphony suggest a newly intensive engagement with birds as both symbol and acoustic object. In the spring of 1915, as he sketched out the finale theme once again, for example, he wrote:

> Today at ten to eleven I saw 16 swans. One of the greatest impressions in my life! God, such beauty! They circled over me for a long time. Disappeared into the haze like a silver ribbon, which now and then glittered. Their call of the same woodwind type as that of the cranes, but without tremolo. The swans closer to that of the trumpets, or rather a sarrusophone. A low refrain reminiscent of a small child's cries. Nature mysticism and life's sorrow! Symphony V's finale-theme. The slurs [*bindningen*] in the trumpets!! God! Nature mysticism + romanticism and God knows what. That this has happened to me now, an outsider for so long. Have been in heaven today, 21 April 1915.[38]

Sibelius was never a committed ornithologist, compared, for instance, with his elder Finnish compatriots the painters Magnus (1805–1868), Wilhelm (1810–1887) and Ferdinand von Wright (1822–1906), whose work revelled in capturing intricate details of avian habitat and seasonal changes in plumage. Rather, his observations of the swans became a way to try and express his experience of sound and place: a deep associative link between instrumental colour, the timbre of the birds' calls and his inner mood. It also reflects the blurring of the boundary between self and environment that was characteristic of his engagement with landscape and nature. Artistic creation, for Sibelius, involved acknowledging the agency of natural elements and forces, including the presence of birds and animals, an ecocritical theology that understood music and sound as aspects of the (non-denominational) divine. Hence he could write again on 24 April, 'the swans are always in my thoughts and give life its gleam. Strange to establish that nothing in the world, neither in art, literature or music has had such an effect upon me as these swans, cranes, and wild geese.'[39]

On 23 May Sibelius became a grandfather for the first time following the birth of Eva's daughter Marjatta. Now aged 49, Sibelius had already begun to reflect on his life and career, writing with a spring-like energy on 13 April:

> The sap still rises in you just as in other fifty-year-old trees – and how! That sprightly age! But the time when one sat on the bank, held each other's hands and swore eternal fidelity are gone. I say that in the hope that it is so. But that *wiederholte Pubertät* of genius, of which Goethe spoke, flatters me.[40]

At other moments, however, Sibelius was plunged once more into his creative depression, and even his decision to give up alcohol and tobacco, in the wake of his throat operations in 1909, had begun to waver. On 4 June, following Marjatta's birth, he was again in pensive mood, contemplating a journey to visit his parents' graves in his old childhood town, Hämeenlinna (which he referred to by its Swedish name, Tavastehus), where he had been a student thirty years before. But summer was preoccupied by the symphony and other smaller works, as well as a visit from Rosa Newmarch and Otto Kling, Breitkopf's agent in London. Later, as summer turned to autumn, he saw the cranes flying once more, and 'immediately immersed myself in their sound again'.[41] What was really driving Sibelius's nostalgia, and his work on the symphony, was the imminent approach of his fiftieth birthday on 8 December: a series of celebrations were planned, including the premiere of a major new work, and, as his country's foremost artist (as he was now widely recognized), public expectation ran particularly high. As ever, Sibelius worked hard up to the deadline, completing the first movement only on 1 November, the second movement a week later and the finale a week after that (16 November), although he was still tinkering with the score the following day: barely sufficient time to have the orchestral parts copied and checked before rehearsals would begin. A photograph of the orchestral sessions survives and gives a good indication of the size of ensemble for Sibelius's work. The group is smaller than would customarily be used today, with four desks each of first and second violins, two or three desks of violas, four or five cellos and a similar number of double basses. Sibelius turns round to face the camera, immaculately dressed as always, but it is hard to escape a feeling of tension and formality in the air, the composer eager to try and crack on with the rehearsal process.

The birthday concert took place in the Great Hall of the University, the venue for so many of his premieres since *Kullervo*. The programme comprised the first Finnish performance of *The Oceanides*, alongside two new *Serenades* for Violin and Orchestra, op. 69, played by Richard Burgin (a former pupil of Leopold Auer in St Petersburg and later concertmaster

Sibelius rehearsing his fiftieth birthday concert, Helsinki, 1915.

of the Boston Symphony Orchestra), and followed after the interval by the new symphony. The concert was enthusiastically received, and was followed by a grand festival banquet at the Finnish Stock Exchange round the corner, a building designed by Lars Sonck, the architect of Sibelius's villa, Ainola, during which the composer was honoured by a generous tribute from Kajanus, among other cultural and political dignitaries. 'Barely had we begun to till the barren soil when a mighty sound arose from the wilderness,' Kajanus proclaimed in grand, mythologizing tones. 'Away with spades and picks. Finnish music's mighty springs came bursting forth. A might torrent burst forth to engulf all before it. Jean Sibelius alone showed the way.'[42] Sibelius's diary entry after the event was characteristically downbeat, as so often after a major expenditure of creative energy, mixing further flourishes of his schoolboy Latin alongside the familiar ironic self-deprecation and misgivings:

> Fiftieth birthday celebrations! Symphony v! Etc. Yes, splendid Ego: *sic itur* [thus one journeys (to the stars)]. *Difficile est satiram non scribere* [it is difficult to write satire]. *Sine ira et studio* [without anger or fondness]. Have written hundreds of letters of gratitude. Received 20-odd paintings. A piano, a fine rug, etc. B[reitkopf] and H[ärtel] sent an address! Yet I tire of all this attention. Long for work. That which gives value to life. Unpleasantly cold circa 20–30 degrees [Fahrenheit]. – Otto Andersson has worked out my ancestry until I'm sick. It's as though I were dead![43]

Sibelius's complaint about Andersson's genealogy reflected Sibelius's long-term obsession with his family heritage, especially the belief (largely unfounded) that he was descended from an ancient line of Swedish-Finnish aristocrats. Attempts the following year by Eeli Granit-Ilmoniemi to 'correct' Andersson's account in order to demonstrate Sibelius's purely Finnish-Finnish background (despite the fact that the composer's first language remained Swedish) caused him a great deal more distress and he resisted any such thinly veiled political attempts to 'authenticate' his Finnishness: an inevitable part of his role as one of the nation's cultural leaders, and an unforeseen emotional cost for someone who was at that time so frequently in the public eye.[44]

Sibelius's restlessness after his birthday was not limited to debates about his family heritage. No sooner had the symphony been performed than he withdrew the score and began to make significant changes to the work's layout and orchestration. The revisions that the symphony subsequently underwent are in many ways the most radical and certainly the highest-profile example of Sibelius's constant discipline and self-criticism. On 5 January, as soon as he was back at his desk after the New Year, for example, he noted that he was trying to get the symphony into publishable shape; two weeks later, he added that he was 'not yet satisfied with the work's form', and on 26 January explained: 'Wrestled with God. I will give my new symphony another, more human form. More earthy, more alive.'[45] The changes took far longer than Sibelius had anticipated, and the revised version of the symphony was not performed until a year after its initial premiere, on 8 December 1916, at his 51st birthday concert in Åbo (Turku) in western Finland. Even then Sibelius was not satisfied, making further changes to the work in connection with a planned performance in Stockholm and then withdrawing the score altogether for almost three years. The final definitive version of the score was only heard for the first time on 24 November 1919, by which time political events, and Sibelius's life, had already moved on significantly from the moment of its original premiere.

The many differences between the 1915 score and the familiar 1919 version of the Fifth Symphony have been tabulated by Erik Tawaststjerna and elegantly summarized and discussed by James Hepokoski. Osmo Vänskä's recording of the two versions of the work with the Lahti Symphony Orchestra has since enabled listeners to gain a detailed grasp of the changes involved in the revision process, and the 1915 symphony has even been performed at the BBC Proms (a prospect that would surely have appalled the composer himself, given the speed with which he retracted the score after its very earliest performances). The most notable change is that the symphony originally had four rather than merely three movements: the opening movement of the 1919 score was originally divided into a gentle pastoral introduction, which ended abruptly with a curious openness, followed by a separate and much faster-paced Scherzo. Although only a double bass part survives of the intermediate 1916 score, it is clear that Sibelius had already combined these two movements into one. His principal innovation was not merely a clever piece of musical dovetailing, but allowed him to unveil his most astonishing example of tempo modulation: the way in which the moderate 12/8 metre of the opening moves apparently seamlessly into the four-bar phrase rhythm, in quick triple time, of the Scherzo. The 1919 score accentuates this effect by extending the coda at the end of the Scherzo, creating an even steeper acceleration curve as the music speeds thrillingly towards its closing bars. Sibelius's changes in the middle movement – the Andante whose material quotes a melodic figure from his music for *Swanwhite* – were more subtle and less far-reaching, and largely involved compressing material and rescoring passages so as to reduce the amount of pizzicato passagework in the strings. Although the scoring of the opening was once much sharper and more piquant, darker chromatic undertones are more prominent throughout than in the later score. A particular loss in the 1919 version is the movement's beautiful, wistfully reflective coda: the revised ending is rather more prosaic. The differences in the finale are especially striking for listeners familiar with the movement's much-loved 'swan hymn': Sibelius initially provided a very different and considerably less effective woodwind counterpoint in the 1915 score, and the manner in which the theme almost immediately starts to unravel foreshadows its much more dissonant treatment in the reprise. Perhaps most startling of all is the treatment of the very closing bars: the dramatic chords, punctuated by silence, with which the symphony famously concludes in the 1919 version, were originally underpinned by a prolonged string tremolo and vigorous timpani roll. One of the symphony's most remarkable and memorable innovations, in other words, was essentially an afterthought.

The origins and fate of the 'swan theme' have provided the basis for many accounts of the symphony. But that is to hear the symphony through only one particular filter or lens. The opening paragraph, for example, evokes a magical nature realm of the kind suggested by the introduction in *Lemminkäinen and the Maidens of the Island* from the *Lemminkäinen Legends* of 1896: a glowing E flat major dawn sequence with florid woodwind cadenzas that pivots on two of the symphony's basic motivic components, the enharmonic pitches G flat/F sharp and C flat/B natural. The string's delayed first entry immediately shifts the harmonic focus to G major, and brings a sense of urgency and restlessness. This effects the second statement of the opening paragraph, which returns to E flat but then gives way to a mysterious development or transition sequence, dominated by strange muttering chromatic figuration in the strings and a lugubrious bassoon melody. Sibelius's brilliant reworking of the end of the original first movement tonicizes the B natural pitch elements from the opening bars, launching the Scherzo in the 'wrong' key: the Allegro's return to E flat hence takes on a much greater long-range significance and weight. The central slow movement consists of six successive restatements and textural elaborations of its gently naive opening theme: hardly a set of variations in the classical sense, rather a feeling of circling round the same material in more-or-less cumulative fashion. The central excursion to E flat obviously recalls the tonal domain of the outer movements – along with a feeling of darker territory that lies ahead, a prospect enhanced by the strange rising brass figures that emerge briefly just before the close. The start of the finale, meanwhile, is breathtakingly energized: the feeling of heightened expectancy that leads to the first pulsating entry of the 'swan hymn'. The Danish composer Per Nørgård (b. 1932) has written in particular about the importance of Sibelius's ingenious multimetrical counterpoint in this passage: the horns, upper strings, and double basses and bassoons play essentially the same material at three different speeds simultaneously, like satellites orbiting an unseen star in concentric orbits or trajectories. There is no real 'development section' in the conventional sense, but rather a giant, expanded second restatement of the opening sequence, which becomes increasingly sluggish and effortful as it encounters growing chromatic obstacles en route. One of the remarkable features of the 1919 score is the way in which the first half of the symphony gradually accelerates whereas the latter half symmetrically loses speed, growing in weight and gravity as it approaches its closing bars. The final restatement of the 'swan theme' hence has an enhanced grandeur and expansiveness, celebrating the symphony's hard-won ability, at long last, to achieve a structural perfect cadence in its tonic key. The hammer-blow chords of the coda themselves adumbrate the intervallic contour of the swan hymn, bringing the work to a brusque conclusion. The question nevertheless remains how far these closing bars should be heard as a straightforwardly optimistic gesture. Despite the affirmative glow of the swan hymn's final play-over, too much chromatic ground has been covered, and too much energy expended en route, for the end to feel unequivocally upbeat. It is at best a contingent and provisional victory, which acknowledges both its human cost and the awareness that much more remains unresolved than can be answered with confidence.

The ambivalence with which the Fifth Symphony concludes reflects a particular turn in Sibelius's biography: that moment, at which he turned fifty, when he felt summoned or called to account, and from where a proper appraisal of his life's creative output might reasonably begin. The balance sheet was not merely financial – although, as always, such matters were never very far from Sibelius's mind – but more broadly artistic-philosophical. How would he justify himself in relation to his contemporaries, or his historical precursors? Had he truly become the great musical figure that he and Aino had originally hoped?[46] It was this idea of a final reckoning, coupled, as ever for Sibelius, with concerns about his health (premature as such thoughts may have been), that no doubt attracted him to his next major project. On 15 May 1916 the director of the Finnish National Theatre, Jalmari Lahdensuo, wrote to ask if he might be interested in writing music for a production of the early modern morality play *Jokamies* (Everyman), the story of a wealthy and well-respected citizen and his departure from the world. After Death appears at one his lavish banquets, Everyman is gradually abandoned by his friends and left alone. It is only after he has renounced his earthly wealth and embraced the good deeds in his life that he can gain salvation and finally enter the Kingdom of Heaven. The allegorical significance of the text for Sibelius could not have been clearer, or more timely, given his recent birthday celebrations and the anxieties that followed in their wake.

The early modern sources for *Everyman* date from the late fifteenth and early sixteenth centuries, but interest in the text had been stimulated by an early twentieth-century revival, produced by William Poel and the Elizabethan Stage Society, and performed at the Charterhouse courtyard, London, on 13 July 1901, alongside the Chester miracle play *The Sacrifice of Isaac*. The unexpected success of the performance led to a touring production that later played at University College, Oxford, the Royal Pavilion in Brighton and other venues across the country, after which Poel sold rights to the actor-manager Ben Greet, who opened at the Mendelssohn Theatre on Broadway in New York on 12 October 1902. The play was even turned into an early film, first in Kinemacolor in 1913 and then a year later by Crawley-Maude features.[47] The version that formed the basis for the Helsinki production, however, was an unattributed adaptation by the Finnish author Huugo Jalkanen of Hugo von Hofmannsthal's composite text *Jedermann*. Inspired by Poel's performances in London, Hofmannsthal sketched his earliest prose draft for the drama in 1906, combining elements from the comedy *Hecastus* by the Nuremberger Meistersinger Hans Sachs, a version of the Belshazzar story by the Golden Age dramatist Calderón, and Robert Burton's *Anatomy of Melancholy*, as well as more modern texts by Maeterlinck and Georg Simmel. Hofmannsthal's *Jedermann* was premiered on 1 December 1911 at the Berliner Zirkus Schumann, directed by Max Reinhardt, only a few months before the Helsinki premiere of Sibelius's Fourth Symphony. It

Closing scene from *Jokamies* (Everyman) at the Finnish National Theatre, 1916.

has been performed annually at the Salzburg Festival from 1920 onwards, with only a brief interruption during the Second World War. Jalkanen's translation opened at the Finnish National Theatre on 5 November 1916, directed by Lahdensuo and with choreography by Maggie Gripenberg.[48] Kajanus conducted the music, and the cast included Sibelius's second daughter, Ruth, who had recently married the actor Jussi Snellman, who also appeared in the production.[49]

The essence of *Everyman* lies in its emphasis on transformation, both bodily and spiritual. As Bruster and Rasmussen have observed, '*Everyman* is a play of coming and going . . . The idea and vocabulary of movement in the play thus remind us that nothing on earth stands still.'[50] It was this idea of mutability, and of the transience of mortal life, that also attracted Hofmannsthal. Sibelius shared Hofmannsthal's acute feeling for a world in transition, of the essentially melancholic, nostalgic experience of passing time and human loss, and of the fragility of beauty and its impermanence. Both were concerned with the impression of modernism and modernity as one of slippage (for Hofmannsthal, 'das Gleitende'), an irresistible passing or letting go: time's insistent onward motion. This sense of 'lost time' permeates many aspects of the score. Sibelius composed sixteen movements for the production in total, arranged in two broad halves: a division broadly consistent with that of the original early modern drama.[51] The prologue is accompanied by a bold declamatory fanfare: a simple rising figure whose basic intervallic content (a rising tone from C to D) anticipates the tonal trajectory of the complete score, and which culminates in the swinging sound of a tolling bell as Death waits to pay his call upon Everyman. The opening scene launches immediately into the preparations for Everyman's banquet and consists of a number of dances and set pieces for individual characters. The mood completely shifts at the start of the second half, which is through-composed (like the score for *Scaramouche*). The opening number, as Good Deeds (Hyvät Työt) approaches Everyman for the first time, is a sparse, searching Largo, resembling some of the most chromatic and remote-sounding music from the first movement of the Fourth Symphony. The light slowly brightens as Everyman approaches salvation: an organ and angelic chorus create a sonic aura that glows stronger as the play's end draws near. In the final sequence, the swinging bell returns from the opening fanfare to announce that Everyman's time is up, and the choir sings in radiant praise as he crosses the threshold.

Much of the music for the second half of *Everyman* is underscore, intended to be played beneath spoken dialogue. But the closing sequence creates a striking parallel with the end of the Fifth Symphony: the bell that calls time for Everyman bears a striking resemblance to the swinging horn fifths of the symphony's climactic 'swan hymn'. Perhaps, then, the symphony is concerned not simply with a mystical nature symbolism, the image of the flying swans as the metaphor for artistic aspiration and creative freedom, but with the summoning and reckoning required by Everyman. As Sibelius contemplated his own career and looked back upon his achievements at a time of unthinkable political chaos and upheaval elsewhere on the continent, events that would all too soon engulf Finland directly, it may have seemed a poignant moment to reflect upon generational questions of inheritance and legacy. And with its images of devotion, sacrifice, pilgrimage and sacred mission, *Everyman* offered a glimpse of the way ahead. As Everyman cast aside his worldly goods and stepped forward, abandoned by his friends and accompanied only by his Good Deeds, it was the faith in art and music alone that ultimately offered release, a trust that Sibelius's last works would seek to affirm.

8

'Some heavenly musicke'

Early in the new year, on 27 January 1916, Sibelius was strolling calmly around the grounds of his villa at Järvenpää: 'worked on Symphony VI . . . A splendid day. Walked in colours of farewell [*adjöfärg*]. The trees spoke. Everything was alive.'[1] After the hectic preparations leading up to his fiftieth birthday celebrations the preceding month, and the premiere of the Fifth Symphony, such productive calm and restfulness seemed especially precious, particularly in the middle of winter. Sibelius was not yet ready to slip into a graceful retirement. The following month brought the opportunity to hear a range of works, even if the war meant that he was unable to travel to Berlin for the winter season, as had become his regular pattern in recent years. On 11 February, for example, he attended a concert with music by two of his pupils, Erkki Melartin and Leevi Madetoja. He described himself as 'utterly entranced' by Madetoja's First Symphony. Reviewing the daily newspaper, Sibelius noted that '*Bis* [the critic Karl Wasenius, writing in *Hufvudstadsbladet*] says that he is influenced by me. This and similar opinions begin to fracture our relationship. I bitterly regret this.'[2] Sibelius's musical instincts were, as always, correct: despite superficial similarities, Madetoja's symphony has a very different mood and character, especially in its magical slow movement, from those of his teacher, and his greatest works yet lay ahead. A week later Sibelius heard Brahms's 'Haydn' Variations, Beethoven's Fourth Piano Concerto and Tchaikovsky's Fifth Symphony conducted by Schnéevoigt. The season also included the Finnish premiere of Mahler's *Das Lied von der Erde* and Scriabin's *Poem of Ecstasy*; although it is not clear whether Sibelius heard those works in person, he stated in an interview with Madetoja in the Finnish daily *Helsingin Sanomat* on 8 August:

'What is written today is already out of date tomorrow. Mahler's symphonies, which I thought were epoch-making some years ago, have already lost almost all their capacity to surprise.'[3] In April he saw the cranes flying overhead once more, 'and heard again my sound!', before attending a performance of Verdi's *Aida* in Helsinki ('completely splendid'). And towards the end of the month he jotted down an even more exhilarating sight at Järvenpää: '12 swans upon the lake, upon the ice. Spotted them with binoculars!! Saw 6 wild geese (not grey geese, as Heikki [Järnefelt] maintained), plus an eagle. A rich day!! – at Puotinokka with Heikki's binoculars. And studied the swans' life. Curious, poetic! Extraordinary!' It was another chance to immerse himself in the environment.[4] For Sibelius, in spite of the tumultuous events taking place elsewhere across the continent, the spring seemed to hold a renewed promise, and some feeling of renewal: 'the earth breathes: mutes and fortissimo'.[5]

For a short while, the shadows of the previous winter seemed to diminish. Sibelius sent a series of small character pieces for piano to his Finnish publisher Lindgren, followed by his five of his op. 86 songs: a sixth would be added the following year. All three of Sibelius's later song collections are on a smaller, more intimate scale than those of his earlier years. Whether he was thinking of a primarily domestic audience, or was mindful of the range of some of his favourite performers, especially Ida Ekman, is uncertain.[6] There is a recognizably vernal quality to the op. 86 set, taking its cue from the setting of Karl August Tavaststjerna's *Vårförnimmelser* (Spring Feelings) with which the collection opens. Shadows never lingered far from Sibelius's mind, however. The day after posting the op. 86 songs, he noted in his diary, 'Thoughts of death! I will never be able to fulfil that which I dreamt of. Pain in my hands. A blood clot?'[7] Sibelius's persistent hypochondria is difficult to understand, especially given his brother's eminence as a medical professional. But it is tempting to draw it back to memories of his childhood following his father's early death, and of course the fact that he had himself lost a daughter at the very turn of the century. In Helsinki political tensions were also darkening. Jalmari Lahdensuo's premiere of *Everyman* at the Finnish National Theatre in early November, for which he had written music, for example, had to be postponed for two days because of objections by the Russian censor: the cause for concern was the use of dark drapes in the auditorium, covering the seat reserved for the governor general.[8] The fact that a staged regicide at the end of Procopé's *Belsazars gästabud* had passed without comment at the Swedish Theatre barely a decade earlier, in 1906, is an indication

Crowds at a political protest in Senate Square, Helsinki, 1917.

of just how far the situation had deteriorated. The First World War had pushed the Russian empire to breaking point, and a much more brutal and unstable mood was already in the air.

Sibelius received direct reports of how things were moving across the Russian border. His eldest daughter, Eva, was in St Petersburg with her husband Arvi Paloheimo, and they could attest to the growing sense of political tension. At home in Ainola, things were also difficult: Aino had likewise been pushed to her limit during Sibelius's struggles with his Fifth Symphony (and no doubt also with his return to alcohol and tobacco), and by the stress that it placed upon the household, and she left to stay with Eva at the start of February 1917. Sibelius's mood was correspondingly bleak. In the middle of the month, for example, he noted 'my new style! And the war that has now touched my life. Surrounded by false friends, I must seriously safeguard my "inner life" and therefore my independence.'[9] It was evidently this need to ring-fence his creative space, over and above the domestic demands of his family, that made life so difficult for Aino. But as the February Revolution took hold in St Petersburg towards the end of the month, the possibility of a much greater existential threat began to emerge. On 16 March 1917, following the abdication of Tsar Nicholas II, Sibelius noted in his diary: 'Great things have taken place in Russia! Can we here shape our own fate? That is the great question. It weighs heavily over Finland.'[10] For Sibelius and his family, the prospect of the Russian Revolution brought a particular political challenge. Sibelius's brother-in-law, Arvid Järnefelt, was briefly placed under arrest for publicly extolling his pro-Tolstoyan views during a political rally in the working-class district of Kallio, north of Helsinki city centre.[11] The Järnefelts' long connection with Russian culture, fostered especially by Sibelius's mother-in-law, Elizabeth, meant they were potentially highly exposed as the power struggles within Russia gained force. The implications for Finland's hopes of sovereignty and self-determination, as Sibelius acutely realized, also remained painfully unclear.

For much of the summer, as war raged south beyond the Baltic and revolutionary unrest gathered speed in Russia, Sibelius worked on a number of smaller, seemingly otherworldly pieces. A series of magical *Humoresques* for violin and chamber orchestra, which he published in two sets (opp. 87 and 89), looks back wistfully to the virtuosic fantasy of the Violin Concerto, now fifteen years old, but has a playful elusiveness that is more characteristic of his later music. The bustling excitement and throwaway conclusion of the second, which he finished on 3 May, for instance, has an effervescence that echoes the opening of the finale of the Fifth Symphony, whereas the shadowy understatement of the fourth humoresque, which was written in September, brings a feeling of remoteness and regret, a lingering farewell.

In June Sibelius and Aino, now reconciled, could celebrate their silver wedding anniversary in the company of Sibelius's brother and his sister Linda: her serious and long-standing mental health issues meant that this was a rare opportunity for Sibelius and his two siblings to gather together. With the weather turning warmer, Sibelius completed a set of songs that turned once again to his favourite poet, Runeberg. Of the six 'Flower Songs', op. 88, the final two seem especially prescient given the political circumstances tightening around Finland. The restrained, dignified 'Törnet' (The Thorn) is a hymn of praise to the wintry stem whose naked branches promise the softest and most alluring of summer blooms, whereas 'Blömmans öde' (The Flower's Fate) is a rocking, melancholic berceuse as the blossom sadly foretells its own autumnal end: 'Solen dalar, stormens röst jag hör' ('The sun sets, and I hear the storm's voice').

That sound of the approaching storm became increasingly loud as the year progressed. Tensions grew between socialist and nationalist blocs in the Finnish Senate, reflecting the country's deepening political tensions as Russia descended further into violence. On 14 October Sibelius noted: 'peace further than ever before. How will this turn out? Oh, my poor country with its divisions.'[12] As a second wave of revolution swept the Bolsheviks into power in Russia, Finland's status seemed ever more uncertain. The parliament's declaration of independence on 6 December only served to increase the instability. Six days later, Sibelius completed a setting of Runeberg's austerely beautiful poem 'Norden' (The North): migrating swans appear again as an idealistic symbol of longing and aspiration. Playing poetically on the geographical conceit of Heine's 'Ein Fichtenbaum steht einsam', Runeberg imagines an observer in the south who looks skyward and calls out: 'Tynande svanor, vilken förtrollning / vilar på norden?' ('Pining swans! What enchantment does the north possess?'). The unresolved dissonance of Sibelius's accompaniment provides a feeling of momentum beneath the soaring vocal line, which twice rises to a climax stressing the emotional crux of Runeberg's text: the idea of longing ('längtan') as an unresolved state of being. Although the song closes affirmatively with a perfect cadence in C major, such confidence and hope in the future must have seemed particularly remote as political events spiralled rapidly out of control in Finland. As with the ending of the Fifth Symphony and *Everyman*, music seemingly offered some means of solace and escape, the vision of a purer and more ideal world, but any attempt at a more permanent resolution proved contingent at best.

Sibelius's diary entries in December provide a vivid impression of the gathering gloom. The week before Christmas he wrote that he had both his Sixth and Seventh Symphonies 'in his head': likely a diary formula or shorthand that may have indicated an idea of mood or thematic content rather than anything more specific or fully worked-out, since it would be several years before either score emerged in their definitive form. Sibelius was instead distracted by Finland's rapidly deteriorating crisis of governance: 'Anarchy increases. My unfortunate country', he noted, 'everything appears dark at present. Misery and lack of culture.' Four days later, on 22 December, he added: 'the anarchists' excesses terrifying', and on the very final day of the year '1917 finished. Could anything be more tragic?'[13] Whether he referred to the state of the young nation, his own prospects or perhaps his close friend Axel Carpelan, who was gravely ill, is uncertain. The start of the new year nevertheless brought some sense of optimism amid all the uncertainty. 'Finland in the process of becoming a free land,' he wrote in his first entry for January. 'After 52 years it is hard to believe. Especially because throughout life one has been so often frustrated over the nation's political ambitions.' In the same entry, he noted with glowing pride the baptism of his first grandson, Eva and Arvi Paloheimo's son, christened Martti Jean Alfred. 'And so my artistic name lives on in a further form,' he added, 'splendid of them to have done this'. On 12 January 1918 he wrote a celebratory march for the Finnish scouting association, a group that had been banned during the final years of Russian rule because of its political overtones. But it was another march, composed in October the previous year, that would bring Sibelius much greater publicity and cause him considerable difficulty.[14]

Inspired by a battalion of Finnish troops serving in the Imperial German Army and stationed in the Latvian port of Liebau (Liepāja), stranded and cut off from events in Finland, Sibelius set a patriotic poem by one of the Jäger officers, Heikki Nurmio, for male chorus. The premiere took place privately, after which copies of the piece began to circulate informally, but on 19 January it was performed with an orchestral accompaniment (presumably by Sibelius himself, though he only noted the arrangement in his diary a week later).[15] After this gala performance, Sibelius deliberately withheld his name from the piece, in the hope that the royalties might benefit the soldiers themselves.[16] But his identity was inevitably leaked to the newspapers the following day, and his authorship became widely known. Tawaststjerna suggests that the march was never conceived as an overtly political gesture: 'Sibelius would not have thought of the possible implications. He may well have imagined its use as a marching song if, in the absence of an acceptable agreement with the Russians, a war of independence were to ensure.'[17] The idea of such a naive approach does not ring entirely true. Sibelius was carefully tracking political events and was keenly aware of his music's capacity to inspire and motivate his domestic audience. At the same time, he had written music for festive occasions and functional commissions throughout his career, and so the *March of the Jäger Battalion*, for all is bellicosity, is in many senses entirely consistent with this familiar aspect of his public role as a composer.

In the wake of the October Revolution in 1917, the prospect of Finland's independence finally seemed within reach, and Sibelius's greatest fear may have been that the new Russian government would seek to crack down on separatist sentiments in the former Grand Duchy. But Sibelius's hopes of a moderate resolution were swiftly overtaken by events, and he could hardly have known that Finland itself would be plunged into the horrors of civil war: Russian-sponsored left-wing socialists ('Reds') versus right-wing nationalists ('Whites') who could draw on German support through their wartime alliance. The timing of the January performance of the *March of the Jäger Battalion* could hardly have been more unfortunate, even if Sibelius still seemed oblivious to the chaos that was about to unfold. As Tawaststjerna notes, 'on the brink of civil war he appeared publicly as aligned with the Whites – his march their symbol – and as a supporter of the Finnish-German alliance. His gesture on behalf of a group of Finnish volunteers on the Gulf of Riga had turned into something quite different and quite out of proportion.'[18] It was a baleful shift of circumstance that would have heavy consequences for Sibelius's immediate safety as well as his later critical reception, not least as the world was engulfed in the flames of another global conflict at the end of the 1930s.

On 25 January Sibelius wrote to the mezzo-soprano Aina Mannerheim, presumably about his new song collections, and to the director of the Society House in Helsinki, William Noschis, seeking to obtain sherry: a fair indication of Sibelius's daily priorities. Two days later, civil war broke out across Finland.[19] Red troops seized strategic positions in Helsinki, which had always had a strong working-class population, whereas in the north and west of the country, Aina Mannerheim's brother-in-law, General Carl Gustaf Mannerheim, seized control of Russian garrisons and ordered the mobilization of White nationalist forces. Sibelius's diary entries record his shock and surprise at the sudden escalation of hostilities. On 28 January he noted, 'Yesterday "unrest" broke out in Helsinki. Red guards with their Russian accomplices! What shame for our people and our land.' The following day, he wrote: 'Red guards in full swing. General strike – arson – murder after murder. That dangerous scum.' And on 2 February he added, with even greater urgency: 'Murder upon murder, and not only those who have taken part in the struggle but anyone of education is unsafe. And proletarian power spreads like wildfire. To such an extent. My turn will come as soon as I am discovered as the author of the *Jäger March*.'[20] Even if Sibelius had not advertised his political allegiances by composing the *March of the Jäger Battalion*, his class and social milieu would inevitably have associated him with the Nationalists (as was also the case for his colleagues Akseli Gallen-Kallela and Bertel Gripenberg). The Russophilia of the Järnefelts meant they had clung to a much older, more patrician view of Russian life: the age of Pushkin, Gogol and Turgenev, and of early Russian support for expressions of Finnish national culture, alongside Tolstoy's utopian idealism. They had no sympathy for either the hardline repression of Nicholas II or the brutal activism of the Bolsheviks. Sibelius's preoccupation with his supposedly aristocratic Swedish-Finnish heritage, which had come under such painful scrutiny from genealogists at the time of his fiftieth birthday, led him equally away from the Red cause. And his long-standing admiration for Germany as the centre for European culture (both musical and more broadly philosophical) drew him even more closely to the Whites. It was a precarious position, especially given Ainola's location in the heart of Red-controlled territory in the south of the country.

At first, following the initial skirmishes, Sibelius and his family seemed to have been barely touched by the conflict. But as the violence escalated, local tensions only became more difficult. On 5 February, for example, he noted with some sarcasm in his diary: 'forbidden from going outside for a walk. Splendid! But what has any of this to do with my symphonies? If only I could distance myself from all of this nonsense!' But a week later Ainola was searched by a group of Red guards, and on 19 February Sibelius and his family were evacuated to Helsinki, where they stayed with his brother Christian at his home in Lapinlahti (Lappviken) in the west of the city. Here they stayed for the short but bloody duration of the war until the Nationalist victory was secured in May. Although the conflict lasted barely three months, it came at a considerable human cost: casualties, including civilians, numbered almost 40,000, but increased after the formal end of hostilities because of hardship and internment. In the absence of any truth-and-reconciliation process, memories and legacies of the war lingered long after the end of the conflict, and the profound social and political divisions at the heart of Finnish society remained unresolved.[21] Although the defeated Red forces sustained by far the greater losses, both sides suffered significantly. Nor was the musical and artistic community left untouched. Leevi Madetoja's brother Yrjö was killed following the Battle of Antrea in the east of the country in April, and Madetoja composed his eloquent three-movement piano suite *Kuoleman puutarha* (The Garden of Death), op. 41, in his memory. The war also influenced the eventual shape and trajectory of Madetoja's achingly beautiful Second Symphony, a work that moves from gentle idyll to a devastated, post-apocalyptic state of catharsis. An even greater loss was felt after the end of the war: Sibelius's former pupil Toivo Kuula was fatally injured in a brawl after celebrations to mark the White victory and died on 18 May in Viipuri (Viborg), aged only 34. Sibelius attended Kuula's funeral ten days later and wrote in his diary: 'today friend Toivo Kuula was buried in the cold earth. How infinitely sad is the artist's lot! So much work, talent, and courage – for life – and then suddenly all finished.' It was a blunt reminder of the senseless violence and human cost of war.[22]

As the conflict reached its bitter end in Helsinki, Sibelius could hear the sound of cannon fire in the distance: 'strange but magnificent. I could never have dreamt of anything so powerful.'[23] He took part in a gala concert to celebrate the contribution of German forces to the White victory that took place on 20 April, with a programme that included *Finlandia* and the *March of the Jäger Battalion*, alongside the German patriotic anthem *Die Wacht am Rhein*. General Mannerheim made his triumphant march into the city on 16 May, just two days before Kuula's death.[24] Sibelius himself was in a desperate mood: 'everything appears dark again. The Reds turn upon themselves. Shall I survive all this and not be murdered? If I now wish to play my part and remain a composer I should seek safety in Germany, for example. But teachers there are worse off than here.' Rampant inflation meant that even if he had been able to maintain his copyright payments from German publishers during the war, they would have lost most of their value. But his worries were not only economic. Sibelius also feared that his music was out of step with the prevailing stylistic tastes of the time, which, he sensed, leaned more towards 'Wagnerian pathos' than the classicist direction of his own work.[25] And the critical reception of his work in Germany still remained equivocal. The musicologist Walter Niemann's 1919 monograph on his work, for instance, claimed that all of Sibelius's symphonies shared the same basic preoccupation with the Finnish landscape and its people (qualities that Niemann esteemed), but that his music was incoherent and lacked sufficient logic, rigour and monumentality: crucial criteria for admittance to the highest reams of the Germanic pantheon.[26] Ironically, many of Niemann's criticisms were the same as those listed by Theodor Adorno in his 1938 essay on the composer, a perspective otherwise presented from the opposite end of the political spectrum. Sibelius was hence increasingly convinced of his own artistic isolation, both in terms of his relationship with continental musical trends and also at home in post-war Finland. An article on Freud's theories in the periodical *Finsk Tidskrift*, for example, only served to intensify his feelings of alienation and his disillusionment with the politics of patriotism and national duty: 'They do not perceive that the symphonist's struggle – to determine laws for the movement of notes for all time – is rather greater than "dying for king and country":

many can do that, and planting potatoes or doing similarly useful things can be done by many more.'[27]

After the cessation of hostilities, life in Finland slowly began to return to some form of normality, even as the war ground on elsewhere across Europe. As Glenda Dawn Goss notes, however, 'that normality was a façade': the divisions and long-held resentments that had first led to the conflict would remain unresolved for many years.[28] Sibelius and his family returned to Ainola to begin to pick up the pieces, and at the very end of the year Sibelius travelled back into the city to hear the premiere of Madetoja's valedictory Second Symphony. 'Much to think about in that respect', Sibelius wrote with characteristic understatement, 'it made a deep impression'.[29] Despite the nationalist victory, the political situation still remained dangerously unstable. In his diary on 3 January 1919, for instance, Sibelius wrote: 'Read Dickens aloud. Truly atmospheric,' but then added: 'politics darker than ever. And I think that my vocation as a composer is impossible now because everything revolves around bolshevism, for and against.'[30] Sibelius's diary entry reflects one important legacy of the civil war on his career, namely the increasingly strong desire to distance himself from politics of any formal, public kind. The very real danger into which he and his family had fallen during the war, and the graver losses suffered by others, were an entirely different proposition from the idealistic, aspirational nationalism to which he had subscribed as a young man, and it was a vision that he could no longer sustain. Hence, when Erik Tawaststjerna suggests that 'Sibelius's active political involvement was a thing of the past, save for the fact that his country needed him as much as ever as a cultural ambassador, an embodiment of its new freedom,'[31] it is essential to recognize how provisional, and painfully achieved, such freedom may have seemed at the time, and the almost impossible challenge facing any attempt at a restorative cultural diplomacy. The war's aftermath brought a further tragedy in the spring: Axel Carpelan's death after a long illness on 24 March. Sibelius was heartbroken, and wrote in his diary: 'How empty life feels! No sun, no sound, no love. How alone I am now with my sounds. On his deathbed he even wrote a card, which I received today. Lucid until the end.'[32] His work on the third and final version of the Fifth Symphony was haunted by the thought of Carpelan's absence, which must have amplified the hollow victory of the work's closing bars.

When Sibelius was offered the position of professor of composition at the Eastman School of Music in Rochester, New York, in 1920, he was sorely tempted to accept the post, despite his long-standing reservations about teaching in academic institutions. The opportunity to renew the contacts that he had made on his visit in 1914 and escape from war-torn Europe must have seemed especially attractive, as well as financially rewarding. And another attempt by the genealogist Granit-Ilmoniemi to demonstrate his authentic Finnish roots had once again provoked Sibelius's anxieties about his class and social background. Ultimately, however, Sibelius did not accept the Eastman offer (despite having initially accepted the post, which was taken up instead by his contemporary Selim Palmgren). Rather, he attempted to pick up the threads of his pre-war compositional projects: sketches for the Sixth Symphony with titles including 'Talvi' ('Winter', over what would become the main theme of the first movement), 'Hongatar ja tuuli' ('Pine-tree Spirit and the Wind', over the secondary theme of the finale), and various references to a work entitled 'Kuutar' (Moon Spirit). Further evidence of his preoccupation with the animating forces of the natural world came in a pair of works for chorus and orchestra: the softly radiant cantata *Jordens sång* (The Song of the Earth), premiered at the inauguration of the Swedish-speaking Åbo Akademi in Turku in February 1919, was followed by his setting of Eino Leino's *Maan virsi* (Hymn to the Earth), which dates from a year later. *Maan virsi* is an intense and moving evocation of rebirth and renewal across the Finnish landscape, the sound of the kantele mingling with the midsummer scent of birch and cherry, the spirit of the 'ever-rejuventating' earth. Lasting barely five minutes in performance, *Maan virsi* must nevertheless have felt like a massive reaffirmation of the consoling power of nature, and the precious hope of recovery in a desolate and broken land. Sibelius conducted a festival performance of the piece at the opening of the Finnish Trade Fair in Helsinki in June,[33] re-intoning the sacred conjunction of environmental resource, economic power and national sustainability.

Though Sibelius would not travel to North America again, he nevertheless paid a final visit to England in February 1921. Staying initially at the Bonnington Hotel on Southampton Row in London, he was reunited with Rosa Newmarch, Henry Wood and Granville Bantock, and conducted performances of the Fourth and Fifth Symphonies at the Queen's Hall before travelling to Birmingham, where he conducted the Third. Before his London engagements, Newmarch held a reception in his honour at Claridge's, at which the other guests included Vaughan Williams, then working on his Third Symphony. Although it was only a brief and fleeting meeting, the encounter left a deep impression on the

English composer, who would later dedicate his Fifth Symphony to Sibelius 'without permission'. The visit equally had a powerful impact on Sibelius. Writing to Aino on 21 February, he noted: 'strange after so many years to make contact again with the world to which I belong'.[34] On his return to London, he stopped overnight in Oxford, where he was awarded an honorary doctorate and stayed as a guest of Hugh Allen at New College, before leaving from Newcastle for his next concert engagement in Bergen. In a letter to Aino, dated 10 March, he wrote: 'strange to have all of the enormity of London behind me'.[35] He could scarcely have realized at that moment that it would in fact prove to be his last visit to the country.

Work on the Sixth Symphony progressed slowly during 1922, against the background of continuing financial pressures and anxieties. In Finland, at least, international musicians had begun to return as post-war travel restrictions eased and markets opened up once more. Visitors included the 26-year-old German pianist Wilhelm Kempff, who visited Sibelius at Ainola on 20 March. Sibelius deeply admired Kempff's performances of Bach, noting, 'he has all the qualities that make a master';[36] Kempff, for his part, would later add Sibelius's piano music to his repertory. But the summer took a much bleaker turn as Sibelius's brother, Christian, whom the family referred to affectionately as Kitti, fell gravely ill. Christian's death from liver failure on 2 July left Sibelius devastated: 'grief is too small a word,' he wrote in his diary, 'he was a wonderful brother and human being.'[37] Sibelius had always admired Christian's artistry and musicianship as a cellist, as well as holding the deepest respect for his professional work as a medical doctor: Christian had been both a kindred spirit and a role model. Given his health scares the previous decade, Sibelius had never expected to outlive his junior sibling. Christian's death rekindled Sibelius's sense of his own isolation and mortality, out of which music again emerged as a form of solace. At the end of September, with the deadline for the new symphony looming, he noted simply: 'Worked. Recognized today life's perfection and my art's greatness.'[38]

Sibelius had set himself a deadline of January 1923 for the completion of the Sixth Symphony, and he finished work on the first three movements on the same day that his younger contemporary Eliel Saarinen won second prize in the competition to design the World Tribune Tower in Chicago. Sibelius proudly noted both events in his diary on 14 January. Saarinen was one of Finland's foremost architects, a member of the group that had included Lindgren, Gesellius and Sonck, and had been responsible for designing Helsinki's distinctively streamlined railway station in a striking modern style in 1911 (the same year as Sibelius's Fourth): his success in the Chicago competition was widely hailed as another cultural victory for the fledging nation. Yet nothing could be more distant from Saarinen's confident monumental plans for the skyscraper than Sibelius's Sixth Symphony, the most intimate and inward-looking of his canon. If works such as *Maan virsi* had suggested a musical rebirth, a vital creative spring renewed, a more autumnal, retrospective tone can be heard in the Sixth. It is easy to suggest the biographical reasons for this change of tone: although initial sketches for the work (alongside material for *Tapiola* and the Seventh) had dated back to the same period as the Fifth, the very early years of the First World War following his return from America, the intervening period had seen an irrevocable change of personal circumstance, from the brutality of the civil war to the death of his brother. In addition, the intense creative struggles he had experienced in revising the score of the Fifth must have reinforced both the strain in upholding the idealized image of the

Christian Sibelius, the composer's brother, late 1910s.

symphony as some kind of grand heroic gesture, the utopian vision of a universal musical community, and also his remoteness from current continental practice, especially the work of Schoenberg and Stravinsky. For many of Sibelius's younger avant-garde European contemporaries, the symphony as an institutionalized genre seemingly held little or no appeal (although Stravinsky would later determine his own characteristically idiosyncratic approach to the form in his *Symphony of Psalms* in 1930). That is not to hear the Sixth as in any sense a defensive or reactionary work. On the contrary, in its quiet, understated manner it is no less formally innovative than either of its predecessors. And as a testament to the consolatory power of musical reflection, in the wake of a period of unimaginable violence and trauma, it is a particularly eloquent and sustained study.

Much of the musical drama in the Sixth Symphony derives from the interaction of a range of modal collections with more familiar diatonic major/minor materials. The work is only notionally 'in D minor', as its title page implies: it might be better described as being in the Dorian mode (a minor mode with flattened seventh and raised sixth degrees), or, more accurately, as moving continually between various related modes and keys (including F major). The work's tonal-modal ambiguity is in fact settled (if not resolved) only in its very final bars. The symphony begins seemingly in mid-air, with a major third suspended high in the violins (suggesting either F or D) that gradually falls towards more solid ground. The strings unfold a glowing polyphonic tapestry of sound, whose luminosity suggests the heightened spirituality of Beethoven's 'Heiliger Dankgesang' from his late String Quartet in A minor, op. 132, or the visionary opening of the prelude from Wagner's opera *Lohengrin*. Despite this early expansiveness, the music is swiftly darkened by the insistent presence of a dissonant C sharp (D minor's leading note), which brings the movement to a moment of chromatic crisis. Out of this troubled harmonic glitch emerges the Allegro proper: a sequential chain of lively woodwind calls and bustling string figuration that suggests a renewed sense of purpose. The initial goal of the development is a cello tune in B minor (or, rather, B Dorian), a point of orientation that in turn gives way to a texturally enhanced reprise of the introduction, swept up by the momentum of the Allegro. As the reprise energetically ascends and attempts to regain its opening sonority, however, the harmonic and textural support dissolves, and the music's energy dissipates. The movement closes instead with a series of enigmatic fragments and a stern modal cadence.

The opening of the second movement cleverly dovetails the broad duple metre of the preceding Allegro with its own triple-beat pattern: the remainder of the movement is a set of simple variations upon a gently rocking violin theme. The figuration slowly accelerates as the variations progress, like a river current draining towards a receding tide. But just as the movement appears about to reach its goal, the expected return of the opening theme is unexpectedly deflected by a mysterious nocturnal interlude, evoking the gossamer textures of the Scherzo from Felix Mendelssohn's incidental music for Shakespeare's *A Midsummer Night's Dream*. It is a strangely haunting passage of gentle forest sounds that seemingly suspends any regular feeling of time or motion. The coda is a brief four-bar fragment of the opening material, curiously foreshortened before the curtain figuratively descends.

If the first two movements both suggest a cyclic process of growth, expansion, withdrawal and dissolution or decay, the Scherzo that follows is a compact burst of cyclic energy, alternating an increasingly wild musical ride with more pastoral elements foregrounding a canonic dialogue between the woodwind and harp. The finale begins in a ballad-like manner, with a series of terse melodic sentences as though intoning the opening lines of an epic poem. The narrative trajectory swiftly intensifies, however, built on sequential restatements of a simple rising melody that Tawaststjerna described as the symphony's basic underlying thematic model. These sequential paragraphs rapidly reach a stormy point of chromatic saturation, cadencing on B natural at a point exactly corresponding to the comparable moment in the first movement (bar 144 in both cases). The second half of the finale briefly regains some of its earlier energy, only to conclude with a wistful hymn-like epilogue, marked *doppio più lento* (at half speed). Though the music briefly promises to close in a sunlit F major, the light inevitably fades, and the symphony turns back once again to the cooler D Dorian domain of the introduction. In that way, the music travels full circle, like a complete seasonal cycle, the pale glow of the final page recalling as it dims to pianissimo the soft radiance of the opening page. To face the world with such a restrained and gracious equilibrium at the time of the work's premiere in Helsinki on 19 February must have demanded considerable creative courage.

The Sixth Symphony was dedicated to Sibelius's friend and contemporary Wilhelm Stenhammar, an early champion of his work in Sweden, and there is something of his Swedish colleague's dignified melancholic interiority about much of the symphony. Stenhammar had dedicated his

Fourth Quartet to Sibelius at the time of the Fourth Symphony (1911), and paid tribute to his Finnish friend via various musical allusions in his own Second Symphony and the Serenade for Orchestra, op. 31. There was a Swedish connection too with Sibelius's Seventh Symphony, which, uniquely among his major orchestral works, received its premiere in Stockholm rather than Helsinki. If the Seventh appeared to follow swiftly after the Sixth, that does not indicate that its composition was in any way easier than its precursors. Indeed, more sketch material survives for the Seventh Symphony than almost all of Sibelius's other works, and its genesis almost brought him to breaking point.[39] On 6 January 1924, barely three months before the work's first performance, for example, he wrote:

> Aino has been very sick for some time. She suffers and groans. I will never get my things ready now. Just hope to get the single one [that is, the symphony] completed. An urgent *necessity*. But – my life has derailed. Alcohol to deaden the nerves and spirit! How infinitely tragic is the fate of an ageing composer! It never proceeds with the same speed as before and the self-criticism becomes impossible.[40]

The confessional tone of Sibelius's diary entry gives a vivid insight into his state of mind and health at the time of the Seventh's composition. His reliance on alcohol had once again become a dependency, as had the crushing sense of insecurity with which he scrutinized and reviewed his own work. Whether his diary was ever a truly personal document, or more properly a performative exercise for future public readership (or posterity), is unclear. The frequent posturing and obsessive nihilism, alongside its frequently ironic and self-parodistic turns, means that it always conceals more than it reveals about Sibelius's actual working methods and domestic routine. For Aino, such mood swings had become unbearable, and she refused to accompany him to the Stockholm premiere.[41] But it is clear that, as Sibelius reached his late fifties, he already felt as though his creative life was rapidly approaching its conclusion. Like Everyman, he was being called to account; the symbolist preoccupation with mortality and death that had permeated so much of his earlier work had now become a more deeply existential state of being, a sense of imminent departure that combined feelings of rage, despair and a visionary radiance.

One obvious manifestation of this obsessive self-criticism was the struggle evident in achieving the Seventh Symphony's final shape. Indeed, for much of its composition Sibelius was unsure whether to describe the work as a symphony at all: his preferred title, right up until after the first performance, was 'Fantasia sinfonica', a reflection both of the work's formal freedom and also perhaps its breadth and expressive range. If the Sixth had seemingly followed the conventional four-movement plan of the classical symphony (superficially only, since the work in almost every other respect adopts very different musical means of articulation), the Seventh is more immediately innovative and original. Various scholars have cited its single-movement scheme as the logical end-point of Sibelius's concern with formal compression and concision, the manner in which from the Second Symphony onwards he had explored various ways of joining movements together or eliding familiar structural boundaries for dramatic or expressive effect.[42] And Sibelius had, of course, contemplated publishing the first movement of the revised version of his Fifth Symphony alone as an independent piece before, fortunately, reconsidering his plans to drop the final two movements. Hearing the Seventh as the ultimate outcome of this process of concentration and compression hence makes reasonable historical sense. The formal structure of the Seventh, however, is more ambiguous than this goal-directed perspective might suggest. Even at the most basic level, there is no consensus over whether it consists of a single movement divided into contrasting episodes in the manner of a 'Hellenic rondo', as Sibelius himself referred to the score, or as several movements spliced together. Nor is it straightforwardly a set of variations, a strophic structure or a massively transformed sonata design, though aspects of all three models inform the music's shape. Rather, it is this underlying ambivalence, in tension with the apparent clarity and simplicity of the symphony's layout, that generates much of the work's drama and momentum.

The whole work revolves around the memorable trombone theme, like the famous alphorn call in the finale of Brahms's First Symphony, which first emerges out of the string's hymn-like introduction and recurs three times in total across the symphony's complete span. Each iteration of this theme is different: the first is reverential; the second stormy and turbulent; and the third resigned and retrospective. The central storm-tossed statement of the theme is framed by two pastoral interludes, both of which accelerate as they progress (much like the scherzo section in the first movement of the Fifth), creating the impression of a cresting wave that breaks and overspills into the return of the trombone motif. The opening and closing trombone statements are then symmetrically bookended by a prelude and epilogue that determine the work's principal tonal argument and ultimately seek to resolve its structural and expressive tensions. The prelude opens with a gradual stair-like ascent, similar to the passage that presages the approach to the threshold of the celestial city in the closing sequence of Sibelius's score for *Everyman*: it is once again the musical evocation of a summons or reckoning. The immediate goal on this occasion is not the promise of salvation, which must wait until the symphony's final bars, but rather a dark, sombre cadence that lands on A flat minor, a world away from the symphony's proper home key, C major. It is this early emphasis on A flat (and its flattened third, C flat or B natural) that generates much of the work's tonal tension, and which is picked up again in the *Affettuoso* with which the epilogue begins. The presence of A flat even overshadows the much-discussed allusion to *Valse triste* that slips in moments before the symphony's closing bars. Sibelius rarely quoted his own works in such a direct and obvious manner, and other cases, such as the parallels between his score for Strindberg's *Swanwhite* and the Fifth Symphony, or between *Lemminkäinen and the Maidens of the Island* and the opening of the Fifth, are exceptions rather than a standard practice. The significance of the quotation in the Seventh has less to do with the particular plot details of Arvid Järnefelt's play *Kuolema*, for which Sibelius had originally written the music, than with the play's preoccupation with the permeable boundary between life and death, and with the notion of the essential circularity of human existence: from birth through death to the promise of rebirth (in an entirely non-religious sense). This is one way in which to understand the gesture in the symphony, namely as a manifestation of the Nietzschean principle of eternal recurrence, Death's presence as a symbol of renewal as much as obliteration. In that way, the remarkably terse conclusion of the final page, which Sibelius drafted no fewer than three times,[43] is notable both for its contingency and its finality or certitude, the simple upward resolution of the opening dissonance (that flattened third – B natural – from the A flat minor cadence) to affirm the tonic once again and draw his own symphonic cycle to what would prove, unexpectedly, to be its final close.

Sibelius's state of mind before and after the symphony's premiere in Stockholm was so gravely overtaken by nervous anxiety that it prompted perhaps the greatest crisis of his married life: Aino, unable to withstand the stress and strain of the process leading up to the performance, gave him an ultimatum and refused to attend the concert. After his return, Sibelius sunk further into one of his periodic depressions: 'The "gloomy spectre" within will be the end of me. To escape it is not within my power,' he wrote on 5 April, adding the following day: 'this life in Death's realm [is] without life and without wonder. Aino has taken it hard and is gloomy – gloomy. Which then robs life of its joy when everything turns to sorrow.' By November things were looking even bleaker: 'one dies alone and then it is easier. Perhaps I must "descend from the mountain" – life is little other than waiting for death,' he wrote, confessing the following day that 'alcohol is the only friend, who never fails.'[44]

The completion of the Sixth and Seventh Symphonies had seemingly brought little sense of creative resolution or relief (and scarce little financial return), but they had consolidated the compositional course that Sibelius had felt compelled to pursue ever since his return from America. The following spring, however, brought a proposition of a different kind. On 27 May 1925 the director general of the Royal Theatre in Copenhagen, prompted by his Danish publisher Wilhelm Hansen, sent Sibelius a telegram asking whether he would be willing to write incidental music for a lavish production of Shakespeare's *The Tempest* directed by Johannes Poulsen and with costume designs by Kai Nielsen.[45] Sibelius wrote back immediately to accept the commission, naming his terms as a down payment of 3,000 Kroner plus 5 per cent of box office receipts and copyright ownership of his music. The invitation had appeared at a propitious moment. Exhausted by his work on the symphonies, Sibelius must have found the idea of a theatre score a far more flexible and attractive prospect, and it reignited his interest in writing shorter atmospheric pieces for the stage. Furthermore, the choice of subject-matter was particularly apt: his visit to Stratford-upon-Avon had been one of the highlights of his fourth trip to England, and Sibelius had always maintained a keen interest in Shakespeare's work, which he had first read at school in Swedish translation. In addition, *The Tempest* offered myriad opportunities for musical response, and its preoccupation with nature mysticism, elemental environmental forces, supernatural magic and creative agency appealed especially strongly to Sibelius's own artistic concerns: alongside *Timon of Athens*, he revealed, it was the Shakespearean drama to which he felt most attracted.

The schedule demanded by the Royal Theatre was challenging in the extreme: they initially requested the complete score by 1 August, barely two months after the initial approach. In the end Sibelius delivered the manuscript by the end of the following month, which still required a remarkable burst of activity. The planned premiere was postponed, however, partly because of the demands of other items in the theatre's season (including productions of Debussy's *Pelléas et Mélisande* and Stravinsky's *Petrushka*), and the first performance did not take place until 26 March the following year (1926). Even then, the conditions were far from ideal, and Sibelius carefully avoided attending the premiere in person. The Danish journalist Gunnar Hauch, who had been in touch with Sibelius throughout his work on the score, wrote diplomatically after the final rehearsals:

> The performance at the Royal Theatre will be without a doubt a great success. There were many extremely fine moments in the technical use of the stage, and the execution was supported by a particularly great effort. But it cannot be denied that the actors' powers at various points were not quite up to Shakespeare's heights. As a whole it seemed that the lyrical scenes worked least well because of the production's fragility. But the comic scenes came out well enough. And that the true aeon of the play's poetry and fantasy was heard so often is due to the music.[46]

Hauch's complimentary remarks about Sibelius's score offered only limited reassurance. The production ran for two weeks and received only mixed reviews (though critics were united in praising Sibelius's music). In more prosaic vein, Sibelius noted that the performances had earned less than two-thirds of what he had been promised. He nevertheless sought to maximize his income from the work: the music was used for a production of the play at the National Theatre in Helsinki the following year (featuring his daughter, Ruth Snellman, as Ariel, and with choreography by Maggie Gripenberg and striking set designs by Matti Warén), and he arranged selected movements from the complete score into two concert suites for orchestra, which were later published by Wilhelm Hansen.

The music for *The Tempest* was Sibelius's largest and most ambitious incidental score, comprising an overture and 34 individual numbers ranging from a few bars' underscore to complete dance movements and interludes. The music's range of mood and atmosphere is similarly diverse: Shakespeare's array of characters and settings, including the theatrical set piece of a wedding masque in Act IV, gave Sibelius ample opportunity to explore different musical idioms and styles. The most powerful moments

Matti Warén, costume design sketch for the Helsinki production of Shakespeare's *The Tempest*, 1927.

are those associated with nature and the environment. For both the Copenhagen and Helsinki productions, Shakespeare's opening scene, on-board ship, was omitted, and Sibelius's overture instead served as a dramatic curtain raiser invoking the howling sound of the gale and the crashing noise of the wreck that first brings Prince Ferdinand and his companions to Prospero's island. At one level, the overture is a remarkable piece of sonic onomatopoeia, the surging walls of sound that rise and fall through the piece vividly capturing the ocean's rolling waves and their irresistible tidal force. At another level, however, the overture is one of Sibelius's most sustained studies in acoustic frequency, almost like the 'sexdecim' sonority that he had first described in a letter to his uncle Pehr in 1882. The shrieking 'white noise' that evokes the storm is actually comprised of congruent blocks of whole-tone chords (that is, chords based on a scale built exclusively from whole-tone steps, rather than alternating tones and semitones), arranged in chromatic sequence. It is among Sibelius's strictest and most systematic intervallic matrices. The bass pedal notes that slowly grind away beneath the texture like a deep oceanic undertow are likewise assembled from resonant stacks of harmonic partials, so that the ultimate impression is of one single resonating block of sound that carries an overwhelming force. The other nature pictures in *The Tempest* music are much more elusive and seemingly immaterial, though no less effective: the gusts of wind that blow Ariel to and from the stage, for example, are little more than a Straussian upbeat, and the breathy sounds of the harmonium in 'The Chorus of the Winds' suggests a soft, murmuring sea breeze that lulls the shipwrecked crew into an enchanted sleep.

Elsewhere in the score, it was the potential for sketching musical character portraits that evidently attracted Sibelius. Ariel's five songs present a series of vignettes, from the glowing pastoral of 'Kom herhid paa gule Sand' ('Come unto these yellow sands') and the funereal shades of 'Fem Favne dybt har din Fader sin Bo' ('Full fathom five thy father lies') to the gentle saltarello of 'Med Bien drikker jeg af Krus' ('Where the bee sucks') in Act V. Miranda appears as a pale, Mélisande-like character in two numbers: first in Act I, where she is lulled to sleep by her father's charms, and then in an elegant entr'acte between Acts II and III, suggesting her graceful innocence and purity. Caliban meanwhile is represented as a cruel orientalist caricature of bestial savagery, an awkward echo of grotesque nineteenth-century colonialist assumptions about race and ethnic origin. Sibelius might have imagined aspects of himself through all of these different figures and roles within the drama, capable of both Caliban's debauchery and Ariel's restlessness. But it was Prospero, the island's wise and ancient magus, who may have appealed the most. Prospero appears in two highly contrasting movements: in the dignified, Purcellian entr'acte between Acts I and II, after he has first set in motion his secret plans to bring Ferdinand and Miranda together, and at the end of the play as he renounces his magical powers and returns, diminished, to his former mortal life at court. Sibelius sets Prospero's famous 'Ye elves of hills, of brooks' monologue from Act V as a powerful orchestral sequence that opens wracked with the towering storm and fury of Prospero's rage as he contemplates his vanquished foes. Then, as Prospero breaks his staff and casts his books into the depths, the music completely changes course and ends with a radiant hymn in B major, a solemn air or 'heavenly musicke' that brings reconciliation and forgiveness. It is this act of absolution, the renunciation of violence and the immersion in nature, which lies at the heart of Sibelius's later work.

That same trajectory – from storm-filled rage to a celestial B major – is traced also by Sibelius's final tone poem, *Tapiola*, which followed shortly after his music for *The Tempest*. Sibelius had received a telegram from Walter Damrosch, musical director of the New York Symphonic Orchestra, early in 1926, and the opportunity to renew ties with his

American connections (and earn American royalties) must have been a significant incentive. The work's title, referring to the domain of the forest god Tapio in the *Kalevala*, emerged only relatively gradually during the work's composition and was prompted by Sibelius's German publisher Breitkopf & Härtel (Aino suggested translating the title into English as 'The Wood', before they finally decided on 'The Forest').[47] Sibelius had nevertheless been thinking of a work inspired by the forest for some time. Ideas for *Tapiola* date back at least to the 1914–15 sketchbook that also contained motifs from the Fifth, Sixth and Seventh Symphonies, and images of trees and woodland feature prominently in his work elsewhere. As Tomi Mäkelä has observed, one of the ironies of the tone poem is that, despite its ostensibly Finnish subject-matter, much of the score was drafted while Sibelius was on holiday in Rome and Capri with his childhood friend Walter von Konow, the same companion who had once written of Sibelius's youthful fantasies of 'extraordinary beings in the gloomy forest depths'. Yet the atmospheric explanatory quatrain that the publisher placed at the head of the printed score ('Wide-spread they stand, the Northland's dusky forests / ancient, mysterious, brooding savage dreams; / Within them dwells the Forest's mighty God, / And wood-sprites in the gloom weave magic secrets') is closer to the German fairy-tale world of the Brothers Grimm (or to Tolkien) than to contemporary Finnish attitudes to their environment. For Finns, the forest has always seemed a place of beauty, solace, wonderment and shelter: the forest served as the nation's most important economic resource as well as a source of spiritual sustenance. Yet the wood that heaves its heavy boughs in much of *Tapiola* has an altogether darker, more sombre quality, which plays on a long-standing continental image of the forest as a site of wildness, fear, terror and panic.[48] A further irony is that the musical means Sibelius employed to evoke such primitive affective responses were among the most sophisticated and refined of any of his orchestral works. *Tapiola* is a miracle of motivic transformation and orchestral timbre, and its constantly shifting instrumental colours within a generally restrained spectrum produce remarkable flashes of light and shade that pinpoint particular pivotal moments of modal inflection and melodic articulation.

Tapiola has often been cited as the most obsessively unified of all Sibelius's works. Certainly, alongside even the Seventh Symphony, its preoccupation with a single modally based melodic phrase seems almost ruthless in its single-mindedness. But in stressing unity over variation, much of *Tapiola*'s vital detail is missed. The way in which the opening prelude sets up the very final cadence, for example, provides an overarching sense of symmetry that belies the iterative quality of much of the local detail. Similarly, the subtle shifts of phrase rhythm that shape the work's continual ebb and flow are deftly achieved: the transition from a broad four-bar rhythm to a tighter three-bar pattern at the end of the austere opening Allegro, for instance, increases the musical tension in preparation for the Mendelssohnian Scherzo that follows. And the weird illumination of the slow central section, with its luminous scoring for divided strings, rapidly gives way from an eerie near-silence to the sudden rage that prompts the reprise. But it is the storm sequence that erupts in the very final phase which most vividly captures the attention. Sibelius had been preoccupied with storm sounds from his First Symphony onwards, both as a powerful musical metaphor for political turbulence and as a purely acoustic resource. The storm sequence at the end of *Tapiola* functions in part as a cadenza. Structurally speaking, it is parenthetical to the principal tonal and motivic argument of the tone poem. Expressively, however, it is absolutely central: the vortex into which the whole piece retrospectively seems to have been drawn. It is tempting to speculate on Sibelius's reasons for introducing such a violently representational gesture into his music. Whether it was the sound of the sirocco gusting through the streets of Rome as he sketched the work,[49] or the memory of the brutal revolutionary winds that scoured the country during the civil war, is ultimately unclear. But Shakespeare's *Tempest* provides a more productive framework for hearing the storm as a creative matrix, a visionary white noise from which something more elemental may emerge. And as the allegory for a radically immersive form of agency, in which human subjectivity is entirely subordinated to the overwhelming motion of the environmental forces that envelop the listener, it is a powerful and moving testament.

Tapiola received its premiere at the Mecca Temple (now the New York City Center) on West 55th Street in Manhattan on 26 December 1926, and its conductor, Damrosch, wrote after the concert to congratulate Sibelius warmly on the work's success. After his troubles with the *Tempest* commission and its convoluted production history in Copenhagen, Sibelius must have been relieved that his new score had fared so well. Writing to Aino from Rome in April, he had claimed, 'I have forgotten the whole story with Tempest. The mistake was that I threw in my lot with Poulsen. He can be fine, but certainly the scenography – as you wrote – was terrible.'[50] *Tapiola*'s success must hence have come as a welcome surprise. At the start of the new year in 1927, Sibelius travelled first to Paris rather than Berlin for the winter season, where he listened to a good deal of contemporary French music. 'I believe I have never gone so often to concerts as here,' he reported in an interview with the journalist Anna Levertin for *Suomen kuvalehti*. 'There is enough here to last a lifetime. Even on my deathbed, I will be painfully curious to know in which direction music's development will lead.'[51] Clearly, then, Sibelius's energies had not been entirely drained by either *Tapiola* or his struggle with *The Tempest*. Sibelius had begun to think seriously about his next major work, the Eighth Symphony, almost as soon as the Seventh had received its Finnish premiere (under Kajanus's baton) on 25 April.

Such early confidence was seemingly well founded. Finland's decision to sign the Berne Convention on copyright in 1928 meant that for the first time Sibelius was guaranteed a regular income from the performance and publication of his work. Stung since the turn of the century by his experience with *Valse triste*, for which he had earned only a fraction of its true commercial value, the prospect of a fixed rate of return for his music was a significant financial step forward. And for much of spring 1928, while he was back for his usual winter season in Berlin, Sibelius reported that he was working well and making good progress with his new scores (including, presumably, the Eighth Symphony). His attention may have been distracted later that summer by an approach from the opera singer Wäinö Sola, who asked whether he might be interested in composing a work to celebrate the construction of a new hydroelectric power plant on the Imatra Rapids in eastern Finland.[52] The Imatra falls are located on the Vuoksi river at the point where the Finnish lake system drains through a single narrow channel into Lake Ladoga (after 1940 territorially part of Russia, but previously shared with Finland) and thence into the Baltic. They had long been a famous tourist site, visited by Catherine the Great (and reputedly also by Wagner), and the possibility of improved transport connections via the Helsinki–St Petersburg railway led to increasingly large visitor numbers in the area. The opening of the power station in 1929 was a significant international showcase for the young nation's political and economic aspirations, and so a group of the country's leading artistic figures, including Gallen-Kallela and Sibelius, were invited to visit the site to undertake a creative response. In the end, Sibelius chose not to participate in the initiative: perhaps, as Tomi Mäkelä argues, because he preferred not to become involved with such an environmentally interventionist scheme.[53] But he had rarely in any case responded to such site-specific programmatic sources of inspiration. Even in his most illustrative *Kalevala*-based works, such as *Pohjola's Daughter*, it was precisely the suggestive, impressionistic quality of the text that most strongly appealed. For Sibelius, in other words, such heavy-duty industrial displays of Finland's new-found independence only threatened to curtail his artistic freedom.

Tapiola was not the only work that moved within the orbit of Sibelius's *Tempest* project. At the very end of the decade, alongside his ongoing work on the Eighth Symphony, he finished three sets of miniatures: the five *Esquisses* (Sketches) for piano, op. 114, and two collections of pieces for violin and piano, opp. 115 and 116. Loose gatherings of little character pieces, strange stylized dances, whimsical improvisations and immersive nature episodes, they are much closer to Sibelius's music for Shakespeare's drama than to either the Seventh Symphony or *Tapiola*. The *Esquisses*, ostensibly Sibelius's final completed work for the instrument, have a particularly protracted publication history.[54] The pieces date from February 1929 but were published only in the 1970s: Sibelius repeatedly withdrew them before print. In a note to the Finnish publisher Westerlund from 1945, for example, he explained: 'I will not make them public now, because they (small pieces) are not exactly my province', adding that 'I do not want to release these until I have published my large work in the making.' Whether Sibelius was alluding to the Eighth Symphony, as late as 1945, is not certain. But when three of the pieces were performed for the first time, from manuscript, in 1932, the pianist Kosti Vehanen quoted Sibelius as suggesting that the pieces 'contain more of my thoughts and impulses than many of my larger works'.

The titles of the individual *Esquisses*, which Sibelius listed at various times in English, German and Finnish, certainly echo many of his recurrent preoccupations: the opening movement is headed 'Landschaft' or 'Maisema' (Landscape), and the second 'Talvikuva' or 'Winterbild' (Winter Scene). The most striking pieces are the two central numbers: 'Metsälampi' ('Forest Lake', or 'Der Teich' in German) revolves around a single modal collection that rises and falls in a series of waves, like a breeze passing across the surface of the water. 'Metsälaulu' ('Lied der Walde' or 'Forest Song') is one of Sibelius's enigmatic tree-works, a blankly obsessive arpeggiated texture that momentarily breaks into a brief melodic fragment before the wood closes in once more. The two sets of pieces for violin and piano are no less imaginative, despite Robert Layton's withering (and surely wrong-headed) assessment.[55] The opening of op. 115, 'Auf der Heide' (On the Heath), evokes a desolate, lonely figure in the landscape before turning to the ambient environmental sounds of the moor for solace. 'Ballade' has a strongly declamatory style that suggests a proud and dignified narrative, whereas the 'Humoresque' that follows has an attractively lopsided gait, like one of the dance sequences from *The Tempest*. The closing number, 'Die Glocken' (The Bells), which Sibelius subtitled 'Capricciettoʼ, is a whirling tarantella whose limpid textures and elusive harmony constantly threaten to slip out of the listener's grasp.[56] The grotesque rhythms and modal flavour of the 'Scène de danseʼ, which opens the op. 116 collection, again recalls the *Tempest* music, perhaps one of Caliban's episodes or the sailor's drunken revelry. The 'Danse caractéristique' is a swaying waltz that alternates delicate, nimble turns with more agitated and heavy-footed passages. The 'Rondeau romantiqueʼ, meanwhile, is a wistful, nostalgic glance back at a long-lost age of Biedermeier elegance and naivety. The coda's simple cadence is a touching adieu.

Innovative and original, as well as warmly retrospective, the opp. 115 and 116 pieces are a last, late tribute to Sibelius's own youthful ambitions as a violinist, and to the continuing vigour of his creative imagination. There is no sense here of a tired or exhausted mind, or of the struggles that would eventually result in the destruction of the Eighth Symphony. And Sibelius himself could scarcely have foreseen the apparent silence that would ultimately fall upon those years, or suspect that his life's work was now essentially complete. For a brief moment still, at the start of the new decade, he maintained his hopes of creating new work on a regular basis. But there would be no more symphonies, tone poems or theatre scores. As the political mood darkened, both at home and abroad, the familiar anxieties and insecurities would return once more.

Page from sketches of Sibelius's Eighth Symphony.

9

Quasi al niente

To review the final 27 years of Sibelius's life is to confront an intractable biographical dilemma. Critical accounts of artists' careers often rely on a series of assumptions, from the intimate link between their life and work to the idea of a creative continuity or unceasing rate of production, the expectation that the artist will remain active until the very end. For some figures who have enjoyed comparable longevity, that is demonstrably the case: Vaughan Williams, Stravinsky and Elliot Carter spring to mind. But others, such as Rossini and Sibelius, evidently did not. It is not that Sibelius stopped composing altogether: the evidence is that he was working on his Eighth Symphony well into the 1930s and most likely completed at least one full draft of the score, and he also undertook a number of important revisions of earlier works, including the *Lemminkäinen Legends*. Rather, the problem is how to interpret the fact that no new works appear after the start of that decade, and to ask what light his apparent retirement might then shed on his work retrospectively. The remaining years of his life also pose irresolvable issues of agency and intention: how far was Sibelius fully in control of his own actions, both public and private, and how might his musical decisions have been shaped by external events, whether artistic or political? The notion of a single, monolithic 'silence' has long since been challenged and debunked by Sibelius scholars, who have studied in detail the documentary legacy of his final years. But for many listeners, the absence of any major works to succeed either the Seventh Symphony or *Tapiola* remains one of the most urgent and compelling questions that hovers over his career, and it assumes especially grave consequences in any attempt to shape and conclude his biography.

The few works that did emerge from Sibelius's hand at the start of the 1930s were tied to particular circumstances or occasions. *Karjalan osa* (Karelia's Fate), a bellicose piece of patriotic militarism with words by Aleksis Nurminen, is especially unfortunate. On 7 July 1930 Sibelius and his wife attended a populist demonstration by the right-wing ultra-nationalist Lapua Movement, a radical splinter group associated with the victorious White side from the civil war that played on fears of the communist threat from across the Russian border. *Karjalan osa* was premiered at Sortvala later in September and taken up in various arrangements across the country. But the Lapua Movement's activism became increasingly confrontational, culminating in the kidnapping of the former president K. J. Ståhlberg in October 1930 and the violent disruption of a Social Democratic rally at Mäntsälä, 65 kilometres (40 mi.) from Helsinki, in 1932.[1] The group was subsequently banned, but the tensions between nationalists and more extreme right-wing factions would continue to grow throughout the remainder of the decade. Sibelius's short-lived association with the group is puzzling. 'Why', Tawaststjerna asks, 'did Sibelius allow himself to be drawn into this movement?' Although Sibelius's sympathies had clearly lain with the Whites during the civil war, his experience with the *March of the Jäger Battalion*, composed just as the storm clouds of the civil war were gathering in October 1917, should have alerted him to the possible consequences of any overt political alignment. Tawaststjerna suggests, reasonably enough, that Sibelius had initially believed that the movement's strong patriotic tendencies may have risen above the nation's language wars and appealed to a higher order of citizenship – although such hopes swiftly proved illusory in the wake of the movement's brutal direct action. More significantly, Tawaststjerna maintains that Sibelius had been persuaded to attend by Aino, who always held more right-wing views than her husband and was taking an increasingly public role in the family's affairs.[2] Certainly by May 1931 Sibelius was writing to Aino about his fears for the country's political outlook, and that he was 'taking valerian for the nerves and ear pain.'[3] *Karjalan osa* was the last time that he would ever permit himself to become so openly entangled in partisan political affairs.

A very different project that Sibelius completed during these years was the *Surusoitto* (Funeral Music) for Akseli Gallen-Kallela, who had died in Stockholm on 7 March 1931. The painter of the 1894 *Symposion* portrait, Gallen-Kallela was an exact contemporary of Sibelius and they had been close colleagues during the heady symbolist years of the 1890s.

Since the start of the century, however, they had grown apart, and the increasingly introspective and reflective quality of Sibelius's music from the 1910s was never part of Gallen-Kallela's more confidently extrovert and colourful outlook. Despite their personal differences, the two men shared so much common history that Gallen-Kallela's death must certainly have moved Sibelius. The two pieces that comprise the *Surusoitto*, Sibelius's only extended work for solo organ, have an eloquent solemnity that evokes a dignified mood of state ceremony. At the same time, Sibelius was irked by the attempts in some of Gallen-Kallela's obituaries to invoke hierarchical categories of class and social distinction: 'Nobility! All these deficiencies! Axel Gallén Kallela. There was the artist. The rest: lies. A farmer's son – "parvenu" – and so on.'[4] Like Sibelius, Gallen-Kallela had in fact been born into a middle-class Swedish-speaking family, and attempts to demonstrate the painter's 'authentic' Finnish roots provoked precisely the same fears and resistance as those that followed discussions of his own genealogy at the time of his fiftieth birthday in 1915. By the 1930s, however, such discussions of class, nationhood and language had gained a more ominous and belligerent tone.

Throughout the decade Sibelius was still committed to working on the score of the Eighth Symphony. Writing to Aino from Berlin in May 1931, for instance, his last trip abroad, he reported: 'the symphony makes excellent progress. I can and must get it done.'[5] At the end of the year he noted in his diary, 'worked on the Eighth Symphony and am young once more'.[6] The new symphony was eagerly awaited, not least by the emigré Russian conductor Serge Koussevitzky, music director of the Boston Symphony Orchestra, to whom he had promised the premiere. Granville Bantock also wrote at the end of 1932 about the possibility of staging Shakespeare's *The Tempest* at Covent Garden with Sibelius's music – and interest in the Eighth in England was particularly intense.[7] In September the following year (1933), Sibelius sent the first movement of the work to his copyist, Paul Voigt, indicating that the following section, a Largo, would continue without a break in the score, and that 'the whole piece will be roughly eight times as long as this.'[8] It seems inconceivable that Sibelius would have sent the materials, or indicated the scale of the remainder, without having completed at least a preliminary full draft of the score. Twelve months later, however, he wrote to his Danish publisher Wilhelm Hansen indicating that it was impossible to say when the symphony would be ready, but that he hoped the score would not have to wait too long.[9] Hansen wrote in 1935 offering Sibelius 3,000 marks for the symphony

– but Sibelius again demurred, and in 1937 wrote to explain that he could not commit himself to saying anything further regarding the work until there was more definitive news to report, a curious retreat if the score had existed in some complete form just a few years earlier. The symphony's ultimate fate remains a mystery, but Tawaststjerna's claim, based on his conversations with the family, that Sibelius had gathered together all of the manuscript sources and copies at some point in the early 1940s and burnt them still seems the most likely explanation. Exhaustive searches among Sibelius's *Nachlass* by both Kari Kilpeläinen and, more recently, Timo Virtanen have identified a number of smaller sketches that may have been associated with the project.[10] Although Nors S. Josephson has argued that these constitute a sufficient body of material to support some form of reconstruction,[11] Virtanen sensibly takes a more cautious approach. The three fleeting fragments of music that he has reassembled, and which have subsequently been recorded by John Storgårds and the BBC Philharmonic, offer a haunting glimpse of what could have been the Eighth's sound world. Based on this evidence alone, it appears that the work was a very different conception from either the Sixth or Seventh, and would have been much closer in character and mood to Sibelius's music for *The Tempest* and the *Esquisses*, op. 114. This difference would challenge one of the most widely accepted readings of Sibelius's later career, namely that the process of compression and formal elision developed in the Fifth, Sixth and Seventh Symphonies, culminating in *Tapiola*'s extreme monothematic concision, could only have been followed by silence, and that the non-appearance of the Eighth was in some senses a logical and inevitable outcome of that teleology. But everything that scholars now understand about Sibelius's working methods, and the numerous transformations and revisions that a piece would undergo before Sibelius ever established a firm definitive version of the score, means that the true shape and character of the Eighth will always remain unknown and out of reach. In other words, the final shape of Sibelius's musical career remains an open question.

The precise reasons why Sibelius destroyed virtually all trace of the Eighth also remain unclear. His crippling self-criticism is well documented, and his struggles with the Seventh Symphony suggest that such large-scale works had become increasingly burdensome and difficult. And it was already clear that Sibelius felt isolated from and alienated by trends in contemporary continental European music. Other writers have been less charitable. Vesa Sirén, for example, argues that since Sibelius had finally achieved a more long-lasting state of financial security in his sixties, as the copyright income from his music finally began to stabilize after Finland signed the Berne Convention and he was able to pay off the outstanding debts on the construction of his villa, Ainola, the commercial imperatives that had previously driven much of his compositional work were no longer so pressing and immediate. But that does not seem to have been the only motivation. Glenda Dawn Goss has advanced the most persuasive explanation: that Sibelius already felt 'out of his time', both stylistically and generationally, mythologized at home in Finland but regarded as an epigone by some of the more progressive voices in European musical criticism.[12] For that reason, there was no longer a creative space that the new symphony could realistically occupy. As Sibelius had already uncannily foreseen in his music for *Everyman*, by the end of the 1930s it seemed as though his artistic life had finished and that at any moment he would be summoned to account before a higher spiritual authority.

That bleak sense of time running out and of shifting political-aesthetic contexts is vividly reflected in his increasingly sparse diary entries and in his correspondence. As early as 1934, just as events were taking a perilously dark turn once again in Germany, he noted in his diary:

> Heard the concert from London on the Radio. Good will and good wishes from the English world. But – how little that is grasped here. Our rawness – which has increased to an alarming degree after they rejected all things Swedish – our self-satisfaction on account of these sporting feats. Uneducated, our understanding of civilization is still in its infancy – all stems from the language quarrel.[13]

Once again, Sibelius felt himself increasingly isolated at home because of his Swedish-Finnish background. And despite the earnest celebrations of his seventieth birthday in 1935, the new nation seemed keener to elevate the athletic triumphs of a younger generation of Finns such as Paavo Nurmi and Vile Ritola than to continue to promote the elderly artistic pioneers of an earlier age. The political tensions that had remained unresolved at the end of the civil war in 1918 erupted to the surface once again as Finland was swept up into a new global conflict after Soviet aircraft attacked the country on 30 November 1939. Finland's recent history of resistance to Russian aggression, and its long-standing cultural and economic ties across the Baltic, meant that the country was aligned with the German axis at the outbreak of the Second World War, and right-wing nationalist elements within the Finnish government were keen to promote closer links with the Nazi regime. The extent to which Sibelius was cognisant of such activities, and actively supported them, has been a difficult topic of debate in recent scholarship.[14] Timothy L. Jackson in particular has argued for greater scrutiny of Sibelius's personal contacts and actions during the war years, and suggested that the composer was eager to ingratiate himself with the Nazi regime at a time when he would have been well aware of the political implications.[15] Key elements of Jackson's case are Sibelius's acceptance of prestigious high-level German awards in 1935, including the Goethe medal, and his apparent refusal to provide an encomium or letter of endorsement for the Jewish composer Günther Raphael in 1934 (although they remained in correspondence after the end of the war). Furthermore, Jackson points to Sibelius's domestic link with individuals, including his son-in-law the banker Eero Ilves, responsible for managing the family's financial affairs, who maintained close contacts with the German authorities throughout the 1930s.

But the historical evidence is equivocal, and Jackson's claims have been energetically challenged, notably by Veijo Murtomäki.[16] Sibelius did not travel to Germany to receive either of his awards in person, for example, and his brief message to the Deutsche Sibelius Gesellschaft (German Sibelius Society), founded by the Nazis at the height of the war in 1942 for specifically propagandistic purposes, is revealing for what it does not say as much as for its actual contents. Sibelius's choice of language is restrained, expressing gratitude for German interest in his work and sending greetings 'from the Finnish forests . . . to Germany, the radiant *land of music* [emphasis in original]', pointedly stressing cultural rather than political kinship and seemingly making no reference to the current military situation.[17] Antti Vihinen, however, has drawn attention to the way that a crucial phrase from earlier in the text, 'in diesen Zeiten der Schicksalsgemeinschaft' ('in this time of common fate'), employs a form of wording that was especially promulgated by the Third Reich, and so the political status of the statement is not necessarily as neutral as it initially seems.[18] Jackson likewise condemns Sibelius's decision to be interviewed by an SS publicity officer, Anton Kloss, that same year. But to have refused to take part in the interview would have seemed a dangerously incendiary gesture, and Kloss's account of their meeting (and his report of what Sibelius may or may not have said during their conversation) must surely be treated with the greatest scepticism. The same is true then of the radio broadcast text. Much of Sibelius's correspondence from the latter phase of his life was ghostwritten, either by his secretary or by other members of his family (including Aino), and so it is uncertain exactly what Sibelius himself wrote or authorized. That is not in any way to seek to exonerate Sibelius or to avoid confronting other unpleasant historical truths. Rather, it is to acknowledge in this particularly precarious and unpredictable context that questions of agency and responsibility are not as straightforward or uncomplicated as they appear.

At worst, then, Sibelius can reasonably be accused of acting out of self-interest in seeking to distance himself from any overt party-political affiliation or support at a moment when virtually all sides in Finland appeared inimical and potentially hostile. This is certainly no uncluttered image of a national hero, as his early twentieth-century reception in Finland might have sought to claim, but a messier, complex and less courageous reality, more concerned with day-to-day pragmatics and self-survival than ideology. Though Sibelius evidently had to try and manage communication with German contacts carefully and sought to safeguard his royalty payments from the German performing rights society STAGMA, whose purse strings and activities were controlled by the Third Reich, he was also actively canvassed by other parties at various times during the conflict. A 1941 telegram signed by Arthur Judson, Executive Secretary of the New York Philharmonic Society and one of the most prominent artist-managers in the United States, for example, promised Sibelius an 'additional royalty payment of one thousand dollars in two instalments of five hundred dollars according to governmental regulations', offered by the Society as 'an expression of gratitude to you for the many great works it has been privileged to offer to its audiences'.[19] A further letter from the Society, dated 26 September 1945 as the conflict reached its close, recorded: 'We are deeply concerned with the state of your general welfare', and stated that 'we desire to do what we can to ease any situation in which you may find yourself a victim of dislocations resulting from war conditions.'[20]

Sibelius's diary entries from 1943, as the conflict began to turn, offer perhaps a more significant insight into his anxieties and preoccupations during the war years. On 9 August, for example, he wrote, 'lineage does not interest me. It belongs to the genealogists for whom it is their daily bread,' and less than a month later, on 6 September, he added, 'this primitive way of thinking – antisemitism etc. is something that at my age I *cannot* any longer condone. My upbringing and culture do not belong with these times. This [is] exceptionally poorly formulated.'[21] Tomi Mäkelä has rightly stressed the contingency of Sibelius's note, and underlined the difficulty of capturing its ironic tone accurately.[22] At certain points of his life, Sibelius certainly had been greatly exercised by questions of his lineage and family origin, and he maintained his belief that he was descended from a venerable Swedish-Finnish line. But at the same time he also believed that he was related to a Jewish family on his paternal grandfather's side, and so it is hard to imagine that he would ever have subscribed to any deeper form of religious or racial prejudice.[23] His sympathies were always essentially liberal-democratic and never authoritarian. But that outlook was not necessarily shared by other members of his family. On 19 September, for example, he wrote, 'in certain countries such as Germany the "Aryan paragraphs" are a necessity to get rid of the talented. Otherwise "racial purity" does not work. Aino quietly sad. She probably guesses one thing and another.'[24] Jackson reads Sibelius's diary as further evidence of the composer's connivance. 'Sibelius did not wake up one morning in September 1943 to suddenly perceive the evil of the Nazi regime's racial policies,' Jackson maintains:

> Rather, the diary suggests that he was grumbling about being compelled to fill in a new 'Fragebogen' demonstrating his racial purity so that he could move to a higher level in STAGMA – and be paid higher royalties . . . coming from an outside, perhaps better informed and more objective Finnish perspective, [Sibelius] did indeed become disgusted with the Nazis yet *still* took their money – as long as he possibly could.[25]

But Jackson's charge is as one-sided as the suggestion that Sibelius was completely apolitical and naive. Despite multiple invitations, Sibelius never, in fact, accommodated himself within any of the major musical institutions of the Third Reich, unlike his younger contemporary Yrjö Kilpinen, and his preoccupation with his family's economic well-being likely had its roots in his long-standing memory of the straitened circumstances of his own childhood and his experience of the First World War. Sibelius never wrote music for the Third Reich. Rather, the tensions, deflections and anxieties noted in his diary and correspondence show all too painfully how Finland's deep political divisions could reach within and fracture even the nation's closest families.

As Sibelius's case shows, music's relationship with the political environment of its creation and reception always remains complicated, confused and contradictory. The myth of music's supposedly transcendent, apolitical character is nothing more than an illusion. But it is vital to recognize that music also offers solace, comfort and a sense of community at even the darkest times. At the end of September 1943, for example, Sibelius was able to record a far more positive and uplifting experience:

> Heard the symphony [the Fifth] which Vaughan Williams dedicated to me. From Stockholm under [Malcolm] Sargent. Culture and rich humanity! Am deeply grateful. Vaughan Williams gives me more than anyone can recognize. A tragic fate has befallen my country. We must suffer brutalism and barbarity – and in any case go under.[26]

Vaughan Williams would write to Sibelius directly himself soon after the war ended, on 27 December 1946, to send New Year's greetings 'from one who admires and loves your music', signing off his letter by adding: 'Please give us the 8th Symphony soon!' But by the late 1940s virtually all trace of the Eighth Symphony had disappeared, and Sibelius had finally given up work on the score. Vaughan Williams would send another greeting on 3 December 1950, five days before Sibelius's 85th birthday, in 'affection and reverence', and stating, 'you have lit a candle which shall never be put out.'[27] By this point, however, Sibelius's musical light was beginning to fade. The critical reception of his work would suffer a slump in the 1950s and '60s, provoked in part by Theodor Adorno's 1938 critique 'Glosse über Sibelius', as the post-war musical avant-garde turned away from ideologically suspect metaphors of nature, environment and race and sought alternative historical legacies and creative precursors.[28] For the Finnish composers who followed Sibelius, such as Einojuhani Rautavaara and Aulis Sallinen, his legacy would prove a heavy burden, a weight or 'shadow' (to borrow Einar Englund's term) that they would struggle to lift. But the wider popularity of his music, especially elsewhere across Scandinavia, the United Kingdom and North America, remained undimmed. At the time of his death, from a sudden cerebral haemorrhage on 20 September 1957, aged 91, the immense significance and value of Sibelius's creative output was beyond question. His memorial service

Sibelius's funeral cortège, 30 September 1957.

at the solemn Tuomiokirkko (Lutheran Cathedral) in central Helsinki was a national event, comparable to that which might have been held for a major head of state: few other artists have been accorded such ceremony or esteem. Sibelius hence did not live to see the renewal of interest in his work from a younger generation of composers, from Per Nørgård and Peter Maxwell Davies to John Adams, Tristan Murail, Thomas Adès and Anna Þorvaldsdóttir. Acclaimed by minimalists in North America and spectralists in France, the imaginative formal innovation of his work and its sheer sonorous affect has been increasingly recognized and admired (and equally emulated by composers of film scores and nature documentary soundtracks). Nor would Sibelius witness the unparalleled rise of Finland as a world-leading centre of musical performance and artistic direction, and watch as a seemingly endless parade of ferociously gifted conductors, from Paavo Berglund and Jorma Panula to Esa-Pekka Salonen, Sakari Oramo, Osmo Vänskä and Susanna Mälkki, went to hold prestigious positions with orchestras and ensembles across the globe. Without the leadership of Sibelius and his contemporaries, it is hard to imagine how such a transformative group of musicians could ever have emerged.

As should now be apparent, there is no single explanation for why Sibelius stopped composing in his final decade. Goss's carefully assessed reasons for his withdrawal are the most persuasive: he was petrified, both in the sense of being terrified of further critical rejection, and also as a figure monumentalized during his own lifetime, an icon who had literally been turned to stone in the form of Wäinö Aaltonen's blank, silent and expressionless bust.[29] But the more prosaic fact is that Sibelius himself had no reason to foresee his own longevity. The early death of his father and the loss of his brother Christian in 1922, as well as his own long-standing hypochondria, was sufficient reason for him to suspect that he would not live far into his sixties, precisely the time at which he finished *Tapiola* and *The Tempest*. And perhaps he felt, rightly or wrongly, that his creative work was done.

Silence alone, however, is no way to remember Sibelius, and it is a poor reflection of his composition and his biography. Having written, almost half a century earlier, that his soul 'hungers and thirsts for music', Sibelius could ultimately have recognized that his life had been full of sound, warmth and humanity, even at its most difficult and seemingly isolated moments. Much better than lamenting the loss of an Eighth Symphony that can never be recovered is to celebrate that life, and applaud a musical legacy of unparalleled richness, depth, range and diversity: not only the symphonies and tone poems, but the piano miniatures, songs, chamber works and (especially) the theatre music. As Vaughan Williams rightly sensed, it is the most moving of legacies, and a generous gift.

SELECT DISCOGRAPHY

Sibelius has always been well served on disc. Although he never recorded any of his own works himself (with the exception of a single moving performance of the *Andante Festivo* for strings for radio broadcast in 1939), he benefited during his lifetime from the advocacy of a number of high-profile musicians, many of whom consulted the composer closely. Since his death in 1957, Sibelius's music has formed a substantial and continually growing part of the recording catalogue, and a full listing would require a far longer and more detailed study than is possible here.[1] The following discography is hence only a very partial and preliminary selection, intended principally as a starting point for comparison and further research. Catalogue numbers were correct at the time of writing but may be subject to change.

An obvious place to begin is the *Sibelius Edition* issued by Bis (Bis CD 1900–1936). Comprising almost seventy discs organized into thirteen volumes, the project aims to record every single note written by the composer and is a remarkable achievement, including premiere recordings of many hitherto unknown works as well as early versions of some familiar scores (including *En saga*, the *Lemminkäinen Legends*, *The Oceanides* and the Fifth Symphony). Many of the performances are outstanding: especially notable are the interpretations by Folke Gräsbeck, Anne Sofie von Otter, and Osmo Vänskä and the Lahti Symphony Orchestra. The accompanying booklet essays by Andrew Barnett are a major contribution in their own right, and contain much ground-breaking information on the origin, chronology and genesis of Sibelius's works.

The seven-disc set entitled *Sibelius: Historical Recordings and Rarities, 1928–1948* (Warner Classics 2564 605317) is equally valuable and contains recordings by many of Sibelius's colleagues and contemporaries, including Robert Kajanus, Thomas Beecham, Georg Schnéevoigt, Serge Koussevitzky, Adrian Boult, Armas Järnefelt, the Budapest String Quartet, Emil Telmányi and Gerald Moore, Marian Anderson and Kosti Vehanen. The repertoire is wide ranging, and includes the seven symphonies, many of the tone poems, songs and chamber works.

Symphonies and Tone Poems

Recordings from the generation following those who had known Sibelius personally give a strong indication of the rapid international dissemination of his work. Notable collections (not all complete) include Herbert von Karajan and the Berlin Philharmonic (DG 825 646 336 197); Eugen Ormandy and the Philadelphia Orchestra (RCA 888 751 085 824); Leonard Bernstein and the Vienna Philharmonic (DG 00289 477 989785); and John Barbirolli and the Hallé Orchestra (Warner Classics 984 706 2). Colin Davis's first symphony cycle, with the Boston Symphony Orchestra, is in many respects his finest (Decca 478 3696), comparable with Alexander Gibson and the Royal Scottish National Orchestra (Chandos 6559). Paavo Berglund's recordings with the Bournemouth Symphony (EMI 973 600 25) are of particular value because of his detailed engagement with the manuscript sources; Berglund's later cycle with the Chamber Orchestra of Europe (Finlandia 3984 23389 2) was genuinely revolutionary in its approach to a more pared-back, transparent sound, the result of working with a smaller ensemble (which may have been consistent with Sibelius's own practice). Vladimir Ashkenazy with the Philharmonia (Decca 473 590 2) offers a very different sound world and approach, as does Lorin Maazel with the Vienna Philharmonic (Decca London 430 778 2). More recently, Herbert Blomstedt's cycle with the San Francisco Symphony (Decca 475 7677) is characteristically sensitive and thoughtful, and preferable to Neeme Järvi's account with the Gothenburg Symphony (DG 477 5688). Of Simon Rattle's two cycles, the first, with the City of Birmingham Symphony Orchestra but with a striking account of the Fifth with the Philharmonia (EMI 5 00753 2), has greater freshness and vitality than his second, with the Berlin Philharmonic (BPHR 150073), despite many beautiful incidental moments.

A younger generation of Nordic conductors, many of whom studied at the Sibelius Academy, have begun to create a substantial new legacy of interpretations. Alongside Vänskä, the most compelling recordings are by Jukka-Pekka Saraste (RCA 1 94397 04812 4), Sakari Oramo's stirring cycle with the City of Birmingham Symphony Orchestra (Erato 25646 6279 5) and John Storgårds with the BBC Philharmonic (Chandos 10809). Outside Finland, Maris Janssons and the Oslo Philharmonic sadly never completed a full cycle (EMI 6971802); Petri Sakari and the Iceland Symphony Orchestra (Naxos 8505179) present a suitably stirring reading. Paavo Järvi's cycle with the Orchestre de Paris marked a significant landmark in Sibelius's reception in France (RCA 19075924512), and Pietari Inkinen has recorded the complete symphonies twice: once in New Zealand (Naxos 8572305/2227 and 2705) and later (more spaciously) in Japan (Naxos 272869). The fact that, to date, no major record label has released a cycle directed by a female conductor highlights the industry's long-standing inequalities.

Theatre Music

Sibelius's theatre scores have experienced a highly mixed fate on record. Some numbers, pre-eminently *Valse triste* from his music for Arvid Järnefelt's *Kuolema*, are among his most popular and frequently recorded works: a complete listing would require book-length discussion. Both *Pelléas et Mélisande* and the *King Christian II* music have likewise fared well, especially given the popularity of the concert suites that Sibelius prepared from the full scores. Notable recordings include those by Beecham (EMI 509 69227), Leopold Stokowski's 1953 account with the Helsinki Philharmonic (Guild 2341), Karajan and the Berlin Philharmonic (DG 410 026 2) and Berglund with the Bournemouth Symphony Orchestra (Warner Classics 569 77358). More recent recordings include Leif Segerstam and the Turku Philharmonic (Naxos 8573301), Petri Sakari and the Iceland Symphony Orchestra (Chandos 9158) and Paavo Järvi and the Stockholm Philharmonic (Virgin 7 24354 54932), whose performance also includes a rare recording of Sibelius's sole opera, *Jungfrun i Tornet* (The Maiden in the Tower).

Sibelius's other theatre works have not succeeded in establishing an equivalent place in the catalogue. The challenges of recording complete scores, which often required extensive dialogue or passages of melodrama (music and spoken voice), have not proved commercially attractive, and it is only relatively recently that the full range of Sibelius's approach to writing for the theatre has become available on record. Osmo Vänskä has done a tremendous amount to promote Sibelius's theatre scores as part of his project with the Bis complete edition. Other notable recordings include Leif Segerstam's account of *Swanwhite*, *Ödlan* (The Lizard) and *Ett ensămt skidspår* (A Lonely Ski Trail) with the Turku Philharmonic (Naxos 857 3341), as well as a striking performance of *Jokamies* ('Everyman', Naxos 8373340). *The Tempest* music has been rather more popular, thanks again to the success of Sibelius's concert suites and the appeal of Shakespeare's text. Early recordings by Beecham (EMI D-152 474) and by Sibelius's son-in-law Jussi Jalas with the Hungarian Philharmonic (Decca 482 3311) have been followed by a number of more recent accounts: Saraste's recording of the complete score with the Finnish Radio Symphony Orchestra is especially compelling (Ondine 813-2). Special mention should also be made of the recording of the complete scores for the 1893 Karelia music and 1899 Press Celebrations by Tuomas Ollilla and the Tampere Philharmonic Choir and Orchestra (Ondine 913-2), which has helped to place some of Sibelius's most familiar works in their original dramatic context.

Violin Concerto

The history of recordings of the Violin Concerto is not merely an account of the reception of one of Sibelius's best-loved scores but a vivid reflection of the way in which the style and technique of twentieth-century string playing has changed and transformed. Given its overwhelming popularity among soloists today, it is surprising that the concerto took so long before it became a regular repertoire item. As Richard S. Ginell has noted,[2] Heifetz's first recording with Beecham from 1935 may have set an impossibly high barrier for other contemporary players (EMI 61591), and it is finer than his second performance from Chicago (RCA 82876 66372 2). Isaac Stern also recorded the work twice, once with Beecham (Sony 45956) and then with Ormandy (Sony 66829), and the performances provide a fascinating comparison of temperament and approach alongside David Oistrakh (Testament 1032) and Itzhak Perlman (two versions: RCA 82876 59419 2 and EMI 5 62590 2). Of late twentieth-century accounts, Anne-Sophie Mutter is outstanding (DG 447 8952), as is Joshua Bell with Salonen and the Los Angeles Philharmonic (Sony 65949). Leonidas Kavakos's heavily characterful reading with Vänskä (Bis 500) is notable especially for including the premiere recording of the first version of the concerto, providing detailed insights into Sibelius's compositional process and revisions.

Voces Intimae

Sibelius's sole mature string quartet has frequently proved a challenge for ensembles: the dense scoring and intensive motivic texture remain difficult to realize effectively both in live performance and in recording. A pair of pioneering accounts from the 1950s began to make a more persuasive case for the work and have since been reissued: the Griller String Quartet from Dutton (CDBP9801) and the Budapest Quartet on Urania (WS121376). Although the work has since enjoyed the advocacy of international ensembles such as the Guarneri (Decca 426 286-2), Fitzwilliam (Decca 442 9486) and Gabrieli quartets (Chandos 8742), it has been best served by Finnish groups: the Sibelius Academy Quartet has recorded a fine set of all of the Sibelius quartets, including his early works (Finlandia FACD209), as have the Tempera Quartet (Bis CD-1466). Of North American quartets, the Daedalus on Bridge (BCD9202) are preferable to the Emersons (DG B0006340-02).

Piano Music and Chamber Works

The piano may have been Sibelius's working instrument, and his early exposure during his student years to players of the calibre of Busoni must surely have brought home an acute awareness of his own technical limitations as a performer. But Sibelius wrote for the piano throughout his career, including some of his very last published works. Wilhelm Kempff's early visits to Ainola were especially valued, but he sadly never committed any of Sibelius's music to disc; nor did other contemporary players such as Emil Gilels or Wilhelm Backhaus. One of the earliest collections of Sibelius's piano works was recorded by the Finnish pianist Cyril Szalkiewicz (Finlandia FA 802), but far more influential has been Glenn Gould's 1977 recording of the op. 67 sonatinas and *Kyllikki* (Sony Classical 86971 48412). Of more recent performances, the monumental cycle of complete works by Erik T. Tawaststjerna (Bis CD-153/367/195/196) is especially valuable, as is Annette Servadei's pioneering set for Alto (ALC5001), Håvard Gimse's for Naxos (85538 99/8554808/8554814/8555363/8555853) and Folke Gräsbeck's volume for the Bis *Sibelius Edition*. Other notable anthologies include two for Sony Classical by Janne Mertanen (888751614222) and Leif Ove Andsnes (88985408502), which offer sharply contrasting interpretations of Sibelius's approach to the instrument.

If Sibelius's piano works have been comparatively neglected in the catalogue, his chamber works have fared little better. Even though the violin was Sibelius's first instrument, and the one to which he always felt musically and emotionally closest, his violin works have only recently begun to attract sustained interpretative attention, notably from players such as Nils-Erik Sparf and Bengt Forsberg (part of the Bis *Sibelius Edition*) and Pekka Kuusisto and Heini Kärkkäinen (Ondine 1046-2). Popular individual numbers such as the *Romance* in F, op. 78, no. 2, secured a relatively early place in the repertoire – it was recorded by Carl Nielsen's son-in-law, Emil Telmányi, and Gerald Moore as early as 1936 (Warner Classics 2564 605317) – but the sparkling *Sonatina*, op. 80, closely contemporary with the Fifth Symphony (with which it shares musical material), remains relatively lightly covered, despite the recording by Ruggiero Ricci and Sylvia Rabinof (RR 022-23).

Sibelius's single large-scale work for cello and piano, *Malinconia,* has gained the advocacy of Heinrich Schiff and Elisabeth Leonskaja (Philips 412 732-1) and Rohan de Saram and Benjamin Frith (First Hand FHR 034).

Songs and Choral Music

Although Sibelius is best known internationally as an orchestral composer, his songs constitute a major part of his output, and were an important part of his early reception, both domestically and overseas. The fact that the development of gramophone recording technology slightly post-dated the end of Aino Ackté's professional career is a considerable regret. However, the other pre-eminent interpreter of Sibelius's vocal works during his lifetime, Ida Ekman (1875–1942), made one of the very first commercial recordings of any of Sibelius's works with her husband, Karl Ekman, in 1904–6 (Artie AMCD 1010), comprising songs from opp. 17, 36, 37 and 50. Understandably, Nordic singers initially took the lead in performing and recording Sibelius's songs, with important accounts from the 1950s by Kirsten Flagstad with Waldemar Alme (Simax PSC 1824), Jussi Björling wth Frederick Schauwecker (RCA 82876 53379-2), and Kim Borg with Erik Werba (DG 477 661-2GM), and later Birgit Nilsson with Janos Solyóm (Bis CD15). Of a slightly younger twentieth-century generation, Jorma Hynninen with Ralf Gothóni (Finlandia 4509-95848-2) and Tom Krause with Irwin Gage (Decca 478 860-9DB4) are both outstanding: Krause's later recordings with Gustav Djupsjöbacka are also exceptionally fine (Finlandia 4509 99320-2). Elisabeth Schwarzkopf's recordings with Gerald Moore and Cyril Szalkiewicz from the 1950s are of considerable historical interest (EMI 3 56526-2 and Warner Classics 2564 602605), and point to the popularity of Sibelius's songs in Germany. Since then, Sibelius's vocal works have become a familiar part of the lieder repertory. Notable collections include those by Anne Sofie von Otter with Bengt Forsberg (Bis CD 1918-20), Barbara Bonney with Antonio Pappano (DG 461 724-2), Karita Mattila with Ilmo Ranta (Ondine ODE 252-2D) and Barbara Hendricks with Roland Pöntinen (EMI 3 88701-2), among many others.

If Sibelius's songs have long held a strong position in the catalogue, the same cannot be said for his choral music, which has not thus far secured strong representation outside the Nordic countries. That is a pity, both given the quality of the repertoire (notably the original version of *Rakastava*), and also because of the role that particular numbers, especially from the op. 18 set, played in advancing Sibelius's reputation, notably during the early part of his career. Two recordings by the University of Helsinki Male Voice Choir, Ylioppilaskunnan Laulajat (YL), an ensemble historically associated with Sibelius himself, have been issued by Finlandia (0927 49774-2) and Bis (Bis CD 1930-32); also recommended are the performances by the Estonian Philharmonic Chamber Choir (Ondine 1260-2D) and the aptly named Tapiola Chamber Choir (Finlandia 0630-19054-2).

REFERENCES

Introduction

1 Fabian Dahlström, ed., *Jean Sibelius: Dagbok 1909–1944* (Helsinki and Stockholm, 2005), p. 41.
2 Autograph manuscript, dated 30 September 1899, National Archives of Finland, Sibelius Family Collection, Kansio 20.
3 Diary entry dated 14 November 1910, quoted in Dahlström, ed., *Sibelius: Dagbok*, p. 60.
4 See Glenda Dawn Goss, *Jean Sibelius and Olin Downes: Friendship, Music, Criticism* (Boston, MA, 1995); and Byron Adams, '"Thor's Hammer": Sibelius and British Music Critics, 1905–1957', in *Jean Sibelius and His World*, ed. Daniel M. Grimley (Princeton, NJ, 2011), pp. 125–57.
5 Undated note, December 1911. Quoted in Dahlström, ed., *Sibelius: Dagbok*, p. 106.
6 Interview in *Helsingin Sanomat*, no. 143, 26 June 1910, pp. 6–7 (p. 6). Quoted in Erik Tawaststjerna, *Sibelius*, vol. III: *1914–1957*, trans. Robert Layton (London, 1997), p. 11.
7 Diary entry, 16 February 1915, quoted ibid., p. 35.
8 Diary entries, dated 14 June and 15 August 1910. Quoted in Dahlström, ed., *Sibelius: Dagbok*, pp. 46 and 51.

1 Country and City

1 Finland remains officially a bilingual country, and place names are given in both their Finnish and Swedish forms, reflecting historical and contemporary usage.
2 Glenda Dawn Goss, ed., *Sibelius: Hämeenlinna Letters: Scenes from a Musical Life, 1874–1895. Jean Sibelius Ungdomsbrev* (Esbo/Espoo, 1997), p. 10.
3 Erik Tawaststjerna, *Sibelius*, vol. I: *1865–1905*, trans. Robert Layton (London, 1976), pp. 2–10.
4 Ibid., p. 13.
5 Andrew Barnett, *Sibelius* (New Haven, CT, 2007), p. 3.
6 Glenda Dawn Goss, *Sibelius: A Composer's Life and the Awakening of Finland* (Chicago, IL, 2009), pp. 21–2.

7 Goss, ed., *Hämeenlinna Letters*, p. 18.
8 Goss, *Sibelius*, p. 43.
9 Goss, ed., *Hämeenlinna Letters*, p. 56.
10 Tawastjerna, *Sibelius*, vol. I, p. 15
11 Ibid., p. 18.
12 Goss, ed., *Hämeenlinna Letters*, p. 54.
13 Letter to Pehr Sibelius, dated 24 October 1888. Quoted in Goss, ed., *Hämeenlinna Letters*, pp. 98–9. On the history of music, sound and electromagnetism, see, for example, Veit Erlmann, *Reason and Resonance: A History of Modern Aurality* (New York, 2010), pp. 190–93. The actual chord in Sibelius's letter does not appear in any of his later works, although similar sonorities can be found: one example includes the start of the main section of the Allegro in the first movement of the Sixth Symphony (bb. 64–5).
14 A. MacCallum Scott, *Through Finland to St Petersburg* (London, 1908), p. 69.
15 Tomi Mäkelä, *Fredrik Pacius: kompositör i Finland* (Helsinki, 2009), pp. 66–70.
16 Goss, ed., *Hämeenlinna Letters*, p. 71.
17 For a helpful overview of Wegelius's life and work, see 'Martin Wegelius', *375 Humanists*, https://375humanistia.helsinki.fi, accessed 29 December 2019.
18 Letter, dated 28 October 1885, quoted in Goss, ed., *Hämeenlinna Letters*, p. 80.
19 Letter, dated 6 July 1889, quoted ibid., p. 105.

2 Young Romantics

1 Erik Tawaststjerna, *Sibelius*, vol. I: *1865–1905*, trans. Robert Layton (London, 1976), p. 54.
2 Glenda Dawn Goss, ed., *Hämeenlinna Letters: Scenes from a Musical Life, 1874–1895. Jean Sibelius Ungdomsbrev* (Esbo, 1997), pp. 107–8.
3 Adolf Paul, *En bok on en Människa*, chapter XIV, trans. Annika Lindskog, in *Jean Sibelius and His World*, ed. Daniel M Grimley (Princeton, NJ, 2011), pp. 307–14 (pp. 310–11).
4 Tawaststjerna, *Sibelius*, vol. I, p. 57. The Latin text is a slightly mangled quotation from Horace's *Odes* 2.10, and should read 'Non, si male nunc, olim sic erit', which loosely translated means: 'things may seem bad now, but they will not always be so.' Sibelius's fondness for (mis)quoting bits of his schoolboy Latin is a frequent feature of his diary entries.
5 Andrew Barnett, *Sibelius* (New Haven, CT, 2007), p. 56.
6 The translation is from Andrew Barnett's excellent liner notes for the Bis recording of Kajanus's music, by the Lahti Symphony Orchestra conducted by Osmo Vänskä (BIS CD 1223, 2004), p. 31.
7 Tawaststjerna, *Sibelius*, vol. I, pp. 75 and 77.
8 Ibid., p. 76.
9 Glenda Dawn Goss, 'A Backdrop for Young Sibelius: The Intellectual Genesis of the *Kullervo* Symphony', *Nineteenth-century Music*, XXVII/1 (Summer 2003), pp. 48–73.

10 Barnett, *Sibelius*, pp. 66–7.
11 Tawaststjerna, *Sibelius*, vol. 1, p. 97.
12 See, for example, his letter to Rosa Newmarch, dated 8 February 1906, quoted in Philip Ross Bullock, *The Correspondence of Jean Sibelius and Rosa Newmarch, 1906–1939* (Woodbridge, 2011), p. 55, in which he insisted that the tunes in his music were entirely of his own creation.
13 'På morgonen fick jag af Krohn en "luettelo" öfver alla de runosångare han känner. Jag gick till honom och bad om det. Äfven utstakade vi en reseplan.' Quoted in SuviSirkku Talas, ed., *Tulen synty: Aino ja Jean Sibeliuksen Kirjeenvaihtoa, 1892–1904* (Helsinki, 2003), p. 17. Krohn (1863–1933) later held the first permanent chair in folklore research at the University of Helsinki and was president of the Finnish Literature Society from 1917.
14 'Tillsvidare har jag ej fåt höra annat än tvenne sångare och de äfven icke om Kalevala. De hafva dels dött dels flyttat bort. Just för en stund sedan kom jag hit från ett fot tur (1 mil) till en som var bortrest. Bättre lycka hoppas jag i nästa by Tschokki.' Letter dated Korpiselkä, 20 July 1892, quoted in *Tulen synty*, pp. 20–21. Tjokki is now in Russian territory, close to the northwestern shore of Lake Ladoga.
15 Glenda Dawn Goss, *Sibelius: A Composer's Life and the Awakening of Finland* (Chicago, IL, 2009), p. 130.
16 Quoted in Erik Tawaststjerna, *Jean Sibelius: Åren 1865–1893*, revd Gitta Henning (Stockholm, 1992), p. 195.
17 Quoted ibid., pp. 181–2.
18 Matti Huttunen, 'The National Composer and the Idea of Finnishness: Sibelius and the Formation of Finnish Musical Style', in *The Cambridge Companion to Sibelius*, ed. Daniel M. Grimley, pp. 7–21 (p. 8).
19 Tawaststjerna, *Sibelius*, vol. 1, p. 107.
20 Glenda Dawn Goss, Preface, *Sibelius: Kullervo, op. 7* (Wiesbaden, 2005), pp. xi–xviii (p. xvi).

3 Sagas, Swans and Symphonic Dreams

1 Tomi Mäkelä, *Jean Sibelius*, trans. Steven Lindberg (Woodbridge, 2011), pp. 102–4.
2 Santeri Levas, *Jean Sibelius* (Helsinki, 1971), p. 139, quoted and trans. in Tuija Wicklund, 'Jean Sibelius's *En saga* and Its Two Versions: Genesis, Reception, Edition, and Form', Sibelius Academy, Helsinki, 2014, p. 48.
3 Erik Tawaststjerna, *Sibelius*, vol. 1: *1865–1905*, trans. Robert Layton (London, 1976), p. 130.
4 Glenda Dawn Goss, *Sibelius: A Composer's Life and the Awakening of Finland* (Chicago, IL, 2009), pp. 175–6.
5 The principal changes involved in the revision are summarized in Wicklund, 'Jean Sibelius's *En saga*', pp. 19–20.
6 Anna-Maria von Bonsdorff, 'Correspondences: Jean Sibelius in a Forest of Image and Myth', in *Sibelius and the World of Art*, ed. von Bonsdorff (Helsinki, 2014), pp. 81–127 (pp. 102–3).
7 A detailed description of the evening, and of Sibelius's music, is given in Goss, *Sibelius*, pp. 150ff.
8 Tawaststjerna, *Sibelius*, vol. 1, p. 147.

9 On Porthan and early Finnish accounts of runic singing, see Anna Leena Siikala, 'Body, Performance, and Agency in Kalevala Rune-singing', *Oral Tradition*, XV/2 (2000), pp. 255–78.
10 Jouni Kaipinen, liner notes for Ondine CD ODE 913–2, trans. William Moore (1998), pp. 4–9 (p. 7).
11 SuviSirkku Talas, ed., *Tulen synty: Aino ja Jean Sibeliuksen Kirjeenvaihtoa, 1892–1904* (Helsinki, 2003), p. 36.
12 Ibid., p. 47.
13 Tawaststjerna, *Sibelius*, vol. I, p. 155.
14 Talas, ed., *Tulen synty*, p. 84.
15 Elias Lönnrot, *The Kalevala*, trans. Eino Friberg, ed. George C. Schoolfield (Helsinki, 1988), Runo 29, lines 149–50 and 167–70 (p. 243).
16 Tuija Wicklund, 'Suomi herää', in *Jokainen nuotti pitää elää: Jean Sibeliuksen vuosikymmenet musiikissa/One Must Live Every Note: Jean Sibelius's Decades in Music*, ed. Timo Virtanen (Helsinki, 2015), pp. 53–73 (p. 65).
17 *Kalevala*, Runo 14, lines 431–2 [p. 126].
18 Fabian Dahlström, ed., *Jean Sibelius: Dagbok, 1909–1944* (Helsinki, 2005), p. 339.
19 See Martti Laitinen, 'Why Kajanus Went to St Petersburg', in *Sibelius in the Old and New World: Aspects of His Music, Its Interpretation, and Reception*, ed. Timothy L. Jackson, Veijo Murtomäki, Colin Davis and Timo Virtanen (Frankfurt, 2010), pp. 148–57.
20 Andrew Barnett, *Sibelius* (New Haven, CT, 2007), p. 115.
21 Erik Tawaststjerna, *Sibelius*, vol. II: *1904–1914*, trans. Robert Layton (London, 1986), p. 31.
22 Dahlström, *Dagbok*, 494; on 'De två systrarna', see Timo Virtanen, 'Introduction', *Jean Sibelius: Symphony no. 1* (Wiesbaden, 2008), pp. ix–xviii.
23 Virtanen, 'Introduction'.
24 Barnett, *Sibelius*, p. 135.
25 Stephen Downes, 'Pastoral Idylls, Erotic Anxieties and Heroic Subjectivities in Sibelius's *Lemminkäinen and the Maidens of the Island* and First Two Symphonies', in *The Cambridge Companion to Sibelius*, ed. Daniel M. Grimley (Cambridge, 2004), pp. 35–48 (p. 38).
26 Eero Tarasti, *Myth and Music: A Semiotic Approach to the Aesthetics of Myth in Music, especially that of Wagner, Sibelius and Stravinsky* (The Hague, 1979), p. 83.
27 Goss, *Sibelius*, pp. 256–62.
28 James Hepokoski, 'Finlandia Awakens', in *The Cambridge Companion to Sibelius*, ed. Grimley, pp. 81–94 (p. 94).

4 New Dawns

1 Tomi Mäkelä has argued that the connection between *Malinconia* and Kirsti's death is unlikely, given Sibelius's businesslike correspondence with his wife after he had finished the manuscript (*Jean Sibelius*, trans. Steven Lindberg (Woodbridge, 2011), p. 295), but the notion that Sibelius may have felt freer to express his feelings musically than verbally is not inconsistent with his work elsewhere.

2 For detailed discussion of Franco-Finnish relations and the Expositions, see Helena Tyrväinen, 'Les Finlandais dans les programmes musicaux des Expositions universelles de Paris en 1889 et 1900', *Musiikkitiede*, 1–2 (1994), pp. 22–74; and 'Sibelius at the Paris Universal Exposition of 1900', in *Sibelius Forum: Proceedings from the Second International Jean Sibelius Conference, Helsinki, November 25–29, 1995*, ed. Veijo Murtomäki, Kari Kilpeläinen and Risto Väisänen (Helsinki, 1998), pp. 114–28. I am indebted to Helena for many conversations about Sibelius and France.
3 Erik Tawaststjerna, *Sibelius*, vol. I: *1865–1905*, trans. Robert Layton (London, 1976), p. 231.
4 Ibid., p. 229.
5 Erik Tawaststjerna, *Jean Sibelius: Åren 1893–1904*, revd Gitta Henning (Stockholm, 1994), p. 147.
6 Fabian Dahlström, ed., *Högtärade Maestro! Högtärade Herr Baron! Korrespondensen mellan Axel Carpelan och Jean Sibelius, 1900–1919* (Helsinki and Stockholm, 2010), pp. 59–60. Both Tawaststjerna and Layton mistake the date of the letter, which is corrected by Dahlström.
7 Kari Kilpeläinen, 'Afterword', *Jean Sibelius: Symphony no. 2* (Wiesbaden, 2004), pp. 210–13 (p. 210).
8 Erik Tawaststjerna, *Jean Sibelius: Åren 1893–1904*, p. 156. Tawaststjerna's original text here differs somewhat from Robert Layton's translation.
9 *Uusi Suometar*, 11 March 1902, quoted in Kilpeläinen, 'Afterword', p. 211.
10 Erik Tawaststjerna, *Sibelius*, vol. II: *1904–1914*, trans. Robert Layton (London, 1986), p. 66.
11 Letter, dated 16 Nov 1902, quoted in SuviSirkku Talas, ed., *Tulen synty: Aino ja Jean Sibeliuksen Kirjeenvaihtoa, 1892–1904* (Helsinki, 2003), p. 301.
12 Letter to Novello, dated 28 October 1897, quoted in Jerrold Northrop Moore, *Edward Elgar: A Creative Life* (Oxford, 1984), p. 227
13 Andrew Barnett, *Sibelius* (New Haven, CT, 2007), p. 163.
14 Entry dated 14 February. Quoted in Fabian Dahlström, ed., *Jean Sibelius: Dagbok 1909–1944* (Helsinki and Stockholm, 2005), p. 218.
15 Talas, ed., *Tulen synty*, pp. 288–9.
16 Dahlström, ed., *Högtärade Maestro!*, p. 181.
17 Hilkka Helminen, 'Ainola – Home of Aino and Jean Sibelius', in *Jokainen nuotti pitää elää: Jean Sibeliuksen vuosikymmenet musiikissa*, ed. Timo Virtanen (Helsinki, 2015), pp. 254–5.
18 Barnett, *Sibelius*, p. 167.

5 Along Modern Lines

1 SuviSirkku Talas, ed., *Syysilta: Aino ja Jean Sibeliuksen Kirjeenvaihtoa, 1905–1931* (Helsinki, 2007), p. 14.
2 Erik Tawaststjerna, *Sibelius*, vol. II: *1904–1914*, trans. Robert Layton (London, 1986), p. 147.
3 Letter, dated 26 January 1905, quoted in Talas, ed., *Syysilta*, p. 25.
4 Letter, dated 6 February 1905, quoted ibid., p. 34.
5 Sibelius's correspondence from England with Aino is quoted ibid., pp. 49–52.

6 Timo Virtanen, '*Pohjola's Daughter* – "L'aventure d'un héros"' in *Sibelius Studies*, ed. Timothy L. Jackson and Veijo Murtomäki (Cambridge, 2001), pp. 139–76 (p. 156).
7 Talas, ed., *Syysilta*, p. 71.
8 Tawaststjerna, *Sibelius*, vol. II, pp. 46–7.
9 On the wider reception of Wilde's work in the Nordic countries, see Lene Østermark-Jensen, 'From Continental Discourse to "A Breath from a Better World": Oscar Wilde and Denmark', in *The Reception of Oscar Wilde in Europe*, ed. Stefano Evangelista (London, 2010), pp. 229–44.
10 Glenda Dawn Goss, *Sibelius: A Composer's Life and the Awakening of Finland* (Chicago, IL, 2009), pp. 306–12.
11 Diary entry, dated 3 November 1901, quoted in Fabian Dahlström, ed., *Sibelius: Dagbok 1909–1944* (Helsinki and Stockholm, 2005), p. 59.
12 Timo Virtanen, *Sibelius, Symphony no. 3: Manuscript Study and Analysis* (Helsinki, 2005).
13 Quoted in Tawaststjerna, *Sibelius*, vol. II, p. 66.
14 Antti Vihinen, *Sibelius ja Mahler: Kohtaaminen Helsingissä* (Helsinki, 2018).
15 Mahler's symphony was not premiered until 19 September 1908, but the first complete draft of the manuscript was dated 15 August 1905, and he spent the following months working on the orchestration.
16 Letter, dated 15[?] November 1907, quoted in *Syysilta*, p. 86.
17 Eija Kurki, 'Sibelius and the Theatre: A Study of the Incidental Music for the Symbolist Plays', in *Sibelius Studies*, ed. Timothy L. Jackson and Veijo Murtomäki (Cambridge, 2001), pp. 76–94, esp. pp. 92ff.
18 Tawaststjerna, *Sibelius*, vol. II, pp. 91–2.
19 Rosa Newmarch, *Jean Sibelius: A Short Story of a Long Friendship* (Boston, MA, 1939), p. 68.
20 Tawaststjerna, *Sibelius*, vol. II, p. 101; Andrew Barnett, *Sibelius* (New Haven, CT, 2007), p. 193.

6 At the Summit

1 Letter to Aino, dated 18 February 1909. Quoted in SuviSirkku Talas, ed., *Syysilta: Aino ja Jean Sibeliuksen Kirjeenvaihtoa, 1905–1931* (Helsinki, 2007), pp. 103–4.
2 Kalisch's invitation, dated 5 February 1909, is quoted in Philip Ross Bullock, ed., *The Correspondence of Jean Sibelius and Rosa Newmarch, 1906–1939* (Woodbridge, 2011), pp. 67–8.
3 Letter, dated 27 March 1909, quoted in Fabian Dahlström, ed., *Högtärade Maestro! Högtärade Herr Baron! Korrespondensen mellan Axel Carpelan och Jean Sibelius 1900–1919* (Helsinki and Stockholm, 2010), p. 234.
4 Fabian Dahlström, ed., *Jean Sibelius: Dagbok 1909–1944* (Helsinki and Stockholm, 2005), p. 58.
5 Diary entry, dated 25 March 1909. Quoted ibid., p. 34.
6 Ibid., p. 35.
7 Diary entry, dated 25 February 1909, quoted ibid., p. 34. In terms of formal design alone, the later Beethoven quartets (from op. 95 onwards) are a more plausible point of departure than Tawaststjerna's comparison with

op. 59, no. 1 (Erik Tawaststjerna, *Sibelius*, vol. II: *1904–1914*, trans. Robert Layton (London, 1986), p. 118).

8 Robert Anderson, *Elgar in Manuscript* (London, 1990), p. 98.
9 Quoted in Talas, ed., *Syysilta*, p. 135.
10 Diary entry, dated 28 May 1909, quoted in Dahlström, ed., *Jean Sibelius: Dagbok*, p. 35.
11 Ibid., p. 35.
12 23 September 1909. Ibid., p. 37.
13 Jeffrey Kallberg, 'Theatrical Sibelius: The Melodramatic Lizard', in *Jean Sibelius and His World*, ed. Daniel M. Grimley (Princeton, NJ, 2011), pp. 74–88 (p. 81).
14 Letter to Axel Carpelan, dated 13 November 1910, in Dahlström, ed., *Högtärade Maestro!*, p. 289.
15 Tawaststjerna, *Sibelius*, vol. II, fig. 23.
16 Dahlström, ed., *Jean Sibelius: Dagbok*, p. 36.
17 Ibid., p. 37.
18 Tawaststjerna, *Sibelius*, vol. II, p. 117.
19 Letter, dated 20 July 1909, quoted in Dahlström, ed., *Högtärade Maestro!*, p. 246.
20 Letter, dated 27 December 1909, quoted ibid., p. 262.
21 Dahlström, ed., *Jean Sibelius: Dagbok*, p. 44.
22 Ibid., p. 44.
23 Ibid., pp. 41 and 43.
24 Ibid., p. 45.
25 Ibid., p. 49.
26 Ibid., pp. 50 and 51.
27 Tawaststjerna, *Sibelius*, vol. II, p. 131.
28 Dahlström, ed., *Jean Sibelius: Dagbok*, p. 55.
29 Tawaststjerna, *Sibelius*, vol. II, p. 109.
30 Diary entry, dated 5 November, quoted in Dahlström, ed., *Jean Sibelius: Dagbok*, p. 59.
31 Ibid., p. 60.
32 Diary entry, dated 11 December, quoted ibid., p. 63.
33 Ibid., p. 74.
34 Tawaststjerna, *Sibelius*, vol. II, p. 171.
35 Andrew Barnett, *Sibelius* (New Haven, CT, 2007), p. 210.
36 Tawaststjerna, *Sibelius*, vol. II, p. 172.
37 Dahlström, ed., *Jean Sibelius: Dagbok*, p. 73.
38 Tomi Mäkelä, *Jean Sibelius*, trans. Steven Lindberg (Woodbridge, 2011), p. 2.
39 For fuller discussion of the work's reception and the question of the programme, see Tuija Wicklund's excellent introduction in her volume for the critical edition, *Jean Sibelius: Symphony no. 4, op. 63* (Wiesbaden, 2020), pp. viii–xviii (p. xi).
40 Dahlström, ed., *Jean Sibelius: Dagbok*, pp. 86 and 94.
41 Ibid., p. 97.
42 Letter to Aino Sibelius, 1 November 1911, quoted in Talas, ed., *Syysilta*, pp. 195–6.
43 Undated diary note, quoted in Dahlström, ed., *Jean Sibelius: Dagbok*, p. 112.
44 Diary entry, dated 16 November 1911, quoted ibid., p. 105.

45 Letter, dated 2 December 1911, quoted in Talas, ed., *Syysilta*, p. 214.
46 Letter, dated 5 December 1911, quoted ibid., p. 219.
47 Ibid., p. 206.
48 Diary entry, dated 17 January 1912, in Dahlström, ed., *Jean Sibelius: Dagbok*, p. 119.
49 Diary entry, dated 15 January 1912, ibid., p. 119.
50 Erik Tawaststjerna, *Sibelius*, vol. III: *1914–1957*, trans. Robert Layton (London, 1997), p. 12.
51 Diary entry, dated 19 April 1912, quoted in Dahlström, ed., *Jean Sibelius: Dagbok*, p. 134.

7 Summoning and Reckoning

1 Quoted in Fabian Dahlström, ed., *Jean Sibelius: Dagbok 1909–1944* (Helsinki and Stockholm, 2005), p. 129.
2 Erik Tawaststjerna, *Sibelius*, vol. II: *1904–1914*, trans. Robert Layton (London, 1986), pp. 212–13.
3 Quoted in Dahlström, ed., *Jean Sibelius: Dagbok*, p. 135.
4 James Hepokoski, *Sibelius: Symphony no. 5* (Cambridge, 1993), esp. pp. 3–9.
5 Dahlström, ed., *Jean Sibelius: Dagbok*, p. 138.
6 Ibid., p. 184.
7 Quoted in SuviSirkku Talas, ed., *Syysilta: Aino ja Jean Sibeliuksen Kirjeenvaihtoa, 1905–1931* (Helsinki, 2007), p. 251.
8 Quoted in Dahlström, ed., *Jean Sibelius: Dagbok*, p. 185.
9 Andrew Barnett, *Sibelius* (New Haven, CT, 2007), pp. 218–20.
10 Dahlström, ed., *Jean Sibelius: Dagbok*, p. 152.
11 Letter to Aino, dated 26 September 1912, quoted in Talas, ed., *Syysilta*, p. 223.
12 Letter to Jelka Delius, dated 2 October 1912, quoted in Lionel Carley, ed., *Delius: A Life in Letters*, vol. II: *1909–1934* (Aldershot, 1988), p. 93.
13 Daniel M. Grimley, *Delius and the Sound of Place* (Cambridge, 2018), esp. chap. 6.
14 'Birmingham Musical Festival', *The Times*, 2 October 1912, p. 10.
15 Undated note, early October 1912, in Dahlström, ed., *Jean Sibelius: Dagbok*, p. 153.
16 Tawaststjerna, *Sibelius*, vol. II, p. 241.
17 Diary entry, dated 30 April 1913, quoted in Dahlström, ed., *Jean Sibelius: Dagbok*, p. 171.
18 Diary entry, dated 8 June 1913, ibid., p. 173.
19 Hepokoski, *Sibelius: Symphony no. 5*, pp. 23–7.
20 Letter from Sibelius to Vaughan Williams, dated 11 August 1949, British Library VWL3161; transcribed online at www.vaughanwilliams.uk, accessed 12 April 2020.
21 'The Gloucester Festival', *The Times*, 11 September 1913, p. 8.
22 Diary entries, 23 October and 25 November 1913, in Dahlström, ed., *Jean Sibelius: Dagbok*, pp. 177 and 178.
23 Tawaststjerna, *Sibelius*, vol. II, pp. 243–4.
24 Lawrence Sullivan, 'Arthur Schnitzler's *The Veil of Pierrette*', *Europa Orientalis*, XIV/2 (1995), pp. 263–80.

25 For a fuller discussion, which analyses the score's concern with erotic desire, see Leah Broad, 'Scaramouche, Scaramouche: Sibelius on Stage', *Journal of the Royal Musical Association*, CXLV/2 (2020), pp. 417–56.
26 Dahlström, ed., *Jean Sibelius: Dagbok*, pp. 182–3.
27 Diary entry, dated 3 October 1913, quoted ibid., p. 177.
28 Undated diary entry, quoted ibid., p. 190.
29 Letter, dated 30 May 1913, quoted in Talas, ed., *Syysilta*, pp. 264–6.
30 Quoted in Dahlström, ed., *Jean Sibelius: Dagbok*, p. 147.
31 Quoted in Tawaststjerna, *Sibelius*, vol. II, p. 277.
32 Diary entries, dated 29, 30 and 31 July 1914, quoted in Dahlström, ed., *Jean Sibelius: Dagbok*, p. 192.
33 Quoted ibid., p. 192.
34 Barnett, *Sibelius*, p. 245.
35 Diary entry, dated 18 October 1914, quoted in Dahlström, ed., *Jean Sibelius: Dagbok*, p. 200.
36 Diary entry. dated 13 November 1914, quoted ibid., p. 204.
37 The themes and tables in Sibelius's sketchbooks are described in the fourth volume of Tawaststjerna's original Swedish biography, *Jean Sibelius, Åren 1914–1919*, revd Gitta Henning (Stockholm, 1996), chap. 2.
38 Quoted in Dahlström, ed., *Jean Sibelius: Dagbok*, p. 225. The passage is also quoted by both Tawaststjerna and Hepokoski, though my translation differs from Robert Layton's in several respects.
39 Dahlström, ed., *Jean Sibelius: Dagbok*, p. 226.
40 Ibid., p. 224. Layton mistakenly lists the date in his translation of Erik Tawaststjerna, *Sibelius*, vol. III: *1914–1957* (London, 1997) as 4 June (p. 51).
41 Diary entry, dated 5 September 1915, quoted in Dahlström, ed., *Jean Sibelius: Dagbok*, p. 237.
42 Tawaststjerna, *Sibelius*, vol. III, p. 71.
43 Undated diary entry, after 8 December 1915, quoted in Dahlström, ed., *Jean Sibelius: Dagbok*, p. 240.
44 Tawaststjerna, *Sibelius*, vol. III, p. 79.
45 Dahlström, ed., *Jean Sibelius: Dagbok*, pp. 242–3.
46 A question Sibelius posed directly in a diary entry dated 11 February 1915, quoted ibid., p. 217.
47 Douglas Bruster and Eric Rasmussen, eds, 'Editorial Introduction', in *Everyman and Mankind*, Arden Early Modern Drama (London, 2009), pp. 41–83, esp. pp. 68–74.
48 Daniel M. Grimley, 'Music beyond the Breakthrough: Sibelius, Hofmannsthal and the Summoning of *Everyman*', in Philip Ross Bullock and Daniel M. Grimley, *Music's Nordic Breakthrough: Aesthetics, Modernity and Cultural Exchange, 1890–1930* (Woodbridge, 2021).
49 Tawaststjerna, *Sibelius*, vol. III, p. 88.
50 Ibid., p. 46.
51 Bruster and Rasmussen, 'Editorial Introduction', p. 49.

8 'Some heavenly musicke'

1 Erik Tawaststjerna, *Sibelius*, vol. III: *1914–1957*, trans. Robert Layton (London, 1997), p. 78. I have amended Robert Layton's translation.

2 Diary entry, dated 11 February 1916, quoted in Fabian Dahlström, ed., *Jean Sibelius: Dagbok 1909–1944* (Helsinki and Stockholm, 2005), p. 244.
3 Tawaststjerna, *Sibelius*, vol. III, p. 89.
4 Tomi Mäkelä, *Jean Sibelius*, trans. Steven Lindberg (Woodbridge, 2011), p. 80.
5 Diary entries, dated 20 and 28 April 1916, quoted in Dahlström, ed., *Jean Sibelius: Dagbok*, p. 248.
6 Tawaststjerna, *Sibelius*, vol. III, pp. 90–91.
7 Diary entry, dated 26 August 1916, quoted in Dahlström, ed., *Jean Sibelius: Dagbok*, p. 251.
8 See Daniel M. Grimley, 'Music beyond the Breakthrough: Sibelius, Hofmannsthal, and the Summoning of Everyman', in *Music's Nordic Breakthrough: Aesthetics, Modernity, and Cultural Exchange, 1890–1930*, ed. Philip Ross Bullock and Daniel M. Grimley (Woodbridge, 2021).
9 Diary entry, dated 18 February 1917, quoted ibid., p. 251.
10 Tawaststjerna, *Sibelius*, vol. III, p. 102. Layton gives the diary entry mistakenly as 15 February 1917.
11 Ibid., pp. 103–4.
12 Quoted in Dahlström, ed., *Jean Sibelius: Dagbok*, p. 263.
13 Diary entries, dated 18, 22 and 31 December 1917, quoted ibid., pp. 265–5.
14 Andrew Barnett, *Sibelius* (New Haven, CT, 2007), p. 271.
15 Barnett suggests that the orchestration used on 19 January may have been by another composer, but there is no firm documentary evidence either way.
16 Diary entry, dated 18 January 1918, quoted in Dahlström, ed., *Jean Sibelius: Dagbok*, p. 268. The score with Sibelius's hastily added name is reproduced in Timo Virtanen, ed., *Jokainen nuotti pitää elää: Jean Sibeliuksen vuosikymmenet musiikissa/One Must Live Every Note: Jean Sibelius's Decades in Music* (Helsinki, 2015), p. 122.
17 Tawaststjerna, *Sibelius*, vol. III, p. 108.
18 Ibid., p. 117.
19 For an insightful critical history of the war in English, see Tuomas Tepora and Aapo Roselius, eds, *The Finnish Civil War 1918: History, Memory, Legacy* (Leiden, 2014).
20 Diary entries, dated 28, 29 January and 2 February, quoted in Dahlström, ed., *Jean Sibelius: Dagbok*, p. 269.
21 Glenda Dawn Goss, *Sibelius: A Composer's Life and the Awakening of Finland* (Chicago, IL, 2009), pp. 394–5.
22 Diary entry, dated 28 May 1918, quoted in Dahlström, ed., *Jean Sibelius: Dagbok*, p. 273.
23 Diary entry, dated 14 April 1918, quoted ibid., p. 272.
24 Tawaststjerna, *Sibelius*, vol. III, p. 126.
25 Diary entry, dated 3 June 1918, quoted in Dahlström, ed., *Jean Sibelius: Dagbok*, p. 273.
26 Tawaststjerna, *Sibelius*, vol. III, p. 144. Sibelius noted the publication of Niemann's book on 17 February 1919, and a year later lamented its influence on his international reception (diary entry, 9 February 1920).
27 Tawaststjerna, *Sibelius*, vol. III, p. 132. Layton's translation (amended here) does not include the date, but it was a diary entry from 7 June.

28 Goss, *Sibelius*, p. 393.
29 Diary entry, dated 20 December 1918, quoted in Dahlström, ed., *Jean Sibelius: Dagbok*, p. 281.
30 Tawaststjerna, *Sibelius*, vol. III, p. 142. Layton's translation mistakenly gives the date as 7 January.
31 Ibid., p. 171.
32 Ibid., p. 149.
33 Dahlström, ed., *Jean Sibelius: Dagbok*, pp. 302 and 474.
34 SuviSirkku Talas, ed., *Syysilta: Aino ja Jean Sibeliuksen Kirjeenvaihtoa, 1905–1931* (Helsinki, 2007), p. 296.
35 Ibid., p. 304.
36 Diary entry, dated 21 March 1922, quoted in Dahlström, ed., *Jean Sibelius: Dagbok*, p. 314.
37 Undated note, quote ibid., p. 316.
38 Diary entry, dated 28 September 1922, quoted ibid, p. 317.
39 The most detailed and revelatory account of this process, on which my discussion relies, is Kari Kilpeläinen's painstaking bar-by-bar discussion of the materials, 'Sibelius's Seventh Symphony: An Introduction to the Sketches and the Printed Sources', ed. and trans. James Hepokoski, *The Sibelius Companion*, ed. Glenda Dawn Goss (Westport, CT, 1995), pp. 239–70.
40 Diary entry, dated 6 January 1924, quoted in Dahlström, ed., *Jean Sibelius: Dagbok*, p. 321.
41 Barnett, *Sibelius*, p. 307.
42 Howell summarizes the structure of the symphony with exemplary clarity in 'Sibelius the Progressive', in *Sibelius Studies*, ed. Jackson and Murtomäki, pp. 35–57 (pp. 43–6).
43 Helsinki University Library (HUL), Sibelius collection, HUL 0353, pp. 98–102 contains the first proposed ending, which is more craggily dissonant and lacks any reference to *Valse triste*; HUL 0354, pp. 98–102 contains a second draft that briefly shifts metre into 12/8. The final page of HUL 0353 is reproduced in Virtanen, ed., *Jokainen nuotti pitää*, p. 151.
44 Diary entries, dated 5, 6 April and 23 and 24 November 1924, quoted in Dahlström, ed., *Jean Sibelius: Dagbok*, pp. 322–3. Sibelius's allusion in his diary entry of 23 November is a reference to the biblical account of Moses descent from Mount Sinai.
45 National Archives of Finland, Sibelius Family Archive, Box 52.
46 Letter, dated 18 March 1926, National Archives of Finland, Sibelius Family Archive, Box 20.
47 Letters, dated 5 and 12 April 1926, quoted in Talas, ed., *Syysilta*, pp. 346 and 352.
48 For a historiography of the forest, see Robert Pogue Harrison, *Forests: The Shadow of Civilization* (Chicago, IL, 1992); on the specifically Finnish context, see Ari Aukusti Lehtinen, 'Landscapes of Domination: Living in and off the Forests in Eastern Finland', in *Nordic Landscapes: Region and Belonging on the Northern Edge of Europe*, ed. Michael Jones and Kenneth R. Olwig (Minneapolis, MN, 2008), pp. 458–82.
49 Sibelius referred to the sirocco in a letter to Aino, dated 1 April 1926, quoted in Talas, ed., *Syysilta*, p. 344.

50 Letter, dated 1 April 1926, quoted ibid., p. 344.
51 Tawaststjerna, *Sibelius*, vol. III, p. 280.
52 Barnett, *Sibelius*, p. 328.
53 Tomi Mäkelä, 'Sibelius and the Ecological Breakthrough', in *Music's Nordic Breakthrough*, ed. Philip Ross Bullock and Daniel M. Grimley (Woodbridge, 2021).
54 Anna Pulkkis, editorial introduction, *Jean Sibelius: Works for Piano, Opp. 85, 94, 96a, 96c, 97, 99, 101, 103, 114. Jean Sibelius Works*, V/3 (Leipzig, 2011), pp. ix–xvii (p. xii).
55 Robert Layton, *Sibelius* (London, 1984), p. 188.
56 For a brief but illuminating discussion of both opp. 114 and 115, see Veijo Murtomäki, 'Sibelius and the Miniature', in *The Cambridge Companion to Sibelius*, ed. Daniel M. Grimley (Cambridge, 2006), pp. 137–53.

9 *Quasi al niente*

1 Glenda Dawn Goss, *Sibelius: A Composer's Life and the Awakening of Finland* (Chicago, IL, 2009), pp. 429–30.
2 Erik Tawaststjerna, *Sibelius*, vol. III: *1914–1957*, trans. Robert Layton (London, 1997), pp. 303–4.
3 Letter from Berlin, dated 22 May 1931, quoted in SuviSirkku Talas, ed., *Syysilta: Aino ja Jean Sibeliuksen Kirjeenvaihtoa, 1905–1931* (Helsinki, 2007), p. 395.
4 Diary entry, dated 18 December 1931, quoted in Fabian Dahlström, ed., *Jean Sibelius: Dagbok 1909–1944* (Helsinki and Stockholm, 2005), p. 332.
5 Talas, ed., *Syysilta*, p. 396.
6 Dahlström, ed., *Jean Sibelius: Dagbok*, p. 332.
7 Letter, dated 20 November 1932, National Archive of Finland (NAF), Sibelius Family Collection, Kansio 16.
8 Tawaststjerna, *Sibelius*, vol. III, p. 316.
9 Letter drafts, dated 19 September, NAF, Sibelius Family Collection, Kansio 45.
10 Kari Kilpeläinen, 'Sibelius Eight: What Happened to It?', *Finnish Music Quarterly*, 4 (1995), pp. 30–35; available at https://fmq.fi, accessed 9 May 2020. Timo Virtanen, 'Jean Sibelius's Late Sketches and Orchestral Fragments', notes for BIS CD-2065 (2013).
11 Nors S. Josephson, 'On Some Apparent Sketches for Sibelius's Eighth Symphony', *Archiv für Musikwissenschaft*, LXI/1 (2004), pp. 54–67.
12 Goss, *Sibelius*, pp. 434–5.
13 Diary entry, dated 4 May 1934, quoted in Dahlström, ed., *Sibelius: Dagbok*, p. 333. The passage is quoted in Tawaststjerna, *Sibelius*, vol. III, p. 319, though Layton lists the date as 4 April.
14 The most sustained discussion of these irresolvable questions of agency and intention remains Ruth-Maria Gleißner, *Der unpolitische Komponist als Politikum: Die Rezeption von Jean Sibelius im NS-Staat* (Frankfurt, 2002). See also Antti Vihinen, *Adorno's Critique of Sibelius: The Political Dimension* (Helsinki, 2001); and Tomi Mäkelä, 'Sibelius and Germany: Wahrhaftigkeit beyond *Allnatur*', in *The Cambridge Companion to Sibelius*, ed. Daniel M. Grimley (Cambridge, 2004), pp. 169–81.

15 See Jackson's chapter, 'Sibelius the Political', in *Sibelius in the Old and New World: Aspects of His Music, Its Interpretation, and Reception*, ed. Timothy L. Jackson, Veijo Murtomäki, Colin Davis and Timo Virtanen (Frankfurt, 2010), pp. 69–123. The issue is also raised with reference particularly to the response to Jackson's argument in Paavo Ahonen, Simo Muir and Oula Silvenoinnen, 'The Study of Antisemitism in Finland: Past, Present, and Future', in *Antisemitism in the North: History and State of Research*, ed. Jonathan Adams and Cornelia Heß (Berlin, 2020), pp. 139–54 (p. 150).
16 Veijo Murtomäki, 'Sibelius in the Context of the Finnish-German History', *Sibelius Reconsidered*, https://sibeliusone.com, accessed 24 October 2020.
17 NAF, Sibelius Family Collection, Kansio 34. The document is a draft script for a radio broadcast, preserved in the Finnish Radio archives.
18 Antti Vihinen, 'Sibelius, the Nazis and the Political Culture', *Sibelius Reconsidered*, https://sibeliusone.com, accessed 24 October 2020. See also Tomi Mäkelä, *Jean Sibelius*, trans. Steven Lindberg (Woodbridge, 2011), pp. 396–7.
19 Undated communication, 1941, NAF, Sibelius Family Collection, Kansio 26.
20 Letter signed by Charles Triller, Chairman of the Board, New York Philharmonic Society. NAF, Sibelius Family Collection, Kansio 26.
21 Quoted in Dahlström, ed., *Jean Sibelius: Dagbok*, p. 335.
22 Mäkelä, *Jean Sibelius*, p. 19.
23 The crucial source is a diary entry dated 5 June 1915, as Sibelius was planning a nostalgic trip to his childhood haunts in Hämeenlinna and Lovisa (quoted ibid., p. 232). He wrote: 'My [paternal] grandfather's grave. Or rather grandmother's. Because grandfather is buried in the Sucksdorff family grave. And what was he, the honourable man, doing there? He was a son of that country and the Sucksdorffs, an immigrant Jewish family, to whom grandfather became attached by marriage. Is this mere sentimentality?'
24 Ibid., p. 336.
25 Jackson, 'Sibelius the Political', pp. 106–7.
26 Diary entry, dated 30 September 1943, quoted in Dahlström, ed., *Jean Sibelius: Dagbok*, pp. 336–7.
27 Letters held in NAF, Sibelius Family Collection, Kansio 31. The British Council had sent Sibelius a copy of the score of Vaughan Williams's Fifth Symphony, carrying its dedication, on 7 June 1946. Vaughan Williams's final birthday greeting to Sibelius was dated 5 December 1955, three years before Vaughan Williams's own death.
28 For an illuminating account of Adorno's essay, see Max Paddison, 'Art and the Ideology of Nature: Sibelius, Hamsun, Adorno', in *Jean Sibelius and His World*, ed. Daniel M. Grimley (Princeton, NJ, 2011), pp. 173–85. An English version of the essay, translated by Susan H. Gillespie, follows later in the volume (pp. 331–7).
29 Goss, *Sibelius*, pp. 434–5.

Select Discography

1 For two critical surveys, see Robert Layton, 'From Kajanus to Karajan: Sibelius on Record', in *Sibelius Studies*, ed. Timothy L. Jackson and Veijo

Murtomäki (Cambridge, 1998), pp. 14–34; and Bethany Lowe, 'Different Kinds of Fidelity: Interpreting Sibelius on Record', in *The Cambridge Companion to Sibelius*, ed. Daniel M. Grimley (Cambridge, 2004), pp. 219–28.

2 Richard S. Ginell, 'Fire and Ice: The Best Recordings of the Sibelius Violin Concerto', *The Strad*, 7 December 2017.

SELECT BIBLIOGRAPHY

The literature on Sibelius is vast, and he is especially well covered biographically. Scholars owe a continued debt to the work of Erik Tawaststjerna, whose five-volume study of the composer, which began to appear from the mid-1960s and was then revised by Gitta Henning and reissued, remains a central resource. For ease of cross-reference, citations in this book usually refer to Robert Layton's abridged three-volume English translation, but some notes rely on Tawaststjerna's original text, either where material has been elided or where minor discrepancies between the two versions emerge. Among more recent studies, the outstanding biographies by Glenda Dawn Goss and Tomi Mäkelä provide essential frameworks for understanding Sibelius's life and his cultural context. Special mention must also be made of Fabian Dahlström's beautiful editions of Sibelius's diaries and his correspondence with Axel Carpelan, as well as his comprehensive thematic catalogue. The painstaking scholarship of the critical edition, *Jean Sibelius Works*, now led by Timo Virtanen, has done much more than establish definitive versions of Sibelius's musical texts: it has shed vital new light on the genesis and reception of his music and revealed many new insights. My discussion has gratefully relied on all of these sources, in addition to those listed below.

Adams, Byron, '"Thor's Hammer": Sibelius and British Music Critics, 1905–1957', in *Jean Sibelius and His World*, ed. Daniel M. Grimley (Princeton, NJ, 2011), pp. 125–57

Ahonen, Paavo, Simo Muir and Oula Silvenoinnen, 'The Study of Antisemitism in Finland: Past, Present, and Future', in *Antisemitism in the North: History and State of Research*, ed. Jonathan Adams and Cornelia Heß (Berlin, 2020), pp. 139–54

Anderson, Robert, *Elgar in Manuscript* (London, 1990)

Barnett, Andrew, *Sibelius* (New Haven, CT, 2007)

Bonsdorff, Anna-Maria von, 'Correspondences: Jean Sibelius in a Forest of Image and Myth', in *Sibelius and the World of Art*, ed. Anna-Maria von Bonsdorff (Helsinki, 2014), pp. 81–127

Broad, Leah, 'Nordic Incidental Music: Between Modernity and Modernism', DPhil thesis, University of Oxford, 2018

—, 'Scaramouche, Scaramouche: Sibelius on Stage', *Journal of the Royal Musical Association*, CXLV/2 (2020), pp. 417–56
Bruster, Douglas, and Eric Rasmussen, eds, 'Editorial Introduction, in *Everyman and Mankind* (London, 2009), pp. 41–83
Bullock, Philip Ross, *The Correspondence of Jean Sibelius and Rosa Newmarch, 1906–1939* (Woodbridge, 2011)
Carley, Lionel, ed., *Delius: A Life in Letters*, vol. II: *1909–1934* (Aldershot, 1988)
Dahlström, Fabian, *Jean Sibelius: Thematisches-bibliographisches Verzeichnis seiner Werk* (Wiesbaden, 2003)
—, ed., *Jean Sibelius: Dagbok 1909–1944* (Helsinki and Stockholm, 2005)
—, ed., *Högtärade Maestro: Högtärade Herr Baron. Korrespondensen mellan Axel Carpelan och Jean Sibelius, 1900–1919* (Helsinki and Stockholm, 2010)
Downes, Stephen, 'Pastoral Idylls, Erotic Anxieties and Heroic subjectivities in Sibelius's *Lemminkäinen and the Maidens of the Island* and First Two Symphonies', in *The Cambridge Companion to Sibelius*, ed. Daniel M. Grimley (Cambridge, 2004), pp. 35–48
Erlmann, Veit, *Reason and Resonance: A History of Modern Aurality* (New York, 2010)
Fewster, Derek, *Visions of Past Glory: Nationalism and the Construction of Early Finnish History* (Helsinki, 2006)
Gleißner, Ruth-Maria, *Der unpolitische Komponist als Politikum: Die Rezeption von Jean Sibelius im NS-Staat* (Frankfurt, 2002)
Goss, Glenda Dawn, 'A Backdrop for Young Sibelius: The Intellectual Genesis of the *Kullervo* Symphony', *Nineteenth-century Music*, XXVII/1 (Summer 2003), pp. 48–73
—, Preface, *Sibelius: Kullervo, op. 7* (Wiesbaden, 2005), pp. xi–xviii
—, *Sibelius: A Composer's Life and the Awakening of Finland* (Chicago, IL, 2009)
—, ed., *Jean Sibelius and Olin Downes: Friendship, Music, Criticism* (Boston, MA, 1995)
—, ed., *The Sibelius Companion* (Westport, CT, 1996)
—, ed., *Sibelius: Hämeenlinna Letters. Scenes from a Musical Life, 1874–1895. Jean Sibelius Ungdomsbrev* (Esbo/Espoo, 1997)
Grimley, Daniel M., *Delius and the Sound of Place* (Cambridge, 2018)
—, 'Music Beyond the Breakthrough: Sibelius, Hofmannsthal and the Summoning of *Everyman*', in *Music's Nordic Breakthrough: Aesthetics, Modernity and Cultural Exchange, 1890–1930*, ed. Philip Ross Bullock and Daniel M. Grimley (Woodbridge, 2021)
—, ed., *The Cambridge Companion to Sibelius* (Cambridge, 2004)
—, ed., *Jean Sibelius and His World* (Princeton, NJ, 2011)
Harrison, Robert Pogue, *Forests: The Shadow of Civilization* (Chicago, IL, 1992)
Hepokoski, James, 'Finlandia Awakens', in *The Cambridge Companion to Sibelius*, ed. Grimley, pp. 81–94
—, 'Rotations, Sketches, and the Sixth Symphony', in *Sibelius Studies*, ed. Timothy L. Jackson and Veijo Murtomäki (Cambridge, 2001), pp. 322–51
—, *Sibelius: Symphony no. 5* (Cambridge, 1993)
Howell, Tim, 'Sibelius the Progressive', in *Sibelius Studies*, ed. Jackson and Murtomäki, pp. 35–57

Jackson, Timothy L., 'Sibelius the Political', in *Sibelius in the Old and New World: Aspects of His Music, Its Interpretation, and Reception*, ed. Timothy L. Jackson, Veijo Murtomäki, Colin Davis and Timo Virtanen (Frankfurt, 2010), pp. 69–123
—, and Veijo Murtomäki, eds, *Sibelius Studies* (Cambridge, 2001)
Josephson, Nors S., 'On Some Apparent Sketches for Sibelius's Eighth Symphony', *Archiv für Musikwissenschaft*, LXI/1 (2004), pp. 54–67
Kallberg, Jeffrey, 'Theatrical Sibelius: The Melodramatic Lizard', in *Jean Sibelius and His World*, ed. Grimley, pp. 74–88
Kent, Neil, *Helsinki: A Cultural and Literary History* (Oxford, 2004)
Kilpeläinen, Kari, *The Jean Sibelius Musical Manuscripts at Helsinki University Library* (Wiesbaden, 1991)
—, 'Sibelius's Seventh Symphony: An Introduction to the Manuscript and Printed Sources', ed. and trans. James Hepokoski, *The Sibelius Companion*, ed. Goss, pp. 239–70
—, 'Sibelius Eight: What Happened to It?', *Finnish Music Quarterly*, 4 (1995); available at https://fmq.fi
—, 'Afterword', *Jean Sibelius: Symphony no. 2* (Wiesbaden, 2004), pp. 210–13
Kurki, Eija, 'Sibelius and the Theater: A Study of the Incidental Music for the Symbolist Plays', in *Sibelius Studies*, ed. Jackson and Murtomäki, pp. 76–94
Laitinen, Martti, 'Why Kajanus Went to St Petersburg', in *Sibelius in the Old and New World*, ed. Jackson, Murtomäki, Davis and Virtanen, pp. 148–57
Layton, Robert, *Sibelius* (London, 1993)
Lehtinen, Ari Aukusti, 'Landscapes of Domination: Living in and off the Forests in Eastern Finland', in *Nordic Landscapes: Region and Belonging on the Northern Edge of Europe*, ed. Michael Jones and Kenneth R. Olwig (Minneapolis, MN, 2008), pp. 458–82
Lönnrot, Elias, *The Kalevala*, ed. George C. Schoolfield, trans. Eino Friberg (Helsinki, 1988)
Mäkelä, Tomi, *Fredrik Pacius: kompositör i Finland* (Helsinki, 2009)
—, *Jean Sibelius*, trans. Steven Lindberg (Woodbridge, 2011)
—, 'Sibelius and the Ecological Breakthrough', in *Music's Nordic Breakthrough: Aesthetics, Modernity, and Cultural Exchange, 1890–1930*, ed. Philip Ross Bullock and Daniel M. Grimley (Woodbridge, 2021)
—, 'Sibelius and Germany: Wahrhaftigkeit beyond Allnatur', in *The Cambridge Companion to Sibelius*, ed. Grimley, pp. 169–81
Moore, Jerrold Northrop, *Edward Elgar: A Creative Life* (Oxford, 1984)
Murtomäki, Veijo, 'Sibelius in the Context of the Finnish-German History', *Sibelius Reconsidered*, https://sibeliusone.com, accessed 24 October 2020
—, 'Sibelius and the Miniature', in *The Cambridge Companion to Sibelius*, ed. Grimley, pp. 137–53
—, *Symphonic Unity: The Development of Formal Thinking in the Symphonies of Sibelius*, trans. Henry Bacon (Helsinki, 1993)
Newmarch, Rosa, *Jean Sibelius: A Short Story of a Long Friendship* (Boston, MA, 1939)
Østermark-Jensen, Lene, 'From Continental Discourse to "A Breath from a Better World": Oscar Wilde and Denmark', in *The Reception of Oscar Wilde in Europe*, ed. Stefano Evangelista (London, 2010), pp. 229–44

Pulkkis, Anna, 'Alternatives to Monotonality in Jean Sibelius's Solo Songs', PhD diss., Sibelius Academy, Helsinki, 2014

—, editorial introduction, *Jean Sibelius: Works for Piano, Opp. 85, 94, 96a, 96c, 97, 99, 101, 103, 114*, *Jean Sibelius Works*, V/3 (Wiesbaden, 2011), pp. ix–xvii

Siikala, Anna Leena, 'Body, Performance, and Agency in Kalevala Rune-singing', *Oral Tradition*, XV/2 (2000), pp. 255–78

Sullivan, Lawrence, 'Arthur Schnitzler's *The Veil of Pierrette*', *Europa Orientalis*, XIV/2 (1995), pp. 263–80

Talas, SuviSirkku, ed., *Tulen synty: Aino ja Jean Sibeliuksen Kirjeenvaihtoa, 1892–1904* (Helsinki, 2003)

—, ed., *Syysilta: Aino ja Jean Sibeliuksen Kirjeenvaihtoa, 1905–1931* (Helsinki, 2007)

Tarasti, Eero, *Myth and Music: A Semiotic Approach to the Aesthetics of Myth in Music, especially that of Wagner, Sibelius and Stravinsky* (The Hague, 1979)

Tawaststjerna, Erik, *Jean Sibelius: Åren 1865–1893* (Stockholm, 1992)

—, *Jean Sibelius: Åren 1893–1904* (Stockholm, 1994)

—, *Jean Sibelius: Åren 1904–1914* (Stockholm, 1991)

—, *Jean Sibelius: Åren 1914–1919* (Stockholm, 1996)

—, *Jean Sibelius: Åren 1920–1957* (Stockholm, 1997)

—, *Sibelius*, vol. I: *1865–1905*, trans. Robert Layton (London, 1976)

—, *Sibelius*, vol. II: *1904–1914*, trans. Robert Layton (London, 1986)

—, *Sibelius*, vol. III: *1914–1957*, trans. Robert Layton (London, 1997)

Tepora, Tuomas, and Aapo Roselius, eds, *The Finnish Civil War 1918: History, Memory, Legacy* (Leiden, 2014)

Tyrväinen, Helena, 'Les Finlandais dans les programmes musicaux des Expositions universelles de Paris en 1889 et 1900', *Musiikkitiede*, 1–2 (1994), pp. 22–74

—, 'Sibelius at the Paris Universal Exposition of 1900', in *Sibelius Forum: Proceedings from the Second International Jean Sibelius Conference, Helsinki, November 25–29, 1995*, ed. Veijo Murtomäki, Kari Kilpeläinen and Risto Väisänen (Helsinki, 1998), pp. 114–28

Vihinen, Antti, *Sibelius ja Mahler: Kohtaaminen Helsingissä* (Helsinki, 2018)

—, 'Sibelius, the Nazis and the Political Culture', *Sibelius Reconsidered*, https://sibeliusone.com, accessed 24 October 2020

Virtanen, Timo, 'Jean Sibelius's Late Sketches and Orchestral Fragments', liner notes for BIS CD-2065 (2013)

—, '*Pohjola's Daughter* – "L'aventure d'un héros"', in *Sibelius Studies*, ed. Jackson and Murtomäki, pp. 139–76

—, *Sibelius, Symphony no. 3: Manuscript Study and Analysis* (Helsinki, 2005)

—, ed., *Jokainen nuotti pitää elää: Jean Sibeliuksen vuosikymmenet musiikissa/ One Must Live Every Note: Jean Sibelius's Decades in Music* (Helsinki, 2015)

Wicklund, Tuija, 'Introduction', *Jean Sibelius: Symphony no. 4, op. 63* (Wiesbaden, 2020), pp. viii–xviii

—, 'Jean Sibelius's *En saga* and Its Two Versions: Genesis, Reception, Edition, and Form', PhD diss., Sibelius Academy, Helsinki, 2014

ACKNOWLEDGEMENTS

It is a privilege to thank friends and colleagues who have generously shared knowledge and advice and have shaped my thoughts on Sibelius over many years. They include Byron Adams, Robert Adlington, Andrew Barnett, Leah Broad, Sarah Collins, John Deathridge, Peter Franklin, Glenda Dawn Goss, Laura Gray, James Hepokoski, Tim Howell, Jeffrey Kallberg, Kevin Karnes, Sherry Lee, Annika Lindskog, Bethany Lowe, Tomi Mäkelä, Andrew Mellor, Sarah Moynihan, Juliana M. Pistorius, Eveliina Pulkki, Edward Rushton, Anthony Sellors, Tom Service, Sam Smith, W. Dean Sutcliffe, Benedict Taylor, Sebastian Wedler and Anna Wittstruck. In Finland, I've been supported by Gustav Djupsjöbacka, Anna Krohn, Pälvi Laine, Sanna Linjama-Mannermaa, Markus Mantere, Helen Metsä, Veijo Murtomäki, Anna Pulkkis, Laura Saloniemi, Juha Torvinen, Petri Tuovinen, Helena Tyrväinen, Mirva Virtanen, Susanna Välimäki and Tuija Wicklund. Timo Virtanen and Paul Prescott read a complete draft of the manuscript and suggested many life-saving changes and corrections. Any remaining errors are entirely my own responsibility.

Particular thanks are due to Philip Ross Bullock, who first suggested the project to the team at Reaktion Books. Ben Hayes kindly followed up, and I am especially grateful to Michael Leaman for his continual patience as the text emerged. This project would never have been completed without the support of my family: my wife Tiffany, sister Carla and nephew Danny. My parents gave me my first love of music; this book is dedicated to them.

PHOTO ACKNOWLEDGEMENTS

The author and publishers wish to express their thanks to the below sources of illustrative material and/or permission to reproduce it. Some locations of artworks are also given below, in the interest of brevity:

Ainola Foundation, Järvenpää: p. 61; Art, Architecture and Engineering Library, Lantern Slide Collection, University of Michigan, Ann Arbor, MI: p. 78; © DACS 2021/photo Daniel M. Grimley, courtesy Theatre Museum (Teatterimuseo), Helsinki: p. 189; Finnish Heritage Agency (Museoviraston Kuvakokoelmat), Helsinki: pp. 29, 35, 39, 42, 171, 181; George Grantham Bain Collection, Library of Congress, Prints and Photographs Division, Washington, DC: p. 149; Hämeenlinna Art Museum (Hämeenlinnan taidemuseo): pp. 14, 48; Hämeenlinna City Museum (Hämeenlinnan Kaupunginmuseo): pp. 16, 18, 19; from *Harper's Monthly Magazine*, CIV/621 (February 1902), photo David O. McKay Library, Brigham Young University-Idaho, Rexburg: p. 84; Helsinki City Museum (Helsingin kaupunginmuseo): pp. 25, 51, 96, 206; © Jean Sibelius Estate/photo National Museum of Finland (Kansallismuseo), Helsinki: p. 196; Kuopio Art Museum (Kuopion taidemuseo): p. 128; Munchmuseet, Oslo: p. 37; Nasjonalmuseet for kunst, arkitektur og design, Oslo (photo Børre Høstland): p. 47; Nationalmuseum, Stockholm: p. 135; Norfolk Chamber Music Festival, Yale Summer School of Music, Norfolk, CT: p. 154; private collection: p. 56; Rijksmuseum, Amsterdam: p. 27; Sibelius Museum (Sibelius-museo), Turku: pp. 32, 83, 161; courtesy the Society of Swedish Literature in Finland (Svenska litteratursällskapet i Finland), Helsinki: pp. 75, 108; Swedish Performing Arts Agency (Musikverket), Stockholm: p. 114; courtesy Theatre Museum (Teatterimuseo), Helsinki: pp. 91 (photo Martikainen & Kni), 167.

INDEX

Page numbers in *italics* indicate illustrations